MIDNIGHT TO MORNING
BOOK 1

BY: H. GLOGAU–MORGAN

IACHÂD

The airport was crowded, and the weather was humid. Warm August moisture leaked into the terminals and made the misery more pronounced. Gareth held my hand tighter as we pushed towards customs. The crowd around us looked much like we did. Escaping the disaster in the United States had taken a toll on them as well. The aftermath of multiple nuclear bombs going off in major cities had led to living in a nightmare. Adding to it was violent illnesses which spread through the entire globe. Nearly one billion people had died this past year alone. Thousands of Americans were trying to escape into any country possible. For some, life in a refugee camp was an improvement over what they had experienced in the last fifteen months. It was for us.

I watched as Gareth held his British passport in front of him so that people would assume he was just coming home and was not one of the refugees. I kept my American passport hidden underneath my entrance papers. The only way we could make it out of the country was to have papers stating we had been accepted into another as a charity case. Although Gareth's citizenship should have been enough, we were not taking any chances. It was nearly two hours before we made it to the front of the customs line. My stress increased when we noticed the large military presence there. The official looked at my husbands' passport, and I prayed he would not ask any serious questions.

"Decided to come home again, eh?" He looked up at us. Gareth just nodded.

"Where's home?" He continued.

Just as we rehearsed, Gareth replied in his best Welsh accent, "Brecon."

The official nodded and then looked at me. He glanced down at the passport gripped in my hand and frowned.

"Is she your wife?"

We both nodded. He looked at the solider next to him and then frowned again. "Unless you can present a proof of residence in Brecon, I can't let you pass, though."

We looked at him confused. "Too many refugees are coming

in, most with illegally obtained visas. Even dual citizenship is not enough to get by anymore."

He looked at Gareth. "She is an American, but even with the papers, we cannot let her in at all right now. The only option is to either pay for a ticket back or go with the soldiers to the refugee camp. You might be able to get a work pass because of your citizenship, but she cannot. I am sorry."

I teared up as Gareth grimaced, "Sir, we have a bank account in Brecon and family waiting for our arrival."

The soldier looked over to the next person in line before answering us, "They will have to petition for your release, and a bank account is not enough. Make your choice now. Next person."

Just like that, what was left of our hopes crashed down. We were so close to making it to the country of Gareth's birth, to Wales and his family. They were all we had left. Everything else was gone in the aftermath. Our only worldly possessions were in our bags. Gareth had a life-long heart condition, and we had been counting on his citizenship for the healthcare he needed.

"We will stay and have my parents contact the embassy." Gareth nearly whispered.

I started to cry. The soldier nodded to the official and then motioned for us to move over to a small, but growing, crowd of people on the right side of the room. I wondered what had happened? When did the change take place that we couldn't even go to a charity willing to take us? I knew the camps in America were horrible. Could this one be any better?

I watched and waited as the hours passed, the crowd gathered, and the lines were shut down. Finally, one soldier picked up a bullhorn, stood on a chair, and spoke.

"You have chosen to stay here in Great Britain. At this time, we will take you to get your belongings. From there, you will be loaded onto buses and brought to Camp Iachâd. It is one of the last camps open to Americans. Please remain calm so the process will go quickly."

I made eye contact with a few of the others. Were they "true" refugees with nowhere to go? Or, were they like us and could not contact the families that were waiting for them? I cringed as we started moving again.

After finding our bags, we were loaded onto an old and uncomfortable bus. I was grateful to be able to sit down. Even more so when a female soldier started handing out water and crackers. It had been too many hours since we'd last eaten.

It was dark outside and no one knew how long it would take to get to the camp. I held onto my husband's arm and tried to close my eyes.

Two hours later, the buses slowed down and then turned onto a dirt road. After several kilometers, they stopped altogether. Slowly, another soldier came onto the bus. He looked all of us over, then spoke.

"Welcome to Iachâd. I am Lieutenant Franklin and will explain the entrance process to you. When you leave this bus, you will be taken to the first warehouse. There, we will do a basic physical exam, write a brief background, fingerprint you, and make your chipped photo ID cards. These cards are your tickets into the cafeteria as well as the ration line, the showers and the clinic. It will help us monitor the activities in the camp and provide adequate services. Families will be assigned tents and singles will be grouped together, by male and female, in bunkhouses. Once everyone has gone through the line, you will be taken to your assigned location and then to the ration line." He looked sympathetic for a moment "I know that you must be tired and hungry. We will do what we can to help you."

It was a slow and sad procession to the warehouse. I was thinking the worst, but hoped for something better. Panic almost set in as we were separated into male and female lines. Gareth's exam could go very wrong. I looked down at my abdomen and sighed; mine could go wrong too. However, it was not as bleak as I had feared. The military nurse listened to my heart and lungs. I hoped that she would not hear anything else. She entered her findings into a digital tablet. Then she pressed on my abdomen and asked if anything was tender. I lied.

She helped me sit up and asked, "How far along?"
I froze.

She smiled softly and said quietly, "It's okay. We have several expectant mothers here and have arranged transport to hospital to ensure a safe delivery."

I placed my hand on my stomach and whispered, "16 weeks."

She nodded and added that to her digital notes. After a check of my eyes and mouth, she sent me to the next station. I breathed a small sigh of relief.

We all moved quickly through the lines and soon Gareth and I were reunited. He looked worried but gave me a small smile.

"How did it go?" I asked.

"They will see what can be done with the heart medication. I might have to be on a less potent generic drug though." He looked towards the guards. "How was your exam?"

"She noticed." I replied, then quickly added, "I think it will be fine though."

"Having a baby in a refugee camp is not fine." He snapped, then sighed, "I hope dad and mum can get us out by then."

"We need to find a way to contact them. Perhaps..." But my comment was broken off by a soldier coming towards us. He was at least six feet tall and very built. He looked bored and slightly angry.

"Are you the dumb citizen who tried to come back with his non-citizen wife after decades with the colonists?"

"If you are looking for Gareth and Nicole Jones, then yes, that would be us." Gareth sounded so calm. It never ceased to amaze me how he could be that way. It was one of the many things about him that I loved.

"Whatever. Because you are still a citizen, you get to live in one of the nicer parts of the camp." He laughed harshly and walked away.

We grabbed our bags and followed. It was night, but there were lights on all around the camp. I quickly noticed the many tows of uniform tents, jammed in close together. Small buildings seemed evenly spaced among them. We had been told that the showers were in a separate building, and I started to become concerned. How often would we be allowed there? What condition were they in? Would there be any privacy? The soldier turned right, and we continued along. Because of the lights, I could see that the tents had turned into small shacks and that we were getting close to a fence. The shacks were not as close together and were made of a combination of wood, cement blocks, and metal. He pointed to the fifth one up, threw a folder at us, and walked away. The folder contained the rules of the camp, a paper to sign stating that we had read it, a note saying that rations will be handed out after we handed in the signed paper, and a rough map of the camp.

The shack was a simple 10 x 10 structure. I looked around and felt the tears well up in my eyes. In one corner was a cot, not quite full size, with a thin mattress, a sheet, and a blanket. A small shelf sat on the other wall, with a trunk below it, and a tiny table was by the door. We put our bags down, shut the poorly hung door, and took out the rules.

There were several pages of rules and notices. A ten o'clock pm to six o'clock am curfew was in effect. Food could only be cooked in specified areas. Rations were handed out weekly and used for one meal a day. Laundry had to be washed on assigned days because only one warehouse held the required equipment. We would receive a container for drinking water when we picked up our rations. Phone calls needed to have prior permission, and visitors were forbidden to enter the heart of the camp. Family, charity organizations, and embassy workers had to have special permission to enter the outer areas of the camp. We had to stay away from the fences and not speak to anyone who came up to it.

Gareth held me as we continued reading. We then signed the paper and took a look at the map.

"Our placement is for show." Gareth noted. "Anyone coming to the fence is going to see us and not the tents and older buildings." I agreed.

We quietly walked to the ration line, handed in our paper and received our package. Too tired to unpack, we opened a self-heating ration pack and split it. After getting on our knees and thanking God for our safety and asking Him for our freedom, we curled up under the blanket and fell into a dreamless, exhausted sleep.

At six the next morning, loudspeakers placed all over the camp began blaring an alarm. There was no choice but to wake up and start the day. With only a few hours of sleep, it promised to be a long one. After unpacking our few possessions, we walked to the line for the bathroom closest to us. I cringed at the thought of what I would find. Surprisingly, it was a row of proper toilets and sinks with running water. We then walked to the cafeteria. At that point, I noticed how many of us there really were. The line was very long, at least five hundred people. Children were crying, and people looked tired. We took our place in line, behind a boy who looked to be in his teens. He turned to look at us and smiled.

"Hey! Are you from last night's bus?" He was around six feet tall, thin-faced, with unruly blond hair, blue eyes, and sounded like he was from New England.

I nodded.

"Well...um...welcome." He hesitated. "I've been here for four months now. It's not too bad. We have food to eat and the weather is neutral enough here that the tents are okay for shelter, except when it rains too much." He chuckled. "It's hard to get used to all the people though, and we are missing some basic things."

I smiled at him before asking, "What is missing?"

"The kids needed a place to play. They are finally getting that, even if it is just a tiny field. We need a school still. The clinic needs to be bigger too. But hey, it's better than where we came from!"

I nodded slightly, wondering what he had experienced.

"My name is Jackson Phillips, Jack for short." He held out his hand.

"I'm Nicole Jones and this is my husband Gareth," I shook his hand and looked him in the eyes. I had an uncanny skill for reading people, and he seemed to have a good heart and a sharp mind.

H continued to tell us about the camp. As suspected, we were assigned to the shack because of Gareth's British citizenship. Jack was quick to point out that we also had nicer bathroom facilities and would probably be given preference in rations. I asked him what the tent bathrooms were like, and he confirmed that they were just pit toilets with hand-pumps for the water. The discrepancy bothered me, but I said nothing. We also talked about our lives in America. Jack was indeed from New England, Vermont to be precise. He was a junior in high school and his father was here in the camp with him. He looked excited when I said that I had been a teacher and told me he only knew of one other teacher here.

Breakfast was plain oatmeal and hot tea. It was just enough to stop the hunger pains. The cafeteria staff were all refugees like us. I wondered if they were being paid for the work. After our meal, Jack offered to show us the rest of the camp. We thanked him and followed.

What I saw reminded me too much of the pictures from the world news many years ago. There were rows and rows of dark green military-style tents. They had been placed on what must have been a field, but now most of the grass had been worn away. There were clotheslines, mud, and many people. Some sat in the few open areas, some at the entry to their assigned tent. Children played wherever they could with whatever they had. Soldiers roamed the perimeter. The warehouses were old but functional. Jack pointed out which one was the showers and which one held the laundry facilities. He also walked us past the clinic, where there was a line to receive services.

"We have been lucky," He said. "There have only been minor illnesses here, nothing major like dysentery or the remnants of the plague." I had to agree with him. Gareth and I had been spared the worst of the plague, mostly because we had been homesteaders and were able to survive off of our own land instead of being forced into the crowded towns and cities.

After the warehouses, we were shown the field that the children could play on. It really was just four small lots, but someone had built three seesaws, a balance beam, and a bench out of scrap lumber. Then, it was back to the rows of uniform tents. After hearing rumors of the abandoned building and razor wire camps in other locations, I offered up a prayer of thanks that we had been assigned to one of the newer facilities.

I tried to greet as many people as possible during our tour. My personality tended to be one of hope, and I tried to spread it as much as possible. Jack helped out by introducing me to those he knew. We met the other teacher, and I mentioned what Jack had said about there being no school.

"That hardly seems right," I stated.

"I agree, but what can we do?" she replied. Her name was Catherine and she, her husband and two children had been one of the first to arrive.

"All we really need is to tell the parents that we are starting a school up, pick a corner someplace and start teaching. The students can sit on the ground and write lessons in the dirt until we can get supplies. Maybe, if the officers here see that we are trying to improve the camp by displaying a school, they will help out."

Catherine hesitated, and I soon became frustrated with her. I had always been the type of person who took on the task, no matter how dirty or difficult.

"Let me know if you want to be involved." I told her when she still did not respond. "However, I am going to look into starting classes as soon as Gareth and I are settled."

Jack gave me a high-five as we started moving down the rows again. It appeared that I might have a teacher's assistant in the near future.

After our tour, Gareth and I went back to the shack and rested until dinner time. A noon meal was not provided through the cafeteria. We were expected to use our rations and any purchased foods. As usual, he was quiet. I knew that he was contemplating our situation and would be announcing his thoughts and plans whenever he was ready. Until then, it was best just to wrap my arms around him and rest.

We met up with Jack again for the evening meal. Every twenty minutes announcements were given over a loudspeaker outside the warehouse where we ate. There was a brief reminder of camp rules along with names of people who needed to report to the main offices there. Then, the list of tent and shack residents who would be able to wash laundry and shower the next day were read.

That night, I thought about the children in the camp and how they needed a place to learn. The decision was made to look around tomorrow for a spot large enough for them. I also needed to start talking with their parents. As my plans were slipping into place, Gareth spoke up.

"Tomorrow morning, I am going to find out who I need to talk to about getting a job either inside or outside of the camp. I'm also going to find out how to contact mum and dad."

I smiled. He was so predictable.

The rest of the first week in Camp Iachâd went by quickly. Gareth was at the main office every morning, trying to get through the proper channels for work and phone calls. On day five, he was finally able to contact his parents. They were, of course, worried about us since we did not arrive in Brecon when expected. They had tracked down our flight and knew that we had been taken to a camp but could not find out which one. Now that they knew, they promised to go to the embassy and start working on our release.

I wandered the camp and talked to both parents and children. Many were pleased that someone was taking an interest in their children but were concerned about how a school would be received. Several offered to help teach the younger ones. A father, who worked on the land management team in the camp, talked to one of the head soldiers about letting us use the small lot that had been set aside as a play area for the children. Another lot had been used as a church, and the man who acted as pastor also offered that spot. Word spread fast, and it was decided that we would try to hold class the next Monday in the lot used by the church.

The day came quickly, and I was as nervous as a new teacher during her first day in her first classroom. I hoped and prayed that no one would interfere and that at least several children would attend. It was silly to believe many would be there the first day. Most parents would be watching from a distance to see if it was safe, to see if the soldiers would break it up. At this point, we had no real reason to fear the soldiers. Most of the time they ignored us. Those who had access to the soldiers told them about the school and tried to get information sent to the main office. However, we were not sure if that message was ever received. So, the first day brought on fresh waves of indecision for all involved.

Gareth was still trying to be hired on outside of the camp, so we kissed each other goodbye after the morning meal of oatmeal and went our separate ways. As I approached the church lot, it became apparent that I was not alone. Jack was walking alongside me, and he was being followed by four children. At the lot, three more children waited for us, mothers in tow. I smiled brightly at them. Seven students were not a bad start. After a fun game where we all introduced ourselves, we got down to business. Two students were middle school age, three were elementary, and two were primary. Using sticks and rocks that Jack had gathered, we separated them into those three groups and tried to figure out what level they were on. I quickly assigned Jack to test the primary group on numbers, letters, and short words. He would write something on the ground and call on a child to say what it was. I tested the older students, but soon realized how difficult it would be to teach them without the help of books they could read. After I had a good idea what level each group was on, I taught a science lesson to all of them.

The hours flew by quickly and it was soon time to wrap up for the day. I looked around at the group of parents who were watching and smiled.

"Will I see your child here tomorrow?" I asked. I did not wait for a response before dismissing the students. Gareth met me at the edge of the lot.

"It looked good to me." He stated. "The soldiers did not seem to care either." I wrapped my arms around him and sighed in response.

By the end of the week, there were twenty-three students. Jack started helping me with the now six middle school students. A parent had offered to help with the ten in primary school. The fathers of the students had grouped together and were gathering scrap lumber to make rudimentary lap desks.

We had been in the camp for four weeks, and the school had been in session for nearly three, when I was called to the main office during the evening meal. I was very nervous but put on a brave face as I made the walk to the front buildings. The tall, nasty soldier from the night of our arrival was there. He sneered but motioned for me to follow him. I was led into a small, sparsely decorated office. Behind the desk sat a middle-aged officer. He nodded at my arrival, but said nothing, reading over a stack of papers instead. Minutes passed before he looked up again.

"Are you the teacher?" he asked.

"Yes, Sir." was my quick reply.

"I was not informed that we had a school."

"I thought not, Sir. We tried to send several messages through the soldiers." I broke off.

"No, they are not the most reliable source for information." He waved his hand in the direction of a chair. I sat down, grateful because of my trembling nerves.

"Why have you started a school?"

I looked at him and said. "Since no one knows how the current situation will turn out, I saw no harm in making sure that the children who leave this camp are performing at grade level. It would make a good impression for the camp itself if the children are not missing out on their education. It will also help them become more productive members of society once they are able to leave here." I had been practicing those lines for this very moment.

The officer stared at me for a minute. "It would make the camp look better if the children were seen attending school. The general public has mixed reactions to the presence of refugee camps here in Britain." He paused. "This could be a chance to show the doubters that the camps are just like the villages where they live." He pulled open a drawer and pulled out a form. "What basic supplies would you need to make the school appear successful?"

I did not like the way he phrased it but instantly came up with a short list.

"We need a chalkboard and mini chalkboards for the students to work on, as well as chalk and rags to erase with. We need books for all ages, but mostly for the elementary and middle school students. Desks would be a bit much right now, but chairs or benches would work well enough." I paused, then finished. "They need their own lot for school, and it should be sheltered."

He nodded. "You have thought this over well. The list is short but enough to make a good impression. I will see what we can do." With that I was dismissed.

Gareth and I held each other tight that night. The emotion of the visit shook me to the core.

As I started to settle down, he sighed and murmured.

"The clinic nurse came by. I will have to be on a different medication." I must have looked horrified, because he forced a smile and quickly added, "I'll be fine, don't worry, remember that it is just temporary. My family is working as we speak to get us out of this place." I tried to put my concerns out of my mind, but anything that had to do with his health always put me on edge.

Within another week, there was an official school in Camp Iachâd. The lot was right next to another fence. It was enclosed with three cinder block walls and a metal roof. Six long wooden benches had been placed inside. An old chalkboard had been hung from the front wall. A stack of lap-size chalkboards was piled below it. The students were so excited that it was hard to teach anything all morning. Suddenly, I had forty-five students, more than a third of the school-aged children in the camp. Jack had recruited a seventeen-year-old girl named Marie to help out. The two of them, as well as my parent volunteer, worked endlessly with the students. Catherine had still not shown up. I mentally wrote her off and focused all my energy into teaching the precious children.

It was only a few days later that I began to notice the faces. They stared at us from the other side of the fence. Sometimes, it was just people walking to a particular destination, but most of the times it was people who seemed to be curious about the camp. They listened in to the lessons and watched the children. At first, they were quiet, but before long they were whispering amongst themselves. I was concerned the children would notice and become uncomfortable. Fortunately, they did not seem to care.

It was around the same time that Gareth finally was given a job working in a grocery store. He stocked shelves from 8:00 am to 6:00 pm every day. He made just seven pounds an hour, less than minimum wage, but at least it was a job. He used his British citizenship to track down the bank in Brecon which had our money and had it transferred to a larger bank nearby. He deposited half of each check into it and spent the other half for supplies that were needed in the camp. Usually, it was bottles of chewable vitamins he would give to a resident who used to be a nurse. Her name was Kris, and she

14

would hand them out to as many people as she could during the morning meal. When possible, he would also purchase fresh foods from the grocery store. I was told that his boss delighted in the fact that what little Gareth was paid was being returned to his store.

Just a short time later, the camp was closed to new residents. One of the soldiers told Jack that anyone making it to Britain was being sent back or sent to another country. Because of the announcement, those who were in Camp Iachâd became much closer as a community. There were one thousand, two hundred fifty-seven of us, and we knew we were in it for the long haul. Many tried to make the best of it. Before the month ended, those precious few who worked outside of the camp began to make small purchases for the good of the community as well. Winter was fast approaching so gloves, hats, and warm socks, as well as fresh foods, were their focus.

In October, the first of the charitable donations arrived. It seemed that some of the outsiders who stared at us day after day had a sense of compassion. One chilly morning, two soldiers came into the school carrying boxes. In the boxes were used paperback books for the students. Three days later, the same soldiers came in with overfull trash bags in hand. It was second-hand child's clothing in various sizes, mostly jeans and sweaters for the upcoming winter. We now had seventy students, and they could not contain themselves as we moved up and down the rows, matching clothing sizes with each child's height and weight. In the middle of the chaos, I looked up and smiled at the group. Several were smiling back. I mouthed "Thank you." and went back to work.

THE COMING DARKNESS

Time seemed to move quickly in those days. With being on the same schedule, doing the same tasks day after day, it was no wonder I seemed to lose track. November was halfway through when the first signs of trouble started. One of the expectant mothers in the camp went into labor. The clinic nurse brought her to the hospital to give birth. She returned without her baby. Then, a second mother came due and the same event happened. They were told that their babies had died. However, the tone of the story did not ring true. One of the fathers decided to spy on the nurse and the soldiers who worked close to her. He soon discovered that the babies had survived and were immediately put up for adoption. There had been papers forged, saying the parents had turned over custody of their babies due to the hardships of life in a refugee camp. Gareth and I were terrified because I was seven months along. His parents were still working with the embassy to secure our release from camp, but very little progress had been made. What would happen to our precious child if I were to go into labor before we were released?

Other events had been happening in the camp that worried all of us as well. It was getting much colder out, and we were anticipating another harsh winter due to the drop in global temperature. It was a result of the multiple nuclear attacks combined with other natural events. Other than the donated jeans and sweaters for the children, no one else had been supplied with warmer blankets or clothes. The men had been petitioning the main office to allow them to visit area charity stores to purchase coats and blankets, but nothing seemed to be happening. Several people had died, and no one had been told the reasons for their deaths. We all began to worry about contagious illnesses and hypothermia. There had also been increasing incidents of harassment and even several events where a soldier hit or kicked a refugee. The conditions in the camp were beginning to decline.

I was called back to the main office the last day of the month. The same sneering guard led me to the same office as before. Inside, I was grateful to see the same officer at the desk. He looked up right away and motioned for me to sit down. The officer wanted to talk about how successful the school had been from his point of view. Of course, that meant how well it made the camp look to those on the outside. After complimenting me and saying Gareth and I were "model citizens" because of the work we did, he tried to dismiss me.

I spoke up instead. I told him about the drafty tents and upcoming winter and how many did not have warm blankets, coats or any way to keep the drafts from coming into the tent. I even went so far as to say I'd give up more donations to the school in order for the rest to have those items. He looked mildly surprised at me, but then said he would see what he could do.

The guard came in and escorted me back out to the main camp. However, as we turned the last corner, he stopped short and stuck his foot out. I stumbled, and he roughly grabbed my arm. "You better watch yourself, model citizen." He hissed. I looked at him, startled. He let go of my arm and stomped back to the barracks.

Warm blankets and adult sized coats were delivered a week later, but nothing arrived to keep the tents warm.

December brought more changes to the camp. Fewer rations were being handed out. It was hard for my students to focus on their lessons because of their near-empty stomachs and cold bodies. We had taken to gathering randomly purchased food items, along with some of the rations, and combining them into a large pot so there could be a hot mid-day meal, but it was not enough. There were more illnesses and several more deaths.

"Gareth, please just stay here. We'll make do with what we have. The others are helping out with purchases now as well." It was another night of me begging. I handed him my mid-day ration, as he was too tired to go to the evening meal.

"No." His voice was almost a whisper. "It is too bad out there right now. They need all the help they can get."

As forewarned, Gareth had been forced to change his heart medication and that came with complications. His heart struggled under the less effective drug.

Jack could tell that something was wrong. It was becoming hard for me to focus on teaching. Without a word, he picked up the slack as much as he could. He also started interacting more with the parents of our students. I never listened to any of the conversations though, because too much was going on inside my head. If I looked over to where he was talking, he would just smile at me and then turn away. It made me wonder, but there was so much on my mind that it was quickly pushed to the side. If I had relied on Jack to help me with the school before, it was nothing compared to how I was dependent on him now.

December 15th started like every other day in the camp. The morning alarm blared through the rows. I moaned at the cold weather, then leaned over to give Gareth a morning kiss. His face was motionless, jaw slack, and he was cold. My heart stuttered as I sat up and tried to shake him. There was no response. With tears welling up in my eyes and a scream waiting in my throat, I laid my head on his chest. Minutes passed as I processed what I heard. Nothing. His heart had stopped sometime in the night. The love of my life was dead. I could not move, could not think. The sun came up and started to warm the shack. The noise from the nearby bathrooms was quieted as residents made their way to breakfast. I continued to lay there, tears flowing, but still holding back the scream.

I did not know what to do, so I chose to do nothing. I had moved so that my knees were on the ground and my head was lying next to his. It seemed like hours passed. Suddenly, the stillness was broken by a knock on the door.

"Nicole?" It was Jack.

Reality flooded back to me like a tsunami. School had started for the day, and I was not there. Of course, Jack would come looking for me. I gasped, and he heard it. The door was opened in a moment, and he rushed in, only to stop and stare in horror at the scene before him. There was silence as he went through the same process as me. Then he too gasped and it sounded like he was choking. I looked up to see tears streaming down his face. It was enough to snap me out of the shock, and I stood up and went to stand in front of him. He looked into my eyes, and then we both collapsed to the ground crying.

More time passed, minutes really, but Jack stood back

18

up and whispered. "We will take care of you, I promise." He looked at the door, but his gaze was beyond it. "I'll force Catherine to cover while we figure out what to do. Stay here." He ran out the door, slamming it behind him.

I poured some water from the container into a bowl and washed my face and arms, trying not to look at the place where the love of my life lay dead. In a ten-foot shack though, that was not easy to do. I ended up covering him with our blanket and then sat at the foot of the bed, facing the door. Jack returned shortly, Kris, the former nurse with him. She checked my vitals. When she was finished, she stared at me and then asked.

"Was it his heart? Or was he ill?"

"It was his heart." I whispered. It was the first time I had spoken, and my voice sounded far away.

"I'm so sorry."

I just nodded, not trusting my voice or my emotions.

"I don't know how long we have until the office finds out that there has been another death. They will come and take...the body...and make sure that you are not ill. But, I do not know what will happen after that."

I looked at Jack, "Gareth was the reason why we were in the shacks and not the tents. I should be prepared to move to the singles bunkhouse."

He clenched his fists and glared out the door. "Not if I can help it. You will need at least a tent because of the baby. With all the work you are doing with the children, they better let you stay here." With that, he ran back out the door, and this time he went left towards the main office.

When he finally made it back to the shack, it was with two soldiers and the officer I had spoken with. The soldiers had a body bag, and I sucked in my breath to hold back the scream in my throat. I wanted to go into hysterics, screaming and clawing at them, but the rational part of my mind knew it would do more harm than good. I leaned over Gareth's body and kissed his forehead one last time. Then, I walked out of the shack and over to the fence.

The officer followed. "I am so sorry Mrs. Jones. The entire camp will be affected by the loss of your husband. He was a model resident."

19

My first instinct was to slap him across the face and start screaming. If he was such a model resident, why couldn't the officer get Gareth the medication he needed? Why did he allow us to continue to live like this? The anger was starting to build. However, the rational part of me kicked in again, and I just nodded, but tears started flowing again. He saw this and put his hand on my shoulder. The soldiers were bringing out the body bag and I fell to the ground, one scream escaping my lips before I regained control.

"Your young friend is concerned about where you will be living. I will write orders to keep you here. Your work with the children alone is enough to allow you to stay. With the baby so close to coming..." He hesitated, and I knew why; they would try to take my baby. I saved him from having to finish the lie.

"Thank you," I whispered.

He nodded and followed the soldiers.

I looked at Jack, but he was looking away staring out towards the hill outside the fence. Someone was standing there, watching us. Even though the hill was far, I could tell it was a man with dark hair. Anger welled up, and I turned towards the hill ready to scream at the stranger peering into the camp and seeing my grief – my husband being carried out to be buried at the far side of the camp.

Jack must have seen it coming because he put his hand on my arm and whispered. "No. Don't say anything. He is one of the good guys."

I stared at him as if he were insane. There were no such thing as good guys when it came to the outside of the camp. There were those people who felt guilty and donated items to us, but there were no good guys. Good guys would be petitioning to let us out, would be at the fence trying to talk to us, encourage us, slip needed items in for us.

"Trust me." He said.

It was becoming too much for me to bear. I ran back into the shack and looked around for something to throw. The screams refused to stay inside this time, so I chose instead to grab the pillow and scream into it. No need for the whole camp to hear my grief, as they had plenty of it themselves.

"Go, Jack. Leave. Go back to the students, they need

you." I choked. He stood in the doorway, not moving. "GO!" I screamed. It startled him enough that he did leave, hopefully, to return to the school.

I lost it. The screams came, and the sobs tore at me. Few heard due to the pillow at my mouth. Not strong enough to walk the three feet to the bed, I laid on the dirt floor and let the sorrow take me. More hours passed. The refugee nurse checked on me again, making me drink a glass of water and eat some stale crackers.

The sun was nearly set when Jack returned to the shack. He sat on the edge of the bed, a ration pack in his hands. I refused to acknowledge his presence, but he refused to leave. Why oh why did he have to be such a good kid? Why was this compassionate, responsible teenager in this forsaken place? Why did he have to care enough to come back and remain here until the storm passed? If he were not sitting there, I could continue to grieve, to scream and mourn my loss. With him in the shack, I had to gather my shredded wits and try to be human again. It took nearly an hour of him sitting there before I could even lift my head.

"Hey." I croaked.

"Hey." He replied. "I brought you some dinner. You really should eat something, even if you're not hungry." He looked at my swollen abdomen.

Of course, he was right, the baby needed food, and I had been skipping meals in order to give the small packaged meals to Gareth for dinner. I forced myself to sit up and reach for the pack, somehow managing to chew and swallow its contents. Jack smiled when I handed him the empty container. He was about to say something else when there was a knock at the door. He stood up and opened it. The camp nurse was standing there, and she looked a little shocked to see that I was not alone.

Quickly her expression changed. "It's good to see that you have not been left to grieve alone, dear."

She walked in and extended her hand to help me up. As with most of the camp, I did not trust her, but it was unwise to do anything to make relations worse. I accepted her hand and used it to help myself up.

"You are called Jack?" She looked at the teenager.

21

He nodded.

"Would you mind giving us some privacy while I examine Mrs. Jones?" It really was not a question.

Jack gave me a knowing look and quietly slipped outside.

"Now, let's see how you are holding up." She pulled out a stethoscope and listened to my heartbeat. She then lowered it and listened to the baby's heart.

"How much longer do you have?"

I had lost track of time, so it took a moment to calculate.

"Seven weeks."

She nodded. "You have had a horrid day, and the next few days will be tough. I brought something to help you sleep. It is safe for the baby."

I did not want to take anything, but she went over to the water container and poured some into the cup. She then pulled a bottle out of her jacket pocket and opened it. She shook two pills into the cap and handed them to me. Remembering that it was probably unwise to go against her, I took the offered pills and water.

She noticed my hesitation and smiled again. "It's safe, really."

I unwillingly swallowed the pills and wondered how long until they took effect.

"I'll be back to check on you in the morning. Sleep well."

As soon as she left, Jack came back inside. "What did she do?" He looked so worried.

"She just checked my vitals, the baby's heart and gave me something to help me sleep."

"I don't trust her."

"I don't either, but there was not much of a choice tonight."

He looked at the bed.

"Well, go lay down before that crap kicks in. I'm staying here tonight to make sure you are okay. And no, do not try to protest, my father already knows I'm here."

The medication did help me sleep, but no living thing could stay asleep once the morning alarms started blaring. My eyes slowly opened, and I looked around the shack. Jack was sitting by the door, his eyes opened, and he stretched.

"Did you stay there all night?" I asked.

He nodded.

"Thank you."

He nodded again.

"I guess we should get this day started." I sighed.

"No."

"Huh?"

"You need to recover from yesterday. After breakfast, you should come back here. We'll take care of the school. Catherine picked up the slack yesterday quite well. It's a shame that it took this to get her to remember how to be a teacher again."

I stared at him, thinking it over. "No." It was my turn.

"Excuse me?"

"I am not going to come back to this shack until after evening meal. It will just make me feel worse. If you will not allow me to teach, then I'll wander the camp. Period."

He thought about that for a moment, "You win."

I followed him to the bathrooms, and then we continued to the breakfast line. It was hard to ignore the stares, but I managed. More stares were met as I walked into the school. Even the children stared at me until I told them it was okay and that I would still be their teacher. Catherine was there and, in those moments where my mind wandered, she picked up the lesson. The day went by quick enough and soon it was time for the evening meal. I was on my way back to the shack, after convincing Jack that I needed the time alone, when I saw the man again. He was still on the hill, still looking towards me. He had dark hair and had on a black leather jacket, like the ones motorcycle riders wore. I stared back for a moment, then shut the door of the shack. Inside, I broke down and cried until the nurse came.

THE END OF MY LIFE

The next day was the same and the next. But on the fourth day, something was wrong, very wrong. I woke up in pain like I had never experienced before. It faded but then came back again and again. It soon dawned on me that I was in labor, and it was too soon. My mind had already been made up that there was no way I would be going to the hospital. They would not be taking my baby and giving it to someone else to raise. As the waves of contractions hit me, I bit the pillow and tried to stay quiet. If he stayed true to form, it would only be a matter of time before Jack came running to see why I was late for school. How was I going to get him to stop running to the main office? How would I explain my reasoning for going through labor and birthing in this dirty shack, away from proper medical care? How was I willing to risk my life and my child's life in order to have a chance at keeping him or her?

It only took an hour before Jack arrived, and he was not alone. He had already come to the conclusion that something was wrong, and Kris was by his side. She took one look at me and gasped.

"What is it?" Jack choked out at the expression on my face.

She pushed him into the room and shut the door.

"When did it start?" She asked me.

"I don't know. Sometime while the medication had me asleep." I cringed at another contraction. "But they are really close together. I think it is going to be fast."

She went right to work. "Jack, I need to examine her to see how far along labor is. Please, go fill up the water container, bring it back here, then go to my tent and get that bag I showed you yesterday."

Sudden understanding lit up his face, followed by horror.

I looked him in the eye and said, "I know, Jack, it's too soon but please go." In an instant, he was gone.

"What bag?" I asked.

"There are two other women here who are expecting.

24

No one wants to go to the hospital because of what happened with the other two babies. I have been working with someone on the outside to procure basic medical supplies and filled a laundry sack with what is needed to help deliver here in camp. I cannot perform a Caesarian but am prepared for most anything else." She smiled at me, and I chuckled.

Kris finished examining me and agreed that labor was progressing fast. Jack came back a few minutes later, and she laid out what was needed. The mattress was lifted and placed against the wall, so it would not be stained. She replaced it with an old blanket. I was propped up on the cot frame with the pillow behind my head and a rolled towel in my hand for stifling any screams. Surprisingly, I maintained enough control to just moan quietly through the increasingly stronger contractions.

The labor changed around noon, and I felt the urge to push. Kris had me sit at the edge of the bed, with Jack supporting my back. He had not spoken through the entire time, and I wondered if he was scared or horrified. The poor kid was having to go through so much because of me. With that thought, the tears started to flow again. Kris looked up from her position.

"Nicole?"

"Just thinking this should not be happening. Gareth should be here to see it, and the baby should not be coming this soon and..." I choked on a half sob, half scream.

"I know, but you need to focus on pushing right now."

I did. I pushed, caught my breath, pushed and caught my breath again. After only fifteen minutes, my daughter was born. My heart caught in my throat at the sound of her pitiful cry. Kris quickly cut the cord with bandage cutters she had swabbed with alcohol and iodine. Jack used some strips of cloth that Kris had in the bag and water to clean her up. She was so tiny but was breathing steady. Once the afterbirth passed, Kris carefully examined the baby. Jack took my hand and asked what I was going to name her.

"Sarah" I whispered.

Kris looked up. "She is small, but her lungs seem to be in good shape – despite being six weeks early. Have you heard of kangarooing?"

I nodded.

"That is what she is going to need. I'll make a sling to hold her close to your body. All she will need to do is turn her head to eat. I have more cloths that can be used to diaper her for now because she is too small for regular cloth diapers."

She looked at Jack. He stared back at her. "Jack has been working on connections with the outside. That is how I was able to get these supplies. These contacts know about your situation and want to help. Yesterday, one of them told Jack that they have been to the embassy and will be pursuing your release."

"Who are they?" I wondered.

Jack bit his lip before answering. "I'm not sure, but they seem to have a bit of power around here. And right now, we need that power."

Sarah started to fuss at that moment, and I looked down at her in wonder.

"You have your fathers' nose, thank goodness, and look at all that hair." I murmured.

"She might be hungry." Kris commented.

Jack realized what that comment meant and decided it was time for him to check on the students. He waved to me and smiled at Sarah before leaving the shack. Kris helped me clean up and put the mattress back in place. She coached me through the process of nursing Sarah for the first time. We were worried that she would be too weak to nurse, but she seemed to take in enough. Afterward, we both closed our eyes exhausted by our efforts. Kris stayed in the shack until I woke again. It was dark outside.

"What time is it? I hope you didn't miss dinner?"

"It is after seven, and I brought rations with me for both of us. Jack has set up a schedule of people to sit with you throughout the next nights." She saw my mouth open in protest and raised a hand. "You cannot be left alone. Once the office finds out about Sarah they may try to take her."

I held my premature daughter closer to my chest at that terrifying thought. She responded by waking up, giving a tiny stretch that made my heart melt and starting to fuss. Kris took her from the sling, checked her vitals again, and placed her back with me to nurse.

At around eight o'clock one of the mothers, whose baby had been taken away, came in with her husband. They looked around at the conditions of the shack and then looked at me. Tears flowed down my cheeks as I realized they would be my guardians tonight. I held a hand out to the woman and she grasped it as if it were a lifeline. Sarah shifted in her sling at my movements, and the woman gazed down at her.

"Her name is Sarah." I whispered.

She released my hand and stroked Sarah's' tiny face with her pinky finger.

"It seems like such a worthless phrase for the circumstance but thank you for being here tonight." I said to both of them.

The man answered with determination in his voice "We can not allow what happened to us happen to anyone else."

Kris gave me a gentle hug and assured me that she would be back at the morning alarm. I thanked her again, and she smiled sadly in return. We both knew that come morning, Sarah's' condition could be worse. Premature babies tend to decline in the first twenty-four to forty-eight hours.

I scooted over against the wall so that the woman could sit down next to me and her husband could sit on the edge. We all listened to her small breaths as the night passed into day. I was happy when she startled and fussed loudly at the morning alarm. The man and his wife left after placing a kiss on each of our foreheads. I began to cry again for their loss.

Jack made it to the shack before Kris. He came right over to me and started to take off the sling. Before I could protest he whispered, "They are suspicious of your absence yesterday. Put on the baggiest shirt you have and get over to the cafeteria line." He paused. "I don't know how observant they will be. Hopefully, just scanning your card will be enough. You need to eat a hot meal anyway. Kris will be here any minute."

I followed his instructions and, after a stop in the bathroom, slowly made my way to the cafeteria line. Fortunately, I had been walking slowly for the last month. The fact that the pain left over from labor and delivery kept me moving at that pace helped the situation. Keeping my head down and my left hand in a protective position around my abdomen, I scanned my ID card and made it through the breakfast line. Most of the morning rush was over. Jack was right, I needed the hot oatmeal. It made me realize how weak I had been feeling and how cold I really was.

As soon as the meal was finished, I slowly got up and wandered back to the shack. Kris was examining Sarah. She brought a fresh towel to wrap her in, and Jack quickly put the sling back on me.

"I have to get to the school. They have been told that the grief over Gareth's death finally caught up with you and you needed a few days alone. My father will be here to guard you." And then he was gone.

Kris placed Sarah back into the sling and sighed.

"What's wrong?" I asked.

"Her breathing seems a bit shallow right now. I'm hoping she is just tired, and after a long rest with you, it will be better."

My heart caught in my throat, but I nodded and went back to the bed. It was noon before either of us awoke again. My eyes opened wide in surprise when I realized Mr. Phillips was in the room. Jack's father was an imposing figure, unlike his sweet teenage son. He had been working on the land management team, and that allowed him to keep the large muscles and strength he must have had before coming to the camp. I chuckled at the thought of some of the average size guards trying to go up again this bull of a man.

The day turned into night all too soon. I made an appearance at the evening meal and quickly returned to the shack. Another husband and wife team watched over Sarah and I that night. The next day was Saturday, and Jack and Catherine stayed with me all day. Sarah was less fussy and that had me concerned. I had to pinch her to get her to wake up enough to nurse. Kris was nervous about the change as well. While Jack and Mr. Phillips would be guarding me, she decided to stay the night as well.

It was a good thing that she did. My daughter stopped breathing at 2 am, then again at 5 am, and a final time at 6 am. It was more than I could handle. This time there was no stopping the screaming. Kris, Jack, and his father cringed as wave after wave of sorrow ripped through me. At some point, a neighbor must have gone to the clinic because the camp nurse and two armed soldiers burst into the room. They shoved everyone out but me, still holding my lifeless baby girl.

"You should have sent someone to get me when you went into labor!" The nurse berated me.

"And let you haul me to the hospital where you would take my daughter to the NICU and come back with the lie that she was dead? Never!"

She looked shocked that I knew the truth but quickly responded. "At least she would have been alive."

"Not to me, she would not have been. The three days I had her were worth the sacrifice. You took my husband from me, I was not going to let you take my baby too!" I was screaming at this point.

She looked angry, reached into her bag and grabbed a syringe. She walked over to me and a soldier came up and held me down as she injected me with it. "You'll sleep for a day with that stuff. I'll be back tomorrow. Hopefully, you will be more reasonable."

Within seconds I was fighting sleep at the same time I was fighting the soldier from taking Sarah's body from my arms.

Gratefully, I do not remember the rest of that year. I was told that I got up in the morning, ate the cafeteria breakfast, taught at the school, ate the cafeteria evening meal, showered and did laundry on the scheduled day, and screamed during most of the nights. The camp nurse gave up trying to keep me sedated after I forced myself to wake up several times after she injected me.

My memories pick up again in mid-January. Since individual days had ceased to exist for me, I'm not sure exactly when it was that daily consciousness returned. However, I think it was the first day "he" came down from the hill. "He," the man with the dark hair and black motorcycle jacket had been watching from the hill nearly every week. My thoughts were that he could not be watching just me, but then he came down, and I saw him while teaching. That evening he was at the bottom of the hill as I came back from the evening meal. The next day it was the same. On the third, I stared back at him – more like glared at him. He shifted his gaze, so our eyes met briefly, and it seemed like he was trying to communicate something. I stomped into the shack and slammed the door.

I wanted to scream at the man up on that hill, looking down on the rapidly deteriorating camp. It was getting much worse here. The soldiers were becoming nastier, showing off their power over us. It was colder than normal, and there was more snow than usual – because of the long-term effects of the nuclear blasts. Everyone was cold and hungry. I wondered why those outside didn't do more to help us. Maybe they were trying, and the corruption was stopping them?

The very next day was what I later labeled as the "start of the end of my life." I was walking back from the evening meal and had not yet made it past the warehouses. Jack, my near-constant companion since the double tragedy of Gareth's and Sarah's deaths was in his tent, sick with a stomach virus that the students had been passing around. I was alone but gave no second thought to it. That was when the sneering soldier came out from behind the last building and grabbed me.

I had not seen much of him since my last visit to the main office. Apparently, he had been watching me though. He pulled me behind the warehouse and through a back door.

"Model citizen." He sneered at me. "Not anymore." I knew then what he was planning to do.

Thankfully, the assault was quick. Horribly painful, but because I did not allow myself to struggle, it was quick. When he was done, he shoved me and my torn clothes out of the back door and stalked off. Somehow, I managed to make it to the shack before collapsing into tears.

Once semi-composed, I cleaned myself off as best as possible, took the needle and threads from our original camp package, and sewed up the tears in my clothes. Someone from the outside had donated several post-maternity outfits to me, and the office had allowed it. Since they were all I owned, they had to last. The next morning, I put on a cleaner outfit which, thankfully, covered the bruises. Jack was feeling better as well, so I felt more secure with having him back as an

30

escort.

Three nights later I found out that an escort meant nothing. At around midnight the same sneering soldier walked into the shack, dragged me to the floor, and raped me again. This time it was much harsher. He held me down with his entire weight and left bruises on my face and neck. It was harder to get up and moving when the alarm sounded that morning. I stumbled sorely to the bathroom and then back to the shack, because I did not think I could handle the walk to the cafeteria.

"He" was at the bottom of the hill. I stopped and stared, the look on his face said it all. He somehow knew what had happened last night. It was not pity on his face, nor horror, just immeasurable sadness in his eyes and fists clenched in anger. Our eyes met again, and he startled me by walking closer.

When he was ten feet from the fence, he spoke. "Tell Jackson."

Before I could reply, he turned around and walked away, past the hill, and out of sight.

I stood, staring at the hill. Part of me wanted to call out to him; another part thought it would be best to ignore him. But in my heart, I knew he was right. Slowly, my head caught up with the rest of me. I was late for breakfast, and since I was too sore to move quickly, I would be late to the school as well. Even if I made it there, all the adults would see the bruises and know that something was wrong.

I went back into the shack, sat on the bed, and waited. True to form, Jack arrived within the hour. He took one look at me and ran out to get Kris.

When they returned, all I had to say was, "The tall soldier, the one who looks like he is sneering at us..." Jack put his fist through the thin door at that point. There was nothing else to say, no need to mention that it had happened another time. There was very little that Kris could do, and she looked upset at her helplessness. We sat and stared at the hole for a few minutes. Suddenly, Jack bolted out the door. I looked at Kris with a questioning expression.

"I think he is going to get help." She sighed. "I hope it is outside help."

I thought about the man on the hill. Who was he? How did he know what happened last night? How did he know Jackson? Was there a reason why he ordered me to tell Jack? There was more going on in this camp then I was aware of, and it bothered me. Whatever was happening, it involved the sweet teenager who had been my friend from the first day in Camp Iachâd. I worried about his safety. If he were talking to people on the outside and was caught, he could be punished.

It was all too much for me again. I broke down crying. Kris quickly wrapped me in her arms and rocked me as if I were a small child. It was so comforting that I ended up calming enough to sleep. When I awoke, Jack, Kris, Jack's father, and four other refugee men were in the room. Panic hit me first, followed by relief when I realized that all of the men were fathers of my students. One was patching up the punched hole in the door with a piece of scrap wood and a couple of old nails.

Jack's father spoke. "They have gone too far this time. Despite the situations that led us here, we are still human, and no human should go through that." He looked around the room. "We are not going to let it happen again."

I wondered what it was that they could do to protect the women of the camp. But when he spoke again, I realized that my thoughts had been in error.

"You will not be alone at any time. Jack will walk you to and from meals and the school. The rest of us will take turns here. There are more of us willing to join in if there are any ramifications."

"But what about the other women?" I whispered.

"As far as we know, there have been no other attacks like this. Even the women in the bunkhouse have been left alone."

"Oh."

Jack spoke up then. "They know on the outside and are doubling their efforts to get you out as soon as possible."

"What about my students?" I could not bear the thought of leaving them. The school was the only stable thing they had. The love between us was strong. They needed me!

Jack looked as if he would punch the door again.

"You are being raped by one of the people assigned to

32

protect us, after losing your husband and baby to this place! People outside are working on a way to get you out of here, and you are worried about your students?" He was almost screaming.

Jack's father spoke up then. "Catherine has come a long way these months, and there are others who will help keep the school."

I sighed and squeezed my eyes shut. Other people had it worse than me and I knew it. It was hard for me to accept help while others suffered around me. It used to be just those in various countries, faces in pictures but so far away...my thoughts shifted. Now, I was part of it, but even then, there were others who had suffered more. I had to help them. With my last breath, I had to help them!

My eyes opened, and I looked around at the men again. "Thank you," I whispered.

"It will not happen again." Jack's father whispered back.

And it didn't. For the next month the only time I was away from one of them was in the bathroom. Women from the camp made sure I was not alone there. We were back into a routine, but it did not feel right. I was always on edge, always looking around, screaming every night. My "guardian angels," as I nicknamed them, would look at me sadly and then we would talk – sharing stories until my eyes closed again.

"He" was no longer on the top of the hill. The man with the dark hair and jacket was now standing closer to the camp. Sometimes he came within ten feet of the fence. He never spoke, just watched. I felt as if he were somehow guarding me as well. One time, a soldier called him out. He walked right up to the fence and they had a quiet conversation. The soldier looked surprised and nodded. No soldier ever spoke to him, or even looked at him, after that.

My life ended on February 20th. Of course, I did not know that when the morning alarms sounded. All throughout the typical oatmeal breakfast, and even during school, there was no hint of what was to come. It was a sunny day, warm for that time of year, and many of us were in high spirits. The parents enjoyed seeing the children play on their small playground lot. Even Jack, who had not smiled in too long, was grinning and laughing. The evening meal was alive with conversations, a change from the glum faces and whispers from the past months. Spring was on its way, and it lifted everyone.

Then, during the announcements, my name was called to go to the clinic. It seemed unusual, but I had no choice but to go. Jack's father was by my side in an instant. He escorted me the short distance to the clinic and remained at the door. After a deep breath, I went inside. To my surprise, the officer whom I had spoken to in the past was standing there. He smiled at me. The nurse was there as well, and she had a small smile on her face too.

"We have good news for you, Mrs. Jones." The officer started. "Your family has been working tirelessly to bring you home from the camp. They must love you very much for continuing the effort after the unfortunate loss of your husband. Tonight will be your last night in the camp. When the alarm goes off tomorrow morning you are to report to the main office with your ID card and any items you brought into the camp. We will then take you to the front gate, where your family will be waiting. We will miss you and the positive example you have been to others here. Congratulations." I sensed that he was telling the truth, so I smiled at him, hope filling me.

The clinic nurse spoke then. "I need to do an end-of-stay exam, and then you will be free to go and pack your belongings."

It was a basic examination. She checked my reflexes, heart, lungs, sight, and hearing. She looked for lice in my hair and checked my abdomen. She then had me shower there at the clinic, mumbling something about wanting the camp to have a good impression and my hair was greasy. When I was finished, she updated my ID card and I was allowed to exit the clinic. Jack's father waited for me, and his eyes were bright with happiness.

"Praise God!" He whispered. He had heard everything.

We went to tell Jack. He was very happy, but strangely did not seem surprised. It made me wonder if the people he knew had something to do with my release. Word spread and soon their small tent was packed with lines of well-wishers. There were many kind words and many tears. We came up with a story to tell the students, and I was satisfied that it would not sound as if I abandoned them willingly.

All too soon it was curfew. The alarm rang, warning that we had only minutes to get to our assigned tents or shacks. Jack decided that he would be the one to guard me on my last night in the camp. He was not part of the normal "guardian angels," because of his youth and thin frame, but none of us thought that there would be trouble tonight. I gave Kris and Mr. Phillips a final hug, and we rushed back to the shack.

We were making the final turn away from the warehouses when the death throws started. The first thing that happened was a large soldier stepped in front of us, blocking our way. Then, another came up from behind and hit Jack over the head with something hard. He was unconscious before he hit the ground. The person behind me clamped his hand over my mouth and started dragging me around to the back of the building, just like before.

It was the same room as the first assault and the sneering guard was waiting. My eyes quickly roamed the dimly lit area. There were four soldiers and, after looking at each of them, I knew what their intentions were.

"Well, if it isn't our model citizen." The sneering one growled as he paced in front of me. "You have put me in a bad situation, being released tomorrow." He stopped and placed his finger under my chin. "There is no reason for you to stay quiet about our little meetings and about why you needed bodyguards." Then he slapped me across the face. "So, there is going to be an unfortunate accident tonight. You won't be alive to prattle on about us."

In the process of death, this was where my heart would have stopped. In reality, it raced with fear. One of the soldiers kicked my legs out from under me. My head hit the edge of what I think was a table. He kicked me again then stepped back. I got up onto my knees, the world spinning around me, and the sneering one kicked me in the chest. I heard ribs crack and my breath came out in a rush. The world started to go gray. He was taking off his belt, and another soldier was ripping off my clothes. Someone punched me in the face and the gray had black edges to it.

"Don't knock her out, she won't be any fun that way." The sneering guard hissed as he started his assault. I wanted to scream, wanted to fight, but I could not take in enough air to do either. He finished, and another soldier took his place. The pain was beyond anything I could ever fathom. My world became darker and darker. In the process of dying, these were the moments before brain death. But, in reality, something else happened.

There was a bright flash, a small explosion, and then my world was full of sound. I heard guns being fired, men yelling, someone screaming in pain. Something heavy was on top of me. I opened my eyes and saw smoke, blood and "him." He was kicking the body of the now dead soldier off of me. I turned my head and saw several men in strange uniforms who were fighting with and incapacitating the rest of the soldiers. I looked back towards the dark-haired man as he got one knee and checked my condition. I winced when he found the broken ribs. Chaos was spilling into the rest of the camp, the refugees had awakened from the flash and explosion, and they were panicking.

He took no notice though, his eyes only on me. "We have to get you out of here, but there is no time for a stretcher." The expression on his face changed from concern to sadness. "I'm sorry, but this is going to hurt more."

With that, he picked me up in his arms and started carrying me out of the warehouse. We made it half way to the main entrance when I passed out.

My life ended in that moment.

NO ONE, NO WHERE

Hazy memories, unfamiliar faces, someone saying I needed surgery to set broken bones and to sew up internal bleeding. Someone was apologizing for the pain I was in. There was the feeling of being moved, being at rest, and then being moved again. "His" voice asking questions to others who had to have been standing nearby. There was so much confusion and so much pain. Sometimes I could open my eyes and see a hospital room, but most of the time I could not make myself wake up fully. It seemed to go on and on and on.

Then it was over. The fuzzy feeling started to leave my brain. I felt that I could open my eyes and keep them open for more than a couple of seconds. Before opening them though, I listened. There was someone else in the room with me. I could hear the breathing and slight shifting. There was the beeping of a monitor and, in the distance, a humming noise. I waited, hoping the person would leave so that I had time alone to process where I was and what had happened. There was the pain, but it was subdued compared to what had happened that night.

That night! I gasped, and my eyes flew open on their own as those last memories rushed through my mind. The other person stopped breathing for a moment. I tried to turn my head in that direction, but a blast of pain stopped the movement. Instead, I slowly turned my eyes toward the sudden absence of sound. In the process, I registered that this was indeed a hospital room with pale walls and a chair. In that chair was "him", the dark-haired man. He registered my gaze and started breathing again. He rose and came to stand by the bed, his eyes wandering over me and the equipment I was still attached to. He was tall and lean, wearing a short sleeve shirt, and his arms were muscular. His shoulders were not broad, but they were firm.

"Welcome back." He said softly and gave me a small tentative smile.

I just stared at him unsure if, or even how, I should respond.

His smile quickly faded. "This must be uncomfortable for you, and I'm sure you have many questions for us."

I nodded. The "us" reference was not lost on me. It was at this point that I noticed his familiar accent, Welsh. "I could answer most of them for you, but traditionally it is The General's duty. I'll let him know that you are awake."

With that, he walked over to the door and pulled out a mobile phone. After a brief conversation in low tones, he placed the device back into his pocket and came back to my bed. He shut the monitor off and then stared at me. He looked as if he were going to say something but then changed his mind. After an endless moment, he did speak quietly. "Try to be open-minded." His expression changed to one of sorrow, and he reached out to brush his fingers across the top of my hand before striding quickly out of the room.

I was alone for only a moment. The man who came into the room next took me off guard. He was average height and weight with short graying hair. His eyes were dark blue, and his face had the early signs of aging. I estimated him to be in his early 60's. He strode over to my bed and smiled kindly, holding his hand out for me to grasp weakly.

"I am General Smiths, but most here just call me The General. I'm happy to see you are finally awake." He was a true-blue Englishman by the accent.

I decided it was time to test my voice. "How long?" It sounded just as bad as it felt. Judging by the sore feeling, I guessed that either my injuries or treatment had left me on a ventilator for a while.

He pulled the chair from its corner to my bedside and sat down. "About ten days. I'm afraid your injuries were quite severe. We had to keep you in a drug-induced coma for the first five." He must have seen the question in my eyes, because he went right into the details. "You had three broken ribs, your nose was broken, there were four other facial fractures, a skull fracture, internal bleeding in your abdomen..." He paused and looked away.

"What else?" I whispered.

"It's lucky we got to you when we did. You were torn up internally." He paused again. "You had some injuries from the rapes and your early delivery."

I sucked in a breath and then tried to suppress a scream as pain ripped through my chest. He waited a moment before continuing, "You were hemorrhaging from those. The surgeon had no choice but to perform an emergency hysterectomy. He still has to do a small reconstructive surgery for the damage done by the multiple attacks." His expression turned to one of grief, and he lowered his head. "I am truly sorry." I could sense that he really was.

We stayed in silence for a full minute. The General was giving me time to think through what he had said. A single tear slipped down my face from the combination of physical and emotional pain. I mentally checked off each injury as I contemplated what it would take to fix each one. I was surprised at how bad it was and even more so that I was still alive. He raised his head back up and met my gaze.

"I'm very lucky that your men came in when they did." I croaked.

He looked relieved. "Yes. But if we had anticipated an attack like that, you would have been out of the camp the hour the orders arrived."

Confusion flickered across my face.

He must have known about what I had been told because his next words were. "No, it was not your family. They would not have been able to get you out of there, not with the way the government has been. The officers were led to believe it was them but in truth..." He paused again. "In truth, they have been told that you are missing and presumed dead. The surviving attackers are being charged as such."

"I need to call them!" The pain didn't stop desperation from leaking into my voice.

He shook his head. "No. Not yet."

I tried to sit up, but there were too many tubes and wires attached. He lifted his hand and motioned me to be still.

"You were asked to keep an open mind. Please stay calm and listen."

I let my head flop back to the pillow. The effort had set off a wave of dizziness.

"It is a hard concept to understand, but to the world, you are already dead. Those who attacked you are sitting in a jail cell, but the rest of those who ran the refugee camps are

39

still alive. Being on the outside, you are a threat to them, however insignificant you feel. Friends of ours have taken over the camp you were assigned to, forcing the government and military to back down. They have already started building residences and a school. They agree with us that the Americans can be productive members of British society. We just needed to open the eyes of the media, and your situation did just that. This has left the military unit we displaced quite sore with you."

I raised my hand to stop him. "If I were with my family, it would not be safe for them?"

"Exactly."

"So where does that leave me? Will I have to go back to America?" I shuddered.

"For the time being, it leaves you in our care. No matter what your decision you will remain with us until completely healed."

"And who is this 'us'?"

He smiled at me, then leaned forward and pressed a button on the side of my bed. Half of the bed began to angle so that I was sitting up. He relaxed back in the chair, looking like a grandfather about to tell an exciting story to his grandchildren. In that moment, I could not help but be open to whatever tale he was going to tell.

"We are a secret agency that has been in existence for about twenty-five years. Not the media or most government heads know of our existence. Several members of the United Nations started us to protect the world from nuclear attacks. We monitor from the smallest idle threat to the largest nations with nuclear capabilities. While we have operations in numerous countries, our main base is here. Through it we have had major successes, like when North Korea test-fired and the missiles kept failing. It was our men on the inside. There has also been one massive failure, the attack on the United States. We knew what was happening, but the masterminds kept one step ahead of us." He stopped to give his words time to sink in.

"Who are the masterminds?"

"A network of terrorists. They are known by many names in many languages. Here, we call them by the name

40

they first used, Unus Universum. It is Latin for One Universe. Their main goal seems to be causing nuclear disasters in key countries and then taking over their governments during the crisis afterward. They believe the world should be under one ruling clan."

"What does this have to do with me?"

I could tell that it was the response he was waiting for. "Nothing. Or everything. The choice will be yours. You know that one of my men had been watching the camp. He had established a contact on your side that had high praises for you and your husband."

"Jack" I interrupted.

"Yes, and he is well. He just had a concussion from the blow. He and his father are settling in nicely to life with us here."

He continued. "We tried to get both you and your husband out of the camp, but even we have to go through the proper embassy channels. The word of your release caused an unanticipated consequence though. My man overheard the soldier planning your attack and called in our special force." He looked grim again. "I am deeply sorry that it took us so long to rescue you."

"You wanted Gareth and I to work for you?"

"Yes. You both had the personality, values, and skills we need for the work we do. You both also had an extraordinary amount of latent talent. Anyways, I had staff placed outside of each refugee camp, because you would all be unknowns in this area and therefore easier to bring on staff. We prefer people with little to no family, because the hours can be long, and the work can take you out of the area for weeks at a time. It is not good for someone with a lot of connections. We were also interested because you came from the area where we had just failed. We need to find out what went wrong, because the masterminds are still out there and, for all we know, they could be planning a global scale attack."

"But I was pregnant."

"Yes, and you both would have been working and raising your child here."

"Where is here?"

He chuckled. "Nowhere and everywhere. Again, the

41

choice is up to you."

"So, if I chose to stay?"

He sat up straight and looked serious. "From what I have seen and heard, you will make a fabulous addition to this organization. I would be proud to have you part of it."

"And if I don't?"

"The medical staff here will help to get you as healthy as possible. Then you will either be placed back with your family, as dangerous as that is, or helped start your life over in another, more secure, area."

"When do I have to decide?"

"Not today. Take the night to think about it. One of us will be in to talk to you in the morning. In the meantime, a nurse is coming in to detach some of this." He pointed to the IV lines and wires. "You must be hungry and thirsty, so I'll have someone send in a meal for you. No rations this time."

I smiled slightly.

"Rest and recover. I will see you soon." With that, he walked out of the room.

I shut my eyes and tried to focus on processing the conversation. Unlike the officer in the camp, everything The General said rang true. I could not detect any deception. There was a lot of omissions but not deception. I wondered what kind of work they could possibly have me do. What skills did I have that would make anyone anywhere want me? I was a good teacher, devoted to my life-long job, but that was about it.

My thoughts were interrupted by the nurse coming in. He was dressed in standard nursing garb but had the air of a soldier. His muscular body left no doubt that he worked out nearly every day. His dark blond hair was cut in a traditional military crew cut. He had what people call a "baby face," but his eyes told me that he had seen more than his share of tragedy.

"How are you feeling?" he asked while checking the leads to the heart monitor. He sounded as if he came from the southern parts of America.

"Overwhelmed."

He grinned, "I figured you would be, but other than that, how is your pain?"

"As long as I don't move, I'm fine."

"I'll give you something for it, but let's figure out what's hurting you the most."

He started with my head and soon found a spot that made me wince. "I figured that would still be sore. You have a couple of stitches and a drain. Your brain swelled a little from the blows, and the surgeon had to get in there." He was omitting something, but I did not have a chance to ask as he quickly moved on to other parts.

My entire face was still a giant bruise, with my nose in a small splint from being broken. He told me that it looked much worse the first week. Back then I had been various shades of purple and red, but now the bruises were fading into yellows. He then checked the bandage that held my broken ribs in place. There was a small incision there too.

"Chest tube" he stated.

"Glad I was unconscious for that one." I gave him a small smile. He nodded.

"I'm going to need to change the bandage here." He pointed to my abdomen. "You'll have to lay back down for a moment. It's up to you if you want to see the incision or not."

I decided that lying down would be a good thing and let him know by shutting my eyes tight. It was a bit more painful then I expected, to have the dressing changed. The nurse said the staples were almost ready to come out and that I'd feel better once those were gone. After the change, he raised the bed back up to a sitting position.

"I'm going to take out one of your IV's and then we'll be done." He smiled kindly. "Sorry that last part hurt. You put on a brave face though."

"It's in my nature." I responded simply.

"I'll have someone bring in your meal, and once you are finished, some more pain medication will take the edge off." At my expression he added. "Not enough to knock you out though."

He walked out and within moments a young woman walked in, carrying a tray. She was also dressed in nursing garb. Without saying a word, she placed the tray on my bed and removed the lid from what was to be my dinner: a small lightly seasoned grilled chicken breast with rice, applesauce,

43

peas and carrots. There was also some grape juice and water. The sight made me realize how hungry I really was. I thanked the quiet nurse, and she nodded before walking out. The meal was delicious but mild enough that it would not hurt my tender insides.

I realized around that time that I must be under surveillance. The moment I sighed and leaned back, the quiet nurse came in to take my tray and the other nurse came in with a syringe of pain medication. It took effect quickly and my thoughts turned cloudy. He was right, it was not enough to knock me out, but it was enough to not allow me to think about all that had just transpired. Honestly, it felt good for the moment, and I let the relief carry my thoughts away.

There was no way of knowing the time. My room had no window and there was no clock. My only indication that night had fallen was the din of noises from the hallway had silenced. I slept for a little longer, but then woke to think about my situation. The choice was fairly easy to make. Living alone in another strange place, with a different identity, knowing there was danger if I were ever discovered, was not a viable option. This was especially true with the current economic situation, and the fact that I had an American accent. Being returned to my husband's family would be like coming back from the dead. It would also put them in danger, which was unacceptable. Essentially, I was a no one with nowhere to call home in a world that would not accept me. It was heartbreaking to realize, and tears flowed for quite some time after the decision was made. Even though they were all strangers, and I had never heard of such a group, they seemed to want me. I would stay.

Whoever was monitoring me must have seen the tears flowing and the change in my expression, because the decision was just settling into my brain when the nurse came back. He looked concerned.

"Oh dear." He tsked. "Did the pain come back that bad?" He moved to the head of the bed and turned on the monitor. "Your heart rate has gone up." He wrapped a blood pressure cuff around my arm and waited for the machine to inflate and take a reading. "That's up too." He took a few steps back and stared at me. A look of understanding came across his face as he registered my expression and the tears that were still silently flowing. In a move that startled me, he reached over and gently brushed them away.

"You cried in your sleep two nights ago. That's how we knew you were starting to wake up." He stayed silent for a moment then offered, "We've been told how you hate medication which knocks you out, but would that be so bad right now? I can make up a quick cocktail that will let you sleep without pain and won't leave you too groggy once you wake up."

How did they know about that? I thought about the offer then whispered an okay. He was out of the room and back before I could second guess my decision. Within seconds I was under. No pain. No thoughts. Just sleep.

When consciousness returned it was amazing how different I felt. The decision to stay had planted itself deep while I slept. A strange peace was around it – like this was how it was supposed to be. I opened my eyes and gasped as the realization that I again was not alone struck. The gasp brought a round of protests from my broken ribs. It was "him," this time in a long-sleeved black polo shirt with an unknown symbol on it. He was leaning against the wall, staring at me.

"Good morning!" He grinned. "Sorry for the fright."

"It's okay." I muttered.

"Our nurse said you had a bit of a tough night. I hope things are better now."

"Did he also tell you that I made my decision?"

He looked slightly surprised at the question but quickly covered it up with a somber expression. "No, Jason didn't specify what caused the rough night."

"Oh." I was not sure now was the time to state it.

"Would you like to have breakfast before letting me know?" I could not be sure if he were serious or not, but I was hungry and nodded. He strode out of the room and came back several minutes later with a tray and two covered plates of food. After sitting me up and setting the tray down, he took one of the plates and sat in the chair. No one had put it back against the wall.

"I hope you enjoy a traditional British breakfast." He grinned again.

45

"Beans on toast is good for any meal of the day." I stated surely while lifting the cover off.

This time I was certain the look on his face was that of surprise. The beans, toast, and eggs were quite good. We ate in silence, and I realized that, even though my decision has been made, I had questions. They seemed to become more and more important as each bite was eaten. He must have noticed the change because his eating slowed down to a crawl as mine sped up.

He broke the silence, "Slow down or you are going to make yourself ill. Questions can wait until after you have eaten."

I slowed, and we finished the meal with more silence. He carried the tray and plates out just as the nurse came in to check on me.

"Don't you ever sleep?" I asked, slightly sarcastic.

"Only when you do." He grinned. "This will be quick; the doctor will be here in about an hour to take the staples out and give a more thorough exam." He checked my vitals, commenting that my blood pressure was back where it should be, and then briefly examined all of the bandages. After saying it all looked good, he left, and the dark-haired man came back.

He stood at the foot of the bed and stared at me. I could tell that he was contemplating something, but his eyes gave away nothing. I stared back, wondering what he was thinking about. His eyes were a brilliant shade of green, almost emerald, and his hair looked as if he had brushed it, but his hands had been run through it several times since. After an endless moment, his expression turned serious.

"You have questions." He stated.

Suddenly, my heart was racing, and my chest hurt. The combination of his expression, and the weight of my decision, was wreaking havoc. I swallowed, took as deep of a breath as the broken ribs allowed and started. "What kind of work would I be doing if I stayed? Are there children here that need a teacher?"

His eyes flashed, but it was too quick for me to tell with what emotion. With the same serious expression, he answered. "To the second question, no. You will not be teaching while here. To your first...If I get my way, you will be working behind the scenes on a special forces team like the one that rescued you."

"Why? What skills do I have that could possibly make me marketable for a position like that?" I was confused again.

He looked sad for just a moment, but then his features softened a bit. "The skills which made you a talented and devoted teacher are the same skills that we need. You have a talent for seeing what is the truth and what is not, and you advocate for what is right and fight against what is wrong with such a passion that you endanger your own life – seemingly without care. You have latent skills that, with the right training, will make you a formidable foe to any evildoer." He had been watching my reactions and was getting quite a show. Currently showing was doubt. There was no way he was talking about me, the teacher who moved from district to district because she could tell when the administration was lying and could not keep a position because of it.

My expression switched to shock when he said. "You are assertive." He paused again. "Do not doubt yourself. It has been a long time since I have seen anyone with such talents. The outside world never understood you, and that had to have been painful. But, what they threw out..." He left the thought unfinished. His expression was still soft, but his shoulders had tensed.

"You seem to know a lot about me."

The expression changed instantly as a chuckle left his throat, "Simple research."

"One more question."

He crossed his arms over his chest and waited, serious once more. This was difficult to ask, I did not want to offend anyone after they worked so hard to save my life.

"Will I be a throwaway? Someone whose life does not really matter, because I don't exist anyway? Frontline, first to die kind of thing..." I stopped because the look on his face had turned fierce.

I cringed. "I'm sorry, really, it was just bothering me and..."

The deep sorrow I had seen when he was on the hill was on his face now – much more potent when he was standing so close. "No. Never." he whispered. "That is not how we are here." He was not lying. I closed my eyes and counted to ten, so my brain could have a moment to process those words. When my eyes opened, he was staring at me again, the same unknown emotion on his face.

"I will stay here then." It was barely a whisper.

His face lit up with the most amazing smile as he exclaimed. "Brilliant!" He then held out his hand for me to shake. "I'm Commanding Officer Jamyson Davies. But most everyone calls me James."

"Hello, James."

"I'm sure you are curious as to where you are. It's an underground bunker on the Wales/England border. One building is on one side of the river and is underground, the rest are in Wales and are part of an old research and development military base. Most are above ground, minus this one. There is a nearby village, where most of our employees live. They work above ground, are paid hourly and such. Agents and Members work below but live in the village too. They do a lot of the hard work, assist in missions to prevent more attacks and such. All have high security clearance levels, even the janitors. It pretty much is a lifetime commitment."

He watched my reactions as he continued on. "We don't have an official name but tend to call ourselves Guardians." He pointed to his shirt. "That's the symbol we've come up with."

"At any point in time, since the invention of the atomic bomb, we are a hair's breadth away from the annihilation of mankind. Of course, world leaders and media want us to believe otherwise, but, deep down, we all know the truth… especially since the attack on the US." As he continued to explain, I asked very few questions, choosing instead to focus on what he was saying and whether or not it rang true.

When Jason arrived with the doctor, I was grateful for the break in our conversation. It really was a lot to take in and my brain was still a bit slow from injury and medication. The doctor was a middle-aged man with a receding hairline that seemed to be in the process of going from black to gray. His dark skin and eyes were enhanced by the wide smile he gave me while walking into the room.

"There's my star patient!" He exclaimed.

"Um, Doc." Jason chuckled. "Right now, she is your only patient."

"Yeah, but only because one of my more frequent offenders is in his bunk and doing his own therapy after breaking his hand, again." He sighed dramatically, "When will he learn to not get into a fight at the pub?"

I looked over at James, who was trying to look serious, but was losing the battle. He ended up rolling his eyes and saying, "There always has to be one bull-headed member. Although after all these years you would think he would get the idea."

The doctor nodded. "Now, if you will excuse yourself, I have a patient to attend to."

James looked at me with that same unreadable expression before walking to the door. On the way out, he spoke to the doctor once more, but in an entirely different tone. "The report will be on my desk within two hours."

"Yes, Sir." was the response from the now unsmiling doctor.

I watched him walk out and shut the door behind him. Glancing over at the doctor I could see that he was still not smiling. He looked at Jason, Jason looked at him, and then they both turned to look at me.

"The Commander has spoken." Jason mumbled.

"Yes, he has, but we have this beautiful young lady to attend to, so he can shove off." And the smile was back.

It was my turn to mumble. "Beautiful young lady? Whatever."

Jason laughed. "Well, you will be, once you get past the yellow stage with those bruises and all the bandages come off."

"I'm not that young."

"Yes, you are, especially now that the surgeon has worked his magic. You did not look thirty-two before you came here. You certainly do not now."

I raised my eyebrows and stared at the doctor. He chuckled and then pointed to the door. "Not me. I just sewed your insides back up. We have a proper surgeon here, and before he switched to neurosurgery, he was a specialist in reconstructive procedures."

Jason interrupted with, "Since it was already broken, he gave you a complimentary nose job and whist fixing the facial fractures he gave you a bit of a lift. No matter what your decision, the slight alteration of your looks will be nothing but beneficial."

I just stared at him. It was shocking to me that any surgeon would take the liberty of modifying a person's looks while performing surgery to fix facial fractures. Weren't there laws about things like that? It raised an entirely new series of questions about the organization. Were they above the law? If so, how far did they take it? Were they really the good guys? They seemed to be. I had not sensed any deception or malice. That train of thought halted when Jason took out a pre-filled syringe. Suddenly wary, I sat up straighter and glared at him. He took two steps back and frowned.

"I told you she would not like it. Think about it, Doc, first you say we should tell her about the facelift. Then you want me to give her pain meds, which we've been told she hates, without time for her to think it all over and ask us questions. It's not very fair."

"If The Commander had not given me that time restraint, we could have taken the time she needs."

"Um...I'm still in the room." I snapped.

Jason turned back to me. "Sorry about that. We are in a bit of a situation here and were not expecting to have you arrive in such bad shape. It has been a challenge for all of us and the legal lines are not real clear. There was little time to go higher up and still save your life." He paused. "Our surgeon did get permission from The General, who agreed to shoulder any ramification. We would have recommended it anyways, once you had decided to stay." He then chuckled. "Most of us have had some kind of plastic surgery."

The doctor, I guessed the staff just called him Doc, spoke up then. "I am also sorry about the situation. We are going to have to leave you in the dark about that for a little bit longer. I have to do a head to foot examination, take those staples out, change all of your bandages, and complete a long report before The Commander returns. It will be easier on you if there is fresh pain medication in your system. Most of it is going to hurt."

50

Jason put the syringe down on the foot of the bed, then came closer to take my hand. "Like James said before, try to keep an open mind. You will understand soon enough. We would tell you everything now, but for some reason, he is being very strict when it comes to you."

Doc added, "It has been a long time since we have added a new member and never under circumstances like this. Focus on healing, the rest will come."

I pondered that for about thirty seconds, before pointing to the syringe. "Only half dose for now."

He nodded, and the doctor started his examination.

Over the next hour, there were several times when I wanted to give in and get the other half. However, I gritted my teeth and forced myself to focus on what the doctor was doing, not on how much it hurt. I watched his every move as he went over my body inch by painful inch. Every healing bruise was drawn and documented. Jason said they did the same thing when I arrived and every two days since. Then, each bandage was changed. The one on my head was not so bad but changing the one around my ribs was. I made the mistake of trying to breathe while nothing was supporting them and nearly passed out from the pain. The staples were next, and I insisted on watching. They raised the top half of the bed up so that it would not be a strain. The fresh scar looked bad, and I had to keep reminding myself that it would fade in time. Finally, they came to the lower half of my body.

The doctor did a quick exam, barely touching me. "I'm not going to take the catheter out. When our surgeon gets the green light to fix this, you will have to have it again anyways."

"How long until that happens?"

"Could be as early as tomorrow."

"The sooner the better. I don't make a good patient and dragging it out will cause me to get quite grumpy." I warned. It was easy to be open with them.

"I'll put that in my report." He chuckled and then stepped back. "We're finished for now. Why don't you rest until lunch and afterward we'll see about getting you to sit up on the edge and perhaps have you stand up for a moment or two?"

I nodded.

51

Jason held up the half-used syringe of pain medication. "Are you done being brave?"

I nodded again, and he grinned, "Good girl." I stuck my tongue out at him and accepted the relief.

After lunch, the doctor came back, this time with the quiet nurse. She adjusted my IV line and pole, raised the top of the bed higher and helped me slide my legs over the side. My entire torso hurt from turning to the side, but once I was sitting up on my own, it was better. Within a few minutes the pain and dizziness subsided, and with my hands grasping a walker, and her hands at my back, I stood up. After a minute, she had me sit back down, never saying more than a phrase and never louder than a whisper. I rested for another hour and she came back, and we tried again. This time it was easier to stand. I even shuffled my feet a little.

James came back at dinner time. As with breakfast, he brought two plates and a tray. He also brought a thin binder. I looked at him expectantly, but he just stared at me with the same unreadable expression and set up our meal.

"Eat first and then we will talk."

Something about his demeanor made me nervous, and I practically had to choke down the grilled fish, rice pilaf and vegetables. If it had not been so long since I had experienced real food like that, I would not have been able to eat at all. James ate in silence, occasionally looking up to see how fast I was eating. We both finished around the same time, so again he took both plates and the tray out. Once sitting in the chair, he leaned back and looked a bit more relaxed.

"Another busy day for you."

"If you can call not leaving the bed except to try standing for one minute busy."

"You did much more than that."

"I guess."

"Any questions?"

"Too many."

He sighed. "Any that you want to ask first, or should I just start talking and you interrupt as needed?"

"The latter."

"Okay. Despite the good doctor and Jason's idiotic explanation of what our surgeon did, I am pleased to see that

52

you are still holding together emotionally. What they said is true, most of us have had some type of procedure to slightly alter our appearances – which brings me to the first part of tonight's discussion."

I just stared at him. He stared back for a moment, then continued.

"We need to start working on your new identity. Try to think of a new name and background information that would be easy for you to remember. We'll see if it works with what we have planned."

For some reason, my heart took that moment to catch up with my brain. Thinking about having to come up with a new identity caused a strange reaction. Quite suddenly, I became angry.

"Why?" I spat out "No one knows me. I am a no one from nowhere with no place to go."

James did not seem surprised by this reaction. He actually seemed prepared for it.

"On the contrary, you are someone with immense skill, here on the Wales side of the bunker which sits below a village that is to be your new home. You were a teacher, loved by your students and their parents, but seen as a threat by your administrators because you were too good at what you did and could sense any deception. You left a positive impression wherever you taught and were friendly to whomever you happened to meet. You were the entire world to several children in other countries through the advocacy group you worked with. You have never been a no one and you never will be. You will continue to be a someone, but you will do it with a new identity because it is safer for you and everyone who ever knew you."

He watched my expressions change from anger, to shock, to doubt and back to anger. When I continued to stare in silence he threatened. "Do I need to pick it out for you? I can come up with something quite horrid."

"No, thank you." I muttered.

He opened the binder and took out the first page.
"Name?"

"Harlie Anwyn Berryman." The name seemed to come to my mind from nowhere.

"Place of birth?"

"Estes Park, Colorado." It was my favorite place to visit.

"Parents?"

"I don't care."

"Parents?"

"Um...Arthur and Glynda."

"College major?"

"Music Education."

He sighed. "Too close. Try again."

"Environmental Science major, Meteorology minor."

"Reasons for some of your scars?"

"Trail riding accident and car crash during a mountain blizzard."

"Languages spoken?"

This time I protested. "I've never been able to properly learn another language. It's too hard."

"It won't be for long. Languages?"

"Welsh."

He rolled his eyes. "Seriously, please."

"I am being serious. My parents would be immigrants from northern Wales and wanted me to know my native language. We spoke it in the home."

He grinned, "Now you're talking! Although you'll need to learn another one more common. You can be honest for the next parts."

I nodded.

"Favorite activities?"

"Gardening, hiking and horseback riding, western style."

"Cottage, apartment or townhouse?"

"Cottage."

"Car, bike, public transportation or motorbike?"

"Public transportation and bike."

He turned the page and announced, "Finished with that. The rest we will fill in with bits and pieces of your former life, but not anything too specific." He stretched, then looked over the next page.

"This is the report I asked the doctor for. Your wounds are healing quickly, and you have responded well to all

54

treatments so far. It looks like we can start with some physical therapy tomorrow. It will be good to get you moving around before the surgeon finishes his work."

"When will that be?"

"Trying for tomorrow morning, after your first therapy session."

"How long will that recovery take?"

He thought about it for a moment. "Should only set you back a day or two, if you stop being stubborn with the medication. Your body needs that downtime to boost its' ability to heal."

"When do I get out of this room?"

James frowned, "A couple more weeks, I'm afraid."

"I'll lose my mind by then."

"That is a possibility, but we will try our best to keep you active enough that you don't." He opened the binder again and pulled out what looked like a manual. "This is required reading, so I'll leave it with you now." It was the history of nuclear weapons in the world.

"Are we finished? You made it sound like this would be a long conversation."

The frown was back. "Well, yes, I was planning on bringing up another topic or two but have changed my mind. I just noticed something missing in this report and need to get that fixed."

He was lying about the report, but I kept silent.

"Have a good night's rest and I'll see you before surgery. Make sure to read over that." He pointed to the history booklet then walked quickly out of the room.

Confused, I sat and stared at the empty chair for several minutes. What made him change his mind? Why did he lie? What was the real reason for his hurried exit? I sighed. There was probably no way to get an accurate answer, so why worry? I opened the booklet and read until my eyes closed on their own.

The next morning was a blur of activity. I had not slept well, waking several times from bad dreams, but no one had come in to check on me. Doc came in first thing to perform a quick examination, then Jason arrived to inject a medication he said I needed before the surgery. After that, James peeked in, but only to apologize for me not being allowed breakfast today. I had figured as much, but the look on his face confused me. He looked excited about all the activity. There was about five minutes of peace and then the quiet nurse came.

"Let's get you up and walking." She whispered. This time she gave me only a cane to help myself up. At my questioning expression, she explained, "Your legs are the only part of you that was not injured, and your back bruises are nearly healed." It was the longest she had spoken in front of me, although it was still a whisper. She detached everything I was hooked up to and then motioned for me to stand.

She kept a hand on my back as I cautiously stood up. The dizziness was not bad this time, although my ribs protested. I took two tentative steps, then smiled and took three more. It felt good to be up and about.

"Do you feel strong enough to go to the bathroom and clean up a bit?" The nurse asked.

"Yes. That sounds great!"

"It will just be a sponge bath, and I'll try to wash your hair."

"That's fine. I figured as much with the drain and ribs."

She nodded and lead me to the attached bathroom. The first thing I noticed was that the mirror was covered. It bothered me, but the idea of getting cleaned up quickly pushed the feeling out of the way. Without talking, she helped me undress and sit on a stool in the shower. I helped out as much as possible with the sponge bath but was still sore enough to need some assistance. When I went to wash my face, she reached over to take the bandage off my nose.

"It should have come off yesterday."

"Oh." I had been wanting to ask her a question, but for some reason had been hesitant. This situation seemed like a good enough moment. "This is all so strange to me. It would help if I knew the names of those around me." She said nothing, so I continued. "James and The General are the only ones who introduced themselves. I found out the nurse was Jason only from a conversation with James. What is the doctors name? And the surgeon? And what about you?"

She paused from helping me dry off and helped me stand up. She guided me to the sink and left me there for a moment. She returned with a chair, which she placed so its back was to the shower, and then helped me sit down. From there, she opened the door under the sink and took out a small box.

"This stuff will clean your hair without water. It does not feel as good as washing it, but it will remove the extra oils and greasy feeling."

I just nodded. It was upsetting that she would not answer my questions.

She put the oversized shower cap on my head and started to massage its contents into my hair, working around the drain. "I'm called Kayla." She whispered.

"Thank you, Kayla."

"The doctor is Marcus Williams, but we call him Doc. The surgeon we only know as Doctor L. because none of us can pronounce his real name."

I nodded. She quickly finished the washing process and then took out a thick comb. Pulling it through the tangles, she was careful about avoiding the bandage. I wanted to see what I looked like but had a feeling that the request would be denied. Putting my fears aside, I hoped it was only because they wanted the bruises and swelling to fade before I saw the changes. Maybe that would make it less traumatic or something.

When she finished, and helped me put on a clean garment, I took the cane and stood back up. It felt so good to be clean that my mood was lifted as well. I was shuffling back to the bed when Dr. L walked in, followed by The General. The latter smiled at seeing me up and about.

"What a wonderful sight!" He exclaimed. He turned to the surgeon, "I told you she was resilient. Just look at her expression and physical progress."

The surgeon looked doubtful.

I made it back to the bed and Kayla helped me get it into the reclined position. The General and surgeon were discussing something in hushed tones. He looked excited, but the surgeon did not. The moods did not match what I had been told about today's procedure. Wasn't this supposed to be repairing the damage done by the rapes and taking the drain out of my head? I stared at them and tried to figure out who was lying. It did not ring of a lie when it was brought up earlier, but then again, there had been the sense of omission when James had spoken about it. Suddenly, they stopped talking and looked at me.

"See what I mean?" The General muttered. Then his expression changed, and he came over to the bed. "You have a big day ahead of you." He smiled, "I am very happy you decided to join our team. Already the papers are being finalized and Commanding Officer Davies is demanding your placement on his team. I don't know what he saw in you that he did not report to me, but he has never been so insistent before." He shook his head, smiled one more time and then walked to the door. The surgeon followed.

Within seconds, Jason was by my bed. Unlike The General, he did not look excited. Actually, he seemed quite miserable.

"Jason, what's wrong?" I whispered, instantly scared.

He did not answer me. Instead, he put the bed back so that I was flat.

"Jason?"

He looked at me this time. Anger mixed with sorrow as he whispered back, "You can tell that they are not telling the whole truth. You can sense that something is not right. Just remember that when you wake up." He paused. "I'm sorry."

He reached up to my IV line and quickly injected something into it. He must have had the syringe in his pocket. My world went black again.

CHANGES

The moment consciousness returned, I knew something was wrong. My head was pounding so hard I wanted to scream. For some reason, I could not move at all. It felt like I was tied down to the bed, like what they do to criminals or the insane. I shook my head back and forth, but it only made the pain worse.

"Her blood pressure is too high!" I heard Jason hiss.

Something that felt like fire spread through my arm and into the rest of my body. This time I did scream, and my eyes opened. Jason was at the foot of my bed, looking horrified. Dr. L was by my IV. He looked calm as he pressed another syringe into the line.

"You're not ready to wake up just yet." He crooned, almost as if he were talking to a child. My world went dark once more.

The second time I regained consciousness, the pain in my head was just a dull throb. As with the other times, I listened first; it sounded like I was alone. There were no sounds of breathing, no slight movements. I counted to fifty before opening my eyes and discovered there really was no one in the room. Of course, I was still under surveillance, but for some reason, that did not bother me for the moment.

My arms and legs were free this time, and I moved all of them to see if there had been any damage. My wrists felt sore, so I lifted my right one to see it. Obviously, I had been struggling for quite some time, as there were deep bruises and some spots where the restraint had cut into the skin. What happened to make me struggle like that?

Next, I tried to tell if reconstructive surgery really had happened. It only took one slight movement to realize at least part of the surgery story was true, as it was terribly sore. I lifted my hand to my head. There was a different bandage in place but no drain. It seemed as if there was some truth to what I had been told.

Then I remembered the moments before being knocked out, the faces and comments. I recalled the excitement from

The General and James, the doubt from the surgeon, the anger and sorrow from Jason. He had told me to remember something when I woke up. It took several moments before my mind picked out the memory. Now that I had time to process it, what he said made me shudder. He knew how I could sense truth and lies, and he knew I could sense when something was wrong. He told me to remember that, but why? Why was it important? That weird ability had always gotten me into trouble. When I was young, it made me unable to relate to my peers, while as an adult it put me in conflict with bosses and others with hidden agendas. In the classroom, it was a gift, but outside it was a curse.

Suddenly, I did not feel like lying down. Even though it hurt badly, I forced myself to sit up. My back leaned against the wall behind my bed, the pillow offering only minimal support to the small of my back. It seemed unusual that no one came to check on me, but at the same time, it was a relief. Something felt wrong. I could not put my finger on it, but I felt wrong. Something had changed since the surgery, but it was hard to tell what. I wanted answers but was afraid of asking the questions. Frustrated, I started tapping my fingers against the side of my leg and waited.

Kayla, the quiet nurse, was the first person to walk in. She silently came over to the bed and turned on the monitor to check my vitals.

"Hello, Kayla." I whispered.

"Let's get you into a better position." was her hesitant response. I laid back down and she adjusted the bed, so I was sitting properly. She then went back to my vitals.

"Why are you scared?" I suddenly asked.

Her face turned white and she backed up three steps.

"What is going on out there to make you scared?" I asked.

"How...how...did you know I was scared?" She looked ready to flee.

I thought about it. "I don't know. Maybe it's the look in your eyes."

She bit her lip, looked towards the far wall, looked towards the door, and then back at me. "There is nothing going on out there to make me scared." She whispered, then she quickly walked out of the room.

Typically, if a person was lying, a slight sensation would ghost through my mind. I called it "my hint" because it was just that, a quiet hint that things were not as it seemed. If I focused and waited for it, sometimes the hint would leave a sub-conscious idea of what the lie was about. However, when Kayla said there was nothing going on outside to make her scared, she was telling the truth. In fact, "my hint" verified it with more of a shout then a ghostly whisper. That was confusing, because she really had been scared, and if the threat was not out there, then where was it? I sat and waited some more.

This time it was the surgeon who came in. Since he rarely spoke around me I sat silently as he walked over and checked the bandage on my head. He then checked my vitals a second time.

"It's good to see you awake." I tried not to look surprised at his decision to speak. "The procedures seem to be successful. Of course, only time will tell how the changes affect you."

He glanced over to see if I was listening. I was, and he was omitting quite a chunk of information. Again, my mind seemed to scream it instead of whispering. I nodded once, and he continued, "Let's get this bandage off. I used surgical glue instead of stitches or staples on the outside. It will give you a less noticeable scar. With the right haircut, no one would notice that I had to get to your brain in order to save your life."

Again, he was telling the truth, but his sudden rambling was saying something else too. He was nervous. I'm not sure how I knew, but I could bet my life that he was very nervous. I gathered enough courage to ask.

"What else did you do to me?"

He looked startled, but only for a moment. "My dear child, I only did what was necessary to save your life."

"Perhaps, but you are omitting a lot of details."

"What I did was only under orders from The General. You should direct any concerns to him."

He was telling the truth, with no omission. He was also no longer nervous but was very pleased. My frustration was starting to lean towards anger.

61

He finished removing the bandage and went to remove the catheter. Now, the only thing tying me to the bed was the IV line. Suddenly, my head started to throb harder. I shut my eyes and hoped it would pass. He noticed.

"That will happen from time to time. It will fade." Again, he seemed pleased. "I'll check in on you later." And he left.

The wait was on again. I hoped this time it would be The General who walked in or even Jason. He might tell me what was happening. No one came, though. Hours passed, and my stomach rumbled. Anger at my helplessness started to build. I looked at my IV line and tried to remember how to unhook myself. That was when Kayla walked back in again, this time with a tray and plate of food. She did not speak, just placed it on the bed and left.

The meal helped to settle my nerves and emotions. After pushing the tray away, I looked around for the required reading book. It was on the nightstand to my right. I used the tray to prop the book up and started where I'd left off.

I did not get very far before my third visitor arrived, and it was not who I expected. James came in, bearing two small hot fudge sundaes. It had been over a year since I had last tasted ice cream, but my excitement was crushed with the frustration that instantly boiled up.

"I hope you like ice cream. I was held up in a meeting and could not make it in time for tea."

"That's okay. I wasn't told what time it was or even how long I've been out, so it could have been any meal. And yes, I like ice cream."

He smiled and handed me one of the sundaes before pulling the chair over and sitting down. I stared at him, suddenly my frustration was gone leaving just questions behind. He noticed my expression change and sighed.

"You are frustrated, and you have a lot of questions, but the same rule applies now as it did before. Food first."

I sighed, and the frustration started to build again, but I ate the ice cream, enjoying every bite. After scraping the side of the glass to get every last morsel, I placed it on the tray, folded my arms across my chest, and waited.

This time, James just placed the tray on the floor. He

looked uncomfortable and that had me on guard in an instant. Of course, he also stared at me. I stared back, trying to see if I could decipher his emotions. When I couldn't, the frustration started to show on my face.

"It won't work." He stated.

"Huh?" I wasn't sure if he meant what I thought he meant.

"You won't be able to read me like the others. We have the same gift, but I've had years of experience with it."

My hands clenched into fists. "Explain."

"I was born with the same talent as you, but yours stayed latent while mine was active from the time I was a boy. It is the reason why you know who is telling the truth and who is lying. It is the reason why you fight so hard for what is good and right. It is why you have had so much trouble in life. And now, it is the reason why you are out of the camp. When Jack told one of my contacts about you, I thought it was an exaggeration. However, while watching you from the hill..." He paused and shook his head. "I've never seen that kind of talent here. It saved your life. Even if Dr. L couldn't activate it fully, you still had enough to make you invaluable."

"What did he do to me?" I spoke through clenched teeth.

"Calm down, Harlie." It was the first time anyone had used my new name. Suddenly, I realized it was the first time anyone here had called me any name at all. I worked to unclench my jaw and hands.

"Simple electrical stimulation. While you were unconscious the first time we ran a few scans and tests. He found where the talent resided in your brain. Once you healed from the brain trauma, he went in and stimulated it. That drain was as much of an access point as it was a pressure release for your injury."

"I was told The General was the one who ordered it."

"It was. I only told him of your talent, he saw it for himself while talking to you and agreed. We are both thrilled that it activated right there in surgery. The change in your scans was instant." He was looking excited again.

"James?" I interrupted, trying out his name.

"Yes?"

"What is this talent?"

"Um, yeah, I guess I forgot to mention it specifically."

"No, you purposely avoided it."

His eyes widened and then quickly narrowed.

"Your face gave it away." I stated.

He looked at me with that unreadable expression again then leaned forward.

"You are empathic."

"I can read others emotions?"

His eyes widened again. "So, you understand the basic concept."

"Anyone who reads science fiction understands the concept. I never thought it was reality though."

"That is because nearly all who have this talent are either labeled as insane and institutionalized or they live as hermits. You and your husband were on your way to becoming the latter as homesteaders."

"Yes, we both were happy being away from mainstream society."

He nodded. "Now you know the reason why."

"What does being empathic entail, and why can't I read you?"

"Mental shielding is reality too." He whispered.

I nodded. Nothing about this place seemed normal to begin with, especially not now. What else would I find out once leaving this room? It was starting to become too much to handle. My head throbbed again.

"You are getting yourself worked up. That will make the headaches worse. Once you learn to control your ability those will fade. It's been months since I've had one, and believe me, I deserved it."

Now I was curious. "What did you do?"

He chuckled. "That is another story for another time. Right now, let's get you up and moving."

"James?"

"Hmm?"

"What day is it today?"

"It is Sunday, March 6th."

He went over to the bathroom and came back with the cane. "Come on, up you go!"

64

"Where are we going?"

He smiled, "I just uncovered the mirror. It's about time you get to see what we have been looking at for days."

I stood up carefully and walked to the bathroom. James stood back while I went in, keeping my head down until I reached the sink. Slowly, I lifted my head and stared into the mirror. I was surprised, but not as shocked as I expected. My nose was smaller, and my chin a bit more pronounced. I could tell where the surgeon had made the slightest of lifts. In truth, I liked it. I had never thought of myself as good looking, but these alterations might just change that. While I was staring, touching here and there, Jason came to stand by James.

"She is beautiful." He murmured.

"Yes, she is, both inside and out." James replied.

"I need a haircut." I commented.

"Yes, we will take care of that." James replied. "There is a salon in the village. Someone will be by in a few days. You also need to put on the weight you lost in the camp."

I turned to face them both. "Now what?"

James and Jason both turned serious. Jason was concerned about something. I looked at one and then the other.

"Come out and sit back on the bed." James spoke quietly.

Once I had, he sat next to me. Jason stood in front of me; he looked very uncomfortable. James was staring at nothing, and he continued to stare at nothing for several minutes. Now I was the one looking uncomfortable. What was making him act that way? I shuddered, and he jerked out of his stare.

"You are very resilient; we saw it in the camp and you are proving it again and again here. However, we know, as you do, that you cannot be this brave and strong for much longer. Sooner or later, all that has happened will catch up with you." He looked at me and switched terms, "I am surprised that it has not happened yet."

Jason spoke up. "We are going to do whatever we can to help you through it. Every one of us, any person on the planet, is bound to break down after going through half of what you have."

"Is that why I have to stay here for a couple more

weeks?"

James nodded. "You need to be in the best shape possible before starting full-time training."

"There are people outside who have been through worse." I muttered. "So, I sit in here, and you wait out there, until I lose my mind and get it back again?"

Jason chuckled, "Not quite. We'll continue as we have been, but no one wants you holding back now and melting down in the field."

James expression changed and so did his tone. "In fact, I will not tolerate it at all." With that, he stood up and walked out of the room.

"The Commander has spoken." Jason mumbled again. Then he turned to smile at me. "Would you like to see a familiar face?"

The excitement was back, "Jack?"

He nodded, then left the room.

Jack came in a few minutes later. The reunion was wonderful as he gave me a careful hug. Once I was back into bed, and he was in the chair, he told me what happened to him since our rescue. I loved hearing all of the details and was so happy for him. This teenager had his whole life in front of him when America fell. His dreams would have fallen with it. He gave up so much living in the camp and put himself in danger by helping me. He deserved this chance, this future.

"So, I hear that you are going to be on James' team." He turned the conversation to me.

"I hear the same thing but have no idea what it means or why."

"They haven't told you?" Jack looked shocked.

"No. But I've been unconscious most of the last two weeks."

"It is the top team in this place. And James told me it was because you have so much talent."

"Yeah, he keeps saying that to me too, but it is a bunch of crap."

He looked shocked again and a little angry. "Don't be so hard on yourself. You are amazing!"

I rolled my eyes. He hopped up, came over to the front of the bed and sat down again. Then he surprised me by turning, leaning his back against the wall and lounging next to me. Leaning over, he whispered.

"I hear things while delivering packages. This place is full of secrets. It bothers me, especially since you seem to be one of those secrets right now. But, I still think they are good guys, and all the secrets are to keep us safe. There is more going on in the world than we ever dreamed, and it seems to be more along the lines of a nightmare." He wrapped his arm around my shoulder like a brother would. "Promise me you will try to be safe once you are out of this room."

How I loved this kid! I wished he had been my son; I would be the proudest parent alive. I nodded, then added. "Only if you promise the same thing."

He smiled. "Of course! Someone has to be here to keep you in line. I know you are going to cause all kinds of trouble once you get out this room."

Jason came into the room then, "Most of us have to be in meetings in five minutes, so visiting hour is over. Say goodbye, Jack."

He hugged me again. "See you soon." He whispered and followed Jason out.

I was alone for the next few hours. During the time, I finished reading the nuclear history booklet and then went back over a few pages where I had questions. No one had reattached me to the IV line, so I was free to walk about the room. In the nightstand, I found an old Bible. It was nice to know it was there and I spent some time going over my favorite passages. It was while re-reading Psalm 139 that the beginnings of what James and Jason warned me about started. "For you created my inmost being, You knit me together in my mother's womb...All the days ordained for me were written in Your book before one of them came to be." This was part of His plan.

The tears began to well up as understanding came. Gareth's death was part of His plan, and I wanted to hate Him for it, but couldn't. My bizarre talents were knitted in the womb, designed before my time began, and I wanted to hate Him for it, but couldn't. The one thing I could do was ask Him why? Why me? Why here? Why this way?

My breathing became more erratic as I cried. My healing ribs protested as the sobs came. The pain in my head got worse and worse, but I could not calm myself down. If the person on the other side of the surveillance saw this outburst, he or she chose to do nothing about it.

At some point, I must have fallen asleep. When I awoke again the hall was quiet, night had fallen inside of the bunker. Every part of my body hurt as I tried to get up to use the bathroom. The pain was worse as I tried to hobble back. I was nearly to the bed when the realization hit me that I was not alone. In the far corner, hidden by the shadows, stood The Commander.

"Harlie." His face was hidden by the darkness, but his voice was laced with some hidden emotion.

I stood, frozen. How long had he been standing there? Could I not just be left alone with my sorrow?

"The most important rule of survival is to be aware of your surroundings at all times." It was the same tone he had used earlier, and it sounded harsh at the edges.

I stayed where I was. The rest of those I had met may respond to that voice, but there was nothing in my experience to make me move.

"Sit back down."

I still stood still.

"That is an order. Defiance is not an option."

This afternoon's anger welled up again. I was drained from the realizations and in too much pain to care what he thought about my actions.

"Go away." I finally whispered.

"No. Your dinner is here and then we are going to talk."

"I don't feel like talking tonight."

"Again, not an option." He moved away from the wall, turned on the nightstand lamp, and nudged the tray that was at his feet. "Do not make me come over there and carry you to the bed."

His stance made it look as if he would follow through with the threat, so I went to the bed and got back into my sitting position. He brought the tray over and lifted the cover from the plate.

68

It was too dark to see what I was eating, but it was good. James stared at me while I ate. After lowering the tray to the floor, he sat in the chair and waited.

"I don't feel like talking tonight." I repeated.

"You should tell your mind that. It is saying quite a bit."

"Get out of my head."

"Until you learn mental shielding, that is impossible."

"Then teach me, Commander." I was growing tired of this conversation.

"Not yet, Ms. Berryman."

"When?" I whispered.

"Soon."

Although the shadows hid most of him, it sounded like he was smiling. That made me even angrier. However, I knew it would get me nowhere. Instead of reacting with a scream or throwing the booklet at him, I sat and stared, eyes narrowed.

He said nothing and made no indications of getting up to leave. I kept completely still and took even breaths, trying to calm the chaos in my head. The silence dragged on for many minutes. I was wondering if he was planning to stay there all night when a low voice came from the chair.

"That was fascinating." He broke the silence. "Did you know that, because we are both empathic, it makes us more in tune with each other's emotions? It has been ages since I have been able to read anyone as clearly as you. Everyone else I have to focus on."

So much for keeping my temper. The tone he used, like I was some kind of science experiment, broke what little control I had. I snapped. The booklet flew towards his head. I screamed at him, letting him know my impression of Dr. L. and General Smiths, as well as my situation, and then the tears started anew.

James sat there until he was sure I was incapacitated by the tears. When he stood up, and I did not respond in any way, he spoke again.

"I had been notified that you broke down earlier today, but the recording made it look more because of sorrow and confusion than anger. From past experience, I know that you must let the anger go as well. Although everything I said was true, I picked the tone that would most upset you, and it worked."

He walked up to where I was curled up on the bed and rested his hand on my tear-streaked cheek. "Cry it all out, Harlie. It will heal you more than anything anyone here can."

And so I did. I cried most of the night, and it was not a quiet cry either. My only relief happened when Jason came into the room, gently took the hand with the IV in it, administered strong pain medication, and silently walked out. With the screaming in my head reduced to a dull throb, I was able to scream into my pillow with more vengeance. At some point, as with that afternoon, the sobs faltered and faded until I slept.

Morning came but they let me sleep until hunger woke me. Kayla brought in a late breakfast, and I was grateful that she seemed to have gotten over her fear of me. Doc came in then to check my vitals. I could feel pity coming off of him but was too tired to react. "Kayla put proper bathing essentials in the bathroom this morning. I'm going to take the bandage off your ribs so that you can take a shower and change clothes."

The shower felt wonderful, I washed my hair twice and stood in the hot water until my muscles relaxed. Afterward, I changed into the outfit provided for me. It was olive green sweatpants and a long sleeve t-shirt which was several shades lighter than the pants. It was not flattering, but it felt great to be out of hospital garb.

Upon my return to the bed, I saw that someone had changed the sheets, placed a pair of basic white sneakers at the foot of it, and left a lap tray. On the tray was a pen, paper, and a binder with my new name on it. Under it was another booklet, this one was on psychology. I positioned myself carefully on the bed and opened the binder. The front pages contained my new life history from birth to current time. My new birthday was the day I died in the camp, February 20th. I read through the pages several times, covering parts with my hand and quizzing myself on its contents. Several tears leaked from my eyes as I memorized the information, but I did not go into hysterics again.

The second section of the binder contained a formal

description of the organization, rules and regulations, and forms for me to sign stating that I understood all of it. There were terms I did not know and questions that were brought up. I wrote the questions down and tried to continue, but it wore me out. Thankfully, Jason came in with lunch.

"Would you like some company?" He asked. My new ability sensed that he was in a cheerful mood.

I nodded.

He took the binder and booklet off the tray and placed the plate of food there. After settling into the chair, he smiled. "Can I take a look at your new history?"

My mouth was full of a sandwich, so I just nodded again. He read it over, nodding his head at some parts and chuckling at others. "So, have you memorized it yet?"

I swallowed before answering, "Almost."

"I heard The General and Doc talking this morning. If you do well, you might be out of here in a couple of days instead of a couple of weeks."

"Where would I go then?"

"We have living quarters here. The team stays underground when there is a high-level alert or in the days leading up to a big mission. Some have bunks and house two of us to a room, others are private rooms." He looked around the hospital-style room. "In either case, it's better than here in the med bay."

I nodded again before asking, "Jason?"

"Yes, Harlie?"

"How long have you been here?"

He paused to think about it. "You need to know that we never ask any member about their previous life. It is something they can volunteer, but that is it."

"I figured that out on my own. It would be rude to ask someone about a past they are supposed to forget."

It was his turn to nod. "Just making sure, and I have been here for seven years now."

"What is your actual position? I'm guessing you are like an RN or something."

He laughed. "Close. Actually, I am the combat medic on the team you will be serving on. The Commander wanted me to work with you from day one so that your transition would be a little easier."

"Oh." was all I could manage to reply.

"Do you want to know about the rest of the team?"

"Yes, please."

"James will pitch a fit for this, but I don't give a rip right now. He has been so moody since you arrived."

I was somewhat surprised, and Jason chuckled at my expression. "Give him time, Harlie, you'll see. It's like Jekyll and Hyde between James and The Commander."

"Anyways, I'm the medic, James is the boss. Some members have special skills like yours. Dara has extraordinary sight and reflexes. She is our driver, strategist, and is a master of hand-to-hand combat. Max was born with a gun in his hand. He is our sniper, and I have never seen anyone who can shoot on the run like he does. He never misses. Rick is our one-man linguistics team as he speaks thirteen languages fluently. He also has an amazing musical talent and is obsessed with songs that tell the histories of people and places."

He paused for a moment. "You are keeping up okay?"

"Yes." I nodded.

"Next, we have Skull, and no I do not know what his real name is. To us, he is just Skull, as in thick skull. You heard Doc reference him before, the one who broke his hand again in a pub fight. He is all muscle, and the only part of his brain that works is the part which makes him a walking atlas. We never get lost with Skull around. The other two are 'normals' like me. Ryan and Mitch are both technology specialists and bomb technicians, but they are amazing none-the-less."

"Normals?"

He turned serious, "Those with enough talent to be on the team, but not the latent super ability that needs surgical stimulation to kick it in gear. Dara and Skull have an implant stimulating their abilities, but the others are like you where all it took was a shock to the right location."

"Right. Okay." That was going to take some getting used to.

He chuckled again. "We hide our skills well. Out in public, no one can tell a thing. It's only when you watch us in training or see us in action that you notice we are not who we appear to be. Our movements are too coordinated, our skills too refined."

"So, will I be a diplomat or a spy?" I was thinking of the uses for an empathic on a military team,

"Both I think. You don't appear threatening, so you will be spying in broad daylight so-to-speak."

Although my full stomach was causing me to become even more tired, there were questions. "How long has this team been together?"

Jason paused. "When I came on, it was James, Rick, Dara, Mitch, and two others. One ended up wounded and the other is working with a different team. Max and Skull joined about five years ago and Ryan has been here about two years now."

"You don't know how long Rick, Dara, James, and Mitch were here?"

He looked bothered. "Not really. James and Rick seem to have been here since day one, but their ages do not match that. Dara and Mitch, I think have been here for at least nine." I could sense that he was puzzled.

"Have there been members killed?"

The puzzlement turned to sorrow. "Yes, we lost a member of our team when the nukes went off in America. Our sister team, whose focus is the Americas, lost three members."

"I'm sorry." It did not seem like enough to say.

He stared out for several moments. "No one said this was a safe career choice." He looked at me for a minute. "You look like you are about to drop. Remember that you are still recovering from serious trauma. Get some rest and someone will be in later to check up on you."

I could sense that he was trying to distract me from the course the conversation had taken. Fortunately, I was tired enough to not protest. My eyes were closed before he even left the room.

The next two days were identical – the only thing changing was the booklet of study and the test to take. James did not visit at all until the end of the third day. I had been getting restless and had taken to pacing around the room. There was only so much sleeping and studying one could do before that person started to get cabin fever. I wanted to get out of the room, if only to walk down a hallway and back again.

I had been testing my newly enhanced abilities and discovered that I could sense how many people were in the hallway and how active they were. The person had to be closer for me to pick up on particular emotions, but even then, my range was increasing. James came into the room just as the night staff was settling in that second night.

"Doc tells me you are getting restless."

I wanted to ask him where he had been for the last three days but just mumbled an affirmative.

He looked at me with the unreadable expression I had seen before. I had asked Jason about it and he said the team called it "That Look." and said no one dared interrupt him when he had "That Look" in his eyes. So, I waited.

He sighed, then sat on the edge of the bed.

"I knew from the first moment I saw you that you were a person of action, never still for long, always looking for something to do. It should not surprise me that you have healed faster than anyone ever expected, but it does. On the outside, you do not look like someone who could ever be that resilient." He looked up at the ceiling. "Once properly trained you'll be... quite dangerous to any enemy."

He looked back at me and shrugged. "Ready or not, your training starts right now." He stood up and held out his hand. I took it, and he pulled me up off the bed and led me to the doorway. I hesitated, unsure what to think of this moment. He let go of my hand and walked out to the hall.

"Follow me." It was The Commander speaking.

I followed him down a long hall. There were three other rooms like mine and what looked like a nurse's station in the middle of them. Beyond the medical bay was a single door on the left. We walked to the end of that hall where it split, and he went right. Again, I noticed doors on the left but nothing on the right. The hall was quiet and only semi-lit. We saw and heard no one. After a hundred feet, he stopped at the only door on the right. It was a large double door like what you would see at the entrance to a school gymnasium.

"Ladies first." He waved his hand towards the door. His expression gave nothing away.

It opened with a slight shove, and I found myself in near total darkness. There was a single light in what seemed to be the middle of the room. James headed towards it, seemingly gliding across the floor. I took a step forward and found that it felt like a modern gym floor, like walking on rubber. Cautiously, I made my way to where he stood at the light – it was much farther than it looked.

"Sit down." He spoke quietly.

Nervously, I sat. He sat on the other side of the light, a small camp lantern. I heard him take a couple of deep breaths, and that made me very nervous.

"Listen."

I heard nothing but our breathing and the slight hum of the ventilation system.

"Look around you."

It was incredibly dark around me. I could not see the door or walls or anything other than the lantern and the part of him that it illuminated. He must have been sensing all my responses because he nodded and muttered, "Good."

"Now, look at me and keep looking at me no matter what."

I did, and he held my eyes with "That Look." Suddenly, a small sliver of emotion whispered in my brain. It was hesitant, cautious, but there. He nodded, reading the recognition in my eyes. The sliver of emotion turned into a shaft of light. Although still cautious, it rang with pride. Again, he nodded, then reminded me, "No matter what."

Instantly, it was like a flash of lightning and roaring thunder. I held his eyes while trying to decipher the emotions. There was pride, but I could not tell whom it was directed towards. There was also hope, and a little curiosity. I kept trying to focus on the thunder and realized that, on the edge, where the lowest rumbles would be, was anger.

Then it was gone. The room was silent and dark, and my mind was clear again. James shut his eyes, and I nearly collapsed. My breath was coming out in broken gasps, pain ripping through my head. I looked at him, focusing my throbbing brain on one question.

His eyes opened again, and he looked surprised. "Yes, Harlie, that was mental shielding. Did you watch as I lowered

75

it?"

I nodded.

He looked away and then back at me, his eyes fierce. "It took me weeks to learn how to focus a thought and send it to another empathic. You just did it on the first night and without any instruction!"

I cringed and looked down at the floor. His expression was too intense for me. Did I do something wrong? I wasn't trying to do what he seemed to be accusing me of. Was that anger towards me? Within seconds, a hand was under my chin, lifting my face and eyes to meet his again.

"No." He whispered. "The anger was not towards you. You keep surprising me though." He let go of my chin and his voice changed back to The Commander, "Never, never let me catch you looking down like that again."

It took a moment to find my voice, "Do you visualize a wall? Does it happen by command?"

He thought it over for a moment, then replied, "A little of both. It helps to visualize a wall between your mind and their thoughts, but it is really like one-way glass. You can sense outside if you choose to, but they don't realize it. What I just did was more like opening a window." He leaned back to his original position, "I'll show you again. This time try to keep me out."

He took several more deep breaths, and it seemed like he was trying to clear his thoughts. When his eyes opened, I met them and waited. It was the same as before, a sliver of light and emotion, followed by a shaft and then the brilliant lightning and thunder. He pushed curiosity to the forefront of his thoughts, and I tried to keep him away. It was almost impossible to visualize a wall of one-way glass, never-the-less make one go up in my mind. I focused, breathing hard, sweat starting to bead on my forehead. At one point, I succeeded in getting what seemed to be a quarter wall up. I felt James curiosity back away for an instant, but then it returned, and the small wall crashed down. I could not keep eye contact much longer. He noticed the strain and broke off.

"It was a good start." He commented quietly.

I could not move. The pain in my head started sending waves of nausea through me. My hands grasped my head and I leaned forward protectively.

"Looks like you reached your limit for tonight." He stood and came around to me, offering a hand. Even with the help up, I was not steady on my feet. I practically stumbled behind him on the way back to my room. Jason met us at the nurse's station.

"Sheesh, Commander!" He scolded, "Do you think you were hard enough on her the first night? She can barely stand." He grabbed my arm and hauled me to the bed. Once hooked up to the monitors he sighed. "Blood pressure is up, but probably from the pain. Did you give her anything first?"

James shook his head and stood in the doorway. "It was not a long session, but it was hard on both of us." It was then that I noticed he was holding onto the frame.

"I'm sorry!" I exclaimed, trying to ignore the wave of nausea that came with the words.

"Don't be." was his quiet response. "You did well, but I was tired before we even started. Next time, I'll be more rested." With that, he turned and left.

Jason left the room as well but was back with a small syringe. I did not protest as he put the cocktail into my IV. Whatever it was, it caused the nausea to dissipate instantly. A wave of dizziness came next and I was out cold.

THE BUNKER

After breakfast the next morning, Jason introduced me to Dara. She was taller than me, perhaps around 5 feet 9 and had short, cropped, dirty blond hair with the tips dyed black. She was dressed in the same outfit as me, but you could see that her arms were muscular.

"The Commander has signed orders stating that you are healthy enough to move into our living quarters." She gave me a small smile, which I returned.

"Grab your binder and booklet and follow me."

This time we turned left at the end of the hall. As soon as we did, the atmosphere changed. The bare walls were painted in various earth tones, and the hall opened up into a large room. Couches, chairs, and tables were strewn about. Books, magazines, music disks, and movies lined a large shelf on one wall and two TV's were on another.

"This is our common room, and those double doors lead to a recreation room with table tennis, game systems and other junk."

She kept walking and at the end of the room was another wide hallway. "Our bedrooms are here." She started walking down it. "This room," She pointed to the first door on the right, "Is Ryan and Jason's. And over on the left is Skull and Mitch." We kept going. "This one on the right is Max and Rick's, and mine is on the left." She paused and pointed to the next door on the left. "This one is your room. The officers must know how girls can be because they are letting us bunk separate." She smiled again, and I could sense that she was waiting for me to respond.

"Thank you, Dara." I paused. "Whose rooms are the last two?" I pointed to the door opposite mine and the room at the end of the hall.

"No one is in the opposite room, although Rick might get it again. It was just refinished and repainted. The end room is The Commanders. We all have places of our own above ground but stay here a few times a month, longer if there is a situation or high alert. You'll be living here for a few weeks at least. We all did when we first arrived."

She opened the door and motioned for me to go inside. It was similar to a hotel room. There was a counter with a sink on the right, just as you walked in, and the bathroom was next to that. A closet was on the other side of the counter. Past that was a full-size bed with a plain gray comforter on it, a nightstand, a small dresser, desk, and chair. On the dresser was a microwave and mini refrigerator. There were several scenery pictures on the wall.

"The comforter is temporary. As soon as you get a catalog or above ground pass, someone will take you shopping for one you like. The same goes for the personal supplies and clothes. We have uniforms, but we also have off-duty clothing. The towels are community property as we all have the same ones." Dara explained.

"Would you take me shopping once I get the pass?" No time like the present to start building a relationship with team members.

"I could probably do that. They might have assigned me to anyways." She smiled again. "In the meantime, uniforms are in the dresser and there are some snacks in the 'fridge. Oh, and something came for you when you were still unconscious. It's in the closet. I'll come get you at lunch and show you where the cafeteria is."

"Thank you so much." I smiled. She had been reserved with her emotions, so she must have known about my abilities. However, she was curious at first, and once I asked about shopping, she had decided that, for the time being, she liked me.

Once Dara left, I opened the closet to see what the "something" was. Instantly, I fell to my knees and began to cry. It was the trunk from the shack in the camp. All of Gareth's and my possessions were in it, nothing was missing. I had kept one of his outfits and had given the rest away, that outfit was folded neatly inside the trunk. On top of it were the pictures we brought from America and my Bible. Inside the cover was a small bag containing a lock of my daughter's hair. Kris must have done that the morning I went to breakfast. Someone had taken a photo of my students and it was in there as well, with each of their signatures attached to a paper on the back. There was an unfamiliar envelope and inside were the contents of our bank account, along with a statement of account closure. My tattered clothes were at the bottom.

It all came back in a rush. Since waking up, I had not really thought about my months as a refugee. I lay right there and silently cried. No hysterics, just a steady stream of tears for the losses.

After a time, I forced myself up and went to wash my face. The basic personal supplies had again been provided. In the trunk were several old hair bands, and I carefully combed my hair into a ponytail using one of them. I then set about exploring the rest of the room. The dresser held five sets of the same outfit that I was already wearing in one drawer and some generic underwear and socks in another. The refrigerator was stocked with various fruit, milk, and snack foods.

I placed the binder and booklet on the desk, then checked out the rest of the drawers. There was a journal, loose paper, pencils, and pens, as well as two more booklets to study. I placed my old worn-out Bible inside the nightstand. There was an alarm clock as well, and I was relieved to not have to guess the time anymore. It was all very basic, but after living in the refugee camp, even the basics seemed like a luxury.

I went back to the trunk and took out all of the pictures. Some were in worn frames, but others were inside a small album. I placed the frames on the dresser so that the pictures were facing me when I laid in bed. Silent tears started to flow again, but I forced them to stop. Lunch would be soon, and I did not want to make the wrong impression by walking into the cafeteria with tear-swollen eyes. To help distract me, I went back to the desk and continued to work on the booklets.

Dara knocked on the door at 11:50. At my invite, she came in and looked around.

She looked me over carefully and nodded. "You are really thin, and it looks like you have lost a lot of muscle mass. Training you is going to be tough. I didn't think we would have to start from the beginning with a team member. The rest of us came in with previous experience and reputations."

I could sense that she disapproved of me being so weak and promised myself right there and then to work harder than ever to catch up

We walked down to the cafeteria in silence. It was beyond the long hallway with the gymnasium doors and up one floor on an elevator. The elevator doors opened into a hallway identical to the floor below. There were no doors on the side with the large room from last night, just windows overlooking it. The other side though had double doors that were open, and the cafeteria was there.

It was very nice inside, with three stations of different styles of food and a salad bar. I had not seen that many food options in years. Round tables were spread out around the outskirts, and I noticed that we were still underground. There were large window frames with scenery painted behind them, and it gave the effect of looking outside.

"All the members eat here. We work a standard eight to seventeen hundred shift, so all of us are here for lunch and sometimes breakfast or dinner. It depends on who is being lazy on what day." She walked over to one of the stations.

I nodded, but for some reason was rooted to the floor. Making decisions about what to eat had become a foreign concept to me. I was uncomfortable here, thinking about those who were still in the camps living on two small meals a day.

Dara turned to stare at me; she was becoming uncomfortable with the way I was standing there. I gave her a weak smile and went to where she was waiting.

"Sorry, it got a bit overwhelming back there. It's been a long time since I've seen this much food." I decided that honesty was the best excuse right now.

Her expression changed, and I sensed a shift in her emotions. Right now, sadness was mixed with curiosity. "That's okay, take your time."

I watched her order pasta with tomato sauce and mushrooms then go over to the salad bar. Although a salad looked good, I remembered the comment about needing to put on weight. So, I went for the pasta as well but with Alfredo sauce and sausage, then made a side salad. Dara was at the drink station getting water, but I chose milk. She nodded in approval at my choices.

"I don't know if they got around to telling you or not, but we all have ID chips." She grimaced. "I hate the thing, but

81

it is the easiest way to keep track of us." We walked over to a small computer. "Run the back of your hand here, put the tray on the scale, and then use the touch screen to pick what you are eating. Someone upstairs tallies calories, frequent choices and stuff and makes a big deal over it." This time she sighed. "It is really annoying."

I put the tray down and stared at my hand. Sure enough, there was a tiny scar there that was just a little too straight. However, I followed her lead and then we went to sit down.

"Judging by your expression, they did not tell you...It seems so Big-Brother or end-of-the-world, but all the military groups have been using RFID tags for years now. Ours is a bit more sophisticated, they constantly update when we pass sensors in the doorways and other locations. The medical bay updates it every time we go there, and we are even tracked via GPS feed. That last part has come in handy during more than one mission."

We started eating in silence, but soon there was a noise coming from the elevators. She ignored it, but I turned my head to look.

"The boys are home." Dara muttered.

Sure enough, five men came through the doorway; shoving, laughing, mock punching, and being boisterous.

"The big one in the cast is Skull, the long-haired one is Rick. The tall, dirty blond is Max, the Asian is Ryan and that leaves plain old Mitch." She took a bite of pasta then continued, "They were on a short assignment in Poland and returned this morning."

"You didn't go?"

She laughed. "Oh, I went, but took the first flight out and was back here before they even woke up."

She did not seem tired, but she had to have been. I continued to watch the five men as they settled down enough to get their food and run their ID. But as soon as they were seated at a nearby table, someone threw a roll and it all broke loose again. Dara rolled her eyes, I laughed quietly, and we went back to our food.

As we were finishing, I noticed that the men had gotten very quiet. I gulped, swallowing a small bit of panic when the thought came to mind that I must be the reason for the silence. Sure enough, when I braved a glance over, they were all chewing quietly and staring at me in between bites. Dara noticed my expression and turned to glare at them.

"Didn't your mothers teach you that it is impolite to stare?" She snapped.

Skull snickered at her, but they all suddenly became interested in the appearance of their food.

"Boys!" She exclaimed and rolled her eyes again. "Are you ready to go back? I'm under orders to make sure you relax before taking you on a tour of the rest of the place."

I stood up and looked at each man at the table before turning to leave. Only one, Rick, met my eyes.

I rested until Jason came in to check my vitals. He also took out my IV line but warned me that if I had to be medicated in a hurry it would hurt when he injected it right into the closest vein. I promised to behave but was bothered when he muttered, "It's not you who I'm worried about behaving."

Then, an elderly man with an unusual accent came in to measure me for the organization uniforms. He was very sweet and said he and his wife had helped make these uniforms for over twenty years. After that, I chose to study until dinner. The latest booklet was an introduction to diplomatic strategies.

When someone knocked on my door, I expected it to be Dara, coming to finish the tour. After calling out a cheerful "Come in!" I did not bother to look up from the desk.

A mumbled, "You seem to be adjusting well." brought me to my feet in an instant.

He chuckled, "You are a jumpy little thing."

I turned and spat out. "Only when someone shows up in my room unannounced and at unexpected times."

"I knocked." He was smiling now.

"That's a first." I came back. For some reason, I was feeling annoyed at him.

Still smiling, he closed his eyes then instantly dropped his mental shielding, "opened a window" as he put it last night. James was in a good mood, made better by my reaction and annoyance. It seems he had been watching Dara and me all morning and thought I handled the team's return quite well. Behind all of that was sorrow from my response to the contents of the trunk. Confusion flickered out from me and he shut the window. I grabbed the back of the chair to hold myself upright.

"I was next door trying to sleep." He whispered.

"Oh." Now I felt bad, all annoyance gone.

"You had no way of knowing. But it reminded me that we must work on getting your shielding up. Living in close quarters with anyone for any length of time is enough to make one empathic crazy, never-the-less two of us with this particular group. You saw how loud they can be."

I nodded and smiled.

"Just imagine trying to sleep when their minds are that loud." My smile faded. It was his turn to nod.

"So, for dinner tonight, we are pushing two tables together and all sitting there. Usually, the first night back we are at a pub, but they are eager to meet you and you don't have clearance for above just yet. Your assignment, and this is an order, is to focus on each person's projected emotions at least once. Of course, I'll be watching for it. Then, I want you to try to block them out, one at a time. Focus on each and then block each. We will eat and then meet up in the common room so there will be time to practice." His voice changed to The Commander, "Do you understand the assignment?"

"Yes, Sir." I tried to sound sure of myself but really wanted to lower my eyes again. He walked out of the room and motioned for me to follow.

On the way to the cafeteria, I tried to calm my nerves. It would be hard enough to not repeat the frozen scene from lunchtime but to have to eat and focus my enhanced abilities as well seemed nearly impossible. It did not help that he was practically marching down the hallways, radiating The Commander, and I was barely keeping up without stumbling. I was relieved when we made it to the elevator and used the brief moment to steady myself. It was very difficult because that unreadable expression was pointed in my direction, again.

The rest of the team were just running their ID's and sitting down when we arrived. I had decided that, no matter what ended up on my plate, I probably would not be able to eat it and went towards the salad bar. James halted mid-stride, turned towards me with narrowed eyes, and my mind changed again. Suddenly, the fried chicken and mashed potatoes looked good, like comfort food. I hurried over to that station instead.   When I went to the drink station for hot tea, James came up next to me and whispered. "If you have that with dinner, then one of the milks better disappear from your refrigerator before you go to bed."

The annoyance returned, and I hissed back. "If you are going to be that strict about my food intake, perhaps a written guide would be helpful. I can pick and choose for the day without you glaring at me."

"Watch your tone, Harlie. It would not help your introduction if I dropped shield while you are carrying that tray." His tone was icy, and he paused to let it sink in before going to run his ID.

I counted to twenty before following him. How dare he use that kind of threat! His mood swings were going to give me a complex. Jason's Jekyll and Hyde comment came to mind, and I figured that if they were able to deal with it, then I would have to as well. I took as deep a breath as possible and turned towards the table.

He was all business as we reached the others. They each stood and greeted me as he introduced each one. He must have known that Jason already told me the positions because he did not bother to add that detail. Finally, he turned to introduce me.

Rick was the first to speak. "It's good to have you on the team, Harlie. The outside contacts we have been using are becoming less and less reliable. There has not been an assigned spy on the team in about two years now either." Dara nodded in agreement.

Max spoke then. "It said in the file we were given that you used to work for a gun shop. Can you shoot?"

For some reason, I was not surprised about him having that information. I shrugged, "I used to be pretty good with a .22 but am really out of practice."

"All the same, you know the basics. It won't be too hard to teach you other calibers."

Skull interrupted with, "What's your favorite beer?"

85

Dara slapped the back of his head, and I had to smile before answering, "I don't drink."

We all focused on our food at that point. Well, most of us. I was back and forth between taking a bite and focusing my mind on each person. It was difficult to not stare while I was trying to read their projected emotion. Somehow, I was able to do it.

Max seemed eager to get a gun in my hands, Dara was curious about something, but I could not tell what. Rick was watching me and felt hopeful. Ryan and Mitch were distracted. Jason was happy to see me at the table, and Skull seemed to want to ask more questions. I turned my mind to James, expecting to sense nothing. I nearly gasped as a sliver of emotion hit me like a laser beam. He seemed pleased by the success but doubt at the second task was on the fringe.

The cue was almost imperceptible, but they all seemed to pace their meal so that everyone finished at nearly the same time. They then stood, fractions of a second apart, and went to empty their trays. I reached out to the group and sensed that it was normally like this when they were on-duty. Something else Jason had told me came back into my mind. "We hide our skills well...Our movements are just a little too coordinated, our skills a little too refined." I was seeing that in action.

I followed their movements and wondered how long it would be until I was working on the same wave-length as them. As we waited for the elevator, Jason came up next to me and slung his arm over my shoulder. I tried not to look startled. He smiled down at me.

"See, I told you it would only be a few days, and you look so much better now that you are out of that room." He whispered.

"Got something you want to share with us, J?" It was Max.

"Not really." He smiled.

"Jason." Only one word, in one particular tone, and Jason's arm dropped. He turned to look at the person who said it.

"We are off-duty and I've known her for a couple more weeks than they have. I was trying to reassure her. Is there a problem with that?"

"She is not off duty." James turned to look at me, eyes narrowed again. "Isn't that correct, Harlie?"

I nodded and looked at Jason apologetically. He grimaced and looked away.

In the common room, Skull and Mitch went to one of the TV's and turned on the latest sports game. They pulled out two headsets and sat on one of the couches. I looked at Dara.

"Yes, that is a wireless hook-up. We begged for it about five years ago after these sports fanatics kept getting into arguments with those of us who like to watch regular TV or movies. Now, all we have to deal with is the outbursts during poor calls."

Ryan, Jason, and Max went to the rec room and started in on video games. James and Dara sat down to watch some show, but I knew that James would not really be watching. Rick came over to me.

"Your file says that you enjoyed singing and you directed a choir a few years back." He smiled. "What kind of music did you listen to?"

I turned to face him, and he motioned to one of the small tables. We sat down, and I risked a glance over at James before answering. He acted as if he were not paying the slightest bit of attention.

"Inspirational music mostly, contemporary from the 90's and early 2000's and a few artists from the last ten years. Country music as well, but it's mostly artists from the nineties. I also enjoy movie soundtracks and instrumentals."

Rick nodded his head. "Those were the better days of music all around. After that, it was just remakes of older songs along with repetitive beats and lines that were quite boring."

"I agree." I let my mind reach out and was happy to sense that he was enjoying the conversation.

"Let me grab my old MP3 player and see what is on there that might be familiar to you." He stood up and walked towards his room.

I took the moment to try and raise my mental shield against one person. Skull and Mitch were distracted by the game. I could sense that they were frustrated by someone's blunder. I focused in on Skull and tried to raise the wall. Because I did not want to sense him at all, I thought of it as a

87

brick wall and not the one-way-glass James described. Out of the corner of my eye, I noticed James shoulders stiffen slightly. It took more effort than I anticipated, but suddenly Skull's displeasure disappeared. It was confusing as to what the trigger was to make the wall go up, but I tried again with Mitch. This time it went up a little quicker, but I still could not decipher the trigger. Sighing, I turned to see that Rick was back and was staring at me.

"Sorry," I muttered. "Got lost in thought."

"It's okay," He grinned, "You are still on duty." He leaned in closer and whispered so low no one stood a chance of hearing it. "Looks like you are in boot camp already."

My sigh was response enough.

"I found some music for you and here is a pen and paper. Write down what you like, and I'll copy it for you."

"Thank you, but I don't have anything to play it on." I lowered my eyes, feeling a little ashamed that I did not have anything at all.

I felt the glare before I sensed the emotions. James "opened the window" and the displeasure at my lowered eyes hit me like a blow to the stomach. I let out a small gasp and quickly raised my eyes to stare at him. He held my gaze for several long seconds, then the shield was back up.

Rick looked uncomfortable for a moment but shook his head quickly and replied, "You will, soon." Then he leaned forward again, "That looked painful." I gave him a quick nod and turned my attention to the task of picking out music. While doing that, I tried blocking out more of the team. Before long, I could get my shielding to block out the front of the room so that Dara, Skull, and Mitch were mentally quiet. It was harder to focus on those in the other room. I could not see them, so it was like working in the dark to picture them – to find whose emotions belonged to whom and block those.

When the show ended, Dara switched stations and turned on what seemed to be a comedy. Rick excused himself to go watch it, and James took a book from the shelf and moved to a loveseat. I kept on with scanning through the MP3 player, listing songs, and completing my assignment. There were nearly 3,000 songs on the player, and Rick had an excellent selection of nearly everything I liked. The hours passed quickly, and I was startled when Jason suddenly came out of the room and tapped me on the shoulder.

"Time to check vitals," He muttered and walked towards my room. I looked at the clock on the wall, it was nearly nine.

No one looked up as I followed him. He still seemed to be in a funk from his encounter with James. When we made it into my room, I reached out to touch his arm.

"Don't." He hissed. "He can still sense you in here."

"So what?" I muttered back. "You had no way of knowing that I had an assignment and, honestly, there is too much going on for me to care."

He looked at me sternly, "Be careful with that kind of attitude. James is a wonderful leader and ally, and he can be quite fun to be around, but it is hell if you go against him. Since you arrived, it has been all business, and we are all on edge."

He checked my heart rate, blood pressure, and reflexes and then carefully prodded my ribs and had me take deep breaths to see how much air I could take in without pain. Finally, he whispered. "You are still healing so be careful, don't let him push you too far."

Jason inclined his head toward James as we came back into the main room. James stood and motioned for me to follow him. When we reached the elevator, he turned to me.

"You did well for your first assignment. If I had not been sitting there, you would have had half the room blocked off. Tomorrow, try to work more on those you cannot see, that seemed to be the hardest for you."

"Yes, Sir," I said quietly, fighting the urge to lower my eyes.

We went up one level and ended up in the nearly deserted cafeteria. He had me pick out milk and a junk food snack, then we went to sit down.

James seemed to be distracted so we sat in silence. As I finished the last of the milk, he reached out and placed his hand on top of mine. I looked up surprised and could not look away. His eyes burned with some emotion I did not recognize. It was similar to "That Look" but much more painful to see.

"I did not like having to do that back in the common

89

room."

I gave a small shudder in response.

"Never be ashamed of who you are or what has happened to you. So what if you came with nothing? It will not be that way for long." His expression turned serious, "And you were warned to never lower your eyes like that. We are all on the same level here, no one is below anyone else. There will be consequences if I catch you doing it again, and I won't hold back like this time."

I shuddered again, and he stood. "Let's go."

"Where?" I whispered.

"To see the rest of the building, with a couple of stops in between."

We walked to the hallway where the elevator was, but instead of going back down, he turned right and headed up the hall. He opened the first door we came to and opened it. Inside was what I had known as a "cube farm" or one large room with numerous cubicles and workstations. On the far wall was a small library. "Research center," Was all he said, and we walked out again.

Continuing on, we went through the next door. The whole area was separated by glass-enclosed rooms and every room was filled with scientific equipment. "Development center," He explained, but then walked into the area. He stopped at one of the rooms and I noticed that Dr. L was waiting for us inside.

"Fitness tests," He smiled again and pointed towards the room. I did not smile back, instantly nervous.

"Can't we just say I am helpless and start at the beginning?" I asked.

"You have never been helpless, if you were, you would be dead by now." He placed his hand on my back and half led, half pushed me into the room.

I spent the next hour on various equipment, pushing and pulling levers as hard as I could, running on a small treadmill, lifting objects, all with sensors on me, recording everything. I was exhausted and annoyed with the doctor's commentary when James finally announced that the tests were over. He grabbed a print out from the computer and read it over while I was detached from the sensors. After thanking the surgeon, we were on our way again.

The moment we were around the corner, I stopped and sat down, pulling my knees up and resting my forehead on them. James stood and stared at me. I chanced a look up at him and saw indecision on his features. Compassion and understanding were mixing with determination and frustration. When he realized I was watching, determination won.

"Stand up; we have two more stops to make." It was the voice of The Commander. I hesitated, and he grabbed my arm and pulled me back to a stand. He was careful not to hurt me, but his grip was firm. The moment I was on my feet, he started down the hallway again.

"This is normally off limits unless you are called up. The General's office and other top-level management offices are here." The carpet and paint rang of the power that sat behind the hardwood doors. He showed me which room was The General's and which one was his own, adding he had one in the training facility too.

"What is across the river?" I asked as we were going back down the elevator.

"Equipment mostly, a bunkhouse for on-duty agents, and a lock-up. It is a smaller bunker and our team only goes there to pick up what we need for missions."

"What is across the hall from the training facility?"

"There is a conference room and tactical facility. You'll be there in the next day or so." We left the elevator and started back towards the living quarters. Suddenly, he stopped at the hallway that led to the training facility. "Time for round two." By his tone, it sounded like I did not have an option. It was not The Commander, but it was close.

"I suppose I am still on duty?" I swallowed.

"You suppose correctly."

"It's late."

"It was late last night too, and you are not in a position to argue." He walked over to the double doors and opened one of them.

"Wait here." I heard a quick shuffle and footsteps. The camp light flicked on and a quiet, "Come, Harlie." came from the other side of the light.

Knowing what to expect did not make it any easier.

The first time, I only got the wall up halfway. The second try, he stopped me and said I was trying too hard. I could feel his frustration. On the third attempt, I managed to get the wall up all the way but could not hold it. I wanted to stop. My head was pounding, and I felt I would collapse from exhaustion. On the fourth attempt, I did just that. James swearing was the last thing I heard before grasping my head and passing out.

The first thing I heard when I woke up was Jason hollering at James. I was still on the floor and it was still dark. "And don't you say I am out of line! It is my job as a medic to keep your team in perfect health. I cannot do that if you are constantly undermining protocol. You pushed her recovery time. You made the surgery earlier than recommended. You put her in the living quarters when all three of us medical personnel refused to clear her. On top of it all, you put her through fitness tests and now this!" He was practically screaming. "You keep pushing her and she will do more than pass out. She will break beyond the point where you can keep her on this team. Back. Off. Commander." He turned, and I could see him facing me.

"She is waking up. File a complaint against me for open defiance or put me on punishment, I don't care. But..." I heard something being thrown and caught. "You caused it, you fix it." Jason stomped out of the room. I wanted to call out to him, to beg him not to leave me here, but he was gone, and James was kneeling by my side.

"Harlie?"

I shuddered and looked at him.

"Can you sit up?"

I could, and I did.

"I'm sorry. I pushed you too far today. I knew it after the fitness tests but chose to continue, and for that, there is no excuse." He waited for me to acknowledge his words. When I did not, he continued. "Jason was correct in everything he said. And even though he thinks I'm going to punish him, the truth is The General is going to be quite unhappy with me when I file this report."

"Why did you ignore them?" I whispered.

"Because I am relying too much on what I saw in the camp and what I see in your mind. Even though your physical capabilities are showing me otherwise, I allowed myself to become too excited by your potential."

I stayed silent, staring at his hand and the object in it.

"It's Jason's cocktail for stubborn commanders." He was trying to lighten the mood.

I glared at him.

"It is the same thing as what we have been giving you, a combination of drugs. One lowers your blood pressure, which skyrockets when you've stressed your ability. There is also a long-lasting painkiller for the migraine and a mild tranquilizer so that your body relaxes enough for you to heal and sleep."

"I hate meds." It seemed he needed a reminder, "And I've been forced to be on one thing or another since before arriving in this place."

There was no mistaking the sorrow in his eyes, "Again, I am truly sorry."

I tried to stand but was very wobbly. He took my arm to steady me, and I noticed that he was being very careful now, not using the firm grasp from earlier. We made our way back to the living quarters, and I was grateful that everyone seemed to be in bed – even though I knew that Jason must still be awake. He led me into my room and then dropped my arm but made no move to leave. I prepped for bed, ignoring him, and he went to stand by the desk. I could see him eying the pictures on my dresser but chose to ignore that too. Instead, I stood next to the bed and glared at him, angry at the entire situation.

"I deserve that." He whispered, and I knew he meant the emotions I was projecting. He moved closer to the bed and took the cap off the syringe.

"I really wish you wouldn't." I was staring at the medication.

"Medic's orders and I plan on following this set." He came over and gently took my arm, turning it to expose a vein.

"I'm going to have Max teach me to use a tranquilizer gun and hit both you and Jason with this junk." Were my last words before the cocktail took effect.

He laughed quietly, "Goodnight, Harlie."

BEGINNING

Someone had set my alarm because it started screaming at 7 am. I wanted to scream back at it, but instead fumbled for the off button and sat up. My head was throbbing, and I felt a bit drugged up from the tranquilizer being injected so late. However, we had to be ready and in the common room at o' eight hundred. I took a quick shower and put on a clean outfit. Wishing I had a hairdryer, I pulled the wet mass into another ponytail and headed for the cafeteria. Mitch and Dara were in the common room, waiting.

"Ready for breakfast?" Dara asked as we started down the hall.

"Yes, I am surprisingly hungry." I smiled, even though it made my head throb worse.

"Not surprising." Mitch pitched in. "You were on late duty and look about twenty pounds under ideal."

I fought the urge to look down.

Dara looked at him harshly, "I swear! You all act like you have been raised by wolves and then moved in under a rock. No manners and no common sense when it comes to basic conversation."

He grinned, "Dara, we do live under a rock."

She slapped the back of his head then turned to look at me apologetically. "There has never been a second female on the team. It's always been just me, and they have gotten away with too much for too long. Personally, I'm grateful to not be the only one anymore. I just hope they can learn to be more civilized."

We reached the cafeteria, and I braced myself for more decisions. Fortunately, Jason was standing in the entryway. He smiled, but underneath I could tell that he was edgy.

"Let's pick out something high calorie and high nutrition for you."

The team was already sitting together so, after making the meal and scanning our ID's, we joined them. The Commander was not there. Jason took a few bites of his meal and then nodded towards the door. Kayla was standing there and came up to hand him what looked like a plastic flip-top container.

"Been sneaking some of this into your IV, but since that has been pulled, have a few pills." He handed it to me.

I groaned. "You know what I'm going to say."

"Yes, and I am prepared with an explanation."

I was on a powerful multivitamin and mineral supplement, and because he knew I would wake up in pain, something to stop it. There was also a small white pill there that he said was for my healing wounds but offered no other explanation.

"You realize I'm not going to accept that for very long." I commented.

"Yes, but the choice is taking it here, or I corner you in the training room with a needle. There is not a person on this team who isn't on something." He was serious about that threat, so I took the foul looking pile and scowled at him.

When the last person finished eating they all rose at the same time again, and this time I was only a second behind. We made it back to the common room with two minutes to spare. The Commander was waiting for us, and I shuddered, remembering last night. His eyes roamed to each team member as we sat down on the various couches and chairs, making eye contact with each one. When his eyes settled on mine, he "opened the window" just a crack, enough for me to sense that he was still feeling remorse for the events of yesterday.

"We have only a brief period of time to mold around our newest member before we must be back in the field." He began. "The current situation is only being held at bay due to shadow recon and short missions like the one you just completed. I estimate we have five to six weeks maximum, and in that time, we all have a lot to cover. With the addition of Harlie, we will be able to take more two-pronged approaches to the situation. That should leave the masterminds reeling as they will not be expecting someone like her to be such a powerful foe. They will be off guard, and we need to make sure they stay that way." He paused and looked at each of us again. "We all have a lot to learn and relearn. New strategies will be in place, new skills, and new equipment will be involved. Ryan and Mitch, you received the reports on their latest weapons development?"

"Yes, Sir, and are working on an answer to it as well as continuing trials on our own little surprise." Mitch answered.

"Max, are you still assisting with the technical aspect of that project?"

"Yes, Sir, and we just received the weapons shipment you requested."

"I'm sure you will let us know how those work out." He smiled, and I guessed that Max would be like a kid in a toy store for a few days.

"Skull?"

"Yeah, GPS updates are being run, but the satellite feed is slow and there were some poor angles."

"Rick, there has not been any new code, but it is only a matter of time. Be ready for it."

Rick nodded solemnly.

"Dara and Jason, your focus will be on getting Harlie trained."

"Yes, Sir," They said in unison.

"I'll be in and out of the office as well as the training facility. Any questions?"

I had a ton but kept perfectly still and quiet.

"Dismissed."

They all stood, and several went towards their rooms while the rest headed for the hallway.

"Harlie, Dara, Jason." The Commander called us back. "She has a meeting with The General at o' nine hundred, and it is not on the schedule. Harlie, you are going to need that binder with all the forms ready. I added a few pages to it this morning. Better work on that first and then go to the facility after your meeting."

So that is what I did. I had not looked at any of it for days and needed to refresh my memory. The new pages had to do with money. Anyone who worked for the organization had an account with the bank in town. Pay was deposited into it once a month, with living expenses already taken out. The estimate for my cottage, electricity, water, and sewer were there, but nothing about my salary itself. I would be given a card that worked only at ATM machines from that bank.

Unless prior approval was given, all purchases must be made in cash. This was for safety and security. There was a catalog behind the extra pages along with a hand-written request to list what I needed by sixteen hundred hours.

At ten until nine, James arrived to escort me to The General. He smiled at my nervous expression and reassured me that it was just to welcome me and to turn in the signed forms. He was correct, for the most part. The General did welcome me warmly to the team, took all the paperwork and quizzed me on my new identity. When he asked if I had any questions, I pointed out that there was no amount listed in the salary section. He looked puzzled and called James into the room. James apologized for the error and wrote in the amount and showed it to me. It took all I had to remember that he was watching for my mental reaction as well as my facial expression. So, I carefully hid my shock and nodded my approval. James turned to leave but The General stopped him.

"Commander, stay another moment. We are almost finished."

It looked like James cringed before turning around.

"I want to talk to the both of you about this report." This time I was positive that James cringed. He continued, "Jamyson, what I read here is unacceptable. I would like to know why you thought that anyone going through her situation would be able to handle that kind of pressure right away."

He lifted his chin, slightly defiant, "You and I both know why. She has shown time and time again to be amazingly resilient. She was restless in the medical bay, and it seemed that the move to the barracks was in her best interest."

"That may be so, Jamyson, but moving her to the barracks and, a few hours later, starting her out like it was boot camp is a bit much."

"Yes, Sir, but you know that she can handle it and the current situation ..." He was interrupted.

"The situation is not critical enough for you to forget that you are normally a compassionate person and that everyone has noticed changes in your demeanor in the last couple of months." The General's voice was very firm. "No, she is not to be pampered, and I agree her potential is amazing, but please listen to your team and support staff and use common sense."

"Yes, Sir."

I had been looking from person to person the entire time. The Commander had his shield up of course, but The General was being totally honest. Now, if I could get them to talk like I was in the room. James sensed that.

"We both apologize, Harlie, for having this conversation like you were not sitting here. It was rude." He glanced at The General who nodded in agreement. Then, James turned to me again, and lowered his shield enough so that I could sense his turmoil.

I stood, thanked General Smiths for allowing me to be part of the team, and followed James out into the hall. We were next to the elevator when he turned to me.

"You'll be with Dara and Jason the rest of the day. Try to practice your mental shielding when moments allow." He turned as the doors opened and walked back towards the offices.

I had an uncomfortable feeling about our exchange but forced myself to shrug it off as I approached the double doors to the training facility. Slowly, I pushed one of the doors open, walked inside and looked around in shock.

The facility was larger than I thought. It was nearly half of an American football field in size and filled with more equipment than I imagined. There was standard fitness equipment like treadmills and weight training items on one side. On another was gymnastics and balancing equipment. The third side held what looked like an obstacle course, and in the middle, was a series of mats. A running track was around the perimeter. On the wall opposite from the entrance was another door. A large window looked into the room on the other side. It was the largest firing line I had ever seen, with stations for basic target shooting as well as a separate section for shooting while on the move. Max was there and looking quite happy with whatever he was firing. Next to that room was another door, but it was shut.

Jason came running over from the fitness equipment.

"You look like you survived the meeting." He was chuckling. It was a welcome sound after last night. "Ready for your first workout?"

I suddenly felt very weak; knowing that what was planned for me was pathetic next to what they would be doing. Jason recognized my expression and chuckled again.

"You'll catch up to us soon enough."

He started walking back to the fitness equipment and my physical training began. I had a circuit to complete on the equipment, followed by time walking and running the track. Jason accompanied me for this, working on his own routine and pausing to check my vitals. From there, it was balance and agility with Dara on the gymnastics equipment. After that, Max got his turn with firearms. From the beginning, that became my favorite part of the routine. He was a great teacher, and it was only minutes before I remembered the skills I had acquired all those years ago at the gun shop. My routine ended with self-defense training on the mats, and Dara was my instructor – with whoever was nearby as her victim. The schedule was set up so that I could stop after one station and leave to study the booklets or attend some other type of non-physical training and then start back up at the next location. Snack breaks and a mandatory rest time back in my room after lunch were on the agenda as well, although that would be shortened as I continued to heal.

During my rest time on that first day, Dara walked me through the catalog. I was used to surviving with just the minimal comforts, not just in the camp but for years before it. Dara quickly became frustrated when I kept commenting that certain items were not necessary and that all I really wanted was a hairdryer.

"This is not your old life. You have a room here in the bunker and you will have your own place soon. This is a chance to have things that have been missed out on for years!"

It was difficult to describe the way I had chosen to live my past life. To make sure that others had enough, Gareth and I kept strict control of our spending. We tried to live debt free and donated what we could to help those who needed it more.

"Dara, please do not be upset with me; it's the way I'm used to being."

She stood up and pointed to the bed and its basic blanket, "Is that yours?"

99

I shook my head.

She walked over to the dresser and pulled open the drawers, "Are these yours?"

Again, I shook my head.

"How about the mattress and pillows?" She knew what my answer would be and kept on going. She pointed to the few items on the bathroom counter, "Did you pick those out for yourself?" Then, she opened the closet and hauled out the trunk. "So, this is all that is really yours?"

"Please do not touch that." I whispered desperately. Tears were welling in my eyes, and I did not want to cry in front of her.

She stopped and stared at me, watching the struggle on my face. I could sense that part of her wanted to make more of a point by emptying the contents and another part was feeling compassion for my situation.

"You will be able to help others once you are above ground. Right now, you need to help yourself. It is okay to let go and make yourself comfortable. There are going to be times, sooner rather than later, where you are going to wish for some of these so-called luxuries that you are refusing."

She took my hand and led me out of the room and into hers. It was decorated nicely, coordinated without being too elaborate. I noticed things like a wicker hamper, portable DVD player, MP3 player with speakers, and a shelf with her personal selection of books and videos. She also had a collection of hand combat weapons decorating the walls.

"See, Harlie?" She opened the closet door, and I saw a handful of outfits and a dress uniform but nothing too fancy. "My apartment is like this but with an amazing sound system and almost every martial arts movie ever made. That part is a bit selfish, but it's nothing over the top."

"What do you do with the extra money?" Despite the potential consequence for the personal question, I had to ask.

There was a long pause before she answered, "My latest donation built the new school at the refugee camp you came from, and I am saving for when my days on the team are over."

I walked back to my room, sat down at the desk, and opened the catalog again. With Dara's help, I picked out a comforter set with a couple of coordinating bath accessories, two down pillows, a hanging cloth hamper, an MP3 player, a small bookshelf, personal items, a favorite brand of shampoo and soap, a hairdryer, and two sets of pajamas.

"Is there anything else? A frivolous item? Off-duty clothes?" Dara was being pushy now that I had given in a little.

"Yes, but I like to try on clothes, not get them from a catalog. Besides we only have a few more minutes until break is over."

She nodded, took my order and tucked it into her pocket. We went back to the facility and to teaching me the daily routine.

The rest of the day went quickly and before too long it was time to stop for the day. Everyone quit whatever they were doing at sixteen thirty and gathered in the conference room to debrief. We then had until eighteen hundred to rest and clean up before the evening meal. If there was nothing pressing, the rest of the evening was spent in the common room, relaxing.

We were just getting off the elevator and walking into the cafeteria when James joined us. He walked over to Jason and handed him what looked like a very small booklet. As the others went to the stations, Jason leafed through it, and I could sense he was pleased with whatever it was. He nodded to James and handed the booklet back to him. Then, as I knew they would, they both turned towards me.

James handed me the booklet. It was so small that it could fit into my pocket and each page was coated for durability. The cover was blank, so I opened it and found that it was a custom-made food guide. Listed was the number of calories and fat I needed to be taking in immediately and what I would need to be taking in after my weight reached a certain level. The next pages were foods commonly served in the bunker and how they could be mixed and matched to make ideal meals and snacks for me.

"Thank you, this is perfect." I smiled at them both. Jason returned the smile and James said I was welcome. We then followed the rest of the team and I used the guide to help pick out the proper meal. It seemed like too much food, but it is amazing what a busy day could do to one's appetite.

As we made our way down to the common room, James leaned over and whispered, "How goes the mental shield?"

Horror washed over my face. The day had been so busy, and there had been so much to learn, that I had forgotten to practice. He sensed my response and placed a hand on my shoulder.

"You had much to learn today, and it must have distracted you. Try to get some practice in while we are unwinding but don't stress over it."

Now shock was the dominant emotion. It seemed he was either trying extra hard not to push me or the compassionate Commander I had seen glimpses of before was back in charge. He chuckled quietly at the change and smiled.

Rick came over with his MP3 player as soon as we were in the room. We picked up where we left off last night, going through his seemingly endless playlist and jotting down the songs I wanted. Dara turned on the television and I wondered if she would turn on the news. It had been nearly a year since I had seen any televised media report. Sadly though, she turned on a car show. When Jason and Skull started a game of Foosball in the recreation room, I practiced sensing their emotions and blocking them out. It was difficult but not impossible.

Time passed quickly and soon enough of the stress from the past few days caught up with me. It was barely twenty-one hundred and my eyes started closing mid-song. Max noticed and laughed quietly while walking over and gently shaking my shoulders. Rick went to get Jason for my nightly exam, and I was wondering how long it would be before those could be stopped. On the way out of the common room, I glanced at James and sent a silent question in his direction. He looked up from his book and shook his head, no late-night practice today.

Moments after Jason finished the exam, I was in the bed and saying a prayer. It was the first night in recent memory that I would be sleeping without the assistance of any medication. Fortunately, sleep found me within minutes.

Come morning, I was ready for the alarm and was up and in the shower within minutes. Despite James warning about how loud the team's minds could be at night, I managed to sleep straight through. I sincerely hoped it would be a trend and not just a one-time event.

Today was Saturday, and I had asked Rick last night what the schedule would be. He said that when the team first starts a training session like this, Saturday was like a weekday. The same went with leading up to a mission. If nothing big was going on, Saturdays would be half days.

Upon leaving my room, I quickly observed that it must be laundry day. Dara brushed past me into the room and grabbed my dirty clothes, checking one and showing me that it had my initials punched into the tags.

"Your order should be here today as well, so those will be punched and ready by end-of shift."

Expect the unexpected, expect the unexpected, I could not let that mantra leave my head for an instant. This place was so efficient it was almost scary. Dara smiled at my expression and turned to leave.

We sat at two tables during breakfast but chatted between them. It seemed that everyone, except Skull, had slept well. I pouted when Jason came up again with the small pill container.

"Put the pain one in your pocket if you feel like you do not need it right now, but I can guarantee that you will need it later."

I wanted to reply that he was wrong but knew it would most likely be a lie. As the team was finishing their meals, I kept myself open mentally as well as scanning with my eyes to see if I could pick out the cue to stand. This time I saw it, a subtle shift in shoulder movement combined with a glance to the person on the left and then straight ahead. I could also feel it mentally. The left glance was to see if that person was finished. If they were then you looked straight ahead.

I was quite proud of myself for deciphering the cue. Suddenly, it became obvious that someone else felt the same. James had come in late to breakfast and was sitting several tables behind us. Because of his mental shielding and my intense focus on the others, I did not notice him until he "opened the window" and projected his pride at my accomplishment. As we were walking out of the cafeteria, I chanced a look behind me. He beamed a smile, then turned back to finishing his toast and tea.

We did not have a meeting and the morning went by quickly, thanks in part to Max insisting that I try out numerous calibers of handguns. We worked with each one until narrowing it down to several I could handle without difficulty and then started on more intense training with those. From there, I went to the tactical facility and worked on the booklets. Towards the end of my study time, Ryan and Mitch informed me that there would be a small laptop assigned to me with video lessons, tests, and Welsh language software installed. It would also have intranet access for daily communications but could not be used for searching the internet until clearance was granted. I was a bit bothered by that fact. It made us seem much more isolated, and I was curious as to what was happening in the rest of the world.

After lunch, I returned to my room for the mandatory rest and was pleased to find that the catalog order had arrived. The plain gray comforter had been replaced with the reversible one I had chosen. Coordinating sheets and shams were with it, and I was smiling and giggling with delight when James and Dara came in to check on me.

"Someone will have to help me with this." I held up the MP3 player. "I've never owned one before, just had CD's and such."

"Since Rick has taken an interest in your musical background, we'll let him have that task." James smiled.

Dara stopped smiling and gave me a stern look, "See? It does not look frivolous. You have chosen a look that is beautiful and practical all at the same time."

I looked around the room, "It makes it feel more like me, less unfamiliar."

"That's the point." She looked around again, "Did you check the dresser yet?"

I shook my head, then went over and looked in each drawer. Half were still empty, but the other half held my newly cleaned work clothes, as well as the ordered articles of clothing.

"Well, we just had to be nosy and see your reaction," It was James again, "And now we will be off. Enjoy your rest."

The afternoon went as well as the morning. I finished all the stations and still had time for another study session. That allowed me to finish the first booklet on diplomatic strategies, test on it, and then start the second one. Rick was still waiting for new code to come in, so he helped quiz me on content and shared a few stories of when he had seen particular strategies in action. I could sense that he had already accepted me as a member of the team and wanted me to be successful.

In the common room, Rick brought out his laptop to transfer my music choices and showed me how to use the new MP3 player. I was sorely out of practice with technology so it took a few attempts to learn it all. The lesson was made more difficult by a rugby game that was on and its fanatics cheers, boos, and less-than-ideal language.

Dara gave up trying to watch another show and retired early to her room. I looked around and did not see Ryan. I checked mentally and could not sense him either. Curious, I sent a silent question out to James. He looked up from his book in mild surprise, then stood and came over.

"Rick, could I interrupt your instruction for a short time?" His facial expressions seemed friendly enough, so the anxiety stayed under control.

"Sure, mate, just don't keep her out past nine." He chuckled.

James laughed in reply and motioned for me to follow him. We walked down the hallway and took the elevator up to the cafeteria.

"I don't know about you, but I am craving ice cream again, and you fell asleep last night without an evening snack." If this was going to be another lesson or something serious, his tone was betraying nothing.

We went over to the snack area, and he opened the lid of a small freezer. When I pulled out a Flake cone, he chuckled.

"You might not have been born on this side of the pond, but your tastes are sure like ours." He looked to be contemplating something, and I caught a brief flicker of what

105

it was.

"Do they ever serve Branston sandwiches here?"

He looked surprised again, and it was my turn to laugh. "You might have super mental shielding, but the context of our conversation combined with your expression gave it away. Remember, I've had that part of my skills since birth."

We ran our ID's and sat down to enjoy the snack. I knew he would wait until we were finishing up before starting in on whatever conversation he had planned. Sure enough, that is what happened.

"You were curious as to why Ryan was not present with us tonight?" At my nod he continued. "Ryan and Mitch are the only two members of our team who are married. Mitch wanted to stay for the game, but Ryan was eager to go home. I asked them both to stay below with us for your first days. From now until the week leading up to our next mission, they will return to their wives after debriefing." He gave me a small smile. "Their wives are both employees here as well. One works as our bank liaison and the other on the base above us."

"Oh." I had more questions but there was no need to ask them, James could sense what was coming.

"Dara is divorced and has not been interested in the dating world, so to speak. Jason was engaged, but his fiancée could not handle all the secrecy. The others are not really looking, as they feel it would distract from the seriousness of what we do."

He was holding something back, even with his shield up I could tell. He had referred to the others but in a tone that did not seem to include himself.

"What about you?" I asked out loud before he could pick it up from my mind.

James stared at me for a long moment before answering, "I am in the same category as you." He looked away, "I married young, and we only had a few years together before a rare illness took her."

My mouth formed an 'o' but nothing came out. The silence lasted for several minutes as each of us gathered thoughts that had been scattered by our shared loss. We both sighed at the same time, startling the other, and we let out a quick laugh. He stood, and I followed.

106

As we slowly made our way back to the common room, he explained the normal weekend schedule. Because so much new information had been obtained from their recent assignment, and because I had been so ill upon arrival, we had worked all today to help catch us up. No matter what, if the team was not in the field, then Sundays were off. The bunker was fairly abandoned then, and only prepackaged meals or sandwiches would be available in the cafeteria. James was not sure if the entire team would stay above ground all day or if some would return to keep me company. Either way, the day was mine to do with as I saw fit. The training facility would be opened if I felt the need work, but James encouraged me to relax.

It was just before nine when we returned. Rick looked up from my MP3 player and smiled. "Excellent timing! I just finished uploading the last of your choices."

I smiled back. Rick excused himself to his room, but not before putting his arm around my shoulder and giving me a quick squeeze. I stayed in the common room, practicing with mental shielding until I could get it around the sports fanatics and keep it up without constant thought. James watched from his position on one of the couches and nodded at my success. I wanted to continue but was starting to get a headache. He noticed and pointed first at me and then to the hallway to our quarters. I went to my room without comment and started preparing for bed.

It felt good to be in proper pajamas after so many months of sleeping in the clothes I wore that day. It bothered me that Jason stopped watching the game to check my vitals, but once he was gone, I climbed into bed with the MP3 player and listened to music until sleep took me.

The wonderful sleep from last night did not return. My dreams were restless, constantly shifting through scenes of my past life. There were good memories, and I could feel the joy, but then it would shift to the difficulties and losses before we left America and from there to events at the refugee camp. I relived the moments before and after the bombs, the billowing cloud which could be seen for miles and the chaos that ensued from it. The days and weeks afterward flashed by partially from the perspective of our home life and partially what the media had shown before it was shut off. I tossed and turned, awoke, and forced myself to try to rest again. It was four in the morning before a deep and undisturbed sleep finally took me.

When the alarm went off at seven, I forced myself to get up and shower. My mind had been made up to keep at least part of the daily routine, even if I decided to go back to bed after breakfast. No one was in the cafeteria, so I had some cold cereal and brought a doughnut and pint of milk back to the room.

Whoever was still in the living quarters started waking around nine. Part of me wanted to go out to the common room and see who was there, but after the conversation with James, I decided to keep a low profile. No one should feel like they had to stay behind or hurry back underground because of me. I tried to tackle one of the booklets, but last night's poor sleep was catching up. The words were becoming more and more unfocused, so I curled back up under the covers and waited for the team to leave.

It was half-past ten when I got out of bed again. There was silence all around me. I picked up the doughnut, milk, and booklet and walked into the common room. It was empty, so the snack went on one of the end tables, and I lounged on one of the couches to study and munch. After finishing the booklet, I went down to the training facility and went through the fitness circuit. It was getting close to thirteen hundred and lunch should have been a half hour ago. Three support staff were in the cafeteria, and they smiled and waved to me. I smiled back, picked out a sandwich, chips, fruit and hot tea, ran my ID and ate there.

James was waiting at the elevator as I left the cafeteria. He had "That Look" on his face until I came to stand in front of him.

"Have you had a relaxing day?" he wondered, although it sounded like he already knew the answer.

"Yes, I have." I smiled at him.

"Hmm. What did you do?"

"I read, took a nap, read a little more while having a snack, completed the fitness station and had some lunch." It sounded innocent enough, but I knew he would sense that there was more to it.

"What were you planning to do next?" He made no move to allow me onto the elevator.

"I'm not sure. Perhaps complete another station or see what's playing on the television."

"The latter." Frustration clouded his expression.

My eyes closed for a moment before addressing his frustration. "James, I am not used to having free time or being given a day to relax. Between that and being cooped up in the hospital for all that time..." I chanced a look into his eyes, "Please be patient. I'm not trying to be difficult. On the contrary, I'm working with everything I've got just to adjust."

His answer was to step aside and press the button to call the elevator for the trip down. When it arrived, he wordlessly followed me inside. I hesitated at the turn for the training facility but chose to keep walking towards the common room. James followed behind me, never more than a few feet away.

When we were at the entryway I turned to face him. "Why are you back so early?"

"To keep you in line. I had a hunch you would not be able to comply with a relaxing day off." He walked past me, sat on the large couch and motioned for me to sit.

I sat but not without reservations. It was moments like this that I wished I knew what he was thinking. He turned on the television and flipped to a random channel. We sat in silence, not sure if the other was actually watching the show or not. When it ended, James turned to me.

"We have not practiced for several days. Since you have been in somewhat of a relaxed state and have had those days to recover and heal, shall we try again?"

Trying to keep the instant panic under control was quite a feat, but somehow, I managed to nod.

"Shh, Harlie, you'll never learn to maintain a shield with anxiety like that. You need to be calmer." James turned to face me. "You have been able to raise it here in the common room during the evenings and while working in the training facility."

"I can't keep it up though, and I don't know what the trigger is to raise it. It takes so much focus."

He seemed to be deep in thought. "It was so long ago

that I was taught, so long ago...let me think." He stood and paced the room for several minutes, then returned to the couch. "You think of it as a wall right now and not the one-way glass that it more closely represents?"

"Yes."

"That's part of the problem. It is not a wall, and it is not something that can be raised and lowered easily. Once you have the shield up, it needs to stay up. You look out when you want to see the others' emotions, but never leave yourself open to attack by another empathic." He laughed. "I really have been going about your training all wrong, haven't I? All those years ago, when I was learning this, it was painful for me. I was taught by being forced to keep out negative emotions or scary thoughts, and it worked because I was so young. But, it was something I felt no one should be put through, and I still feel that way. I tried a different approach with you and it has not worked. With all you have been through, causing you more pain is unacceptable."

It was difficult to follow him, not everything he said was making sense. "James?"

He heard the change in my tone and mind and his face reflected that.

"We could keep trying the way we have been, but with me making it into a one-way glass. I do not like knowing the teams' feelings all the time, and I'm sure being around more people will make it more uncomfortable. There isn't an element of fear though, and I hope that I can learn to keep it up without having to know that fear."

His answer was to let part of his shield drop. It was more than just "opening the window" and the sudden flow shocked me. First and foremost was a wave of emotion for me. There was concern, pride, compassion, sorrow, and something that seemed to border on the desire to protect. Behind that wave was emotion towards the team. Again, there was pride and concern but also a feeling almost like love. Following that was emotion about the world, particularly about the future. It was there that I sensed fear and urgency. There was something in those emotions that he was hiding, but I did not press. I was amazed at the complexity and beauty.

"Harlie," He whispered. "I'm going to raise the shield

110

back up. Reach out with your mind and try to feel it, sense it, try to understand it."

I thought about how I was able to ask a question mentally and tried to focus my mind in the same way, but on doing just as he said. Suddenly, I could see the shield! It looked like liquid opal or mother-of-pearl – cloudy, shimmering, and moving up like a translucent bubble to cover and protect the emotions he had just shown me. As the last of his thoughts disappeared, he sent out a tendril of pleasure at my recognition.

We both collapsed into the back of the couch, gasping for breath. Coherent thought evaded me for several moments. When my breathing returned to a somewhat normal pattern, I asked.

"Do I sound like that all the time?"

James chuckled weakly. "No. I chose to show you all of those emotions. I let that part of my guard down completely. You..." He paused to breathe again. "You actually have a thin layer of unconscious shielding; only the more potent emotions come through. Most people have something like that, just not as strong."

"Wow."

We rested for several more minutes before he turned to face me again. "Now that you understand it a little better, see if you can block me." Not waiting for my response, he "opened the window." This time he seemed to be like someone holding a stopwatch, impatient to see if the task could be completed.

It was easier now to visualize the shield. I could feel it trying to rise up and protect me from the intrusion into my thoughts. With some effort, it came all the way up and James' thoughts were again separated from mine. He smiled his brilliant smile, and my shield dropped again. The instant after it did, James' smile disappeared, and I nearly screamed. Through the opened window in his shield I felt anger stronger than anything I had ever experienced before. In a heartbeat, my shield was back up, and I was curled into a ball trembling.

"As much as I hate it," James' voice was choked. "It worked." He got up from the couch, came to stand in front of me, then knelt down so he was at eye level. "That anger you

111

just felt..."

I could not respond other than to curl myself tighter into a ball.

"That is what I felt when I realized you had been raped. The day I told you to tell Jackson, you saw my clenched fists, you sensed my sorrow, but this is what I was holding back."

"The shield popped right back up." Was all I could whisper.

"Your minds' way of protecting itself. Hopefully, it will stay up for a time and you can get used to the sensation. If we can get you desensitized to the feeling of having to force it to stay up, it should unconsciously stay on its own." He looked away. "I don't want to keep frightening you like that in order for it to stay up permanently."

I nodded slightly but didn't move from my position. Sometimes the things that were happening in the bunker were just too much for me to handle. I needed time to process the last scene. He turned back to the television, waited several minutes and then turned it off. "Can you play table tennis?"

I laughed nervously, "That was random."

The brilliant smile came back as he stood up and held out his hand to pull me up as well.

"Yes, it was, but we have a couple of hours before Dara returns with pizza. Let's head down to the med bay and see how much damage I did, then play a few rounds."

I agreed only because I was feeling unusually dizzy, and we made the short walk to the medical bay. As predicted, my blood pressure was up, although not as high as it had gone before. When asked about my head, I had to be honest. It hurt, but nothing like before, and I told him it was tolerable. James looked pleased with my answer. The on-duty nurse did insist on a smaller dose of the blood pressure medication and something for the pain, to which I balked. The Commander made an appearance at that point, and after he spoke, I knew the choice would end up being: take the liquid medication the nurse was pouring, or another version would be forced.

"Why liquid?" I wondered, holding the foul looking stuff in the little plastic cup.

"It takes effect faster than pill form." The Commander

replied and motioned for me to drink it.

As we walked back to the common room, I was still a bit put off by the disappearance of James. "Do you ever have to take that crap?" He stopped in his tracks, slowly turned and hit me with "That Look." I was still glaring at him, but it quickly turned into a curious stare. What was he thinking when he was looking at me like that? Thank goodness my shield was still up.

"Yes. When I push my abilities too far, yes, I end up having to take 'that crap.'" He took a step closer. "I have a bottle of a custom mix, as well as injection form, in my quarters and another in my apartment. Jason has learned to let me handle the consequences myself."

I had not expected a reply, never-the-less a serious one. I wanted to ask how often he had to take it but chose not to since the unreadable expression was still present. Instead, we continued back to the common room, where he opened up the recreation room doors and ushered me inside.

Since this was my first time in the room, I took a long moment to look around. James handed me a paddle and motioned for me to pick a side.

It was a wordless game for quite awhile. There was still a hint of "That Look" in his eyes, and I knew not to push him. It took me stumbling after a particularly wild return before it disappeared, and me sending him a revenge-laden serve after he cremated me in a round before he smiled again. When Dara arrived, with four large pizzas in hand, we were laughing at a return, which had slammed off the table and hit the ceiling before I had sent it back his way.

"It's good to see the two of you playing nice. I was concerned when James said he was returning early."

Rick and Max arrived minutes later carrying sodas, chips, and cookies. Jason and Skull were at the pub and would be by later to finish up any leftovers. The mood was light, and we were all joking and being loud. It was the first time I had seen the team relaxed and enjoying themselves together. It made me happy that they already seemed to accept me as one of their own. Max sat next to me and asked about my likes and dislikes in food and entertainment. I was just as interested in his responses as he was to mine. It was surprisingly uncomfortable to not be able to tell what his emotions really were, but I leaned on my natural ability to read others and that helped. Of course, I could have just looked out from the one-way shield, but did not trust it to stay up, not just yet.

The hours passed quickly, especially after Jason and Skull stumbled into the common room. Skull was loud when he had a few drinks, but Jason was just more happy than usual. James seemed to be concerned about how I would handle their behavior, so he and Rick kept close, talking and laughing amongst themselves. Before we knew it, the clock said twenty-three hundred and we really needed to get some sleep. I helped Dara clean up the mess, although there was nothing in the way of leftovers.

Unfortunately, even with the relaxing day, my sleep was still restless. The same pictures kept flashing in my mind, over and over: Scenes from the camp, mostly of my husband and daughter, flashbacks from my first days in the medical bay here. Tonight though, I woke up with a scream in my throat. I had remembered the night my old life ended, the blows, the pain. I stood up, stumbled to the sink and washed my sweat-drenched face. I remembered that, when I went to sleep, the mental shield was up. A quick check and a small amount of relief passed through my terror. Somehow, it managed to stay up, and I wondered if it was because of the terror in the dream. After pacing the room for several endless minutes, I turned on the MP3 player, found the instrumental category, and listened until sleep found me again.

BECOMING

I was kept incredibly busy during my first full week with the team. Monday started with a complete physical and Doc was happy to see that I had put on three pounds already. I looked tired because of the last two restless nights, so he decided to not reduce my rest time until the following week.

On Monday afternoon, a beautician set up shop in the common room and gave us all haircuts. I had already decided on having mine so it rested just above my shoulders and then thinned and layered. When it was my turn, I felt like a two-year-old getting her first cut. The woman laughed, and we joked as the hair fell to the ground. When it was finished, the entire team either hooted, wolf whistled, or clapped in approval. We both took a bow.

For the most part, the daily schedule was the same and only minor changes were made to the stations I practiced on. Max was encouraging me to practice shooting from various positions and was pleased when I took right to it. I was also learning quickly under Dara's self-defense training.

I received my laptop on Tuesday, complete with language software and training videos. There was also a college-level course on international relations for me to complete. Three hours each day were spent in the tactical facility working on the laptop. A new code came in on the same day, so Rick was happy for the company as he worked tirelessly to crack it. Sometimes, Mitch would pop in and visit during those hours and teach me short lessons on what it took to make and diffuse bombs. He had a very dry sense of humor, but we seemed to get along well enough.

When I returned to my room for rest Tuesday, my new uniforms were laid out on the bed. There were three sets of camouflage, a dress uniform, three pairs of slacks and five polo shirts. While trying on the pants I noticed that the tailor had expertly folded and sewn in extra fabric in the waist and thighs. A few snips with a pair of tiny scissors and the uniforms would continue to fit even after I had put on more weight. It felt good to have more choices than the sweatpants

115

and t-shirt uniform.

James and I continued to work on keeping my mental shield up. The first time, it stayed up until I became really focused on my physical training on Monday. That evening, I was able to raise it up without him scaring me, and it stayed up until Thursday. Tuesday night and Wednesday night, there were more nightmarish flashbacks in my dreams, so it seemed unusual that with the terror it would have fallen. I was tired and a bit grumpy Thursday morning and decided that the shield could wait. However, while in the tactical facility, James walked in with the air of The Commander all around him. He stood in front of me with his arms crossed and dropped his shield with no warning and no words. The shock was enough for me to quickly raise my own, and he gave a quick nod before walking back out. This time it stayed up for nearly five days. I was beginning to be able to sense when it was starting to slip and was able to focus on the shimmering cloud picture from when James had me watch and raise it back up.

We were only training for a half day on Saturday, and everyone seemed to be in lighter spirits. Max, Skull, and Dara would be moving back to their individual residences that afternoon, just as Ryan and Mitch had last week.

As noon rolled around on Saturday, James called me aside from where Max and I had been trying out some of the rifles. Max continued to be delighted by how quickly I took to each weapon and how accurate my aim was becoming. To be quite honest, I was delighted as well. It seemed that since I had been moved into the living quarters, it had become much easier for me to learn all these new skills. I had always been the type of person who needed to study hard and practice frequently in order to learn anything new. In this last week, nearly everything I had read, watched, or tried was sticking with me.

When we walked into his office, James turned and smiled at me. "You have had an amazing week, Harlie."

I returned the smile, "Yes, Sir. I had my doubts about being able to learn all of this new content, but it has been almost easy."

"Excellent!" His voice was enthusiastic, but his eyes

said something else. There was a hint of omission rushing through my brain. He walked over to his desk and sat on the edge. "How do you feel about your mental shield?"

"Well..." I thought about it for a moment, "I am becoming more aware of it and just yesterday recognized when it was starting to slip."

"What triggered it to slip?" He wondered.

"I was really focused on keeping Dara from knocking me down, but at the same time, I was nervous from you staring at us. When Skull crashed into Jason, it startled me."

"Your mind was going in several directions and your anxiety was up. It makes sense, but we have got to train the shield to stay up all the time. Have you been able to look out and sense through it yet?"

I nodded. "The last two nights while in the common room. It takes a bit of effort though."

"Keep practicing, it will get easier." He smiled again and reached behind him. When his hand reappeared, it was holding two items. He handed them to me.

One item was a debit card. It was issued by the bank in town and had my new name on it. The other was an ID card with an electronic chip on it. I looked at him questioningly.

"I think it is time for a short visit above ground." His smile grew bigger. "As long as your shield stays up you should be fine while getting to know the area."

I was shocked, "Thank you, Sir!"

He rolled his eyes, slid off the desk, came over and placed his hands on my shoulders. "Enough with the 'Sir' stuff, Harlie. It's James."

The closeness caught me off guard, but I managed to reply with a soft, "Thank you, James."

He gave my shoulders a quick squeeze before dropping his hands and heading towards the door. "Dara and I will be with you the whole time. We'll drive the main roads of the village, then park the car and do a little shopping." With that, he walked out, and I went back to the living quarters.

As I walked into my room, a wave of anxiety hit me. Tomorrow it would be a month since my old life ended and I was brought here. It would be a month since I had been above ground and seven months since I had known life outside of the

117

refugee camp. I thought back farther, to life in America. It would be nearly two years since I had experienced anything like a shopping trip.

My legs suddenly felt weak, so I quickly sat on the bed and put my head in my hands. Jason came into the room several minutes later to check my vitals. I looked up and he shut the door.

"Hey, what's wrong? You should be happy about going above ground." He carefully placed the blood pressure cuff on my arm, pressing the button to run its program.

I stared at him for a second before answering. "Not sure. I think I just panicked a little."

He shook his head at the results and started searching his bag for what I could only guess was a syringe. "He caught you off guard, huh? I shouldn't be surprised though." He laughed harshly. "The Commander acts like he has never had experience with Post Traumatic Stress before. You really need more than a few seconds warning."

That last line brought me to my feet. "Excuse me?"

Jason saw the reaction, stood and gently took my hand before trying to lead me to the chair by my desk. I planted my feet, jerked my hand away and waited.

"Harlie, no one can go through anything close to what you have and not come out unscathed." I started to deny it, but he held a hand up. "Your reactions to stress, your lack of sleep due to nightmares...and yes I know about that. The bags under your eyes are worse, and first thing in the morning, your vitals are off. The near constant anxiety is a factor as well."

"I've always had issues with anxiety." He was not going to win this argument.

"That may be so, but I bet it did not cause you to panic like you did just now. Not that I blame you. A month underground is enough, but all that time in the camp before it did not help at all. You have no idea of what the world looks like anymore." Jason gently pushed me down in the chair. He paused, looked towards the door, then added, "If James were to walk in here right now, you would be condemned to another week below."

At that comment, the fight went out of me. He was right. I remembered James response earlier today "Jason, did they do anything else to me?"

"Explain that question." He was digging through his bag again.

"I noticed this week that it has become easy for me to learn new content and remember what has been learned in the past. I have never been a good student and had been worried about being able to learn this new life quickly enough."

His hands paused as he brought up liquid medication; I noticed it had my name on it. "That's the little white pill kicking in. It enhances the brains memory functions, the ability to learn, retain and recall in long-term memory. Top secret stuff but it works really well with very little in the way of side effects."

He poured a dose and handed to me, but I refused it "I knew you were lying last week."

Jason's head lowered. "You want to know something?" His words were strained. "I hate having to deceive anyone, but when I have to deceive you it feels so much worse. It must be because I know that you will see through it." He put the dose on the desk and sat on my bed. "But then sometimes I think it is because, out of all of us, you are the most innocent. You have experienced so much evil, but you have not been part of it. You were not a soldier in your past life and are not used to this world like the rest of us are. It makes it so much harder to lie to you."

"What's in the liquid?" This side of Jason bothered me. It struck too close to the protectiveness I sensed from James on Sunday.

"Blood pressure and pain. I was not prepared for the panic attack." He sighed. "Tomorrow, I'm going to add to your pile, and you'll have to understand why."

"For the Post Traumatic Stress?" I frowned.

He nodded. "It's mild compared to what the others have been on at one point or another, and I do not want you to be on it for more than a month or two. The high levels of anxiety bother me, and this will give you the time you need to finish your physical recovery and start working on methods to control the anxiety yourself."

I pondered the situation, trying to see it from his point of view as well as mine. Looking at the big picture was tough, but it could be done. "Okay. I won't make a scene."

The look of relief on Jason's face was priceless. I swallowed the dose and made such a face that Jason doubled over laughing. As it took effect, he left the room, and I quickly changed into one of the pairs of slacks and a polo shirt. I found myself hoping there was a store in town that sold clothing so that I could have a pair of jeans for the weekends. No sooner did I have my hair brushed and a barrette clipped on one side then Dara knocked on my door.

She was dressed in a pair of tight jeans and a floral button-down shirt that accented her eyes. She nodded at my uniform before making a comment about how desperately this trip was needed. We both laughed and made our way to the elevator.

"Do you have your cards?" She asked as the doors closed.

I took both cards out of my pants pocket and flashed them in her direction.

"Good. See the red light over here?" She pointed to a tiny light above the open and close door buttons. I nodded.

"Place the chip on your card in front of it, like this." She demonstrated. I mimicked her, and the elevator began to go up. However, it did not stop at the cafeteria floor. It continued to trek upwards.

"There is a sensor in there and a camera in here. The amount of people in the elevator needs to match the cards scanned for it to go up beyond the cafeteria level."

It took longer to get to the next stop than it did to make it to the cafeteria level so that meant we were farther below ground than I had originally suspected. When the doors finally opened, I was frozen inside the elevator. Dara smiled at my hesitation and motioned for me to follow her.

It was a corner in a small warehouse. Dara explained that we were in one of the buildings which were part of the above ground base. This was where many in the village were employed, but many did not know the details of the underground bunker. The entrance was facing away from the rest of the buildings, so we were not seen going in and out. We went out a side door where James was waiting with a sedan. I stood at the open car door for a full two minutes, inhaling the fresh air and looking around.

The warehouse was several hundred meters from the gates for the rest of the base. James informed me that most of the team parked in a strip mall on the other side of the fence and used a small secure entrance behind the travel agency at the mall. The strip mall also held the beauticians shop, a coffee shop, and the tailors dry clean business. It sat on the edge of the village and several streets and homes could be seen from the tiny parking lot. As James drove, Dara pointed out where some of the others lived. As we approached the main part of town the narrow road widened slightly. The main street had a row of small shops, and I quickly noticed a pharmacy, shoe store, restaurant, and a small department store. James pulled over into the bank at the end of the road. Dara showed me to the ATM machine and the panic returned. I did not know my pin number! She saw the expression and laughed.

"Oh, they got into all your old information. It is whatever your last bank card pin number was."

"How much should I take out?" Whatever her answer, I knew it would make me cringe. Taking out more than forty dollars used to set off a feeling of guilt. She asked what I wanted to buy, then gave an estimate for those things.

Somehow swallowing the anticipated feeling, I punched in the numbers and stuffed the money into my pocket. The machine printed a receipt, but I pocketed it without looking.

James continued the tour of the town, showing me where the rest of the members lived as well as where the park was. We drove through the parking lot of the grocery store, and then he pulled over at a pub several blocks away.

"This is where we all hang out. There is another pub on the north side of town, but we like this one better." He pointed up the road to a hill. "There is an apartment building up there and my place is on the third floor. It looks like your cottage will be on the same street, just a little farther down."

When the tour was finished, James went back to the main part of the village and found a place to park the car. He and Dara got out, but I just sat there. People were walking to and from the stores, children wandered by walking a small dog. It was as if time stood still inside this small village in Wales. As if the nuclear attacks in America and the crushed economy in the rest of the world did not exist. James, leaning against the car, tilted his head in my direction and whispered.

"A bit overwhelming at first, eh?"

"Is it like this in all of Britain?"

"No. There are areas economically devastated by current events, but the smaller villages like this are relatively unharmed. They are used to living on their own, with what can be found here and, as of late, what can be grown here. It is like the Victory Gardens of old, many people are growing as much of their own food as possible and sharing the bounty. That spreads into other areas like crafting and has kept the businesses afloat."

"Wow."

He nodded and turned to open my door. "Come on then, let's have some lunch and a little walk-about. The cafe across the street serves Branston sandwiches." He winked.

That made me laugh a little, and I was able to get out of the car and follow Dara into the cafe. James walked behind me. Inside the café, several people nodded or gave a short wave towards us. They also stared at the newcomer, me. Dara muttered something about them needing lessons in courtesy just as much as "the boys." James reminded her how it had been quite some time since any member of the team had been in the cafe with someone who was not only unfamiliar but unfamiliar and wearing the organization's uniform.

The Branston and cheddar sandwich was delicious, and the silent reaction of the other customers when I ate every bite with a smile was priceless. They had heard my American accent when I ordered, and Branston pickle was relatively unknown in The States. James was glancing around the room, occasionally laughing under his breath. When I asked what was so funny he said he was looking out, which meant he was taking advantage of the one-way glass that was our mental shielding and picking up on the customers' emotions.

After our meal, Dara led the way to the small department store. James had the sense to look embarrassed at the thought of women shopping and quickly escaped to the electronics section.

122

"Thank goodness!" Dara exclaimed when we were out of earshot. "I did not want to have to shop with a sitter."

Her expression made me laugh, and she looped her arm through mine and pulled me over to the ladies clothing. Despite my anxiety, the familiarity of shopping with a friend brought on a glimmer of joy that I had not felt in too long. Dara, as I had suspected, was secretly a shopping maniac. Within minutes she had four pairs of jeans and five shirts in my arms and was dragging me to the dressing room. There wasn't a moment to protest her choices. The look on her face screamed that she was the boss in this situation and all I had was veto power on the final selection.

It was easy to decide on three shirts that looked good, were loose enough to still fit after I put on more weight, and were comfortable. Dara was pushing for me to buy more, but I put my foot down.

"Dara." I sighed and rolled my eyes. "Have some mercy here! It has been years since I have been able to shop, and it is taking all I've got not to panic and run."

"Sorry, Harlie, I don't have time to shop anymore and it was something I used to love to do. I can't even tell you the last time I had a shopping partner." She smiled at me and I returned it.

Over the next hour, I found two pairs of jeans, socks, hair bands, a wallet, bras, and a miniature backpack which was designed to be a purse. Dara was the perfect combination of a dedicated soldier who could incapacitate anyone with a single blow, and feminine grace and beauty. I was in awe while watching her shop. We were getting ready to check out when my eyes roamed over to the jewelry section.

"Dara, wait a moment." I walked over to the case that held necklaces as Dara practically danced with delight at my pause.

"I used to have a gold cross necklace." I whispered, as my eyes found what they were looking for. "I had to trade it for supplies."

Dara got the attention of the employee behind the counter, and she took out the cross for me to see. It was white gold, almost the same size as my old one, and it had tiny lilies engraved on it. It was a simple, yet beautiful. I looked at the price and mentally added up the amount of the items in my arms. I would have to go back to the bank. Dara must have been doing the same thing because she suddenly took the cross from my hands.

"We have wanted to get you a welcome gift; pick out a sturdy chain and the boys will pay me back for it."

"Dara..." I started to protest.

"Don't even try it." The look she gave me stopped any words that would have come from my mouth. And I thought only The Commander used a tone and expression like that!

"Thank you." Was all I could choke out as she helped me choose a chain which could handle the rigors of our work. It was then that I realized that James was watching and had probably been watching since I had turned towards the jewelry department. He must have picked up on Dara's emotions.

When the purchase had been completed and Dara handed me the box, we went to check out the rest of our items. The total came up, and I was pleased to find out I was thirty pounds under budget so quickly added two reusable bags from the endcap.

James waited for us outside. "Well now, that looks like a successful shop." He smiled at my two bags. "Shall we head back?" His eyes moved to meet mine, the question burning there as well.

I surprised myself by answering, "Would it be okay if we stopped by the pharmacy? I noticed they had a shelf with candy on it by the window, and I have a weakness for dark chocolate."

He continued to stare, "That Look" replacing the questioning in his eyes. Next to me, Dara shifted uncomfortably from one foot to the other. I held my breath. Finally, he broke contact.

"Put the bags in the car first, then we'll walk over."

Dara and I both exhaled in relief.

On the way back underground, we stopped at the dry clean business and dropped off the jeans and shirts, since laundry had already been completed for the week. I would hand wash the rest with some gentle detergent purchased from the pharmacy. Dara had chosen to walk to her apartment, so it was just James and I as he parked the car behind the travel agency and we headed through the small entrance and into the warehouse. I took one more look around outside, not knowing when I would be allowed above ground again.

James smiled grimly and sighed as we rode the elevator down, "Again, you have surprised me with your resiliency and ability to quickly adapt. I really did not think you would do so well today."

I turned to him, slightly annoyed, "Then what did you think? That I would stand there cringing and looking about wildly like a feral child?"

"No, not to that extreme."

"Not to that extreme." I muttered. "You're still waiting for me to break down again, though, like I did in the medical bay."

"I'm expecting it, especially since you have not been sleeping well. Can I assume the nightmares have started?"

Now I was getting angry and my tone showed it, "You assume correctly." The doors opened, and I brushed past him, hurrying down the hallway to the common room.

James grabbed my arm to stop me, his grip tightened when I tried to keep moving forward. I stopped, dropped my packages and turned on him.

"Today has been a wonderful day for me" I hissed. "For the first time in over two years, I felt some sense of normalcy. Do not ruin it now with negativity, Commander." He dropped my arm, and I picked up my bags, rushed into my room, and loudly shut the door.

With emotions dangerously close to anger swelling up in my mind, I chose to keep myself busy with the new purchases. I unpacked all of them and proceeded to hand wash what had not been brought to the cleaners. After putting away the weekly laundered clothes from the bed, I moved on to the small box from Dara.

The white gold cross was so beautiful. It made my heart swell knowing that the yellow gold one that I had been forced to trade for basic supplies back in America was now replaced with something that looked so similar and yet so amazingly different. I took the cross and its strong chain out of the box, undid the clasp, and then placed it around my neck. I peeked in the mirror to see how it looked, smiling at the result.

Now I was faced with a dilemma. It was time for the evening meal, but I had a suspicion that James was still nearby, and that Jason and Rick had not returned from their trip above ground. I was not sure though and knew that there was one way to find out without leaving the safety of my room. It was difficult for me to look out from my still shaky mental shield, but that is what I would attempt to do. My emotions were still in an uproar, which made it difficult to get focused enough.

I could see the shield as a creamy opalescent bubble. I carefully looked around inside the bubble, still in wonder that such a thing really existed. My mind felt safe and secure here. The murmur of my own thoughts was in the background, but beyond that was silence. Carefully, I eased closer to the shield and focused my mind on seeing outside of it. I had to make sure my mind was just looking out and not "opening a window" for James to sense. I looked outside of the shield and hoped to see the glimmers of Jason or Rick's mind. Disappointment struck when they were not there.

James was not in the common room, nor was he in the cafeteria, although about a dozen of the support staff was. I quickly picked out a meal with the proper range of calories and fat, ran my ID, and sat down at a corner table. Rick walked in as the first bite was being chewed. He smiled when our eyes met and was soon sitting across from me.

"I had the option to cook for myself tonight, but it would have meant a trip to the grocery store. This sounded like the better route for now."

"When will you be moving back above ground?" I figured it would be soon and that Jason would not be far behind.

"Was given the option this week but decided that someone else needed to be here to keep Jason and James from fighting too much."

"Oh." I chewed and swallowed another bite, "Do they usually not get along?" It seemed odd to me that Jason would still be on the team if he and the boss did not agree.

Rick contemplated his answer, "There have been moments of conflict in the past, but lately there have been more. Jason wants your recovery to be slower; he does not like

126

any of us to be in pain either physically or emotionally. James is in a hurry to have you trained and in the field. That undercurrent of discord has made their typical personality conflicts more frequent. However, they both have one thing in common..." He paused to eat several forkfuls of food.

I waited.

"They both seem to feel protective of you." He finished.

My nod let him know I had already realized that fact. It was not a good thing for any of us. People make rash decisions when they are trying to protect someone, and in the field, that could be catastrophic.

"They can both get over it because I won't be helpless for much longer." Sarcasm dripped from my voice.

He laughed. "With that attitude, I don't doubt it, although you really were not that way to begin with."

"I'm happy you stayed, Rick, thank you."

He smiled warmly, "Anytime."

We were finishing the meal when I felt something pressing on my mental shield. The only time I had ever felt that was when I had been learning to use the shield. In the moments it rose, I could feel that pressure, but it quickly stopped. This was not stopping. If anything, it was getting more persistent, almost as if someone was knocking loudly on a door. I paused in the middle of chewing and focused on keeping the shield up and intact. Rick noticed the change in my expression and looked around the room.

"Perhaps you do need protection. He does not look too happy right now."

"He tried to ruin my first day above ground with pessimism and analyzing when we returned. I was not about to allow it and gave him a bit of an attitude."

"That explains his expression then." He sighed, still staring at James who was still pressing in on my mental shield. "His recent mood swings have us all in a bind. I have known him longer than anyone on the team and am about ready to put in my two cents. It is bloody annoying, and we do not need the added stress."

"He'll get over it." I mumbled, finishing dessert. "I need to restock the drink and snack supply in my room, want to follow along as a guard?"

Rick's roaring laughter turned heads all over the room. Suddenly, the pressure on my shield disappeared. I turned my head and saw the back of The Commander as he left the cafeteria. Taking a deep breath, I went to dump my tray then headed over to the snack shelf and cooler to pick and choose what to bring back to the room. Rick waited at the door to the cafeteria, still smiling.

"James might be waiting to ambush us in the common room." He commented as we rode the elevator back down.

"Bring it on. I'm aggravated enough to give The Commander a challenge tonight."

Rick chuckled again, "I like this side of you, Harlie. Is this the way you were before?"

The compliment caught me off guard for just a moment. I thought it over. "Yes, this is pretty much the attitude I had in my past life. At least, it is the one I had when things needed to be done."

"You won't need much protection then. If James is set on a fight, it looks like you will give him one." He turned serious as we exited the elevator and started down the hallway. "But, let's try to avoid it. I think when we get back, I'll bring out the digital piano, and we can share some music."

Somehow, it did not surprise me that he had a digital piano here. I expected his residence probably held a baby grand. It had been fifteen years since I had played seriously, but up until a year ago I had an upright piano and had played for my own enjoyment. I hastily tried recalling the songs I had previously memorized.

The Commander was not in the common room, so Rick was able to wheel out and set up the piano without hassle. He placed it in front of the entertainment unit then sat down and played a cheerful tune.

"What was that?" I had never heard it before.

"Ukrainian folk song. You know that Mitch is from there right?"

I could tell by his accent that Mitch was from somewhere around Russia but had not asked him for specifics. Rick played another ethnic tune, then turned the piano over to me. I played an old song called "All My Trials" and grinned when Rick knew it and sang along.

The rest of the evening continued in the same pattern. We took turns on the piano and shared about the music we had chosen to play. If James was in the building, he had made himself quite scarce. Exhausted by the excitement of the day, and by the interrupted sleep during the week, I excused myself earlier than usual for bedtime. Rick put his arm around my shoulder and squeezed before launching into a series of soothing lullabies. I could just hear it through the door and, within minutes, my mind was drifting with the notes. Sleep came soon after, this time without the nightmares.

Sunday morning, I woke at normal time but took an extra long shower before going to the cafeteria. When I returned, Rick was up and getting ready to leave.

"Do you think I'll be able to attend church today?"

He grimaced, "Don't think so. James was looking for you a few minutes ago."

At that moment, the door to The Commanders' room opened and footsteps came closer. "Ah, there you are! Up and about early for a Sunday." He seemed to have gotten over last evening's negativity, but I was still upset.

"We were wondering if Harlie had a pass to go above ground and attend church this morning." Rick was smiling, but I could sense an edge to his voice.

James shook his head, "Not this week. Let's give it a little more time. We will go above ground another day or two for exercises, then next weekend we can try for two-day clearance."

If I could have read his emotions, I am sure that revenge would have been a predominant one. This had to be my consequence for yesterday's attitude. "Even though yesterday went so well?"

"Yes, but you are still recovering. And while yesterday did go well, you should rest today."

I could not help myself, "Funny how that reasoning can be used some days and ignored on others."

Rick and James both looked a bit surprised at my response, but both chose to ignore it. Instead, Rick gave me an apologetic look and went to finish getting ready. James left the common room without a word. I went back to my room,

129

hooked up the MP3 player, and sat on the bed to listen to music. Just as I was settling in there was a knock on the door. It was Rick. He had brought the piano back out for me.

I thanked him, and he was gone. Turning up the music so that it drowned out anything outside of a bomb blast, I propped myself up on pillows, stuck my legs under the covers and stayed there for the next two hours.

After that, I decided to work some of the stations. However, James' silent revenge was not just keeping me below ground for the day. The doors to the training facility were locked. I searched the bunker for him, ready to give him a piece of my mind, but he either left or was back in his room and not responding to my repeated knocks. It seemed I was alone. I could not locate the remotes for the televisions, so the rest of the day was spent either napping or playing the digital piano. By evening meal, I was getting restless and eagerly anticipating the others coming back. Rick and Jason came in just as I was leaving for the cafeteria and my second full week in the bunker began.

Only one major event happened that week, the rest was minor details. I had put on several more pounds and my rest time was reduced to thirty minutes. I worked out harder, studied longer, and we began practicing maneuvers as a team. Dara had stopped working with me on self-defense and was attempting to teach me offensive attacks. I hated it. It was against my nature to punch, kick and try to maim someone. I knew that offensive tactics had to be learned, and this line of work meant that there would be times that I would have to rely on those skills to survive. Still, I hated every minute.

It was Thursday, and we had been above ground, practicing inside an enclosed field. James, who had continued to be pleasant, and whom I continued to ignore as much as possible, was working alongside us. Everyone was taking turns with defensive and offensive moves against each other in hand-to-hand combat. Depending on whom they were against, sometimes weapons like switchblades were used. We were careful to only bruise if contact was made.

I had been holding my own defensively but was really struggling with having to attack other members of the team. I

130

was peeking out from my shields and could sense that Dara was becoming increasingly frustrated with me. Jason, sympathetic as always, was praising all that I was doing well and trying to downplay how bad my offense was. We were halfway through switching partners when it was James' turn against me. He walked closer to one of the walls, away from the others, before turning to face me.

He started on the offense, but I no sooner set up my defense when he jumped to my side, grabbed my arms, pulled them behind me and shoved me into the wall. With my face pressing against the cool concrete blocks he used his left arm and leg to hold me against the wall and stuck a switchblade against my back with his other hand.

There was silence in the field. No one moved. No one breathed. James held me there for too many seconds. I could feel the point of the blade, millimeters from piercing the skin.

"Enough with the pathetic attempts at offense. This is exactly what would happen in the field. It is unacceptable. You will NEVER be helpless again, understand!" he hissed harshly into my ear.

I nodded quickly.

He let go and walked to the far side of the wall where he leaned, seemingly casual, against it and watched the aftermath.

I stood, still facing the wall, until I was sure he was gone, then turned around and slid down to the ground. In the instant it took him to put me in that position, the memories of the attacks in the camp flashed through my mind. My heart had started racing and my mind froze in fear. Now that he had walked off, it was taking all I had to convince my mind and body how this had only been a lesson, and I really was not in any danger.

No one else moved for at least a minute. Skull finally broke the silence by clearing his throat. I peered out from my shields. Rick and Jason wanted to come to my side but were unsure of what James' reaction would be. Dara was hoping that I was planning on putting more effort into learning offense. The rest were wondering if such a scene was really necessary, and Max was positive that it was not.

The team finished with whomever they had currently

been paired, but no one's heart was into it. I stayed where I was and watched them, nervously glancing over to where The Commander was still leaning against the far wall. Dara called off the practice soon after and we piled back into the van we took to get there. Jason, Max, and Rick sat around me on the trip back and stayed with me until we reached the training facility. James disappeared into his office and did not come out until debriefing.

The next two weeks continued with the same schedule and same increase in the amount of work. We did more and more training together as a team, practicing outside in all weather and all environments. We had live-fire instances, practiced escape and evasion maneuvers, and ran obstacles in the woods. It was feeling more and more like I was working for a military-style organization.

It was during this time that I received my nickname/codename. All of the others had these names, and over the weeks, I had learned all of them and the contexts of when those names could be used. Of course, Skull was still Skull, Dara was called Bruce after the martial arts legend and Rick was called Jaws for all the languages he spoke. Ryan and Mitch were Twin Ka and Twin Boom because of their skills with explosives, Max was named Root, and James was The Guard or Boss Guard. Jason was called Stitch, and I was called Bear. Bear came about due to my last name and because Skull said I was as grumpy as a bear some mornings.

James watched every combat practice, and I never gave him another reason to make an example of me. Truth be told, I had started to fear him. Day in and day out I worked harder than I ever had in my life. Most nights I retired early, exhausted from the effort and the continued nightmares. Jason was only occasionally checking my vitals but, when he did, I sensed he was disturbed by the results. Late one night, I heard Jason and The Commander arguing again, my name was said several times. Come morning, though, everything was still the same. Figuratively, I was keeping my head down even if physically that was not allowed.

MISSION ONE

Our orders came during the first part of week five. We were needed in Poland, to follow up on the mission the team had when I first joined. The Guardians had been monitoring this particular cell for several years now and were convinced they had nuclear technology. No one was quite sure where the cell had originated from, but most started somewhere in the Middle East. This cell had been testing their equipment by setting off IED's with their newest technology hidden inside. Other terror groups were claiming responsibility for most of the attacks, but some remained unsolved. Their latest attack was at an embassy in Dubai the week before my arrival.

We had three days to prepare for the trip and everyone moved back underground. Max and Dara brought me to the smaller bunker on the English side of the river via a tunnel that ran under the river bed. We rode a high-speed cable car through the tunnel. Once there, we picked out all the equipment we would need. Tiny cameras, micro-chip sized voice recorders, travel packs, and more were checked out. The smallest earpiece I had ever seen was carefully custom fitted to my ear. Someone would have to be inches from the side of my head to see it.

That evening, Dara and I were informed that something needed to be done with my wardrobe. I knew this moment was coming and had already prepared myself for the inevitable. To be a spy, especially one who was hiding in the open, I needed to be able to dress for all parts. We received clearance to travel to Cardiff. I tried to let go and have fun with the time there, even though we were in a hurry. It helped that, in my past life, I had shopped in Cardiff twice. The city looked more worn down then I remembered it, but many of the larger shops were still there as well as the indoor markets. We left at seven in the morning and were back by four. The laundry crew was ready and within two hours the five new outfits were washed and packed, along with accessories which were quickly fitted with the cameras.

On the day before our departure, we all had physicals.

When my turn came, I knew there would be trouble. Fortunately, Doc was not too hard on me, but I had a feeling his report to The Commander would state something about my bad stats.

Jason chased after me on the way back to the living quarters. "Wait up!"

I did not want to talk to him; he probably would give me a hard time about the physical. I went straight to my room, packed the container of medication Doc had given me, including something to help me sleep better, then headed back out. Jason was standing on the other side of the door, waiting.

"Just stop for a moment, please." His voice was pleading.

I stopped.

"When you are out there, out in the field, take a good look around. Pay attention to what's going on, what is really going on. Use your freedom wisely. No one is hiding remotes or newspapers out there."

My head tilted to the side, listening, but unsure of what he was really saying. I just nodded in reply

With that, we both walked into the conference room.

We went over the mission step by step – the details that would be needed once we arrived tomorrow in order to quickly be on the move. We would be on three separate flights and our seats were far apart in the airplanes. Once we arrived, one of our contacts would pick some of us up while the rest of us took taxis to three different hotels. From there, the individual phases of the mission would begin.

My part of the mission would take me to a precise area of town, where I would pretend to be a student observing human reactions. That area held what we believed was an office for this group's cover company, but we were not sure of its exact location. It also held several national monuments, and it was the reactions to those that I would be "observing". Of course, I would really be looking mentally towards the offices and only minimally watching the rest of the world.

Ryan, Max, and James would be trying to pinpoint the location using James' skills and information that Ryan and Rick had been able to obtain. Their goal was to sneak into the place and gather as much evidence as possible, while potentially laying down some form of sabotage.

As I had learned over the month, whenever you make bombs, especially ones with nuclear capabilities, residue is left behind. Dara, Mitch, and Skull had state-of-the-art devices to help them detect particles from the bomb-making process. The technology this cell was using was similar to what Unus Universum used in the American bombs. They were hoping to find a link, because the masterminds could not have completed the attacks on their own.

After the meeting, we all went our separate ways to finish final preparations. As I stood staring at the packed bag there was a knock on the door. I peered out my shield and saw that there was a dark spot there. In that moment, anxiety, fear, and anger competed for dominance in my own mind.

"Come in, Commander." I sighed.

James walked in, looked around the room, stared at my bags for a moment then turned to me. I was surprised to see that he was out of uniform and wearing the black jacket I saw him wear on the hill next to the refugee camp.

"We need to talk." His voice was low and calm. The last two weeks I had been quietly observing him, trying to figure out emotional triggers, changes in tone, anything to help me understand the person who had saved me, but whose moods now scared me. I had also continued to avoid him as much as possible.

"I'm a bit busy." I lied.

"No, you are not, and even if you were, this cannot wait. Come."

I knew that there was no choice but to follow. He led me past the common room and the nervous glances from the rest of the team. We went straight to the elevator and he scanned his ID card then waited for me to scan mine. The lift went up past the cafeteria level and into the warehouse. Without saying a word, he motioned for me to follow him out the side door. A motorcycle waited there, and he handed me a helmet. I hesitated.

"Have you not been on a motorbike before?" He looked serious.

"No." I did not add that I was afraid of them.

"Put on the helmet, climb on behind me and just hold

135

on. We will not be going far." He settled onto the bike and waited.

I did not want to be alone with him, did not want to be anywhere near him, and now I was being made to leave the bunker with him. Why? I could feel that he was very tense as I wrapped my arms around his middle.

We drove to the edge of the village, to the stone-walled field where we had practiced live rounds and maneuvers. He parked the bike. We both got off, took off our helmets, and I followed as he started walking towards the middle of the field. I remembered there had been a couple of small boulders around that area and, sure enough, that is where he stopped.

He was facing away from me, looking up towards the stars. I wanted to look as well, to observe every detail of the night, but the person in front of me was making that impossible. He stood completely still for several minutes, then his shoulders slumped, and he turned around. His expression confused me, it was sorrow like what he had displayed in the camp.

"Harlie." His voice was soft, but tortured. "I cannot keep doing this. It has to stop tonight. I don't know what it is about you that makes me react the way I do, but I keep having to apologize for my behavior." He paused to study my expression, which managed to stay blank.

"After your first visit to town, those things I said...it was wrong. I was so proud of you up there, happy that you were adjusting so well. What I wanted to do was to give you a hug, tell you all of that, and ask if you wanted to stay above and celebrate by going to dinner with me, but that would not be professional. I should have just said you did a great job and walked away. Instead, I said those negative things and it was horrid. Then, when I decided to try to make it right, there you were in the cafeteria laughing with Rick. I tried to get you to step away by knocking at your shield, but you ignored it."

I stood perfectly still, listening, trying to understand his words.

He laughed harshly, "I locked the facility doors the next day to force you to relax. I watched you from my main office. You looked so angry that I regretted it instantly, but the damage had already been done."

His expression changed again, this time he looked angry. "I tried to talk to you, tried to find a way to make things right, but you were so determined to avoid me. And, when we were outside, and I heard in Dara's mind the frustration at your lack of effort in offensive training, knowing that it could be your only means of survival when this mission was finally called..." He did not finish because, at the memory, I visibly cringed.

James took two steps closer, and I backed up two steps. The sorrow came back full force on his face. "You really are afraid of me, just like Jason said." He whispered.

"I never know what you are going to say or how you are going to react, and I don't want you to make an example out of me again." My voice wavered.

"Harlie." He sounded like he was choking. "I was not making an example out of you. I have wanted to protect you from the moment of your first loss at the camp. When your daughter died and then you were attacked, I swore I would do everything in my power to make sure you were never helpless again. It made me so angry that you were balking at the very thing that could save your life..." He sat on one of the nearby boulders and put his head in his hands.

This was getting very uncomfortable.

As I was thinking his words through, James stood back up and walked slowly to where I was standing. "I cannot bear for you to be afraid of me, and I want you to understand what has been happening. I am torn between being a proper commanding officer or doing what is right for someone whom I wish to be a friend, someone whom I want to protect, but know that I can't."

He reached up a hand and gently laid it against my cheek. My eyes instantly met his and he dropped his shield completely. I felt the difference between us. He was letting me choose whether or not to look out from my own shield and sense what he was feeling. Still frightened, but still looking into his eyes, I held my breath and peered out. It was all there, raw emotion laid out for me to see. It was exactly as he had described it, nothing was being held back. I almost cried out at his pain. No one should have to feel that way, especially not over me. I looked away mentally and physically, and James

137

protected his mind again.

"Please, Harlie, please forgive me. I cannot promise to not mess up again, but at least now you know why. I want us to be able to work together on the team and still be friends at the end of the day. Is there a chance that could happen?"

It took me several moments to process it all and to think up an honest answer. "I don't want to be afraid of you. I want the team to be able to work together without being on edge from your mood swings and would like you and I to be able to work together without conflict."

He looked sad that I did not respond with wanting friendship from him, but it was something that I could not allow, not yet.

"I will not give you a reason to be afraid of me, and we will not be in conflict like this again." He promised.

Before the sun rose, we were on the way to London. Max sat with me in the van, chattering on about the small handgun he placed in my travel pack. It could not leave the hotel though, and my only means of protection would be the techniques Dara taught me and the pepper spray in my shoulder bag. Jason, Rick, and I were on the first flight out that day and were setting up in the hotel when the second group landed. The third would arrive an hour later. We had to be very careful to avoid detection, and that meant multiple flights and all of us having aliases. The groups would be staying in separate hotels on opposite sides of the city. I was not allowed to speak to Jason or Rick, even though we would be in the same hotel.

There would be very little communication between the groups. We would be leaning on James' and my abilities more than anything. This was the reason why the Guardians needed a second empathic. The others had been taught years ago how to focus an image so that James could actually sense the picture and its meaning. They had practiced the skill with me the entire way to the airport, with Jason and Rick continuing once we arrived at the hotel. It was eerie how in-tune I was becoming to their minds, even being able to pick them out of a crowded hotel. It wasn't enough detail, though, and more could be communicated via another empathic.

The first night there, the guys ordered room service while I ate in the hotel restaurant. They needed to remain hidden, and I had to be out in the open, portraying a professional student. While at dinner, I wrote in a notebook and had a textbook with me. Back in the room, I was too nervous to relax enough to sleep, so one of Doc's pills had to be used.

The next morning, we put our plan into action. Rick sent me a mental go, and I left for the closest coffee shop. I had memorized a map Skull had made just for this mission and knew where all the stops needed to be. While having a breakfast of pastry and coffee, I set up my notebook for the day, listing various facial expression responses to the World War II statue and memorial I would be sitting near. It looked like a student hard at work, the same as many others in the shop that morning. When it was set up, I ordered a sandwich and bottled water to go. From there, I walked slowly, observing my surroundings until reaching the bench which would be my destination for that day. I would be facing the statue and to my right would be some of the office buildings under suspect.

With a racing heart and sweaty palms, I took a deep breath and then looked out from my shield into the mass of humanity around me. Within a half hour, I could decipher that there were four separate businesses in the building and each had someone like a secretary in the front. Potential customers came in and out, and I focused on each one. It was hard work to keep that kind of control while still appearing to be tallying responses to the memorials.

I had just finished lunch when the action started. I noticed a gentleman who did not seem to belong with the tourists hanging around the statue, but he did not appear to be a local either. He was dressed nicely, but his skin tone was just a bit too dark for this area of the world and his eyes did not look quite right. Focusing on his mind, I found that he was feeling a little edgy but also annoyed. It was difficult not to stare, but somehow, I managed to continue to look like I was writing observations. I lifted my notebook just a little and pressed a button hidden inside the cover. It snapped a picture in his direction, just in case. The man stood across the road, looking towards the office building for at least two minutes before crossing over and going inside.

I followed him with my mind while scanning mentally for James. There had been no time frame set for when he, Max and Ryan would be in the area. For all I knew, they could be doing surveillance in another part of the city. I stood up, stretched a little, then sat to focus some more. The man was feeling more nervous now. He was farther inside the building and it was harder to hear him. Suddenly, his nervousness turned to anger, then just as quickly to fear. I forgot all about my facade and tried to pick up on the source of his fear. There was someone else with him, someone who seemed to be quite arrogant. This other person was also angry, and I could sense a hint of deception. My head began to hurt from the effort.

The emotions stayed the same for around ten minutes and then the original man I had followed was moving from that part of the building. The moment he reached the outdoors, relief gushed from his mind. It flowed through my mind as well, whatever I had just witnessed, it was not normal business for this tourist area. I chanced a glance in his direction and he was coming towards the bench where I sat. He looked like he would collapse. I crossed my legs so that the notebook was resting on one knee, facing where he was going to sit, and tried to look intent on my supposed assignment while snapping more pictures. He sat and stared at seemingly nothing for quite some time, then stood and walked in the direction of a nearby bus stop.

The rest of the day went without incident; no one else visited the office. I made several attempts to read the emotions of the person who had been with the gentleman, but it seemed that no one was there other than the secretary. No one had left the building via the front door though, so it seemed odd.

At seventeen hundred hours, I stood up again and started to make my way back to the hotel. That was when James made his presence known. He started walking in my direction from the other side of the road, radiating curiosity. I opened a mental window and sent him a series of focused phrases and mental pictures, reflections of what I had witnessed. We both paused at a crosswalk, and he visualized the number two, our signal for me to repeat the details again.

My head was throbbing, and nausea was building, but I sent over another reflection of the man's emotions as well as the supposed cause for it. I reached the hotel, and he was one block away. This time James seemed satisfied with the information.

Exhausted and in pain, I collapsed onto the bed in the hotel room. All the emotions that I had been suppressing during the day came back at once: Nervousness at my first mission, fear that I could not pull off the student facade, and concern that the cell might have picked up on me sitting in the same spot all day. I shook like a leaf under all of it. Come evening, I ordered room service and waited.

At twenty-one hundred hours, James knocked on my mental shield. I had gotten my emotions under control but was not sure if they would stay that way once I opened up to whatever he needed to communicate. Breathing slowly, I let the mental window open. Pride and happiness was the first thing I felt; it seemed that we all had some form of success today. Then a mental picture came through, it was me on the bench. It seemed I was to repeat the assignment again tomorrow. He laughed mentally, and I sensed that his group was planning something. When I questioned it, he laughed again. Suddenly, his laughter turned to concern. I could almost hear the words, *Are you okay?* I sent back a feeling of accomplishment, but he sent back what my mind had slipped out... pain. In return, I thought one word, *Headache* and shut the connection. I could not allow him to get too close to my emotions; there was still fear and now worry about his admissions. Despite the pain, I was asleep in minutes, too tired to dream.

The next morning was dreary. There had been rain during the night. I dawdled in the coffee shop before making my way to yesterday's location. Today, I picked a bench closer to the office, even though it meant my back was to it. Nothing unusual happened all day. As far as I could tell, the secretary was alone. I was just getting ready to go back to the hotel when it happened. James started tapping on my shield, and I opened up to him. The thought was perfectly articulated words, *Watch this.*

Quickly tuning in, I realized that Max and Ryan were

141

approaching, but I could not see them. Then it dawned on me, they were underground! Scanning the area, I could sense that James was with them and Dara was two blocks away with Skull. Using the emotions coming from them, I could piece together what was happening. Max was quite proud of himself when he broke into the lower level of the office. Ryan hot-wired the security systems and reprogrammed the cameras to play back the last five minutes over and over. All three worked their way up to the main floor and into the room where yesterday's exchange took place, taking pictures and scans the whole way. They were all surprised by something they found and quite pleased when Ryan broke it. It was then that I noticed the secretary seemed confused. I sent a warning to James, who also picked up on her emotions. In a flash, they were out of the building and Ryan erased all evidence of his tampering. James asked me to stay at that position again the next day to see if there were any ramifications, but nothing came about.

On the fourth day, we returned to the airport in a different order than we arrived. Several vehicles took us back to the bunker via several different routes just in case we were being followed.

We were brought immediately to the conference room and given something to eat while filling out our reports and waiting for the rest of the team to arrive. Once they did, The General made an appearance and we each explained our part of the mission. It seemed to have been an incredible success. Dara and her group had been able to find the environmental traces we had suspected were there. I had pinpointed the correct office, and James' group were able to sneak in, gather evidence, complete some sabotage and get out before being detected. The General was very pleased and gave us the next four days off.

General Smiths was barely out of the room when all professionalism broke down and we were cheering, mock punching and hugging. It was just like the scene from my first visit to the cafeteria but with all of the members present. Of course, James was a bit more reserved than the others, but his radiant smile spoke volumes. I was also reserved, but only because I was not sure how the team perceived me just yet.

But then Jason rushed over, picked me up in a tight hug, swung me around and put me back down, laughing the whole time. On the way back to the common room, the team started sharing stories of the mission from their point of view. James came alongside me and placed his hand on my shoulder. I knew what he wanted and dropped my shield just a little. He did the same, and my mind was filled briefly with the pride and satisfaction he felt towards the team. It then focused to overwhelming pride towards me and how successful I had been on this first mission. I glanced over my shoulder at him and sent him my relief that it was over and that I had not messed up in any way. I added a question as to what would happen next.

"Get cleaned up, then the pub." He whispered before taking his hand off my shoulder and walking towards his room.

DISCOVERIES

We were at the pub within an hour. All of us crammed into one giant u-shaped booth, and it seemed that this was their normal spot. It also seemed the seating was always the same too. The only change happened when I was seated next to James – who was in the middle of the U. Rick was on his other side and Max was next to me. Menus were passed around, but I had a feeling it was out of courtesy and they already knew it by heart. I had no sooner started looking over the menu than what appeared to be the owner of the pub stopped by. He smiled and greeted us in a hearty manner, welcoming us back from "whatever mischief" we had been making. He kept glancing over at me though, and finally, Skull introduced me via my nickname.

Ever since the name had been bestowed upon me, it was all Skull used. Max, who had been frequenting the name as well, leaned over and informed me that nicknames were generally used here as well. I nodded at the owner and then he and Skull went over to the bar. Several minutes later they returned with nine beers of various brands. I blushed in a combination of annoyance and embarrassment until the owner left again.

"Skull!" I hissed, "I told you I don't drink!"

He laughed, "You used to."

I was a bit surprised at how he knew that little fact.

I turned to Max and glared at him. "Root?"

Max had the nerve to sound innocent. "Yes?"

"When you and I had that conversation about the foods and drinks we liked, and I told you how I used to enjoy an occasional wine or beer but had abstained for the last two years... Did you happen to spread that to a certain pub loving team member?"

"It might have come up one evening." He gave me his most innocent expression.

"Root?"

"Yes, Bear?"

"I will find a way to make you pay for this."

144

"No, you will thank me for it." He smiled, and mock punched my shoulder. I turned towards Dara for assistance.

"Sorry, Bear, this is their territory." She grimaced. Looking through the mental shield it became apparent that she was in with the conspiracy.

The others were quite intent on their menus with James and Rick discussing the mission in hushed tones. Since it appeared I was on the losing end of this conversation, my attention turned to the menu as well. I enjoyed many of the traditional British and Welsh foods, so it was difficult to decide. Skull memorized our whole order and repeated it to the owner, who sent it on to the staff. It seemed we received preferential treatment here, but no one else in the pub seemed to mind.

As we waited, the stories from the mission started flowing again. Outside of the official reports, the real mission was much more interesting. The whole team wanted to hear how I did and what I thought. If I could have hidden under the table I would have, but instead told them what they wanted to know in as short of a story as possible. It made me very nervous to have James sitting right there. Now that the mission was over, I was worried if anything said might be turned against me later on. I kept looking out from my mental shield, analyzing the team's reaction, wishing that the dark space next to me would drop his own shield so I could know if there was an issue. But instead, he listened along intently with the rest of them, never saying a word and only nodding a few times.

Thank goodness, our food was ready quickly and the team's attention turned to eating and then to their own stories from the last few days. They also got a good laugh in when I tried the beer Skull had picked out for me and promptly made a face. It was quite bitter and foul.

"Skull, this stuff is awful! If you will not let me have water or a soda could we try something a little milder?"

He came back with a brand I was more familiar with as well as a water. I promptly finished the water, but it took me the rest of our time there to sip down only part of the beer.

After the meal, half of the team left the table to play billiards and mingle with several off-duty bunker employees. I remained at the table, watching and listening to everything around me.

Most of the team chose to go to their own residences for the days off. James drove me back to the bunker, and I wondered if I would be spending the four days alone. He seemed to be deep in thought as we arrived and rode the elevator down. We were nearing the common room when he finally spoke.

"I'll speak to The General in the morning about getting you a pass for above."

"Thank you." If the pass was granted, it meant I could hang around the park or cafe instead of being stuck inside.

He looked as if he had more to say, but instead, he stopped at the entryway to the living quarters and wished me a good night before turning and walking back towards the elevator. It appeared he would also be spending the night above ground. It was past midnight, so I chose to go straight to bed. Thankfully, sleep came without nightmares.

The first day off was lonely but wonderful all at the same time. James had not returned with permission for me to go above, but I made the best of the situation. I slept in, took an extra long shower, went back to bed for a nap and then listened to the MP3 player while completing two of the training stations. Because it was a regular workday for the rest of the bunker, there were hot meals and plenty of snacks. Jack heard about our successful mission and found out I was off duty. We had lunch and dinner together, catching up on each others news.

When I returned to the common room, James was waiting. He had a huge smile on his face and was holding a large envelope and an even larger catalog.

"I apologize for not getting your pass for today, but it looked like you did well despite. How is young Jack doing?"

"He's wonderful, really taken with his work here and nearly finished with school. I'm so happy that you were able to give him another chance at life."

James' smile grew even bigger. "I have a good excuse for not getting you outside today." He handed me the envelope.

Inside was a rental agreement for a cottage in the village. There was also a small album with pictures of the

146

exterior and inside each room from numerous angles. It was adorable, white with a light brown roof and stone walls surrounding the lot. It appeared the lot had been landscaped and was quite a nice size. The inside had a small living room, a decent size kitchen with breakfast nook, one bedroom, and the second bedroom had been converted to an office.

"It's lovely!" I exclaimed.

"It is yours and is a clean slate. You are going to choose the paint, furniture, all of it." He handed me the catalog. It was to a worldwide chain of build-it-yourself furniture stores. I had shopped in one several times, and a person really could fill an empty house in a day with their products. "We will be going there tomorrow. Dara already rented a box truck. So take a look through this and get ideas for what you want tomorrow. We have a crew to build it all, as well as one to paint the walls and get you moved in before the break is over."

I was shocked and had to sit down. James plopped down next to me, his enthusiasm was very apparent, almost like a child.

"Look at the last pages in the envelope."

It was a bank statement, and the amount on it staggered me a bit. James chuckled and took the paper from me.

"You never bothered to look at the receipt from last month, did you? And you probably ignored your pay-stubs too. You are exempt from most taxes, and the last two months you did not pay rent or utilities. You have permission to use a combination of cash and your card tomorrow, and I expect to see that number go down quite a bit. Do not be reserved, this is for your house, your future."

The sting of tears made me turn away from him. I had never had much in the way of money my entire life and always said that if I had more, then more would be given to those who needed it.

Somehow, he knew what was going on in my mind.

"Harlie." His voice had turned from cheerful to stern. "Don't do it. Do not let yourself go down that road. Yes, there are plenty of others out there who need money, but you have been without a place to call home for quite some time now. You don't have to go all out and make it look like you make

147

the salary you do, just make it look nice and comfortable, like a home. You cannot stay in this bunker forever, for you love the outdoors too much. Use future paychecks to do good in the world, we all have done that."

I gave up fighting the tears and turned back to face him. "It's not just the money, James."

He sighed sadly, "I know. You have handled everything so well. It can be difficult to remember the hell that brought you to this point."

I nodded, wiping away the tears which were slipping slowly down my cheeks. For the second time since we returned, James looked like he wanted to say more. Instead, he picked up the catalog and handed it to me.

"Let's try to get some ideas for the cottage, okay?"

After going through the catalog twice, I was too tired to make any more decisions. That night, however, the nightmares returned with a vengeance.

At the crack of dawn, Dara was pounding on my door. She did not even wait for me to get up and open it – letting herself in and pulling an outfit from my dresser.

"Let's go! Yesterday was the lazy day. Today we are filling up that empty house. Move, move, move!"

"Yes, drill sergeant," I mumbled, dragging my sleep deprived self out of the bed and into the shower.

She was still in the room when I got out, throwing clothes in my direction and heating up her hair straightener. Within minutes my hair was dry and straight, and we were on the way to breakfast.

"Get it to go. We have at least a two-hour drive."

I sighed. "Dara, if you make one more demand before I have had something caffeinated, I will go outside and slash the tires on the box truck."

She rolled her eyes, grabbed my arm and hauled me to the cafeteria. James and Rick were there, placing their meals into a to-go box and running their ID's.

"Good morning, Grumpy Bear." Rick greeted when he saw my expression.

"Will someone call off Bruce? Her shop-till-you-drop attitude is going to make me drop before we even get there."

All three laughed, and I growled while putting together

148

breakfast and getting a large vanilla cappuccino. We then made our way outside. Dara and James would be in the box truck while Rick and I followed in a pick-up. I was pleased with the arrangement and Rick seemed happy to have me with him as well. We talked music, sang along to whatever was on the radio and had a fun trip to the massive store.

We spent all day inside the place too. They had been warned ahead of time and assigned a manager to us for the day. Rick and James seemed to enjoy watching me pick out furniture while Dara tried to find accessories I approved of. The two-story showroom could be overwhelming to anyone, but especially to someone who was furnishing an entire house in one visit. Having pre-shopped the catalog helped quite a bit though.

James stayed with me as the final items were rung. When the manager pressed total, I felt James tapping on my shield. Fighting panic, I lowered it just a little and he radiated calmness towards me. It helped as I counted out the bills and then rang the rest on the bank card. James took the lengthy receipt as we both thanked the manager for his time and effort.

The box truck was full, and Dara was beaming at it when we arrived outside.

"What a beautiful sight!" She exclaimed.

"No. When it is built, and in the house, then it will be a beautiful sight. Right now, it looks like bonfire material." Rick chuckled.

"I need a nap." I yawned. It was nearly time for the evening meal, and we still had the long drive back to the village.

"You nap. I'll drive." James smiled. I was not thrilled with the arrangement and the expression on Ricks' face showed that he wasn't either. However, we did not have much of a choice.

As soon as we were on the road, I leaned the seat back and shut my eyes. I must have fallen asleep quickly because, when they opened again, we were stopping for dinner. A quick look at the clock showed an hour and a half had passed.

After we ate and were back on the road, James spoke. "You did well today. I cannot wait to see what the cottage looks like with your choices."

149

"It will look like someone tried to decorate it country-themed while using modern style, prefabricated, mass-produced stuff."

He looked surprised, and I could see him think about the choices I made. "Oh. Yes, you did do that didn't you?" He smiled. "Quite an impressive feat considering the choices. Have you thought about paint yet?"

"James! I just found out last night about the place and spent all day today in a monster-sized store filling a box truck full of things for it. No, I have not thought about paint."

"Tomorrow then, we only have two more days off, you know."

I growled and turned to watch the sunset.

"Harlie."

I groaned internally, as he sounded serious again. I knew there had to be a reason behind him wanting to drive back. It looked like I was about to find out what it was.

"You have been calling out in your sleep." His voice was soft.

"Yes, I've woken up screaming too."

"Hasn't Jason given you anything to help you rest?"

"Doc did before the mission, but I think Jason just figured my lack of sleep had to do more with our conflicts than the nightmares. And you both know how I hate medication."

I saw his grip tighten on the steering wheel and tried to calm the fear that crept up. He did not speak for several minutes. When he did, the words caught me off guard.

"Did you know that your skills might run deeper than being empathic?" He looked at my reaction briefly before facing the road again. "The General and I have both noted how easy it was for you to adjust to becoming a full empathic. The way you instantly picked up on how to focus emotions and images and send them to another empathic mind, it hints at deeper abilities."

We turned down the road main road to the village. "I worry if your past trauma might be affecting those abilities; it is not a good combination." He glanced at me again. "I would like to be able to help you with both issues but am not sure if you will allow me."

150

"You are my commanding officer. Do I really have a choice?"

He pulled the truck over to the side of the road and turned to pin me with "That Look." It took all I had to not look down. Fear stopped me, and I looked away instead.

"It hurts to see you in so much pain. Last night, I sat up and waited for the screaming to start. I wanted to come over to comfort you and perhaps show you a way to make the dreams less traumatizing. The whole team has suffered from horrifying flashbacks at one time or another, but they have not been through the nightmare you had to live in first." He sighed, "And yes, you do have a choice."

"If there are other skills you think I have, teach me how to use them, but leave the night to me. I'll be in the cottage soon enough and then you won't have to listen to me scream."

His hands tightened on the wheel again before turning the pickup back onto the road. We remained in silence the rest of the trip. Dara stopped the box truck outside of the cottage, but James kept driving to the bunker. As I turned to my room, he reached out and gently grasped my wrist.

"I hope you will change your mind."

Torn by curiosity at the potential skills but determined to keep James distant, I pulled away. "Goodnight, Commander."

In my past life, I had been determined to make as little of an environmental impact as possible. Because of that, I picked out low VOC paint the next morning, and the painters went to work immediately. By the end of our fourth day off, all the furniture was built, the paint was dry, and my few personal possessions were moved in. The team came together to help me put all of the furniture and accessories in the right spots and set up the kitchen.

Sleeping in my own house, alone, was a harrowing experience at first. Every noise woke me, every memory of sharing a home with loved ones made a sob catch in my throat. The return to a full schedule, combined with lack of sleep had me starting to use some of the medication Doc gave me.

The team soon fell into a routine again. Most evenings

I was too tired to grocery shop and was not sure of how much canned and prepackaged food I could handle. It was difficult to keep fresh foods in the house because we never knew when we could be called up. If I wanted something fresh, I would have to buy it and eat it within a day or two. Many evenings I ended up eating in the cafeteria and having just breakfast at the house. I started using an electric assist bike for the daily trips to the bunker, but on many days, someone from the team picked me up along the way.

We were only home for two weeks when Max, Mitch, Rick, and I were called out to Poland again. This time I was with the team as they slipped into not just the office I discovered, but into another one the evidence collected during the last mission led us to as well. We were at the second location when Max let loose a string of whispered expletives. He was looking at a pile of aerial photographs found in a file cabinet. It was two in the morning and we had been in the building since right after midnight. I had been looking out of my shield and heard the words at the same time dread came pouring out of his mind.

"Root? What's wrong" I whispered back. Rick had rushed over and was looking at the photos now. The same dread and alarm started to fill his mind as well. Max began snapping pictures of the photographs, while Mitch checked to make sure we still had not been detected. The building was empty, with the exception of two security guards at the front door and two at the back. Apparently, no one in this terror cell realized that they had been discovered to such a degree.

We finished up with the investigation and were making our way out of the building when I sensed something was amiss. One of the guards had left his post; it seemed as if he was headed towards the restroom. Something made him stop though and he was heading towards the area we just left.

"Jaws, we have to move quickly." I hissed.

Max reached behind him and grabbed a gun from his pack. It was a strange looking device that was more tranquilizer gun than anything. It shot out a medicated dart that would both knock the person out and erase the last few hours of that person's memory. Of course, the dose could not be precise for weight and height, so no one could be sure how

152

long the person would be out. However, it would give us time to escape without having to injure or kill anyone.

We made our way out via the roof entrance we arrived through. I had not been thrilled about roof hopping on the way in but had no choice but to get over my fear and follow Rick. On the way out, we had a complication. We had just made the jump to the next building when someone came up to that roof. It was what we call an "innocent," someone who was not involved in the mission but was in the wrong place at the wrong time. In an instant, Max had the person shot, and Rick ran over to ease the man down and check his vitals. It was a janitor and we all felt horrible about having to tranquilize him.

"Jaws, Root, we should lower him back down the ladder he came up on, make it look like a fall."

Max looked annoyed, "We don't have time, Bear."

"She's right. We don't want to raise suspicion and he will be groggy while waking up. It could be dangerous if he wakes up on the roof." Rick quickly picked up the man, while Mitch held the hatch, and Max climbed down to help settle him. I kept scanning for trouble. There was none, and we were able to make it back to our hotel without any other complications.

I was curious about why the photographs had set off such a reaction but did not have a chance to ask. Rick pulled me aside as I was heading towards my room.

"We will be leaving as soon as possible. Change out of your camos, put on a travel outfit, and be totally packed before trying to get some sleep." He turned towards his room, but then came back and gave me a hug. "Wonderful work out there tonight."

I did as he said and sure enough, two hours later, we were on the way to the airport. Whatever they found, it was urgent enough that we all flew on the same flight and were picked up by the same vehicle. The Commander, The General, and the rest of the team were waiting in the conference room the instant we finished filing our reports. It was nerve-wracking, and I wished someone would give me some information before debriefing. We had strict rules about no conversation during travel and had been rushed back to the bunker so fast that I had no time to corner anyone about the photographs.

The Commander wasted no time. "Max, you were the one who found the surveillance photos?"

Max nodded.

"It appears this terror cell must be linked with the masterminds that attacked America..." He projected the photos onto a screen. "These pictures are of Rio."

Perhaps it was a combination of the all-night mission followed by a plane and car ride with very little sleep. Perhaps it was the memories of the blasts and the devastating situations that followed which hit me full force as he spoke. Whatever it was, at the same time the rest of the team gave a sharp intake of breath, my shield fell for the first time in a month. James' eyes widened slightly, and he glanced over at me. Instantly, I was wide awake and afraid. However, he turned away and continued.

"These pictures look fairly recent. Skull, you need to figure out how recent and exactly where in the city they are. Rick, contact our North American team and provide them with the information we have obtained. The rest of you will be going over the other evidence that has been brought back. We must find out if they are, in fact, part of the group that attacked America. Even if they are not, we do not have much time to take them down. Heads of State and other world leaders will be converging on Rio within three months. The Summit will be shortly after that."

Rio. World leaders. These were photographs from Rio De Janiero, the location of this years' World Summit! I had studied the reports about the potential targets that The Guardians had been protecting, ones that they had already saved: Dublin, Oslo, Paris, London, Vancouver, Tokyo, Copenhagen, Kabul, and more. It had not crossed my mind that any type of bombing, especially one with nuclear technology, would be devastating to the entire world if it happened during the Summit. I quickly thought back to the other major world meetings I had watched and how the media had reported threats during every single one. My eyes and mind found James. He nodded imperceptibly and continued with his orders.

"Rick, Max, Mitch, and Harlie, go get some sleep.

Take the rest of today and tomorrow to recover from this mission. The rest of us will use the time to research. After that, we will move back into the bunker and prepare to disable this cell." He looked grim, "The situation has just gotten more complicated."

We all nodded, waited for The General to exit, and then stood to leave. I had just placed my hands on the table in order to assist my tired legs when James lowered his shield and told me to stay. I sat back down and tried to get my shield to go back up, but again he spoke mentally. This time I could hear actual words inside my mind.

It is okay, Harlie. Wait until you are rested.

Even through my exhaustion, there was enough left in me to look surprised at how clear his words came through.

Dara came up to me then, "Do you need a ride home, or are you going to stay here?" She glanced at James as she said it. Of course, my attempt to stand had not slipped past her.

James mind gently prodded me to answer. "I think I'll stay here until morning. Thank you though." I smiled weakly.

"Okay, have a good rest." She glanced at James again before leaving the room. Once she was gone, James came around from the head of the table. I tensed up as he came around to stand behind me.

"Quite a show going on there," He murmured. I cringed, having my shield drop the way it did was inexcusable to me. Not being able to get it back up quickly, letting him sense my emotions, was even worse.

"Let's get you back to your living quarters." He waited for me to stand. It took a moment until I was steady enough, but I stood and walked out of the conference room and towards the common room. James followed close behind. We passed Jason and he looked very concerned. James halted and whispered something to him, Jason nodded and changed his direction in order to go to the medical bay. I sighed, this could only mean trouble.

At the door to my room, James stopped me with a hand on my shoulder.

"No, Harlie, it does not mean trouble, and no I am not angry with you, and there is no reason to be afraid."

He opened the door to the room and motioned me inside. I hesitated, and another sentence came through my mind. *Either here or my quarters, you choose.*

Shuddering, I walked through the doorway. James followed and shut the door behind us.

"Get cleaned up and put on one of the sweat suits. I'll be here when you are finished." His voice was low and calm. It set my nerves on edge because I did not know what he was planning or why he was acting so calm. It was hard to swallow the fear that crept up. Of course, he sensed all of that and sighed loudly.

"I deserve it, but really wish you wouldn't be that way." Slowly, he closed the gap between us and reached a hand up to touch the side of my face. He lowered his shield enough for me to sense what was behind: Turmoil at what we had discovered, worry that it was part of the larger organization, and right at the front of his mind was concern for me.

I tried to think positively, that I just needed sleep and would be fine tomorrow. He answered by running what felt like a mental finger along my fallen shields and pondering about the nightmares I'd been having.

"Nice try." He whispered, letting his hand drop. The Commander appeared then, "Get cleaned up." How I hated that tone, but I grabbed the requested clothing and went to shower. It felt good, but what I needed was time to think, alone, and it seemed that my mind was not planning on being protected again until I had some sleep.

James was standing by my desk, a dose of liquid medication next to him, and that unreadable expression in his eyes as I came around the corner from the bathroom. I caught myself wondering once again what was going through his mind when he had that expression.

"Believe me, you don't want to know." He answered my unspoken question.

"I've followed your orders. Can I go to bed now?" Exhaustion was making it too easy to be grumpy. I grabbed the liquid and quickly swallowed the whole dose, so it could not be used against me.

"It is bothersome that your shield dropped, it is also

156

interesting how you could hear my projected sentences in their totality. One shows weakness, the other shows more skill than anticipated." He moved over to the bed and turned down the covers then waited for me to climb in.

"I'm not a child, Commander."

"No, you are not. However, we have already discussed my feelings concerning you." He let that sink in for a moment as he walked to the door. "If you have a nightmare while in the bunker, I'll be back in here." I held back a cringe, but he sensed it. "That is not a threat, Harlie. I want to help you and you need to trust me. Sleep well."

I slept the rest of the day and through the night, waking only for a light meal from the cafeteria. When daytime came again, I felt much better but could not remember what day of the week it was. Since my shield was still down, I scanned the bunker and realized it had to be Sunday. The place was nearly empty. There was, however, a dark spot nearby.

I started to raise my shield but heard him think to me, *Not so fast. I want to try something first.*

I moaned but stood up and got ready for the day. James was in the common room, smiling.

"Good morning! You look well rested."

I nodded, and his smile grew bigger. "What am I doing here and why am I smiling?"

Another nod.

"We have the day off. You need to go to the cottage and gather some things before moving back into the bunker and need a ride. If I know you as well as I think I do, you will find a way to fit everything into a pack and stow it on your bike in order to get right back here and work. That is not going to happen. You and I are going to go on a little hike instead."

"What if I don't feel like hiking? I'm sure another member of the team would be available to pick me up, or I could just stay in the cottage until tomorrow morning."

"You could, but you won't. Besides, we are all meeting up at the pub this evening."

"You seem to be confident." If he was trying to make things right between us, he was going to have to work for it. I started walking towards the elevator, but James was quick. He blocked me by putting his hands on either side of the doorway.

157

"That is a bit over the top, Commander."

His expression turned serious, "I have a reason for it." He looked up for a moment then dropped his shield. This time his thoughts were not focused towards me like before. He was just there, like everyone else around me. I could feel how powerful his mind was, and it astonished me.

"Let's try this for the day, shall we?" He lowered his hands from the frame and stepped towards me. "You know what I'm thinking. I know what you are thinking. It's fair enough and should give you some insight."

I started to step back, but in my mind his voice said, *Don't.*

Just as with the shield dropping, what I did next was something I knew was unacceptable. However, some part of me wanted to see just how far his promise of us not being in conflict would go. Acting quickly, I tried to raise my shield. If successful, there would be no reason for him to stay open and I could get out of the hike. Just as quickly though, I felt it stop moving up and fall hard. It felt as if someone were holding the shield down. I struggled again to raise it but could not. I looked over at James and saw he was focused. I stopped trying to raise the shield and he turned away from me.

"Don't ever try that again." His voice was firm.

"Were you holding my shield down?" That kind of power scared me.

The expression on his face said it all.

"I need breakfast." It seemed like a good time for a subject change. He sighed and motioned for me to lead the way. We ate in silence. He was lost in thoughts I could not reach, and I was numb from the encounter. The motorcycle ride to the cottage was silent, and he waited in silence while I packed up what was needed for an extended stay at the bunker and wrote detailed instructions to the gardener I had recently hired to help with the landscaping. We then traveled in silence back to the bunker, my bag strapped to the back of the bike. At the elevator, he spoke.

"I'm going to get two boxed lunches while you bring the bag down. Meet me back here in ten minutes."

Still numb, I followed his directions, and we were soon out of the bunker and on the road out of town. We rode for nearly an hour before he pulled the bike over into a small but empty parking lot. I could see several trailheads and wondered which one we would be taking.

This one. It has the best view.

Something struck me just then and I had to try it, *James, why am I not surprised at being able to hear mental words?* It seemed easy to focus the mental sentence at him.

Because you have been sending them to me since our first practice.

But I thought it was just an impression, images.

No, that is why I was so shocked. It was words.

James?

Yes, Harlie?

These abilities are starting to scare me.

He turned to me then and I could feel concern flowing out of him. He spoke aloud. "It is more than we expected, I'll be honest, but they are nothing to be scared of."

"The things you can do scare me."

"Sometimes they scare me too, Harlie. Be grateful you were not born with abilities this vast." He motioned to the trail, and we started to hike up the hill.

We stayed in silence again for an hour, stopping only to eat lunch at a fallen tree. I was surprised how it was not uncomfortable. We heard each others' thoughts and were each letting our minds wander in the beauty of the trail. Sometimes we would chuckle when a certain bird or another sound would make us think the same thing at the same time. I was curious though, and he picked up on it.

"Not today. Yes, it is not fair that I have your file and you know practically nothing about me. I promise to tell you soon, at least as much as I am allowed to, but not today."

We continued to the top without speaking. He was right, the view was amazing. I felt like I could see all of Wales from there. We sat down and reflected in silence, each in our own minds, not really caring what the other saw. He was remembering other times at this same spot, once with the team and several times alone. I was trying to take in the beauty and not focus on thoughts of past hiking trips with loved ones. We sat for nearly two hours then started down the hill. At the bottom, he smiled.

"This worked out well, didn't it?"

"I agree. It was very relaxing." It was also unsettling; how easy I had put aside our morning conflict.

"We should do this again sometime soon."

I surprised myself by nodding in agreement. His brilliant smile made me smile in return and we made the trip back to town in a strangely happy silence. He drove back to the cottage and I wondered why.

Shields.

I tried to focus, but he stopped me by opening the gate and walking towards the building. I sent a mental question. He replied by saying there was one more thing he wanted to try.

Inside the cottage, I found out what that was. "This is more testing my own ability than yours, but it could prove helpful in the future. Hold still and cooperate with me okay?"

"As long as it won't hurt."

"No, it won't."

He reached up and rested his fingers on my temples. I could feel him running a mental finger along my fallen shield again. Then, the strangest thing happened. He somehow managed to tug part of it up. I could sense he was pleased as he slowly and gently started to raise my mental shield for me. At the half-way point he stopped and I took over. Once it seemed secure he poked at it a few times to make sure it would stay, then quietly withdrew his hands.

"Wow." He breathed.

"It is a good thing to know, but it's terrifying too." I gave a slight shiver.

"I wondered if me lifting your shield was possible after I prevented you from doing the same this morning."

"Can we not do that again, unless it is an emergency?"

"Of course." He snapped his own shield back up and we went to have dinner with the team at the pub. It had been a week of discovery and who knew what tomorrow would bring.

OF JACK AND JAMES

Before the week was out, most of us were back in Poland. Rick and I stayed behind to monitor chatter on the terrorist networks we knew about and to set up the next target. Whoever reported what the team did first was most likely part of the cell we were going to sabotage. I had a feeling I was left behind because no one really wanted me to witness the destruction they had planned.

The rest of the team split between the two buildings and, after gathering more evidence, set up explosives and packs of highly flammable liquid. While it would have been better to take out as many members as possible, the buildings were too close to too many innocents to take that chance. The explosives were set off in the early hours of the morning. The goal was to make the fires burn so hot and thorough that nothing would be left of the target buildings, but there would be no loss of life in the others. The devices used would make the fire look like arson but were common enough that no one could be targeted for setting it off.

The chatter we had hoped for came within thirty minutes of the fire. It came out of Pakistan, then went to Central America. Rick clenched his fist at the code coming in.

"These are part of a Unus sub-group we have been fighting. It is their code and being received in a location we know them to be."

"We can't get in there, can we?" I knew Pakistan was insanely difficult to access and had been since before the nuclear attacks, but I was not sure about this other location.

"We can, but it is dangerous. Both Max and James were injured in our last attempt inside Central America. Our best hope is to track down whoever they have working for them and stop the plans there. With the exception of America, in which we were only partially successful, it has been a good strategy for us."

I thought back to the blasts: Washington D.C, New York, Colorado Springs, Los Angles, and Chicago, and the smaller, non-nuclear bombs at fifteen other key locations around the country. If the Guardians had some success, where was it? Rick read my expression.

"There were more targets that would have crippled the country even more. We stopped the bombs coming into twelve military bases, as well as six going to bases overseas. That was the cell out of Pakistan; the one in Central America was responsible for the larger blasts."

"They were planning on taking out the potential for military assistance as well then?" It was shocking.

"We were under the impression that it was only Pakistan and did not even discover the main group in Central America until a day before the blasts." He lowered his head, sorrow tearing through him. There was nothing that could be said. We continued to monitor, taking turns resting and eating until the team arrived back home.

When Rick gave his report in front of the team the sight was one I will never forget. Skull started swearing like a sailor, The General and Dara lowered their heads into their hands, and Max stood up and kicked the wall. Ryan, Mitch, and Jason sat stiffly with clenched fists, and The Commander...I cringed at the ferocious expression on his face. The power of their emotions was overwhelming, and I shied away from it, looking at my copy of the reports instead.

The General was the one to call order, "The success at Poland is not going to be enough if we are to stop them from making an attempt at Rio."

"I agree." The Commander nodded, "However, both locations are incredibly dangerous and will need to be planned carefully. It is not something we can come up within a day or two. We are going to need several weeks."

"You have two from today. That will put us in the last week of May and will give us enough time in case we need to dig in and camp it. I want everyone out by the end of June because, success or not, we must be at Rio."

Next to me, Jason sighed, "Gonna be a long summer."

We spent the next two hours sketching ideas and assigning duties for the time leading up to our ordered departure. The General was gracious and allowed us to live above ground for the first week. He ended the meeting by wishing us the best of luck and said that he would be flying to

Canada in the morning to assist the North American team with their part of the plan.

Dinner was a silent event that night. We all ate in the cafeteria instead of going to the pub. While the mission had been a success, what it uncovered shadowed any joy we might have felt. I could sense that they were all frustrated and angered by this group who not only had a success in America but who kept returning via smaller cells all over the world. After the meal, transportation was arranged to get everyone home for the night. The team tended to carpool as much as possible since we all lived in the village. Of course, I ended up on the back of James' motorcycle because we lived on the same street.

I figured he would be so tired from the mission that he would just pull over and let me off. It was surprising when he parked the bike on the side of the road, shut it down, and took off his helmet.

"Could I come inside for a moment?" It sounded serious, so I nodded, and he followed me to the door.

Inside the house, he sat wearily on the sofa and I heated up water for tea. He seemed lost in thought and stayed that way until I handed him a steaming cup and sat down on a nearby chair.

"Thank you, Harlie." He sipped at it for a moment. "I think we were all caught off guard by Ricks' discovery. Our reactions must have been overwhelming to you."

"I had to look away."

"It was our worst nightmare come to life." He was referring to the attack on America. "Having them creep back up puts us in a dangerous situation emotionally. The team wants revenge, but we need to focus on the mission and take that threat out for good. Let the world judge once we have them exposed."

It looked like he wanted to say more, so I kept my questions to myself, fairly sure that those would be answered in the next two weeks. He drank more of the tea and turned to face me.

"It is going to get much more intense for you. How are you feeling about that?"

"Nervous. But at the same time, I'm ready for it.

163

Physically, I would like to have more endurance though."

"It takes time to build endurance. You are at your peak in strength training though, and Max said you have a gift for accuracy with most of the guns we use. It seems your abilities are not over-taxed as easily either and that is the most important thing right now. We are going to have to go at this two-pronged in order to have a chance at success. You are I are going to have to closely work together."

One of my questions suddenly could not wait. "James, how far can we receive and transmit emotions or words? That is going to be important if we are in the same general area."

He cocked his head to the side. "I know how far my abilities reach in sensing general emotion, but as to how far you and I can communicate? You are very correct; we need to test that as soon as possible."

Another question became urgent and James read it on my face. "What's wrong?"

I looked away, worried about how he would react. I perceived myself as the weakest member of the team and this would make me seem even more so. James came over to where I sat and knelt in front of me. "Harlie, tell me."

"No. It's not important right now. You need to get home and rest." My voice was a whisper.

"Sleep can wait. What is it that makes you look away from me?" He started tapping on my shield, but I did not drop it, did not want him to see my feelings about this particular issue. He placed his hand on the side of my face and tried to turn my head back towards him, but I jerked it away.

"Don't make me pull rank." He threatened, and I could hear a hint of The Commander in his voice. "If it is something that concerns how you perform on this team, then you need to say it."

I took a deep breath and turned back to him. "There is a very real possibility that I might have to be responsible for the death of someone this summer, isn't there?"

"Responsible as in using the skills Max said you have? Yes. It is almost guaranteed." He paused, pulled me up from the chair, led me over to the couch and gently pulled me back down. Sitting next to me he looked sad. "You have seen death; you have seen and experienced violence. That gives you

164

insight on how it would feel to put someone else through both. Remember though, that we go above and beyond to protect innocents. Those whom we face are the evil we need to stop."

I stared out. What if some of that evil was just people trying to support their families, no matter what the position was? He seemed to know my thoughts, even though they were protected.

"It is the chance we take, the price we all pay for the choices that we have to make for humanity." Again, he looked up and I could see "That Look" in his eyes as he thought. It was a full minute before he turned towards me. "Let me try to show you what it is like. It might help you be more prepared for that moment."

I bolted to my feet and tried to step away from him. I did not want to see someone die at his hands. My whole life I had been against any kind of violence, even though I knew from the instant I signed on here that it was guaranteed. But, I was not in the field and that moment had not come yet. James stood up too, grabbing my arm and spinning me to face him. My heart started to race, and fear began building.

"Are you trying to run, Harlie?" His tone sounded mocking. "That doesn't seem right. Always eager to learn, constantly working to succeed on the team, been through hell and back but now you turn to run?" He saw my expression change. "Don't you dare look down, Bear. Don't you dare." He threatened.

I pulled away. "I don't want to see it."

"Tough." We stared each other down for what seemed like an eternity. "If you had said something to the other members they would have found a way to show you as well, probably through surveillance footage in the archive. Personally, I prefer to be the one."

He was right; I would have asked another team member. Squelching the fear that threatened to overwhelm me, I sat back down and slowly dropped my protection. He remained standing and "That Look" was in full form. His shield dropped, and my head fell into my hands as several of his memories were projected into my mind.

I watched a suicide bomber taken out by Max in a sniper mission, just moments before detonation, and then a chase scene that ended in a firefight. In both, I could feel James' emotions from that moment in time. The final memory was the hardest to witness. Skull, Rick, Max, and James were running in the dark. They climbed up a tall chain link fence with barbed wire at its peak, quickly cut apart the top, and jumped to the other side. They then ran to the back of what seemed to be a large building. I could see the gun in James' hands as Skull kicked down the door and set off the flash-bang bomb. His memory slowed down enough so that I could see more details: the dim room, the uniformed men, the battered girl on the floor being attacked by a man on top of her. James raised the gun, rage turning his vision almost red, and a bullet flew straight into the man's temple. He collapsed on top of the girl and the vision showed James' foot kicking him off. Then it stopped, and I was back in the cottage.

We both had tears of pain in our eyes, both stared at each other. My mind kept flashing back to his memories. He kept searching my face, watching my reactions. Time stood still.

"I should go." His sigh was both sad and tired. "Be ready in the morning to see how far our abilities can go. I have an idea about how to test it."

I stood to see him out, still going over what he had shown me. At the gate, he turned to face me once more. "Do you have any more of the stuff Doc gave you?" At my nod he added, "You're going to need that tonight."

He was on the motorcycle and gone moments later.

The next morning, I was ready and waiting, surprised when he pulled up in a car instead of the typical motorcycle. The surprise turned to joy when the back door opened, and Jack came bounding out. It had been several weeks since we had last met up, and his long embrace let me know he missed me as much as I missed him. When he finally let go, it was only to jump up and down like a small child and ask.

"Guess what?"

I laughed at his expression but asked what.

"I graduate next week, and I've been accepted into a distance learning program through Swansea!"

"Wonderful, Jack! I am so proud of you!" I gave him

166

another hug but quickly stepped away at the sound of another closing car door.

James was smiling as he came around to us. "We have reserved the pub for the night after the ceremony. It is the day before we are due back underground. Jack here has been a wonderful student. His teachers have been thrilled to have him in the evening program."

"It will be a great party!" I was so happy for him, it made last nights difficulties fade away.

"We should be going. Jack is going to work with us today to help test how far our abilities can reach." Jack bobbed his head happily as we climbed into the car and were off.

James drove us far out into the countryside. From what I knew of Wales, we had to have been near Brecon Beacon National Park when he turned onto a dirt road. He drove a few more kilometers, before pulling onto an unpaved parking lot. There was another trail head here, but it went through a clearing instead of the woods and hills. He popped the boot as we got out, and I was surprised to see an all-terrain bike in there. Jack set about putting the front tire back on as James explained the test. He explained that it was a rarely used trail, so there would be very little interference. Jack had an earpiece in and would stop ever fifty meters for me to try to sense him.

"After we have your limit with sensing emotions" James continued. "Jack will bring the bike back here and I'll take it out. I'll stop at the same points and send you a message; you will send one back. That way we test both of our limits."

It sounded like a good plan. The weather was stunningly sunny and warm, so I was pleased with the idea of spending extra time outdoors. Jack had finished reassembling the bike and had hopped on. With a smile in my direction, he began to peddle to the first point. I could sense his happiness loud and strong. He peddled to the second point and third point and it was still the same. At six hundred meters, I had to really focus in order to sense his now questioning mind. Somewhere between six hundred and six hundred fifty meters he became a whisper and by seven hundred he was gone.

"Impressive." James complimented after calling Jack to come back down.

I was feeling a bit dizzy and sat on the ground, resting

my back against the car. James came to sit next to me. "Now for the fun part. I don't think we should repeat the same line over and over. It could lead to shadows, false communication where we think we hear but do not. You expressed curiosity about my past during our last hike, so listen in for facts. Respond in a way so that I know you understood me. Also, we need to do this with shields up. It is unsafe to stay open during a mission." The moment Jack arrived, they switched places, and James began his trek.

He started off at fifty meters with, *I siarad Cymraeg*. I had to smile as I responded in both Welsh and English. *You speak Welsh, m heyfyd*.

At one hundred meters: *I was born near Colwyn*. I repeated him but added, *By the bay*.

One hundred fifty meters: *Yes, and I loved visiting the water's edge*. I responded with how it must have been beautiful. He sent an affirmative while peddling again.

At the next stopping point he stated, *I was sent to boarding school at age 12*. I asked why.

There was a pause as he biked to the next point, *Father was in the military*. He did not wait for a response before moving to three hundred meters. *And my mother had recently died*.

This time he waited until I responded, and I offered my condolences at losing a parent while so young. At the next stop he changed the subject. *My father and General Smiths helped with founding the original Guardians*. I asked how long he had been part of the organization and I heard him hesitate. *Since I was fifteen*.

Fifteen!

Yes, fifteen.

At five hundred meters I could still hear him. *Did my time with the military, then joined a team*.

So, you have always been here.

Pretty much.

I asked him what his real rank was since it was a long time to be stuck at Commander. His reply was, *Other than The General, we don't officially have ranks*. I wondered what his unofficial rank was then, and he answered that it would be Colonel.

168

You seem a bit young for that.

He laughed at the next stop.

How old are you?

Not a chance, try again. It was hard to tell at this distance, but it seemed that he was suddenly uncomfortable. Although it made me curious, I changed the subject – asking what his least favorite food was. Come to find out, he hated fish. I laughed and told him I avoided mushrooms at all cost. At the next stop, I asked about his favorite food and was pleased to find out it was one of my favorites as well, pasties.

At nine hundred meters we had to focus a bit more. *Are you still there, Harlie?*

Yes.

This time he stopped the bike. *I can barely hear you.*

I mentally shouted back at him.

Heard you loud and clear that time. He shouted back.

It was at one thousand, one hundred fifty meters where I heard him last. It seemed like a whisper. *I really want us to be friends.*

He started peddling down before I could answer. Since the entire test had been completed without spoken words, Jack was anxious to find out how it went and what he said. While I eagerly let him know that we made it over a thousand meters, I felt bad telling him that what James said was confidential.

James pulled up soon after, jumped off the bike and grabbed us both in an enthusiastic group hug. "That was amazing! Harlie, you are a bloody natural at this. I cannot believe you were born with these skills in a dormant state."

We drove back to the bunker and all three of us had a late lunch together in the cafeteria before Jack went back to his position delivering packages and mail.

The technology team inside the bunker was working with Rick to analyze the messages sent between Poland, Pakistan and Central America for hidden code and changes in reception which could help us narrow down where to look. The team knew that the Unus Universum had a base of operations in Panama but were unsure of its exact location. It seemed to have moved from where transmissions came out of during the attack on America. As they narrowed down the reception points, I was assigned to lead a small group to research the areas around it. Skull helped out when he could, but The General had him busy with mapping out the mission to Rio.

Max and Ryan spent the first two days in the smaller bunker pulling out the supplies we would need. Most of it was new to me, so Max and I would stay after debriefing to get me caught up. Mitch was working endlessly on anything and everything bomb-related. Dara and James were developing strategies, schedules, plans, back up plans, and how the teams would be split. Jason was preparing for any kind of illness we could possibly pick up.

He had recently changed my medications around and for that, I was quite grateful. I had been complaining that my body was not used to all the added chemicals and I preferred natural solutions. Jason had researched and found a food-based multivitamin as well as a natural hormone supplement since my body had finally figured out that there had been a hysterectomy. He let me stop the anti-anxiety medication. The only thing that had failed was a reliable natural way of getting me to sleep. Since I was facing weeks of close quarters with the team it would not be good, or safe, if I were to scream myself awake.

The days flew by like hours and all too quickly it was the night before we had to lock down in the bunker. I helped Jack's father decorate the pub for the graduation party. The owner, as with most people in the village, had grown fond of the dirty blond teenager with the contagious smile and heart of gold. His staff had made a feast of classic American foods for the event.

Most of the employees from the bunker came to the party. The pub was full to overflowing. Even though several other village teens had graduated that week, none were as celebrated as Jack. In a world that had gone terribly wrong, he was becoming a symbol of hope in the community. They all knew his story, they all admired his father, and they all were proud of him. The party was an amazing success.

As the evening turned to night, the villagers said their farewells. The team went from mingling to sitting at our usual table. The mood was growing more and more somber as the realization of what we were about to do set in. I kept a smile on for Jack and his father, but the moment they left so did the smile. We stayed at the table, barely talking until it was quite late. Rick took most everyone to the bunker in the van. I stayed behind to help with clean up and would join the group first thing in the morning. But, when I went to leave, there was a motorcycle on the side of the road. Its owner was waiting for me, helmet in hand.

"Hop on."

Trying not to look disappointed at losing a night in the cottage, I took the offered helmet and climbed behind him. He started driving towards the bunker, then suddenly spun the bike around and headed away from it and the village. I questioned his sanity and he dropped his shield, sending back laughter.

I don't get to be impulsive very often, hang on! The bike nearly doubled its speed.

We raced through the countryside, which passed by in a blur. Minutes passed, and he still did not slow down. Just as my anxiety was building, he pulled onto a gravel road. Several hundred feet later the bike stopped, and I breathed a sigh of relief.

It wasn't that bad! Even in the darkness, I could see the excitement in his eyes.

Tell that to my stomach, which was left somewhere by the bunker. I groaned for effect.

"Drop shield and follow me." He spoke aloud.

Since his shield had been down since the impulsive turn, I let mine drop as well and followed him. James walked on for about two hundred meters then stopped and turned to face me. When I stopped a couple of meters away, he smiled and pointed to the sky.

"Look, Harlie."

I hesitated, unsure of what to think of his impulsive behavior and wondering why we were out here.

Just look up. The answer is there.

"Trust me." He added, a pleading edge to his voice.

Slowly, I lifted my head and eyes and my jaw dropped in awe. The sky was perfectly clear, and because we were so far out in the country in a sparsely populated area of Wales,

171

the stars were amazingly bright. There were more visible than I was used to seeing and the sight nearly took my breath away.

"If we end up in a remote part of Central America, they will be even brighter. You'll be able to see millions." He whispered. "But, I wanted you to witness this first and tonight the weather was perfect."

I plopped down on the ground, pulling my knees up to my chest, and looked up again while gathering scattered thoughts. "Why did you want me to see this? Why did you have this impulsive moment when you knew it was not professional, and I could have reacted negatively?"

He sat down next to me, in the same position, and also looked at the stars. "I did not know if you had ever seen the stars like this before and wanted you to experience it. There are many things I want you to experience that your previous life did not allow. As for the impulsive moment, I agree it was not professional. You still could react negatively, but I'm not sorry for it. A couple others on the team have seen this side of me." He chuckled, "Ask Max about it sometime."

We sat in verbal silence, letting our minds wander like on the day of the hike. He was picking out stars and listing them off. I could not help but listen to it.

It seemed like hours before he broke the silence. "It is very relaxing, coming out here and star gazing. It's something that I enjoy doing but rarely get the time for anymore."

"Oh." I whispered, trying to not give away the fact that I was once again comfortable in this moment with him. It was relaxing, and I was not afraid.

He sighed and stood up, "It is past midnight and I don't need to remind you what today is the start of."

We rode back in silence and quietly made our way back to the living quarters in the bunker. At my door I paused.

Thank you, James, it was very relaxing.

He smiled gently. *I hope there will be more moments like it.*

PANAMA

After a week of intensive work, we were on our way to Panama. Half of us boarded a jumbo jet whose final destination was Panama City. The other half flew into a nearby country and hopped onto a smaller airplane to meet up with us.

We had to be very careful to appear as strangers to each other as we waited at the chosen central location, a marketplace which was popular with tourists. Once everyone was present, James sent me a mental cue. I checked my watch and began walking around as if I were looking for someone. In fact, I was looking for Rick, who had arrived with the other team. We had already registered under our aliases for the same hotel. Once we were within sight and pretending to have a grand reunion, I sent a cue back to James. He was sitting at a small cafe two hundred meters away. James stood and had the same kind of reunion with Mitch and Skull. Once that had been registered by me, I nodded to Max, who was browsing a small shop within eyesight of me. He set off to meet up with the others in a different part of the city, and our mission officially began.

Rick and I were to portray hikers who had just arrived in the country and had to stock up on supplies before trekking into more remote areas of Panama. It wasn't a total lie. We had all packed light for this leg of the mission and would need supplies, especially if the masterminds were where we thought they were. Preliminary information showed part of the cell to be in the jungle. While portraying hikers, we would really be spying, scanning the area for evidence of those responsible for the attacks on America, and looking for the ones we believed were planning an attack on Rio. If all went well, in five days we would join up with one of the other teams and head out to a more rural location. I could sense that Rick was unsure of how much success we would have. I hoped those doubts would prove to be in error.

We checked in at the hotel and were having a good time with portraying our parts. We had both studied maps

173

Skull had made for us as well as information on what we would be seeing and where we might see it. To anyone listening in, it would sound like we were avid hikers and knew what we were doing.

Once in the room, we sighed in unison and then went to work. Because we were portraying hikers, each of us only had a back-country pack and frame. We had been very clever about making it look like a one-person tent and sleeping bag was on the top and personals were below. What we really had was a small camp roll and inside the roll was the electronic equipment we would need. It had been kept from detection using a new fabric that hid the metal parts. There were also some food bars, first aid, and survival kits, several changes of clothes and personal items. We both had attached water bags, which had been filled with safe water and a filter. Rick's bag carried a small tent as well.

We set up the equipment in near silence then took turns getting showered. From there, we inserted earpieces and placed mini recorders on our smaller backpacks and went back to the marketplace. Some of the other members were there, but we were not allowed to look at each other at all. Instead, I reached out with my ability. It showed they also had been to their hotel and were eager for the mission to have success.

It was a slow walk back to our hotel. I was exhausted from the multiple flights and jet lag but also excited at the chance to help stop another attack. My mind wandered to the person next to me. Over the last month, I had come to realize that Rick had a strong sense of intuition. He could read me like a book and very little made it past him. It did not scare me the way James' abilities did, the way my own abilities sometimes frightened me. With Rick, it was nice to know that someone had an idea of what I was feeling, even with the mental shield up. He had become a good friend and for that I was grateful.

As I was pondering this, Rick stopped in his step and turned to me. "Out of all the rest of the team, I'm glad it is you and me together in this part of the mission."

I smiled up at him.

As we went about our nightly routines, Rick started humming a familiar tune. I hummed along in harmony, and at the end, we broke out into a fit of childish laughter. I thought it would be uncomfortable to share a room with him, but he was very courteous and aware of personal space. The trials of the day soon left us both in a deep dreamless sleep.

The following morning, we were up early and ate breakfast while discussing where we would be "shopping" that day. Skull had made a series of maps, broken down into a grid pattern using stores and vendors, which we could visit for needed pauses. The area we had to cover was, thankfully, in the better parts of the city. It seemed that this group was into hiding in the more popular areas of a country. Evidence showed that, like Poland, there would be a cover business and we needed to find it.

Our first stop was at a proper outfitter. We were greeted, in English, by a young woman behind the counter and a burly man who was arranging various dehydrated foods. Rick started in his direction while I pretended to browse. Stretching my ability as far as it could go, I also searched the minds of those in my range. It was an uncomfortable exercise, one which made me feel intrusive, but I kept at it. We looked around for about thirty minutes, purchased two dehydrated meals and then went back out into the city.

We walked for a mile and found another store to pause inside. This time it was a bookstore and one of us headed for the travel section while the other went towards the magazines. Nothing seemed amiss and we left after forty minutes. The rest of the day was the same. There was not a single hint of deception that was strong enough to make us pause in our search.

The next day we worked another part of the grid, making sure we overlapped the edges of my abilities. We were closer to where a few transmissions had come from and spent more time at each stop. We chose larger shops or bookstores, so we had reason to be in one spot for longer periods of time. Like the day before, sometimes we purchased items for the rest of our mission. It was another disappointment when late night came and there was still no hint of what we needed.

Before we had left the bunker, transmissions had been increasing. Rick carried a modified mobile phone that would vibrate if certain frequencies were being used within a five-mile radius. It would also receive email and multimedia messages if something with the masterminds' codes or anything similar was pulled off the internet. While it had gone off several times, it had all been false alarms.

By the fourth day, I was starting to wonder if we were going to have to be in the city for longer than scheduled. The brief communications I had with James showed that his team was meeting with the same lack of luck. We had decided to go over the grid again, but this time spread out a bit more. It meant that we were walking more into areas of the city that were not as nice, but we maintained our disguise and kept at it.

Five days into the mission, I was getting worn out from the days of waking early and walking until it was past dark, all while keeping my mind out for trouble. Rick decided that lunch should be at a nicer sit-down restaurant, so we could both rest for a bit. The server sat us near one of four televisions inside the establishment. We were waiting for our meal when the noon news came on. Without thinking I started to watch it, becoming more and more absorbed in what was on the screen and what the anchor was saying. First, it was local news which covered a recent murder and a legislative battle. When the anchor switched to international news, my world started to change. There was a video clip of America and it was sheer chaos. I could not hear his exact words, but it seemed like this was something which had been happening for awhile. Another clip showed what had to be one of the refugee camps, and it was violent.

Our food arrived at that moment, and I tore my eyes from the screen and noticed the look on Ricks' face. He looked upset, and I sensed he was troubled. Initially, I was unsure of why he was that way. As we ate, my mind started to backtrack in order to figure out what could be wrong. It was something Jason had said, something before Poland, about remotes being hidden. I was in the middle of putting two and two together when I heard a sharp intake of breath. Rick was glancing at two men who had entered the restaurant and were walking unescorted to a side room.

"Bear, when they walked in a two-second transmission came from the room they are headed to." He whispered and then took a bite of his food.

Being so lost in the televised news and my own thoughts, I had not really been looking out. When I did, it instantly became obvious that we were in the right spot at the right time. Rick deftly adjusted his earpiece to focus in the correct direction and we waited.

The meeting lasted about twenty minutes, and we had to order dessert in order to make it seem as if there was a reason to stay. Using our own system of code words and conversation topics, we were able to combine my skill and his enhanced hearing to piece together what was happening. Since it was too dangerous to discuss openly, we left the establishment shortly after the suspects did and took a taxi back to the hotel.

In the room, Rick wrapped me in his arms and held me for a moment before stepping back. "We will talk about what you saw later. I promise." He shook his head sadly then sat on his bed. "What did you sense?"

"Deception. To me, it seemed they were trying to convince the visitors to deliver a package to a location and the visitors were not happy about it. One was afraid, but they both seemed shocked at something that was said. Whatever it was, they were thinking really fast. It was hard to keep up, but I sensed surprise, fear, relief, and then hardly anything. The other side was pure deception at first and then almost gloating. Both sides were somewhat pleased when the meeting ended."

Rick looked relieved. "That matches up with the bits and pieces I heard. It is a package, a large one which must be trucked to a rural location. I heard the coordinates and need to get those to Skull. The men were offered a sum of money if they agreed to make the delivery and another much larger amount if they returned successfully. The two men..."

He was interrupted by the modified mobile. It was a multimedia message and he took several moments to read it, then grabbed a small notepad from his pocket and began to write furiously. The more he wrote, the happier he seemed. After ten minutes he shut the phone and smiled.

"That was a transmission from the restaurant and in the latest code the organization has been using. Bear, it confirms everything we were just discussing!"

"Wonderful! Now we need to find James."

He agreed, "It looks like a jungle trip will be in our near future. The drop is happening one week from today."

James, Skull, and Mitch could be anywhere within their part of the grid. We were not scheduled to be within each others ability range until twenty-two hundred. Rick flagged down a taxi while I found spots on the map where my range would cover the largest part of their assigned area. Rick explained to the driver that we were looking for a friend because there was an emergency and offered a large tip if he would drive us to certain spots in the city and wait for us. The driver agreed, and we began our search. At the first stop, I got out of the taxi and pretended to look around a small park. I called out mentally to James several times, but there was no answer. The next stop put us at a museum and Rick went inside to supposedly have him paged while I repeated my mental calls. There was still nothing, so we drove to the third corner of the grid. This time a mall was close by. I headed in that direction and called as loud as I could.

James! Jamyson! Where are you?

Harlie? Did you find something? His reply was loud enough that I knew he was close.

Yes. I looked at the taxi and gave a signal to Rick. He picked up his mobile like it had vibrated a call and had a fake conversation. As he was doing that, I glanced around like I was still looking. *We are at the mall; where should we meet you?*

There was a moment of silence.

The market where we first arrived, inside the cafe on the south side of it.

Rick called to me as he slapped the mobile shut.

"The idiot had his phone off all day! He is a couple blocks from here." He thanked the driver and gave him the promised tip. As soon as the taxi was out of sight, I relayed where we were to meet, and we made the short walk to the market place.

The fake reunion was a brilliant drama which played out perfectly. The others made it look like a surprise and then shared tales of hiking adventures. James and I spoke as little aloud as possible, instead sharing mentally what had occurred.

We witnessed an entire transaction, and it was

followed up by a multimedia message in the newest code.

Where were you when this happened?

We were having lunch in a proper restaurant. I tried to show him with mental pictures but, in my haste, forgot to edit out the scene with the television. I felt him back away mentally, shielding himself for an instant. My puzzle from before was starting to solve itself without me having to work at it.

James came back a moment later, all business. *What is being exchanged and where?*

A package that has to be trucked into in the jungle. Rick has the coordinates. It will occur a week from today.

Skull had out his pocket GPS and was pretending to show the others where he hiked. What he really was doing was pulling up the location Rick had slipped to him. We all appeared to be intrigued. The rest of the group started up a conversation about how we should hike together and where we should go.

Can you see what he pulled up? James asked.

I leaned over and Skull showed me the map while mentally focusing on the name of the surrounding area.

At the same time, both James and I leaned over a pointed to the same area on the map, "We should hike here!" Where we pointed was in the middle of the Parque Nacional Darien, a protected jungle.

Skull, Mitch, and Rick looked at us and started laughing. They agreed, and we laid down plans of where and when to meet up. It all sounded innocent enough to anyone listening in. There was no way anyone could have realized we were planning on either intercepting the package or following it to its' destination and attacking. We decided to leave tomorrow to have enough time to arrive, set up and run recon before the delivery. James informed me that he would try to contact Dara's group but not to expect them because they were tracking a transmission from near Balboa.

We did not stay too long at the cafe, choosing instead to use the time to get ready for the next day. It was early evening when Rick and I arrived back at the hotel. While we were both happy with the success of today, we were also thinking about the next part if the mission.

"We have a lot to put together." I thought about the electronics in our bags as well as what the others carried. Each team carried an light tent, made for those who are hiking for multiple days. It was just large enough for four people to sleep in. Since two teams would be going into the jungle, we would have two tents. One person would guard the equipment, which would be set up in the second tent, while the others were in the first. We each had a sleeping bag and pad as well as bits and pieces of cookware and survival gear. Two teams combined would leave us with enough supplies to make the trek almost comfortable.

We worked in silence, packing up what we could and getting cleaned up. No one knew when our next real shower would be. I had just finished my turn, dressed in sweatpants and a t-shirt and was reaching towards the television remote when Rick spoke up.

"You and James seem to be getting along a bit better."

"Before Poland, he apologized for the seemingly split personality and promised that we would not be in conflict again. He's been trying ever since to prove it."

"You both seem more comfortable around each other; there isn't as much stress."

I thought about how to answer him and decided on honesty. "Rick, remember when we talked about how Jason and James both seem to feel protective towards me?"

"Yes." I heard the question on the end.

"It's a bit more than protective with James. He really wants us to be friends and has been trying to get me to feel the same way."

"You sound as if there is something wrong with that."

I tried not to show the surprise I felt with his response. "Isn't there? I would have thought it not very professional or very safe."

"James and I are friends, have been for most of our lives. You and I are friends, and I am technically your senior. You learn quickly to separate work relationship from off-time relationship. Sometimes the lines get blurred but never too much. It's safe enough."

I was thinking it over when Rick picked up the remote. "It's against orders for me to turn the news on."

180

Sitting on my own bed, I turned to face him. "Why?"

"When you decided to join the team, we all received a file with some of your history in it. You were supposed to get a short bio on each of us, but for some reason it never happened. However, in the file was an order. We were not allowed to watch televised news, read the newspaper or be on the internet around you."

"Why?" Rick seemed calm enough about it. Jason had seemed upset about the order without me even knowing it existed.

He shook his head. "That, I do not know."

"Who gave the order?"

Before he could answer, I jumped up. James was tapping on my mental shield. I went around Rick to the window, where James was standing in the parking lot two levels below.

"I really hope that was not on purpose. He is out there tapping on my shield." My eyes turned to Rick.

"No, he would not know."

The tapping became more urgent.

"You better be right, because he is getting impatient. I'll be back, I think"

Rick stood up and pulled me to him with an arm around my shoulder. "First, I do not think it was him. Second, remember what I said about being friends." He laughed as I turned an annoyed look towards the window where James was now pounding on the shield. "Finally, be safe out there." He let me go and I grabbed my daypack and headed out the door.

I'm coming.

Quickly, we do not have much time.

Rushing down the stairs and out the door I was by his side in less than a minute.

What's the issue?

I cannot contact Dara or Max, they are on radio silence. All I have is their search plan and the hope they are in a hotel for the night. He handed me a black hooded sweatshirt, and I noticed he was wearing the same style. I put it on, and he walked towards a waiting taxi.

He will take us in but refuses to wait for us. Getting out might be hard.

Where are we going?

Balboa. What used to be the main building center of the Panama Canal and is now a run down, crime ridden mess.

The ride there was quiet. James was deep in thought and keeping his distance mentally. I could sense he was disturbed but did not press. Instead, I took careful observation of each street we drove on. The buildings were getting more and more run down, trash littered the streets. We started hitting potholes and had to slow down. James started to look agitated.

"Stop here." He told the driver.

The driver looked incredulous. "Your funeral, but I warned you before, stranger, this is not the place to be at night."

"I appreciate your concern but would appreciate it even more if you stayed until our business is finished. We will not be long."

"No, Señor. You will have to find another way back. It is not worth the risk for me."

We stepped out of the taxi and James came around to where I stood on the broken sidewalk.

"We will separate to 800 meters and walk parallel. Listen for their minds. Try to find them and let them know we must speak." He looked around. "Walk quickly and take this." He took a small handgun out of one of the hoodie pockets and handed it to me. He started walking away.

I hesitated then started to ask a question.

Focus on your mission. The air of the Commander could even be heard mentally.

His attitude bothered me, but there was a task to complete, and we had to complete it quickly. Trying not to look too much at the world around me, I put the hood up and started walking. Keeping my mind open to Dara, Max, Jason, or Ryan, I walked in the opposite direction until we were at 800 meters. At that point we started walking up the streets, scanning for the rest of the team.

The problem with looking out broadly is that you sense nearly everyone around you. By a half mile in, I was becoming disturbed by the increased level of evil. Many people were high on drugs, their emotions flickering from euphoria to anger and back. Someone had recently flagged down a prostitute, and I had to shut my mind until I was past them. Several people were contemplating some kind of wrongdoing, more were fighting. There was sorrow everywhere, the feeling that nothing mattered, and levels of desperation that brought tears to my eyes. The humidity pressed in around me, making me feel even more weighed down.

We walked and walked, never communicating, always searching. When we finished one stretch of the grid Dara's team was to follow, we turned and made a large U shape 1600 meters out so that he was 800 meters from where I walked, and I was 800 meters out from him. I hoped that if we walked fast enough, kept our heads low and said nothing aloud, we might make it back to the city without trouble. Several times, my mind caught someone staring at me from the alleyways, their thoughts vulgar. Each time I shuddered and reached into the pocket to place my hand on the small gun.

It was near midnight when James found them. I hurried towards their location and arrived just as he finished whispering the events of the afternoon. He handed Ryan the coordinates of where we would be. Jason pulled me aside.

"What was he thinking, bringing you out here?" He whispered fiercely.

"We were able to search twice as fast. If he were out here alone it would have been 2 am or later before he found you."

"You should not be anywhere near this city!"

"You need to get over that protective streak, Stitch. I am one of the team, not some helpless thing down in the med-bay." I was still whispering but getting angry.

STOP! I cringed at the mental yell.

Dara and Max were nodding at something James had just said. If they had noticed our conversation, no one was letting on. I went back to where they stood and waited for it to end. Finally, Max turned to me.

"Sounds like you had a great day. Be careful out in the jungle." He pointed to my pocket and the gun inside of it. "Hope you don't have to use that tonight." Dara nodded in agreement.

"We need to head back to the city. Hopefully, a bus or taxi will still be out here." James waved the team off and we started walking back towards the main stretch of town. We walked quickly to the main road, but there was no taxi in sight.

"Maybe near the bars?" I chanced to whisper.

"Perhaps, but we will start heading back to the city. If we find a bar, I'll call for a pickup." He looked around. "It could be a long night for us."

"I'll be praying a cab pulls over as we walk."

He pinned me with "That Look" so fast and hard that my breath caught in my throat and I backed up a step. We stood there, the silence deepening until I broke the stare and started walking. He caught up quickly and our hike back to the city began.

It was after one in the morning when we walked up to a bar and found a taxi. He was unhappy about the long drive, but when James showed him a sizable tip, he nodded and was more pleasant. The trip back was just as silent. I was thinking about what we had seen and sensed in Balboa. I was also wondering what was making James so quiet. The taxi stopped at the hotel Rick and I was staying at and I quickly got out.

Good work tonight. We will debrief later. Debrief, not talk.

Sure, whatever. I didn't even bother to turn.

The taxi sped off, and I made my way up the stairs, exhausted. The moment our rooms' door was open, Rick had me in an embrace.

"Thank goodness you are back safely. What in Hades was that all about?"

I polished off a bottle of water before replying. "The other team was on radio silence. We had to find them using our empathic abilities."

"You were roaming the streets of Balboa looking for the other team?"

Oh, no. He was starting to sound like Jason. I went over to my bed, laid the gun on the end table, took off the hooded sweatshirt, and climbed in under the covers.

"Yes, and it was depressing, terrifying, and exhausting all at the same time. We found them around midnight but had

184

to hike halfway out before seeing a taxi."

Rick looked disturbed, "Did you know that Balboa was where Max and James were injured the last time we encountered this group?"

"No. The Commander barely said a word the entire time."

"There are people in that city who know us, who would be looking for us. You are very fortunate to have gotten in and out so easy. James was probably stressed by returning there with you."

"The Commander was probably quiet because he does not want to deal with what he saw in my mind earlier today." The emotion in my voice was stronger than intended.

Rick tilted his head and thought about it for a moment. "The news broadcast at the restaurant?"

I nodded, the scenes coming back to me.

"It would have been a combination of both." He climbed into his own bed and shut off the light. "Try to get some sleep. We will be moving out in a few hours."

My eyes were closed, but sleep did not come. The things I had sensed in Balboa, the images from the news, the silence from James, it all ran through my head. First slowly, then faster and faster until I thought I would scream. If I dozed it was only for brief periods and daylight came all too fast.

We were out of the hotel soon after dawn, met up with the group, and were in a rented van on the way out of Panama City before o' eight hundred. Mitch had found the rental company after we left the restaurant yesterday and had reserved it for three weeks. It took a little extra cash to keep it for so long, but the guy seemed to believe the story stating we were a group of hikers whose original rental vehicle had been given to another customer.

I was able to nap for a few hours in the van while the others looked at maps and recon information which had been sent to us last night. When my eyes opened again, Rick and James were both sleeping, Skull was now driving, and Mitch was working on the plans. I picked up the now marked maps and tried to find where we were at and how much farther we had to go. It looked like we would be driving all of today and hiking into the jungle by tomorrow.

185

Even though all of this was new, I did not allow myself to dwell on the unknown. It would not do me or the team any good to think too much about what it was we were doing, or to allow fear and doubt to creep into my mind. Instead, I looked out the window and reflected on the uniqueness of the country, comparing and contrasting it to all of the other places I had been. How could anyone look at the world and believe such diversity and strange similarities all happened by accident?

It was the sensation of being watched that eventually made me turn away from my contemplations.

What is so fascinating out there?

I blushed just slightly but answered mentally, *Diversity,* and turned my gaze back outside.

The tap on my shield made me turn again, this time with a sigh.

Tell me what you sensed last night.

Debriefing this way? How can there be a record?

There was a slight pause. *No debrief, we'll combine it with the general mission one.*

The memory of last nights' silence, of him yelling for me to stop arguing with Jason, and the mental distance between us, it all came forward and I was suddenly very agitated.

I would rather not talk about it this way.

He frowned, *I could order you to.*

That would be out of line; there is no reason for us to talk mentally. The others are part of the team and there is no immediate danger of us being spied on.

You need another nap. His frown deepened.

You need to not be so moody.

He spoke aloud. "Pull the van over."

Skull did as he was told. James ordered Rick to the front passenger side and Mitch to the middle seat. He then climbed into the back seat with me. Rick gave me a look full of concern and questions. I sent him a look that I hoped conveyed both my agitation and now my own concern.

The moment we were back on the road, James turned to me.

Explain.

I fought the urge to roll my eyes. *Going into this*

186

mission, even with all the added stress, everything was fine between us. Even yesterday when we met up, it all seemed to be okay. Then, you back away from me mentally when I forgot to hide the moments with the televised news. When you call me to help with finding Max's team you are silent and cold. And do not tell me that was just being focused and professional, you were far too distant.

There is that temper again, I see.

I glared at him then turned to look out the back window.

Look at me.

I wanted to act like a child and tell him to make me but instead chose to ignore the order.

Do you want to make a scene here in the van? There will be one if you do not turn that head back in this direction.

I sighed. *James, if this conversation were being held out loud, would you have dared to say those last two sentences?*

There was silence all around. He knew he was out of line and that I was going to expose it.

No, I would not have.

Who gave the order, James?

Harlie, this is not the time or place for that conversation.

It obviously affected you last night or you would not have been so distant. I was not going to drop the issue.

He sighed, *The General gave the order.*

Did you agree with it?

At the time, yes. Have I asked for it to be lifted? No. Should I have? I am beginning to wonder.

I turned to look at him. *Do you know what it felt like to see those clips on that screen? To see what is going on in America and not having a clue as to when it got that way? It was bad when we fled, but what was on the news was much worse. And then having to spend the night wondering what else is going on in the rest of the world?*

Haven't you wondered before yesterday?

I thought about it. *At night, when my nightmares wake me...*

He interrupted, *Exactly.*

187

Oh no, he was not going to get away with pinning this issue on my well being, on his desire to protect me. If he meant for that to be a conversation stopper, he was in for a lesson.

Why did you react the way you did? Why back away from me? Why the silence?

Harlie, there is a lot of pressure on us to complete this mission successfully. At that moment, realizing you had seen what we all had been trying to protect you from, it made me think less about the mission and more about you. That cannot happen.

He did not give me a moment to reply. *Quite a few factors played into my silence. I thought you would be angry with me. You seemed so close to accepting me as a friend and not just as your commanding officer. I became angry with myself, partly because you had found out here in the field, where I could not explain right away, and in part because I had not removed the order beforehand. Also, bringing you into Balboa, a place where I had failed before, played a part. I had to distance myself until we were out of there.*

He stopped long enough for me to reply, *I was angry, James. However, I did not know who to be angry with at that time. All I wanted was answers as to why this team, the one you say we are supposedly all equals on, keeps trying to protect me from reality. How can we be equals when this order is in place?*

His eyes closed, and his head moved slowly from side to side. *While I can see the situation from your point of view, try to see it from ours.*

"No." I spoke out loud. "I am not going to be open-minded on this, try again."

Now he was angry, I could see it flash in his eyes. Rick turned to look at us. Skull smirked but kept driving, while Mitch shifted uncomfortably in his seat and rustled some of the maps. For a moment, I was afraid that there would be a scene. However, James turned and faced the window, brooding.

There was silence in the van as we continued our journey. We ate lunch while driving, pulling over only for a silent fuel and bathroom break. Rick grabbed my hand and squeezed it quickly when we stopped but did not speak. As we were gathering back at the van, James ordered Rick to drive, then motioned for me to go to the back seat again. The rest understood.

I faced the window and waited, unsure about what he was planning.

I'm sorry.

In my surprise, I turned towards him.

The order will be lifted as soon as we return to the bunker. I will talk to The General about it. You are right about it not making you equal with the rest of the team. He clenched his fists and I leaned away. He noticed the movement and his hands relaxed again. *It's not towards you, Harlie. Please, do not be afraid of me.*

Who is it towards then?

He turned away for a moment. *Myself.*

Then it might as well be towards me because I caused you to feel that way.

Why do you keep doing that? I could hear his frustration.

Doing what?

Trying to alleviate another persons' pain by either changing your own behavior or taking the issue onto yourself. Your file is full of examples, and now you are doing that here on the team. He stared hard at me, a hint of "That Look" playing on the fringe.

I shrugged. *It's just the way I am, James. I hate to see anyone suffering, especially if I have a part in that pain.*

Sometimes I wish you wouldn't be. This is the kind of pain and anger a person can learn from.

How so? I tilted my head.

I've learned about how narrow-minded we were about having you on media blackout. I've also seen just how close you were to accepting me and now I'll have to start over again. He was trying to hold the pain back from his mental voice, but it could still be heard.

I sat in silence, quickly going over the conversation I had with Rick last night and processing my own feelings on that issue. The pain from his voice was now noticeable on his face, but I could not let that affect my decision.

No, James, you will not have to start over again.

A small smile lit his face and Rick turned to see what the change in emotional atmosphere was about.

"Looks like the two of you are done fighting." He smirked.

"We weren't fighting." James and I both said at the same time.

Mitch chuckled, "Ha! You might have hidden the conversation from us, but you forgot about the body language. You were fighting."

Skull couldn't be left out, "Who won?"

James looked at me and winked, "Strangely enough, she did."

"That's not strange. I expected it with the all the attitude she keeps hidden from most of us. She probably hit you with every trick in the book." Rick smiled at me.

James turned serious, "Actually, it was her determination to be honest that won."

The other three shrugged and the hours rolled by without further incident. At dusk, we made it to our destination. It was a tiny town that was popular with hikers and tourists. There was a proper motel but also a hostel. Mitch had called the hostel and told them we would be coming and made arrangements for us to leave the van there for the duration of our supposed trip.

The woman in charge of the hostel was called Tinka and was very sweet. We were allowed to clean up and her children helped make a late evening meal for us. When Mitch had spoken with her earlier, she had asked if he could pick up supplies she had ordered from the city. Mitch took it a few steps further by paying off her balance there and adding a few more items. She was overjoyed at our generosity and we had a great evening around a fire ring, listening to the legends of the area.

As sleep was taking me, I heard James ask, *You still did not tell me what you saw last night.*

I sent back a mental grumble. *Goodnight, James.*

There were nightmares that night, but I was able to stay asleep and managed to not scream.

THE JUNGLE

Somewhere in my past, I had wondered what it would be like to see a real jungle. Now, I was hiking into one, and it was astonishing. I wanted so bad to stop and look at everything around me, to touch and smell and experience more of it. We had a deadline, though, and it was a two-day hike to where we needed to be. I had to experience it while on the move.

We were on a fairly visible trail for the first five hours. The animals seemed to understand that they were safe. There were parrots high up in the trees, and we saw or heard an occasional Capuchin monkey. When we stopped for water, Skull found a tree frog and motioned for me to see it. My face must have betrayed my awe because, at one point or another, each member had smiled or laughed quietly after glancing at me.

The terrain was tough, but since we were all in excellent physical condition, we made good time up into the mountainous area. There was very little conversation, and by mid-afternoon, we had left the main trail and gone off into more dense foliage. Skull had purchased a machete but only used it if absolutely necessary. We did not want to make an obvious path. Despite the rough terrain, thanks to frequent checks on the pocket GPS and sheer determination, we made it to our first goal early. I thought we should press on, but James called a stop and we set up camp.

We set up on the banks of a stream, so less had to be cleared out and the sandy soil made it easier to cover our imprints. I started cooking a hot meal using a back-country burner while the men set up the tents and equipment. Rick brought me water for the small filter we had and, before darkness fell, dinner was ready. I made pan bread with dried fruit and grains as well as re-hydrated vegetable and beans. We had prepackaged camp meals, but tonight time was on our side and we enjoyed the home-cooking.

As it became dark, reality hit. While I had been accepted as one of the team, this was the first time that we all had to spend a night in close quarters. I was pondering all the issues it could bring up when Rick came to my rescue.

"Boss, do you remember when Bruce first came to us? How she demanded we go off and "be men" while she dressed, and how she insisted on sleeping against the tent wall so only one of us was next to her?"

Skull laughed, "Now she doesn't care at all."

James nodded and tried not to smile. "I've got the late watch. Jaws, why don't you take up position next to Bear tonight?" We took turns staying up to guard the camp. The first shift person took a position close to the tent entrance. The second shift person would sleep in the equipment tent.

"Sounds good… Also, we have the stream here too, so we can clean up a little before breaking camp as well. It's possible that we will not have access to that kind of water again."

We finished cleaning up from the meal and setting up for the next day. After placing the mosquito netting, we climbed into our bags and tried to sleep. Before I could relax though, there was a tap on my shield.

Are you going to tell me tonight, Harlie?
No, James.
I'm proud of how you handled today.
Today was easy. I know that the hard stuff is yet to come.

I could feel his agreement more than hear it.

The next morning, we washed our arms, legs and faces in the stream, filtered more water, had a breakfast of energy bars and some fruit Tinka gave us, and were back hiking in short order. Our progress was much slower as we were now completely off any kind of trail. We needed to stay as hidden as possible and knew the area trails were most likely being watched. Our story was that we had misinterpreted a map and had gotten lost. So long as whoever found us did not look too deeply into our bags, the story would hold up.

Again, the conversation was kept to a minimum. For some reason, James stayed closer to me today than he had yesterday. At times, our arms would brush, or he would pause to hold a branch away from me. I quickly sent a mental message to quit with the gentleman act because I was no

192

refined lady. He laughed back and let a branch snap into my shoulder.

As the day wore on we moved slower and stopped more often. Mitch was setting up sensors, attaching them to trees we were passing. The one inch around devices would report the movement of any larger creature. Other than humans, the only thing that might set it off would be a jaguar. We actually circled part of the camp by a mile before moving in and setting up. For the first night, half of a circle of sensors had been placed. Two of us would finish in the morning while the rest stayed in the camp.

It was nearly dark when we set up, so dinner was reconstituted meals using water I heated up the back-country burner. There was a stream nearby, but we could hear animals near it and it was too dark to be safe there. Exhausted, we turned in shortly after finishing our meals.

Tonight, I had first watch and Skull had second. I sat where we had placed the burner earlier, the handgun I had been carrying since Balboa positioned next to me. Unlike last night, when I was inside and feeling somewhat secure, now I was sitting in the middle of the two tents in the middle of a jungle. The only light was a dim glow from the sheltered equipment. That secure feeling was gone. I listened to the unfamiliar world around me, trying to make sense of each sound. The insects out here were incredibly loud and, from the few I saw scurrying by, incredibly big too – like big as my hand. As the hours slipped by, I taught myself to pick out certain sounds. If I could learn what was normal here, then it would be easier to pick up what could be a threat. I was picking up the sounds of something four-legged and obviously nocturnal when there was a small beep from the equipment tent. The hours had passed quickly, and it was Skulls turn now.

It was difficult to fall asleep after that. My mind refused to tune out the sounds, and when I could finally get my eyes to close, scenes and feelings from Balboa flashed through my mind. The hours passed slowly, and I slept little. Come morning, it was harder to get up and moving again, but it had to be done. Fortunately, Skull had decided to make breakfast and there were reconstituted eggs and coffee ready.

After a couple of cups, I started to feel a bit more like myself and helped Mitch and James get ready to place the other sensors. Skull, Rick, and I would continue to set up the camp, including the rest of the electronics needed to complete our mission.

It was tedious work to put together the pieces of equipment, and we spent most of the morning hunched over various projects. Skull registered each new sensor as they were placed and activated. The transmission receiver was turned on, and Rick started scanning the airwaves for any information. I set up the small radio transceiver and even smaller earpieces for it. Each of us would be wearing one whenever we had to leave the camp, even to go relieve ourselves. The guys were quick to share stories about some experiences in that department, and I shuddered.

The jungle really heated up in the afternoon, even under all the trees. Until living it first-hand, I had no idea that humidity levels could really get so high that you could see water droplets hanging in midair. The insects were hungry and tried hard to make us the main course. Along with the mosquito netting, the team had brought along a couple bottles of a special repellent to spray around the camp. Combined with the repellent we wore, not many insects were able to feast on us. Skull and Rick both had small battery powered fans and we set those out to make a slight cross-breeze. As they rested and talked, I took out the maps and recon information to study again.

James and Mitch returned around sixteen hundred. I started making dinner shortly after their arrival. Tonight, it was pasta and sauce made from a powdered mix. There was barely enough food to last the entire time here, so plans were made to start looking for edibles inside the sensor range. Hunting had been something I had always shied away from but had learned to do out of desperation back in America. With enough seasonings, most any animal can be made palatable. James and Rick could both identify safe foods, so we decided to search in two teams tomorrow. One team would stay in camp, listening to the receiver and watching the sensors. The other would go out in one direction, hunt and then circle back to the stream to wash up at noon. Once they returned, the second group would go out in the other direction.

James had first watch and Rick had second. When sleeping bags were set up, I noticed that James had placed his next to mine. I thought it would make me uncomfortable but soon discovered that it really did not bother me that much. Next to Rick, I was closer to him than the other two here. Besides, I was hoping to be long into sleep before his shift ended and made sure of it by taking a sleeping pill.

James, however, was either bored or feeling chatty. It is difficult to unwind when someone is nagging you.

Harlie, I still want to know what you saw and sensed.

I sighed and rolled over to face the sidewall of the tent. *I did not sleep well last night, James. Can we please go over this another time?*

Just show me, don't use words.

It takes too much focus.

He stood up, moved so he was on the other side of the tent wall and sat back down again. "Please." He whispered aloud.

Why are you so interested? You saw and sensed it too.

Yes, but I've been at this a lot longer than you. He paused and dropped his shield. Sighing, I did the same and showed him my experiences from the night in Balboa, holding back on the emotions concerning him.

It's how I imagined a place like that would be, but sensing made it much worse.

I wanted to add how it was nothing I could not handle but knew that would be a lie. The truth was, the images were constantly in my mind, blurring together with ones from America and then the refugee camp.

The sleeping medication was kicking in and it was harder to focus. I raised my shield and felt him do the same.

The next thing I knew the sun was coming up. I had slept in the same position all night, so my muscles were a bit stiff. Rolling over slowly, I opened my eyes. James' eyes were already open and looking right at me. I could see several emotions flicker through them before he smiled.

Good morning, looks like you slept well.

My mind seemed a bit fuzzy, but I smiled back. After a careful stretch and slight grimace at the stiffness, I sat up and

195

started the day.

Rick, Mitch, and I were the first team to go out hunting for edibles. James and Skull stayed behind to monitor the channels. Since we would be following the nearby stream for a time, we each took a change of clothes and items to wash up with. We were about a half mile out before Rick noticed some edible roots that we were able to dig up. At the stream bed we quickly found sticks that were whittled into makeshift spears. Mine did not come out so well, but since Rick and Mitch had more experience, they finished in no time.

"Bear, we are going to go downstream a bit while you clean up. Come to us when you're finished." Rick smiled gently. I was very grateful that he and Mitch were giving me some privacy. I knew there would be times when it would not be possible.

After washing up in the cool water and changing my clothes, I joined up with them. They had also cleaned up and were waiting for me, fishing spears in hand. As we followed the stream, I spotted a few plantain trees. Mitch shocked me by climbing right up and cutting down a large bunch.

"These are about ripe too!" Mitch called out as he jumped down from about halfway.

We stopped soon after to fill the water jugs we carried along and tried to spear fish – with very little luck. When we returned to the camp, it was with only two fish. Hopefully, the other group would have more luck. They took our spears along to save more time.

The afternoon went quickly with Rick monitoring and translating increased transmissions from the enemy camp. It sounded like the package we had learned about had left Panama City and was en route. We used our GPS unit and other devices to trace out the probable paths they would take. As I was scanning through radio frequencies, an alarm came across in a weather report. There was a tropical depression coming through tonight and tomorrow. While we had experienced several brief showers since our arrival, this would be something more dramatic. Mitch set about making sure the tents were secure and laid out a larger tarp to run between them. I ran all the water we brought through the filter and into a larger, collapsible container.

The second team had much more luck with fishing than we did. As soon as James was within reception range for our skills, he bragged about the seven fish they caught. I replied that they better already be cleaned, because I was not about to leave the camp and get eaten alive doing their dirty work. He laughed, but the fish arrived cleaned and ready for the small, low-smoke fire we made.

"Better make sure the ration packs are handy for tomorrow." Mitch commented in between bites of roasted plantain and fish.

"Are we prepared to move out in the rain if something comes up?" I asked.

"Very good question, Bear," James smiled. "We have ponchos, guns, rations, med-kits and water packs. Let's get them next to the door of the tent. We might have two days until action, we might not. Best be ready to move out at a moments' notice."

Skull laughed quietly, "She is one of us for sure."

The rest of the evening was filled with preparations for the upcoming days. I had second shift so, after moving my sleeping bag into the equipment tent, I went back to the main group to see if anything else needed to be finished up. Rick was at the remnants of the fire and looked up at my approach.

"We are ready, Bear, you should get some sleep."

James came from the inside of the main tent, "He's right. You have done a lot today. Your head is probably hurting from the incoming storm so try to rest."

My head was starting to throb from the dropping barometric pressure. I nodded to each of them in turn and retired to the equipment tent. After checking the electronics one more time, I curled up in the bag, put the mosquito net in place and tried to sleep.

The rains came as second shift began. My head was pounding at this point, and it was hard to focus on the world around me, but I mentally scanned the area – lingering on the sleeping minds in the tent. The extra tarp helped to keep out some of the rain, but when the wind picked up, things started to get wet. To protect the non-electric equipment, I moved everything into the second tent and zipped up the flap until I could just see out. The rest of the night passed slowly, and

197

come morning, I was wet and chilled, but the equipment was dry.

There had been several transmissions during the night, but none with the key phrases Rick had made me memorize. He listened to the recordings and translated that the transport had been stalled due to the weather. It would be taking an alternate route. The new route would bring it within a mile of our location, on a trail that crossed the river via a raft transport. We had seen the raft on our way in. James got a faraway look in his eye with that information, and I wondered if we would be making a quick, soaking hike back out of here.

He turned towards me, "I wish it were possible, but no. Some of us, however, will be arranging a little surprise for the transport when it reaches the river."

Skull smirked, and Mitch whispered, "Ka-boom."

Rick turned to me, "You'll be staying here."

I scowled.

"It's no big deal; we'll just be blowing up the raft once the transport is on it. Big boom, little to no fire, and some falling debris. Besides, someone has to stay at the camp and monitor transmissions. There is bound to be an increase in activity once we take it out."

"Not like I have any idea what they are saying, and it will all be recorded anyways."

James looked up from the map he was studying. "That will be enough, Bear." His expression and The Commander in his tone was enough to silence me.

The team worked all day on their plans to blow up the raft while the transport was on it. Mitch and Skull assembled the bombs and detonators while Rick continued to monitor transmissions. It was pouring down rain, so I stayed mostly in the tents, feeling useless. We ate lunch from our stack of self-heating rations and afterward, James came over to talk.

"Have you been looking out?"

"Yes, and there is nothing human out there."

"I get nothing as well. So, we are yet undetected." He picked up a small stick and started snapping it into smaller pieces. "Are you feeling a bit left out right now?"

My brief nod was all the response I dared to give.

"Remember, you are still new, and this is your first

long mission. As you get experienced you'll be more and more involved."

I nodded again, not trusting the right words to come out.

He said nothing more, but he did not leave the tent either. Instead, he continued to sit and make pictures with the stick pieces. I watched, but still did not speak – there just did not seem to be a reason for saying anything.

After a time, James left the tent. I followed soon after and ended up helping Rick with some of the equipment. The rain stopped in the early evening, so cooking dinner became my priority. After the meal, the guys stayed by the fire and started sharing stories from their past. Sometimes it was events that happened while they were on the team, and other stories were from their time before. I listened intently but continued to stay quiet. It annoyed Skull.

"Bear, are you really listening or just randomly nodding and making faces?"

"I'm listening," was my quiet response.

"You should speak up. Tell us a tale, and make it a good one."

I gazed at our small fire to stop my first instinct, which was to lower my eyes and head. "There isn't much to tell, at least nothing that is exciting."

Skull looked like he was going to pout. I felt a little remorse for my response but really did not think anything could compare to the stories they were telling.

The evening passed into night, and it was Rick who put an end to the sharing by waving us off into the main tent. He had volunteered for second watch tonight in order to keep a careful ear out for trouble. James had put his sleeping bed next to mine again, and I hoped it would not be much different having him there all night as it was when he had first watch.

As with the last time, he seemed to feel the need to say something. And, just as he had for most of the mission, no one else was going to witness the conversation.

Harlie?

We were both laying facing up. Me with my hands folded on my stomach and James with his hands behind his head. Mitch was facing the far wall.

Yes, James?

Why are you not talking? Are you still upset about tomorrow's assignment? There was a hint of disappointment in his mental voice.

I turned my head to face him. *I did not have anything to say and sometimes a person just feels like being quiet.*

The disappointment faded, *About tomorrow...* He turned to face me. Our close proximity inside the tent caused me to feel like I had to catch my breath. James continued with just the slightest hesitation. *Don't move from the receiver and transmitter, as we will be wearing the earpieces. Listen for the play-by-play; Mitch said he will keep you informed. You'll need to be armed as well, especially since we will be a mile away and our abilities cannot go that far.*

I nodded.

He smiled gently. *Are you nervous about being out here alone?*

I won't really be alone.

He opened the window into his mind and I could feel a wave of emotions, comforting, calming, his pride towards me, his happiness that I had accepted him as a friend, and hope for tomorrow.

As far as I am concerned, you will never be alone again.

The next morning was so humid it was hard to breathe. The guys were packed and on their way shortly after dawn. I sat in the equipment tent, turned one of the fans on and waited. Once the team arrived at the river, Mitch began dictating what was happening. His dry sense of humor was at its peak, and I could not help but laugh at the mental pictures he was creating. He and Rick had crossed over at a shallow spot farther upriver and ran a line between them and the other side. The explosives were sent over and Mitch attached them in between the floater logs. Those would be detonated remotely. On the other bank, James and Skull set up a small claymore that would be set off remotely as well. They then cleared their tracks. Mitch made it sound like a song and dance versus setting up devices that could very well be deadly.

It was two hours later that the hired delivery team arrived. According to Mitch, there were ten men. Four rode in an old jeep and the other six walked in front and behind. Mitch waited until they were halfway across the river before detonating the bomb. I heard the blast and said a prayer for those I knew could not have survived it.

The radio was strangely silent for around seven minutes, then there was a series of questions, followed by louder and more urgent questions. It went silent again, and I sat, waiting and wishing I could translate what had been said. Ninety minutes later, one of the sensors we had placed on the way in went off. I pressed the talk button on my headset and Rick picked up.

"We have a target, coming in from west south-west."

"Confirm, target coming west south-west."

While waiting for the next closest sensor to go off, I started scanning the area using my abilities. Once the next sensor blinked, I contacted the team again. They were sifting through the debris, tying up the survivors, and decided to wait until the last moment before taking cover again.

Twenty minutes later, everything changed. The incoming enemy was just within my range when I noticed a dark spot. At first, I was confused, but realization quickly came to me. I focused on the dark spot, and it was moving along with the others. Was it possible? Was this something James knew about but did not tell me? Who was out there?

Answers came quickly. I felt pressure on my mental shield. The pressure got stronger, but the shield held. Suddenly, an emotion flashed at me. It was curiosity. Then an image of question marks.

I risked making contact, *Who are you?*

There was a long pause. *You....not...old...mind.*

Whoever was out there, they did not seem used to communicating mentally, especially with using words. The mental voice sounded young. I quickly reflected on that. James mental voice sounds like his own physical one, so this person might be as young as his voice.

Old mind? I dared to ask.

The image of a question mark came at me again. The other minds were still as if they were all holding their breath.

Keeping with our cover story and remembering the diplomatic tactics I had been studying, I answered. *I am a*

201

hiker and got stuck in the storm.

Where....is....old....mind?

I do not know of an old mind. Who are you?

LIES! The scream made me cringe.

I thought quickly. *Not lies, I really do not know. Please, help me understand how you can talk to me like this.*

No! Lies! An image of fire came into my mind with amazing power. It took my breath away. Several long moments passed before I regained enough control to look out again. The enemy group was leaving the way they came and moving quite quickly. I kept as much of a focus as possible until they were outside of sensor range. My head hurt from the new contact and intense work to watch them, the fire image still fresh in my mind. Time seemed to stand still as I processed what a possible empathic on the mastermind's side could mean. I did not hear the beeps of an incoming call on the headset. I could only register the sensor board and my own lost thoughts.

HARLIE! I jumped and nearly screamed out loud at the mental voice.

James, you startled me. I called back.

Why aren't you answering our call?

Oh dear, how was I going to relay what just happened? *There was an incident, but the site is safe.* I hesitated on what to say next. *James, there is more trouble than what we planned. We need to talk.*

There was a pause on his side. *Harlie, are you aware that right now you sound scared?*

I'm not in danger here, James, but yes, I am scared.

I looked at my watch and was surprised to find that thirty minutes had passed since the enemies had left sensor range. It made me uneasy at the thought that I had been so focused that time had passed by so fast. I really should have been more aware.

The team returned within the hour. All of them were carrying pieces from the destroyed transport, presumably what was left of the devices we were sent in to destroy. Mitch and Skull looked quite pleased with themselves while Rick and James were more somber. Rick went into the equipment tent and brought out our mini voice recorders. All of us had been assigned one for longer missions and had used them back in Panama City. We recorded the details of major events so that, when it came time for our official reports, nothing would be forgotten. The others went to separate corners of the camp and started to speak into their devices.

James followed as I walked over to behind the sleeping tent, pressed record and began relaying the events of the day. When I got to the part about the dark spot and first contact with the empath my voice broke. It took four false starts before I could continue.

"I asked mentally who it was and received a reply. The voice sounded young and inexperienced with talking mentally. It sounded confused and said I was not the old mind..."

"WHAT?"

The recorder flew out of my hands and landed on the ground. I jumped as he grabbed my arm and pulled me away from the camp. The fear I had barely squelched came back full force. I tried to plant my feet, but James kept dragging me deeper into the jungle. Once we were out of sight of the camp, he stopped but did not let go of my arm. Instead, he grabbed the other one so that I was facing him.

"Tell me exactly what happened." His voice was quiet but very firm.

I couldn't speak and instead started to shake.

"Bloody...augh!" He let go of my arms, and I sank to the ground. James stood over me for a minute, then knelt down and took my face gently in his hands.

"Bear, please stop shaking. We are still close to the camp; you are still safe."

I tried to still my trembling body. He waited calmly, keeping one hand on my face.

"No." I was able to say at last. "No, we are not safe."

"Bear, tell me what happened." He tapped on my shield, but I could not bring myself to drop it, instead choosing to tell him verbally. When I got to the part where the voice asked about the old mind, he let go of my face and clenched his fists at his side. While I had no idea why I also had no time to think about it. I finished relaying the event, ending with the fire image. James just sat there, completely still and quiet, but his eyes were looking far off.

It took immense effort to not start shaking again. James sighed, took my hand, pulled me up then gently placed his hands on my shoulders. A moment later he raised one hand and gently brushed my hair away from my face. The urge to shake stopped and a small sense of calm started to spread.

"No wonder why you were shaking and scared. That would have upset me as well. But you managed to stay calm during the situation and did exactly what you were supposed to do." His voice was barely above a whisper. "I'm very proud of you."

James let go of me and took a small step back. "You know what we have to do now, don't you?"

I nodded. "The other empathic knows our location. We have to get out of here fast."

James grabbed my hand this time and rushed us back the way we came, stopping only to pick up the discarded recording device.

"We have to pack and head out. Now!" He barked the second we came around the tent.

The rest of the team looked perplexed for just a moment, but then jumped up and started tearing down the camp. In five minutes we had the electronics back into pieces and the bags rolled up. Within fifteen minutes what was in each backpack on the way in was in the same pack for the way out. All of the evidence carried from the transport was placed into plastic bags and then into stuff sacks that Mitch brought. We had hidden the camp well, and there was very little damage to repair. Once the tents were down and back on the frames, we covered up the area as much as possible. In less than an hour we were lined up and ready to head out of the jungle. I had never seen people work as fast as we did.

"Single file, step on step as much as possible until we reach the river." Rick ordered. "We will need to be silent."

It was tough to walk in another person's footsteps quickly, but somehow, I managed. I prayed the whole way to the river that the dark spot would not appear. We grabbed sensors as we walked, hoping the ones left behind would not be found.

At the river, we waded in part-way and walked as

quietly as possible. We would be able to stay in the river for almost two miles before it met up with a different trail than the one we came in on. It took us past the blown transport, and it was there that I hesitated. Skull paused with me.

"We were talking about bringing you down here to see it if no one from the other side arrived. Didn't think it would happen though." He looked somber.

I had to fight off the shaking again. There were three bodies in the river, and I could see a severed arm on the shore. James' shared visions were not as grotesque as the scene before me.

"Keep moving." Rick called calmly.

No one said another word as we continued down the river, guns drawn in case of trouble. Men with weapons were not our only concern. There were large snakes in the river and possibly other carnivorous creatures. Skull kept checking the hand-held GPS to make sure we did not miss the trail.

Back on the trail, the high humidity kept us from drying out much, but we pressed on. It was nightfall, and Mitch grabbed water and energy bars from my pack and handed them out as we walked. Skull was in the lead with the lantern, and the rest of us followed close. The thick undergrowth hid parts of the path, and branches stuck out at all levels. We were still walking single file and step in step as much as possible – hiking through the night, rarely stopping. After midnight, it was becoming harder and harder to keep up. I just did not have the stamina that the others had. I stumbled several times, and Rick slowed down to help me along.

"I'm sorry." I whispered.

"It's okay. You are doing fine." He whispered back.

We stopped right before daylight and rested for an hour, then made the rest of the trip out. It was around noon when we arrived back at the hostel. Our gracious host, Tinka, was a bit shocked at our early arrival and even more shocked at our appearances after the all-night hike. James pulled her aside and talked quietly with her while we loaded up the van. Even though it had been over thirty hours since any of us had slept, the decision was made to keep moving. All of us took turns driving while the others finished their recordings and started to plan the next steps. We drove for five more hours before checking into a motel at a decent size town.

James decided to park the van at another location nearby, so we made sure it was completely empty. Rick thought we should stay in just two rooms and wait until we were back in Panama City before spreading out again. The rest of the team agreed, including James, who immediately announced he and I would be sharing a room. I hoped that Rick would speak up and it would be the three of us, but he remained silent. We placed our frames and packs into our rooms and then met up in front of the second one.

James spoke, sounding like The Commander "Since we have minimal information on this area, we should play it safe and eat from the packs."

While I gave no outward indication, mentally I groaned. Mitch went into the room and came out with five meals. Each of us carried four and we had used the ones in my pack first plus one of Rick's. We looked around to make sure the meals would not bring too much attention to ourselves and sat back down. As we started the heating process, I made a face.

"What's wrong, Bear, the instant heat-and-eats not to your liking?" Skull asked sarcastically.

Exhausted but hungry, I turned on him. "Skull, I spent seven months of my life eating some pathetic form of MRE nearly every day. Forgive me for making a face at the thoughts of choking down the memories along with the food." James and Rick grinned when Skull mumbled an apology, along with something along the lines of getting his head bit off.

After the meal, we retired to our rooms for much-needed showers and sleep. The moment James and I were inside, I became very nervous. How was I supposed to act around him? He was my commanding officer. He also had repeatedly said that he wanted more than to be just my commanding officer. He wanted to be friends. Before all of that, he was my rescuer. It was easier to share a room with Rick. Rick was, well, he was just Rick. Always seeming to say and do the right thing, there when I need him, quickly becoming a good friend, Rick.

James threw his pack onto the bed by the window and started rummaging for a set of clean clothes along with his

206

personal bag. I followed his actions, pulling out all I had left that was clean, my own bag of personals, and a tiny notepad I had brought along.

"Will we need to set up any of the equipment?" I asked, trying to remain business-like.

James turned to look at me, "Rick will set the receiver up in case they get close to us. Other than that, just keep the clip in the gun."

I nodded, then took the gun out of its holster and placed it on the end table. It felt weird to not have it on my hip after so many hours of carrying. I had been sleeping with it next to the pillow and everything.

Unsure of what to do next, I stood and looked out mentally. James saw my expression.

"Nothing out there." He pointed to the bathroom, "Ladies first."

The shower water was barely warm but felt good anyway. It was nice to be able to clean up properly. The fresh clothes felt good as well. James smiled as I walked back into the main room to get my hairbrush.

"Feel better?"

I nodded again.

He got up from his bed, picked up what was needed and took his turn. I picked up the notepad and started sketching pictures and phrases that were in my mind. It's something I had done for years. After a few minutes, I started to feel the effects of nearly two days without sleep. Not sure if it was alright to pass out, I stood up and went to the sink mirror. There were scratches and insect bites on my face and arms. We each carried a small first-aid kit, and I was applying a little packet of ointment to the scratches when James exited the bathroom.

I must have tensed up, and he must have seen it. He came over, gently took the packet from my hand, placed it on the end table, then moved to stand very close to me.

"Bear, Harlie, I'm just James, not The Commander, not here. We are all working together in this." His voice was low and calm.

I nodded.

He frowned, "I'm starting to grow weary of that

response."

There was an uncomfortable silence as I tried to think through what to do.

Please say something. He prodded.

The silence continued as I thought of what to say. Although I contemplated trying to end the issue with a simple "okay," I decided on something closer to the truth.

"Sometimes," I spoke just as low, and hopefully just as calmly. "I need time to think things through before replying. There is still so much that's new. Sometimes, there really isn't anything to say or worth saying."

His eyes narrowed ever so slightly, "So which was it?"

There was a hesitation in my answer, "The first."

James head tilted to the side, "Why?"

I did not want to go into details, did not want to give away any of my hidden emotions and fears. I slowly turned to face him and took a step back to give myself more room to breathe and think.

"James, it has been over 45 hours since we have experienced anything close to sleep. Can it wait until I am functioning on more than a few brain cells?"

It was very subtle, so subtle that, if I had not been looking into his eyes, it would have been missed. "That Look" was there and, once again, I wondered what he was thinking when he looked at me that way.

"Yes," He finally muttered. "It can wait. There are more important things, more urgent issues to address once we have rested." He turned away and moved to turn down the covers on his bed.

I had nightmares, fierce ones, fire-filled ones. Nightmares of a young voice laughing and flames coming at me over and over. I was running through the devastation of Washington, D.C., the rubble of the Lincoln Memorial, the hole where the White House and National Mall had been, the damaged buildings all around. Before we had left the United States, I had seen some of it from the plane and the rest in pictures before the media had been cut off. In my dreams, it was even more vivid. No matter how fast I ran, the laughter and the flames kept catching up to me. Then there was an explosion right in front of me.

I bolted upright, awaking in the middle of a choked scream. It seemed to take an eternity to catch my breath and slow down my heart. As I was calming down, memories of where I was and who was in the room came to the front of my mind. Mentally swearing, I turned to look at the other bed. James was propped up on the pillows, sitting with his back to the wall, watching me. I held my breath, trying desperately not to panic, but remembering our past conversations about my nightmares.

Standing up and walking towards the sink, his eyes followed my every move. Although it was futile, I wished that this room was just mine, so I could pace the bad feelings off. James was still watching as I washed my face, walked back to the bed and propped myself up the same way he had. Staring straight ahead, I tried to calm my thoughts enough, but he continued to stare.

"What scared you so much?" James finally asked.

I told him as much of the nightmare as I dared to.

"We do need to be concerned," he agreed, "About the existence of an empathic on the enemy's front. It will make our job much more difficult." He sighed, and I could feel the weight of the discovery as well.

"You need to rest," He told me while laying back down.

"You do too." I stayed in my current position against the wall, hoping he would doze off before me.

"Not until you are asleep." He turned so that he was laying on his back and looked at the ceiling. Placing his hands behind his head, he continued. "But, you are not ready to sleep again. The nightmare is too fresh."

I froze, knowing he was right and guessing at where the conversation was leading. Still staring at the ceiling, he kept on speaking. "I can guess where your thoughts are taking you. And yes, I did say that if you awoke screaming in the bunker that I would come into the room for a late-night lesson on how to help calm the dreams." In the darkness, one fist started to clench, and he paused, "But I am leaving it up to you." His head turned and pinned me with a stare that looked like pleading. "If you want me to show you, to help you, then I will – but you must ask."

209

I stared back at him, comprehending what it took for him to give me a choice like that. As much as I hated the dreams, hated to medicate in order to get a decent night's sleep, I did not want to appear weak and ask him right away. Slowly, I turned my head to face forward again.

"Thank you, Jamyson, for giving me the choice." My voice was barely a whisper.

He just nodded.

It took nearly an hour for me to fall back asleep. Thankfully, the two days it took to get us out of the jungle caught up with me. The sleep was deep and nearly dreamless. Daylight came and, though my body said it needed more time in bed, my mind knew the facts and was active. After a food bar and water, we gathered in the other room and worked on plans.

Rick and Mitch had come to the conclusion that the only way we were going to get out of Panama safely was through military extraction. While we had notified them of our presence in the country, no one had thought we would require a pick-up. The issue was with the evidence we carried out of the jungle. It would be impossible to hide it enough to get onto a commercial airplane. James agreed with them and the decision was made to contact the U.N. forces once we were back in Panama City. I went to get the van, Mitch checked it over for tracking devices, and we were back on the road.

It was a quiet trip. The driver and one other were awake and keeping a look-out while the other three slept. We arrived in Panama City in the early afternoon and quickly found two hotels to stay at. I was surprised when we kept the same arrangements, thinking that it would have made more sense for James and me to use our abilities to keep track of each group. There was little time to question it though. James immediately activated his phone and started calling the proper channels to get us out. Since we were in a larger hotel, I was able to order room service, and we stuffed ourselves on the meals. Other than that, there wasn't much for me to do.

At dusk, he called the rest of our group to meet us. I was surprised when they came into the room, followed by Dara, Jason, Ryan, and Max. Their job must have been to find the rest of the team. As we settled onto the beds and chairs,

James updated us on the situation.

"The United Nations presence should be able to take us out of Panama and fly us home within three days. We will not have an exact time, so be ready to ride at a moment's notice." He looked around at all of us. "They picked up on an unusual transmission for medical assistance out in the region we just left. It happened while we were hiking out. Now that they know what it was about, they are sending their own men to scout out the area."

James turned to Dara, "Was your mission successful?"

I looked at her and noticed she had a bruise on her cheek. Switching my gaze to Max, I saw he had a bandage wrapped around his knuckles.

"Yes, Commander. We were able to find the members of that particular drug cartel and eliminate them. As suspected, they were smuggling chemicals for homemade bombs as well as drugs. Root and I had to go one-on-one with a few and that is where the minor injuries come from."

Max smiled, "It felt great to punch the dude who shot us last time."

"I'm sure it did." James mumbled, and I wondered if he wished it were him who threw the punch.

He looked at all of us again, "We will need to lay low until the extraction, only essential contact and no face to face meetings. Be ready to go but enjoy the moment to rest." He shook his head sadly, "Who knows when our next real break will be. Dismissed."

There were a few moments of shaking hands and a couple of hugs before we separated. Then they were all gone, and it was just James and me. I looked around the hotel room and sighed.

"It's not that bad, Bear." He spoke softly. "At least we have a microwave and refrigerator in here. No rations."

"Why are we sharing again? It makes more sense for us to split up so there can be contact between the groups."

"Right now, we do not know who is listening. Calling out across a distance is too risky. Even though we were not followed, the original contacts are here and the empathic may be on the way."

"Oh." I suddenly felt stupid and struggled keep myself

from looking down.

James walked up to where I was mentally kicking myself and waited until I looked at him. "Remember, you are still learning. This world is still very new to you."

The attempt to make me feel better fell on deaf ears. "I should have remembered the contacts here. The empathic could easily meet up with them and search for us."

"It's okay." He searched my face. "We both are still sleep deprived. Let's call it a night and we'll talk more in the morning."

THE OTHERS

The next morning, we ordered a large breakfast via room service, and then I gathered our dirty clothes for a trip to the guest laundry room. If we had still been in the jungle, the river would have been our washing machine and time would be the dryer. James went to the small convenience shop on the main level before joining me. He brought down two snack bags of chips and two sodas. He also brought a weekly news magazine.

At my questioning expression he responded with, "Commander's prerogative, the ban was lifted at midnight. Read it over and I'll answer your questions as best I can."

I looked at the cover of the magazine. It was a hand-drawn map of California, Oregon, and Washington, with factory symbols, city labels and tent symbols all over it.

"I'm almost afraid to." I whispered.

He looked grim but said nothing.

I read the main article and fought back tears. When the attack first happened, many countries came to America's call. Europe had set up camps and helped maintain farms, so we could feed the masses. Middle Eastern countries had amazingly cut the price of oil for the first six months. China had set up refugee camps up and down the west coast. Japan, Russia, and Australia had made supply drops all across the nation. All of that I remembered hearing about.

But then there was the media blackout, and for a long time, no one knew what was going on. Now, I was finding out. China had called in the massive debt we owed them, and since the United States could not pay up, it had to make a horrible decision. What was left of the leadership "rented out" California, Oregon, and Washington. The Chinese took over the government of those three states. They signed a treaty to maintain rights given under the Constitution, but now it seemed that it was not being enforced. Those in the refugee camps were hired out to build or remodel factories and then made to work there. First, they were paid in dollars, but recently the Chinese changed it to the Waun. That meant the

213

workers could only spend their pathetically low pay at certain stores and those stores were very overpriced. As the situations in those states became worse, more and more people who had been able to avoid the camps were having to work for the Chinese just to make ends meet. The schools were forced to teach Chinese, and the major surviving corporations had to have a certain percent of Chinese nationals in management. The riots I had seen on the television were of this deteriorating situation on the west coast of America.

The next article was about how the United States was trying to call in debts from other countries in order to pay off China quicker. The government was still too shaky to demand anything though. There was very little military presence available to enforce anything. Central America had a sudden influx of its own people racing back across the border, those who had come over legally or illegally. Its own resources were stretched, and chaos was breaking out. African nations could only lessen their demands for imported food. It was a useless endeavor. I looked up at James, and he reached over to put his arm gently around my shoulder.

"That's some of what we were trying to protect you from. The General thought it would be better if you did not know those things as you were adjusting to your new life."

"Those poor people," A tear slipped down my cheek. "They are little more than slaves right now. They could be friends or family too; we lost track of so many..." My voice trailed off.

"I know, Bear, I know. The North American team has been doing what they can, but the best we can do is to try to prevent this tragedy from ever happening again. Just like with the rescue of you and Jack, some have been taken from there to work for us. Others have been taken in well-planned group rescues and brought into Canada or Australia through our connections there." He smiled, "Other groups are doing the same thing. We are helping to rebuild, bit by bit."

I just nodded, it would be better to not say anything. I missed my family, missed Gareth, and missed my old life of homesteading, where the evils of the world seemed so far away. It all seemed so long ago and so terribly distant. James and I sat there, lost in thought until the clothes were dry.

214

Back in the room, James turned on the television and found a news station with English subtitles. I tried to watch as we folded the clothes and rearranged our packs. We set them up for easy access to outfits and personal supplies but still ready for us to leave instantly. I could only take a few minutes of the anchor droning on about something wrong that someone in power had said before picking up the remote and turning it off.

"I've seen enough for the first day."

"That's fine. Give yourself time to process what you have learned." Then he grinned wickedly. "What are you going to do instead?"

Thinking quickly, I walked over to the alarm clock and turned on the built-in radio. It took just a moment to find a station playing decent music and a moment longer to prop myself up on the bed.

"I was hoping you would be agreeable to just switching to another television channel." The grin faded.

"Anything other than the news would be too far from reality and most likely stupid."

"Not true, there are documentaries."

Rolling my eyes and sighing at the same time, I made the compromise. "You find a documentary that has nothing to do with war and I'll watch it."

We ended up watching an educational special on the Dead Sea Scrolls and spent the rest of the morning debating what was said during it. After lunch, the heat and humidity were leaking into the room – despite the air conditioner. James decided that we should check out the hotel's exercise room and the next few hours were used up on treadmills, rowing machines, resistance training benches and exercise cycles. We were both hot and sweaty once finished and took turns with showers before settling down to rest before the evening meal.

"We should go to the restaurant here for dinner." James suggested. "I bet it would be a grand meal."

"Perhaps. But aren't we supposed to be laying low until extraction?"

"Yes, but it's not as if we are leaving the hotel." He looked hopeful.

A proper meal in a proper setting did sound a lot better

than another room service meal. Besides, I told myself, the staff might think it suspicious if all we did was order in.

"Okay. You win."

"Excellent!" He beamed.

The restaurant was indeed quite nice, and the food was wonderful. I ordered a mixed seafood dish with crab cake, shrimp, and scallops. James had steak with a mushroom topping. We chatted about different restaurants we had been to and the strangest foods we had tried.

As we settled back into the hotel room, James came over to me. "Thank you. I really enjoyed that and hope you did as well."

I nodded, then added, "I enjoyed it. It was nice to do something pleasant after the last couple of weeks." We found another documentary to watch and then went to bed early.

When James had not heard anything from the United Nations by breakfast, we set up for another day at the hotel. We worked out in the exercise room for two hours then went back upstairs. I sat on the bed and started sketching while he made a phone call.

When finished with the call, he turned to me and grinned. "I have an idea for something we can do."

"You know, I'm beginning to grow concerned when you start smiling like that."

He laughed and sat next to me on the bed. I stopped sketching and turned to him.

He stared at me for several moments and seemed to be contemplating what to say. "You still know hardly anything about me or the rest of the team," he started. "You cannot tell me that you aren't curious about us. While I can only answer for them with facts from their personal files, I'm right here and can answer for myself."

It was an interesting proposition. Indeed, I had been curious about my counterparts since the beginning – but figured eventually their files would be sent to me, like mine had been sent to them. Finding out it was not the case had disturbed me, but there was little that could be done. I turned to stare straight ahead. It was the person sitting next to me right now whom I was the most curious about.

"Okay, I'm game." I turned back to him.

216

He tucked his knees to his chest and glanced over at me, "Would it be alright if I asked a few of you as well?"

"I guess, but isn't it all in my file? You seem to have a book on my life."

James rolled his eyes then looked my way again, "No. Strange as it might seem to you, there is quite a bit missing."

It was my turn for dramatic expressions, "I doubt that but will pretend to believe you. So, who is going to start this round of Twenty Questions?"

"You."

The rest of the day was spent learning about the team. In order to not make it obvious where my real interest was, I asked about other team members first.

Dara came from the American/Canadian border. Her mother was Canadian, and her father was American. She lived in both worlds, but chose to be a United States Marine and, because of her martial arts training, ended up on a Special Forces team. She married a serviceman but the marriage only lasted nineteen months. During her fifth year in the service, she was critically injured. The Guardians had already been in contact with her about signing on with them after her time. While she was still unconscious from the injury, the Marines handed Dara over to them. Unlike me, she had a chance to tell her family a type of goodbye. She told them she would be on a series of top secret missions and it would be a long time before she could contact them again. She "disappeared" and was listed as MIA.

Mitch was a teenager when his family moved from Ukraine to England. Already a top student, he was quickly enrolled in an advanced placement program and was accepted into University at age fifteen. By twenty he was on his third master's degree and working towards his doctorate. At age twenty-five, he was at the top of a successful career with an international company that designed and developed weapons when a false accusation, made by a jealous coworker, and some backdoor sabotage brought it all to an end. He was working a series of dead-end jobs when he answered an advertisement for the Guardians' above ground base. Impressed by his credentials and skills, they quickly moved him into a position on the team. He married a coworker and

217

settled into his new life quickly, happy to be considered valuable again.

Max was the youngest member of the team, joining the Guardians when he was just twenty. At a very young age, he had shown a talent for accuracy, not only with weapons but with most anything else that required precision. He was orphaned at age five and had been raised in a series of foster families and group homes in Britain. As soon as he could, Max joined the Royal Air Force. While running joint missions with a U.N. team, his talents were revealed to a Guardian scout. They offered him a position and he accepted instantly. There was a planned "accident" to explain his disappearance to the Air Force. While he chose to undergo the enhancement procedure, his skills were already so dominant that it only made a slight improvement.

Skull was another orphan case. He was from London, and his parents had been killed in a violent crime when he was twelve. After a bad experience with a foster family, he ended up living on the streets and was frequently in trouble. He turned to the military in order to get his life back on track. A freak accident after a long battle left him near death and with no memories of the previous five years. When the military could not locate any living relatives, he was listed as an adult ward of the state. The Guardians picked up on his case through a contact inside the military hospital, and the General brought him to the bunker. He had severe brain trauma and it took months of rehabilitation before he could join the team. Almost as soon as he was allowed above ground, Skull was "taken under the wings" of the owners of the pub. He still spends his days off with them, and they have become his family.

Ryan was born and raised in Saudi Arabia. His father was an American working for an oil company and his mother was a Saudi native. Ryan spent his early life with his parents in a community of Americans. The year he turned twelve, he was sent away to a boarding school in Indiana. After graduating, he chose to go back to the Middle East for his secondary education. He moved to Qatar and attended an extension program for a major U.S. university. After completing his degree in Criminal Science, Ryan was hired by the CIA. Because of his Middle Eastern background, he was quickly promoted and was trained to work with explosives of all varieties. While working on a joint operation with a U.N. task force, he met James and learned about the Guardians. James approached the CIA and pulled several very important strings with those higher up. Even though Ryan had no say in it whatsoever, he was reassigned to the Guardians

Jason was a pure southern boy, born and raised in Alabama. His father was a truck driver and his mother was a nurse. In high school, he enrolled in a program for students interested in the medical field. Because he could not afford college, he joined the Air Force itself after graduation. Through them, he became a medic and eventually received his R.N. license. Even though he was engaged to his high school sweetheart, he served three tours in Afghanistan and earned quite a reputation for his bedside manner and his skills. When his mother became terminally ill with cancer, he requested a leave to be with her. The request was held up and she passed on without him being able to say goodbye. A second request to assist his father with moving to a retirement home was turned down. Jason became angry with the Air Force and his performance deteriorated. He went AWOL, and that was when Dara found out about him. She had been sent to recruit a medic and had just arrived on base when Jason disappeared. She quickly tracked him down and convinced him to join the Guardians. The Air Force dropped charges against him and he was able to make sure his father was taken care of before leaving. However, his fiancée could not handle all the secrecy around his new position and left him.

Rick's story was similar to what little I knew about James. They had grown up in the same neighborhood and were close friends; they even went to the same boarding school. He had a talent for music and languages from an early age and his mother encouraged him in both areas. His father had left when he was two and had been shamed by the town for doing so. He had lost his position in the Royal Army and had not been seen for quite some time. The town rallied around Rick's mother and that allowed her to enroll him in piano and guitar lessons. He grew up speaking English and Welsh but had taught himself Spanish and German before turning age ten. At the boarding school, he took Latin and French and then took an online course in Mandarin. Rick was also very involved in choir, band and a quartet. It was here that he became interested in songs which told the history of a people. After graduation, he was in the same basic training as James but was transferred to the Linguistics department soon after. The next time James saw him was when he joined the Guardians.

James paused at this point and looked hard at me, "He'd already had the enhancement procedure and was having a hard time adapting to it. With so many languages in his head, he would open his mouth to speak and there would be a long pause before he could get out whatever it was he needed to say in English. Quite often another language would come out. It took nearly a year before he was able to control the ability. During that time, he rarely left the bunker. It was hard on our friendship, but we made it through. He is different from when we were young, but I love him like a brother."

He stood up, stretched, and added, "He seems to have taken a liking to you, feels as if he has to protect you somehow – like a little sister or something."

I also stood up to stretch, "I've noticed that too. He is becoming a good friend and I enjoy our time together. The musical connection has helped me adjust."

A far away look came to James' eyes, "Seems like there are three of us looking out for you all the time. Does it bother you?"

"Sometimes."

"Specify, please."

This would be difficult. I started to pace the floor. "While I appreciate Rick, Jason, and you looking out for me, it really is not in the best interest of the team to be so protective. Destructive events and accidents will happen at some point. It's not safe for all of you to be worried about me. One of you might hesitate on a decision because of it and the results could be catastrophic." I turned to face him, "I am a grown woman and have learned much since starting here. You thought I would be perfect for the team which means you must have thought, at some point, that I was capable of taking care of myself."

James' hands started to clench. I noticed and started pacing again. Part of me hoped he shared that information with Jason and Rick so I would not have to repeat it, but part of me did not want Rick to know. If he was feeling protective, it did appear to be on the lines of an older brother watching out for his kid sister. With Jason though, it bordered on over-protective. I thought back to his reaction to me being in Balboa. With James...my thoughts were stopped by his sudden appearance in front of me. I started to walk around him, but he gently took my arm and pulled me back in front of him.

"Jason has been spoken to before about his behavior towards you. He can be spoken to again. However, I will not speak to Rick about it. He would not endanger the rest of the team, and he has been good for you."

There was a more than a hint of omission in his words and I pressed. "What about you, Jamyson?"

His grip on my arm tightened slightly. "Yes, you are a grown woman and a beautiful one at that." His voice took on a tone I did not recognize. "Every day you are becoming more and more capable of taking care of yourself in this new world." He stepped closer, leaving only a couple of inches between us. "Your opinion has been noted, but I will not likely cease in how I feel about you."

That was not acceptable. "Commander," I started but his other hand came up and two fingers were held to my lips.

"Shh." He whispered. "I will not put the team in danger because of you, but I cannot put aside what you have been through." I started to back away, but the hand on my arm shifted, refusing to let me move so much as an inch. "Yes, you are very resilient. Yes, your skills are much more developed than we ever imagined. And yes, you are quite independent. Do not use the "others have been through more than I have" line on me either, Harlie. It is a moot point to argue. Just give in and let me be a little protective. We are having more and more good days together, starting to develop what I hope will be a strong friendship. Think of me as another Rick but with more determination."

He waited for me to respond, emerald eyes piercing, a firm grip on my arm. For some reason, although I wanted to be angry with him, I was not. Part of me wanted to be far away from him, but another part wanted to stay right here close to him. As much as I wished he were not so protective, the thought of someone wanting to keep me secure in this frightening new world was strangely welcome.

"You are very obstinate." I sighed.

He laughed, "Almost as obstinate as you." He let go of me, but neither of us moved at first.

I ended up being the one to step back. "We should break for a meal before going back to the question and answer session."

He nodded, went to the phone, and ordered late lunches to be brought up. We ate in silence, but as soon as the trays were empty and in the hallway, James spoke. "My turn for a bit."

"Sure, but you'll be bored and need a nap."

"I doubt that." He scoffed.

James then proceeded to ask about what I grew back on the homestead, how it was preserved and what meals were cooked with it. He wanted to know about holidays with my extended family and places I had visited.

"If you could revisit any place in Britain where would you go?"

That took some thought. "I've always liked Brecon Beacon National Park and visiting the older castles in Wales. There is something about Mumbles Beach too that attracts me – and not just the tide pools."

James was silent for a long while.

"Jamyson, where would you go if you could see only one more place on earth?"

He looked startled, as if I had interrupted a long train of thought. "My childhood home." It was a simple answer. "But that's impossible. It washed away in a bad storm."

"So that would be your answer to the Britain question too?"

"Actually, no. I am also fond of Brecon Beacon. Have you ever been to Snowdonia?" He smiled at me.

I shook my head.

"I'll have to remedy that situation." He looked serious about fulfilling that statement.

This seemed like a good time to get to the heart of our

day-long conversation.

"Tell me more about you, James."

"What would you like to know?"

I wanted to say "everything" but settled on, "Do you have an extended family?"

He nodded, "Yes, but we were never very close."

"Did you have plastic surgery like the rest of us?"

"No. Neither did Rick. He just grew the beard and long hair."

"How old are you?"

His eyes narrowed for a moment. "How old do you think I am?" The question was very slow and careful.

I pondered my own real age versus the one I pretended to be, thirty-two versus twenty-seven. "Upper thirties?" I guessed even though it did not make sense with what Jason had said about how long James and Rick had been here.

He laughed nervously, "Close enough."

We had both been sitting on our own beds, but James stood up and came over to sit on mine. He carefully took my hand, turning it over in his own. Strangely, I did not feel the knee-jerk reaction to pull away.

"What do you miss the most about the outside world, Bear?"

The question took me off guard and it was difficult to answer. "I miss having time to cook meals from scratch and having time in my garden. Since I do not have as much training to cover now, I might be able to do more of that." I turned to face away from him. "I miss caring for pets too. They were my children, and I loved them, but it would be impossible to care for an animal now."

"I had a dog when I was young. Tell me about your animal children and I'll tell you about the best friend I ever had." He moved his hand from mine and lifted it to turn my face back towards him.

We shared animal stories until his phone cut us off. He rushed to answer it, said a few words then snapped it shut. I stood up, and he came over and gave me a quick hug.

"Extraction time." He whispered.

THE RETURN

James had been told to check us out of the hotel and meet up with our first transport, a silver pickup truck with a driver who wore a black hat. Once we were inside and moving, a black sedan pulled in behind us. James whispered that it was probably Dara, Jason, and Max. We continued through the city, and three more vehicles joined us. They were all different makes, models, and colors and blended into the daily traffic. Once all five vehicles were in visual range, we turned off the main roads, split up then regrouped at the edge of town. It was a standard maneuver to lose anyone who might be watching or following. The five-vehicle convoy drove us to a U.N. military installation and we were taken, bags and all, into a large building.

Inside the building, several armed men waited for us. We were asked to declare all weapons and equipment. They did not check to see if we were telling the truth though, and we were not. James tapped on my shield and let me know it was safe to look around but stopped just shy of ordering me to do so. From that point, everything was moved into a spacious room. We were left alone, and I scanned each person in the room to see how all of the team was holding up. No one spoke. We stood silent and still, waiting for what was coming next.

Two U.N. doctors came in and completed brief physical exams on each of us. Since Jason had already taken care of Dara and Max's minor injuries, and we had several days to recover from our jungle experience, there was not much to do, and they left quickly. The next to arrive were three officers and two privates. One stepped forward and spoke.

"Which one of you is Commanding Officer Jamyson Davies?"

James tilted his head in a brief nod.

"I am Colonel Stofsko, and this U.N. base is under my command."

"Then it is you I need to thank for our quick extraction.

225

My team and I express sincere gratitude towards those who were also involved."

The Colonel kept a straight face, but I sensed he was slightly surprised at the words. "You are welcome. But I do need to ask, why we were suddenly called on to extract you?"

There was a slight flicker in our Commanders eyes. "Were you not informed of our presence in Panama?"

"We were, but there was little information given. We were told that you were a terrorist reconnaissance group under the power of the U.N. and should be prepared to provide assistance."

James nodded. "That is true enough. To answer your first question, we were prepared to enter and exit commercially, but in an encounter with the terrorist cell, came across evidence too vital to risk in a common flight. It has been our experience that even the papers we carry have not been enough to stop others from trying to see what we are needing to hide. There was no way to secure these items, so we required you to take us out of here and back to Britain."

"I see. And you will not be informing us of what you located either?"

"Not in as much detail as you would wish."

The Colonel nodded. "I do not know who you really are or what you are really doing, but the orders I received came from the highest level of the United Nations."

James expression turned serious. "You must realize that my team and I are under the strictest orders as well. The best thing for all involved is to get us back over the Atlantic as soon as possible. The final report will answer some of your concerns, I promise."

"I expected an answer along those lines. Introduce me to your team and then we will discuss the rest of your extraction."

"Thank you, Sir." James turned to us. We had silently moved to stand in formation whilst he was talking, and he started on his right, using our code names. "This is Jaws, our linguist, Root is our weapons specialist, and Ka is one of our bomb technicians." Moving slightly to face the middle he continued, "Bruce is our combat specialist and Bear is our diplomat." He then looked at the left line. "This is Skull and he is our transportation coordinator, Stitch is our medic and Boom is our other bomb technician."

We gave the Colonel a resounding, "Sir!" and saluted.

He smiled slightly, "A pleasure to see such a well-trained force." Glancing over to the other officers he introduced them, then moved on to what would happen next. "There is a transport fueling up as we speak. As soon as it is given the all clear, you and your equipment will load up with ten of our own men for the trip to London. I wish you the best and am looking forward to seeing that report. You are a most curious group, and I am wondering what all of those specialties in one team could be needed for."

James saluted him, "You will know soon enough, Colonel. Thank you for your hospitality."

We were given a light meal and escorted to the restrooms. We were then marched to the large airplane that would be bringing us across the Atlantic. I was becoming nervous, and my head started to hurt. I had been scanning as many minds as possible, looking for any sign of deception. Thankfully, there had been none.

The plane was quite large, and it seemed very little was on board other than us. I sent a trickle of curiosity towards James. He responded.

Yes, Harlie, other than the assigned escorts, we are all that's on the transport.

What a waste of resources.

I know, but it is necessary to get us back to the bunker. They did not have time to plan out equipment transfers or personnel changes.

I looked around the nearly empty plane and the seats we would be sitting on for the next nine hours. It was just like what one would see in military action movies, with the seats facing the inside and looking very uncomfortable. Max was watching my observations.

"Welcome to our world, Bear. It is as bad as it looks."

Jason pitched in with, "I'll give you something for motion sickness."

Although I felt bad about it, I turned on him. "Who said I needed something for motion sickness? I don't get motion sick."

"Thought it would make the trip easier on you, that's all." He sounded defensive, but there was hurt on the fringe.

"I'll be fine Stitch. I'm not as pathetic as I look, remember?"

"You do not look pathetic." Now the hurt could be heard.

"Then stop acting as if I cannot handle anything new."

James threw us both a warning glance, and we were silent. We strapped our bags into a location where we could see them and went to take our seats. As I moved to sit next to Rick, James brushed up against me and tucked something into my hand.

It's one of yours. You'll need it later, trust me. It was one of the pre-filled liquid doses of the combination medication I took when my skills were overworked. All I had to do was twist the top off and swallow the contents. James took a seat across from me, Rick sat on my left and Dara sat on my right side. In minutes we were in the air.

The trip was torturous. James was right about the medication. If it were not for the sedative effects from taking it, I would have lost my mind in those nine hours. It was difficult to tune out all the emotions while keeping alert to any change. Three of the escort troops were positively vulgar while staring at Dara and me. James and I kept up a mental conversation about what we were sensing, and he seemed surprised at the details I could decipher just from the emotions.

Jason stared at me for most of the trip, and I guessed he was waiting to see if I was going to show signs of distress. That made me more determined to sit still and keep a straight face. Every hour one of the soldiers would start asking us questions. It was mostly small talk, but we answered as briefly as possible, never asking them anything in return. To me, it seemed rude, but James was quick to remind of our rule about silence until debriefing.

Nine hours, one ration bar, and a bottle of water later we were back on land and being picked up by our ground team. Within sixteen hours of our extraction, we were back in the bunker and making our way to where The General was waiting.

Debriefing took several hours. We all had reports to write and spread out around the conference room. Each of us hooked earpieces to our digital recorders and went to work with only a salute to the General. He wandered from person to person, like a teacher in a classroom, looking over our reports and asking questions about what he read.

As each of us finished, Doc took us to the med bay for physicals. Thankfully, mine went well. Unfortunately, Dara, Jason, and Ryan tested positive for a virus common to that area of the world. Doc said there was a forty percent chance that they would become symptomatic, but the chances of us catching it from them during the plane flight were a low five percent. They had to be symptomatic for it to be fully contagious.

At the group meeting, we all took turns with our reports. Dara and Max knew from the last time the Guardians were in Panama that a gang in Balboa had contacts within Unus Universum. Before they took out the cartel members who carried the chemicals for some of the bombs, they had been successful with another task. They found out the location of those who worked with the contacts and set up a reconnaissance operation. Jason and Ryan played unaware tourists and searched for connections in a style similar to what we had done in Poland. Together, they had been successful in locating sketches of potential targets in Rio as well as information on what type of explosives would most likely be used. It appeared there would mainly be nuclear technology involved in the form of two trunk bombs and one truck mounted airborne. The equipment needed to launch those had been in existence for about ten years but had been closely monitored. We were all disturbed at the evidence of one being in the wrong hands. That team had also discovered that smaller explosives would be used as well to ensure most of the city was destroyed. It was essentially a smaller scale version of the attack on America.

When it was our group's turn, the others learned about how we discovered the detonator and wiring transport and how we were able to take the transport out. However, no one was expecting my part of the report, after Mitch recalled the success of the explosion and recovery of equipment.

"It was at that time when Harlie called in with a report of potential enemy activity within our monitored zone. By the time we arrived, she announced the targets had left the vicinity." He looked at James, who nodded for him to continue. "We were making our individual recordings of the event when The Commander took Harlie away from the camp, presumably to discuss the intrusion. They returned in a hurry and The Commander announced our immediate departure." Mitch turned to look at me before sitting down.

"General, Commander." I acknowledged them. "The activity happened at our south-western sensor, number 8 on the map. The sensor registered five large bodies moving north, north east. The path would have avoided our camp and brought them to the river in approximately twenty minutes. I used my mental abilities to sense their numbers and intentions. Immediately, I sensed what I have been calling a "dark spot." The only other times I have sensed these "dark spots," are when The Commander has his mental shield up and is within my range."

The General signaled for me to pause and looked at James. "Does this phenomenon happen to you as well?"

James nodded.

The General looked back at me, "Continue."

I went on to describe the encounter, quoting word for word our conversation. At both mentions of the "old mind" James and the General glanced at each other uncomfortably but said nothing. When I finished with the fiery last contact and sat down the others started talking all at once. I had been looking out to monitor their emotions the entire time. Initially, there was a mixture of surprise and doubt, but then reality struck all of them.

Dara spoke first, "The presence of an empathic on the enemy side makes our mission to Rio much more dangerous."

Ryan added, "Hopefully, what Harlie sensed is accurate, and he is young and not well trained."

Max leaned forward, "But now James and Harlie have to watch out for him sensing our every move. There will be no way we can get around Rio unnoticed if he is there."

James stood up, "That is not true. He probably has the same limited range we do. We will have to come up with a

230

method for keeping track of his movements so that any major task we have to complete can happen safely. Remember, he may not be aware of the extensiveness of The Guardians' work. He will also be tuned in to the minds of his own people, looking for hesitations or betrayal. I can teach you a method for blocking out any random scanning he does. It will not help if he is focused on you though – at least I have been led to believe that it won't."

The General motioned for silence. "We will have to leave for Rio in just two weeks. I will be overseeing this mission from the Canadian bunker. Look for transmissions from them about what further actions they will be taking. They have already deployed fifteen men to go undercover using various professions. We must work together closely to ensure success. Take the next two days off to recover, then report back here. Are there any questions?"

Something had been bothering me for the last few days. Something I had not been able to put into words until now. Suddenly, I had to say it because it seemed vital to what we were planning. I raised my hand and waited until the General acknowledged it.

"Sir, two questions keep repeating in my mind." All eyes were on me now. "Who made him and why is he looking for an old mind?"

James was quick to answer. "We can only assume he was made, but it is possible that he was born with the ability and was recently discovered by the enemy. As to why he is looking for an old mind, that is up for speculation."

The others stared at us, and I could sense they were bothered by James' response. Something was being omitted and we did not need my enhanced ability to figure that out.

The General dismissed us, and we calmly made our way to our rooms to prepare for two days in our own homes. Pub night would be the night before we went back to the bunker. As I headed to the elevator, Jason caught up to me.

"Need a ride home?" He smiled.
"Yes, but it's awfully out of the way for you."
"It's not that far. Besides, we can grab a bite to eat on the way. I'm craving pie from the cafe on the main street."

Over the last couple of months, Jason had been asking weekly to take me out to a meal. Every time I either had other plans or made a reasonable excuse. Still feeling bad about snapping at him back in Panama, I acquiesced. His smile grew wider, and we walked out to his pickup truck. Even over here in Britain, where trucks were unusual, it seemed natural that a southern boy like Jason would be driving one.

Despite being exhausted, we had a good time. Outside of work Jason was very nice to talk with. He was full of southern charm and compliments. Unless he was being snapped at by James, Jason was generally a happy person. I enjoyed the meal and our conversations. We both had hot sandwiches and pieces of pie. He drove me home after the meal and walked me to the door, where I turned to face him.

"Thank you, Jason. Hanging out for a meal helped me unwind a bit from the last few days."

He smiled and then laughed, "Being locked up with The Commander must have been hard on you."

The comment bothered me, "Actually, only the first couple of hours were nerve-wracking. The rest was fine, emotional because he lifted the media ban and I was catching up on the rest of the world, but we were comfortable."

"'Bout time he lifted that thing." Jason's eyes turned hard, then brightened again. "We should go watch a movie together soon, now that it's lifted."

I was becoming concerned about how he was feeling about me, "We are not going to have a chance any time soon. Let's get through Rio first, okay?"

"Okay." His expression became soft. I dared to glance at his emotional status and knew there would be trouble if I did not get him to leave soon. I started to turn away and unlock the door.

"Thanks again, Jason."

Even with my back turned to him, he wrapped his arms around me and stayed there for a moment. I started to move through the door and he let go. "Thank you, Harlie, for finally letting me take you out."

I went inside and shut the door. What a mess! I needed to get him to not be so absorbed in protecting me, but this might have made it worse. There had to be some way to let him down without hurting him too badly.

It would have to wait though. I was so tired that coherent thought was a struggle. After changing to a pair of pajamas, I climbed into bed and was asleep in minutes.

The next day was a beautiful one weather wise. I spent the morning with the gardener, being updated on the edible landscaping he had planted for me. All of it was up and in various stages of development. It made me look forward to a great harvest with extras to freeze and enjoy over the autumn and winter. After lunch, I decided to walk to town. There were several items that needed to be purchased before Rio. However, the main street was barely in sight when the familiar sound of a motorcycle approaching made me stop and sigh. I really wanted a day to myself, but that looked to be impossible.

"Harlie!" James called.

I sighed before turning around and smiling at him, "Good afternoon, James."

He turned off the bike, dismounted and came around to stand by me. "Did you get enough rest last night? Jason didn't keep you out late did he?" James was not smiling.

"I slept quite well, and Jason was limited to just dinner and a ride home. Although he is fun to talk with, I do not want him getting any other ideas."

James just nodded and pressed his lips together. "Good idea. Don't want him getting delusional."

His comments seemed a bit harsh, so it was time for a subject change. "Is there anything you wanted to talk to me about, James? I was on my way to pick up a few essentials before being locked back in the bunker again."

He took the hint. "Yes, I wanted to see if you had plans for tomorrow."

In my relief that he was not going to take the rest of my day away, I hurried my answer. "No, there are no plans."

The pressed lips turned into a smile. "You have plans now. Be ready by nine."

I asked why but was fairly sure it was a waste of breath.

James' smile got even bigger, "You'll find out tomorrow. Ta for now." He hopped back on the bike and was out of sight in moments. I sighed and continued to the store.

Our second, and final day, off dawned bright and warm. Even though my nerves were a little on edge about what James had planned, I was cheerful while getting ready. It was a t-shirt and shorts type of day, but since I still did not own any, my best jeans and a button up short sleeve top had to do. I pulled my hair back and took a good look in the mirror. The face looking back was becoming more and more familiar, her expressions similar to the ones I had known for thirty-two years beforehand. I noticed the scratches and insect bites were nearly healed and was grateful. A knock at the door brought me out of my musings.

James was smiling like a child at Christmas as I greeted him.

"Ready to go, Harlie?"

I grabbed my mini backpack, locked the door and followed him to the waiting motorcycle. He hesitated while handing me the helmet.

"You look very nice today." His eyes looked me over from head to toe. "That shirt matches your eyes. I like it."

Much to my horror and his delight, I blushed. He gently laid his hand against a now red cheek. I looked up into his emerald eyes and my heart skipped a beat. The response confused me, but I was able to turn away and take the offered helmet.

"Where are we going today?" My voice did not sound right but at least the words came out.

"You know me well enough to realize I'm not going to answer that." He chuckled.

"Well, then shouldn't we be going? Or are we waiting until I have a panic attack?"

Once we are out of town James dropped his mental shield completely and increased speed. I was still thinking over my reaction to his words and touch so did not do the same. After twenty kilometers he slowed down a little.

"Harlie? You going to relax at all today or am I going to be the only one?" He called over the roar. "Your muscles are so tense I can feel it through my jacket."

"Once I know where we are going and what we are

234

doing."

"Look at the signs and figure it out." His voice sounded a bit harsh, and I fought back a cringe.

At first, all I could tell was that we were heading towards Cardiff and Swansea and not towards London. As time passed, he turned the bike towards Swansea. It was at that point I started to relax a little. When we turned onto one particular road, old memories started to surface. Somehow, I knew this road. When we passed the University, the memories came back full force, and I dropped the mental shield.

James spoke mentally, *I take it you figured out where we are headed to?*

I squeezed my arms around his waist tighter in a form of hug.

His mental voice was gentle, *Thank you.*

Are the tide-pools still there?

Yes. And the ice cream parlor you mentioned.

We arrived at the parking lot next to Mumbles Pier and started walking towards it. It all seemed the same, the walkway, the arch that said "Croeso I Pier Mwmbwls," and the steep climb to the wash house. Once we reached the steps, I stopped to look at the inlet. There were boats of various sizes scattered along the shore. It was in the middle of the tidal cycle, and I remembered how extreme the tide seemed to be here. At the low point, the boats were on sand and the rocks by the tide pools were high up and dry. Come high tide, the boats were floating in feet of water and the rocks were covered.

James interrupted my thoughts, "I figured we could get something to eat since the cafe has more than just ice cream. Then we can walk out towards the lighthouse and over to where you saw the tide pools last time. You thought they were close."

"Yes, they are." I turned to face him, "Why are you doing this? Why use up a rare day off taking me here?"

He looked out towards the water, "Because I wanted to." He glanced over at me, "And typically, I do what I want." We stood in silence for a minute before he added. "I also thought visiting a place that meant a lot to you in your past life would make you happy, and I want you to be happy."

We walked over to the cafe, which stood at the

entrance to the pier itself and had a quick lunch. There were few other people around us as we made our way to the lighthouse. I reflected how most of who we saw seemed to be locals and not the tourists of my past visits. The pier looked more run down than before. I remembered when there had been a play area and other attractions at the end of it and you had to pay to walk down that far. Now, it looked deserted.

"These last few years have been rough everywhere in one way or another. Nothing is as bright as it once was." James sounded worn out, ancient with sadness.

I put my hand on his arm. "I know, but we can still look forward and try to make things better with whatever resources we have."

The emotions coming off of him were full of turmoil, but then he turned to face me, and the turmoil was replaced with caring. He turned back to the lighthouse and we continued our climb in silence.

The lighthouse was smaller than most and was painted in the classic white with red trim. Up close I was happy to see that someone had been taking care of it. Unlike the pier, the lighthouse had a new coat of paint and the landscaping around it was well maintained. It was not open to the public, but we enjoyed walking around the premises.

"Did you walk to the tide pools or drive over to the parking lot and steps there?"

"We drove, but there is a sidewalk."

James expression turned devious. "I think we should take the rocks." I looked doubtful and he added, "Is your spirit of adventure only active when you are on duty?"

"My spirit of adventure is just fine, thank you very much. It is common sense and self-preservation that is active right now. Missing Rio for an extended stay in the med bay is not an option."

He laughed for a moment then grabbed my hand. "We'll be safe enough. Let's go!"

I hesitated for a moment, freed my hand, and followed him. It was a fairly difficult climb over the rocks, and we were right at the ocean's edge for several hundred feet. I tried not to think about the crashing waves below and what those would do if either of us were to fall. I was not a strong swimmer. In fact, I could barely swim at all.

An electric shock of mental surprise stopped me in my tracks. James turned to face me from the boulder he had just jumped to.

"What?" I asked, then looked at his face. "That Look" was in his eyes, and he seemed to be looking right through me. I froze. It was an immeasurable moment before he shook his head and moved to the next rock.

We arrived at the tide pools a few minutes later. It was just like I remembered, and I gave a child-like squeal of delight while kneeling at the first one. It was about two feet around and the water was less than a foot deep. Inside were numerous seaweed stalks, mussels, and two tiny shrimp that moved from plant to plant. The next one was hardly six inches around and only seaweed lived inside. As I moved to the third, I glanced up to see where James was. He had stopped at the top of the rocks and was staring down at me. A slight smile played on his lips.

"Jamyson, come look." I called. He came down and we sat at the next pool. It was one of the largest and housed a starfish as well as shrimp, mussels and seaweed. Together we watched their activity. Time passed, and I still was not tired of watching the to and fro movements of the plants, even though the water seemed still. In the back of my mind I was in tune with James' emotions, and he seemed to be enjoying this simple time of observation as well.

We stayed at the tide pools for over an hour. Sometimes we laughed at the movements of creatures inside their salty oasis, other times we just sat in a comfortable silence. It was very relaxing, and I felt refreshed when James finally stood and held out his hand to help me up. On the way back, I paused again to watch the water. The tide was coming in quickly, and we could not linger very long. As we turned up towards the lighthouse, James spoke mentally.

Harlie?

Yes?

Would you answer a question for me?

I did not notice the edge to his voice so answered with an affirmative.

Please be completely honest. Can you swim?

237

Instantly a feeling of dread came over me. Of course, he would have been following my thoughts when I stopped to reflect on the way to the pools. This could be very bad...

Barely. My answer was a whisper.

There was no response from him until we were at the ice cream shop. *That will have to be remedied in the next couple of weeks. Rio is at the ocean's edge, and we might need to take a boat in for some of the mission.*

While the whipped soft serve ice cream was as wonderful as I had remembered, it was not as enjoyable because of my revelation. How could I possibly learn to swim strongly in just a couple of weeks when, for most of my life, I avoided water that was more than a foot deep?

What made you afraid? The gentle voice reminded me that my thoughts were still open.

I sent the memories in his direction.

I can see how those three events could make a person wary.

I just nodded, and he grew silent again.

We finished eating the treat and walked back to the motorcycle. As I reached for the extra helmet, James reached out his hand and took my arm. I stopped mid-action and turned around to face him.

"I'm very sorry that training will have to be rough on you again. You must have been looking forward to less intense work in the bunker."

"I'm okay." It was not the truth. "I still have a lot to learn, and it's better that particular secret came out now and not in the middle of a mission."

He reached to tap two fingers on my temple. "You're fibbing, but I expected it." He smiled gently then stepped back. "We need to return to town. The team will wonder if both of us are late to the pub."

The ride back went quickly. I enjoyed the flashing scenery as he drove recklessly fast in between villages. We both raised our shields before reaching our own. James dropped me off at the cottage to freshen up then drove to his apartment to do the same. After finishing getting ready, I started to walk towards the pub. James caught up with me halfway and we walked in together.

238

Skull and Max were already there and smiled from the bar. We ordered our drinks and sat at the traditional rounded booth. Rick came in as we were sitting down, with Dara close behind him. Ryan and Mitch were the last.

"Where is Jason?" I looked around.

Dara answered. "He became symptomatic with the virus this morning and confined himself to the med bay."

James seemed surprised at this news, and I realized that, since he had been with me all day, he would not have gotten a report. But what about his phone? I looked at him questioningly.

I turned it off. Didn't want it bothering us.

Our expressions had not been lost on Rick or Max who both gave us curious looks.

"Well, at least Doc will have something to do for a few days. He has been getting bored." It was James who made the comment.

We ordered our meals then went to throw darts while waiting. As always, the food was wonderful. During the meal, we chatted about how our days off had been. After the meal, Max worked with me on the billiards table – since I was practically clueless. The evening went by quickly, and we all left at a decent hour in order to be ready for our morning move back into the bunker. Max and Rick had requested that the extra quarters be used to give them their own space. Since Rick had seniority, the request went through, and we would be helping him move first thing. While walking home, James came alongside of me.

"Did you have a good day, Harlie?"

"Yes, James, thank you for taking me to Mumbles. It was very relaxing and refreshing."

"Good. I enjoyed the time there as well. The tide pools are a wonder, and your reactions to them made me happy."

We were at the gate to my cottage. Against common sense, I reached out to give him a hug.

He returned it and smiled. "Tomorrow, I have to be tough again, sorry."

"I know."

He turned to walk back to his apartment and I went inside the cottage. Sleep came quickly, and it was a peaceful one.

BACK AT THE BUNKER

It did not take long to separate Rick and Max's belongings and move Rick into the spare quarters. We set up all of the basic furniture and left the rest for him to work on later. There was quite a tangle of wires surrounding his digital piano and other electronic equipment. From there, we settled into our own rooms then met up in the conference room to discuss the next two weeks.

Positions were assigned, and once again, I was leading a small research team. This time our focus would be the region of Brazil where Rio was located. It was a narrower focus, and we had to find out many more details about the area. Max, Ryan, and Mitch were eagerly taking apart and analyzing all the debris we brought back. Their main task was coming up with ways of remotely disengaging devices with that technology in it, as well as others we knew about. Skull again had the job of mapping out everything and anything we might need as well as arranging locations for us to stay in. Dara and James worked through the split teams and potential missions. Rick was listening in to all the current and select past transmissions, picking out what was important and documenting. Jason was under the care of Doc and would join us once the virus ran its course. His position was to keep in contact with the ten undercover operatives whom we had deployed from our own resources.

When sixteen-thirty came around, we were so into our assignments that the decision was made to forgo the daily debrief and work until it was nearly eighteen hundred. The evening meal was a noisy event as we broke down what had been accomplished.

I had just picked out a book and curled into a corner on one of the couches of the common room when James tapped on my mental shield. I watched as he quietly spoke first to Dara, then to Rick, and stood as he motioned for me to follow him.

At the elevator door, there was a backpack which he handed to me, "I informed them that, because of the other empath, we have to practice with different mental defense techniques and it was best to do so away from the others." At my grateful expression, he added, "Which was only a partial truth. We will be practicing while at the pool."

I frowned.

His motorcycle was waiting, but he paused before getting on it. "Did you think that just because we worked late, practice would not happen tonight?"

I had been thinking that but did not want to admit it. "I was hoping, but figured it was improbable."

If he had a response, he kept it to himself and saddled the bike. I did the same and wrapped my arms around his middle. He felt very tense, a far cry from yesterday's relaxed and happy demeanor. Flashbacks from my early days on the team whipped through my mind, and I cringed as he slowly drove towards the back of the base. There was a recreation center with a large indoor pool for the personnel who actually lived on-base. We had occasionally visited it for team building activities, but I had been successful in avoiding the pool area.

The building seemed to be closed, only the lights inside the pool itself were lit. James parked the bike next to the front door and flashed his ID badge at the scanner, motioning for me to do the same. The door clicked open and, once inside, James pulled out a flashlight and led the way to the locker room. He flipped on one of the lights.

"Your suit is in the bag. It's the kind we wear under our uniforms during missions where water could be involved – like in Rio." He turned and walked out, "You have three minutes to be at the pool."

I hurried out of my polo, slacks, and undergarments and into the suit. It was a dark blue single piece that covered nearly to the neck and had one-inch thick straps. The bottom half looked like a pair of shorts and came to mid-thigh. It was a close fit and seemed to be much like what professional swimmers wore. At the three-minute mark James started tapping on my shield again. I left the locker room but hesitated at the sight of the pool. James stood at the edge in an identical suit.

He turned to face me. "I am unsure of how to teach you to strengthen your mental defense and how to attack another mind if need be. However, it must be done. Just as you getting over your trepidation around water and becoming a stronger swimmer must happen as well." He motioned me closer, and I went to stand by his side. I stared at the water, trying to breathe slow and steady, trying to hide my embarrassment. James was staring at me. I could feel "That Look" and held back another cringe.

"Let's try this." He finally said, and I was surprised how his voice sounded lighter than before. I pulled my gaze from the water and saw he had the slightest trace of a grin on his face. "We know that you can hold your mental shield up consciously and unconsciously. We also know that I can pull it up when it's down. Let's try the opposite. Keep your shield up while I try to pull it down." The grin spread. "If you are successful, there will be no pool time tonight. If you fail," he pointed to the water, "In you go."

"I'd rather not." My embarrassment deepened when my voice came out shaky.

Instantly, his eyes flashed, and The Commander was present. "Too bad."

Those eyes closed for a moment, when they opened again determination was dominant. He lowered his shield part way but was careful to keep his emotions hidden. I took a step back and prepared for what was bound to be a painful onslaught. He reached out and ran a mental finger down my shield, just as he had before. Then he tapped on it like when he was trying to get my attention. I focused on each sensation and how the opalescent bubble responded. When James started poking at the shield, I closed my eyes to shut out the rest of the world and focused more on what was happening. Suddenly, it felt like he had mentally grabbed a fistful and was pulling it like a child would pull on a parent's shirt. The tugging became more and more insistent as I fought to keep the shield from slipping.

Impressive.

I dared not respond, especially mentally. It was a good thing too because the next instant James' mind changed. He stopped tugging, but now it looked as if a knife was coming at me. It slammed into the top my shield and, for just a split second, I could sense a small hole. I quickly pictured the hole healing and it did, but James let slip a feeling of victory. The mental knife came at me again, and before I could fix it, he tugged at the hole. I could not get it to close and struggled to keep it from getting larger. Sweat dripped down my face from the effort, and my head began to pound.

Please, James, stop. It's too much.

Instead of answering me he pulled harder and the shield began to collapse. A physical shove landed me in the water. It was cold enough to take the breath out of me. As my head went under, the old feeling of panic came back. Somehow, I was able to push the flash of memories aside and came up sputtering, tears of frustration forming in my eyes. When those eyes focused on James, he was sitting with his feet in the water. At first glance, he seemed calm, but when my eyes met his, I could see determination. He was breathing hard and that made the tears stop. At least he appeared to have struggled with the exercise as well.

There was silence as we both slowed our breathing and tried to calm our minds. The Commander spoke first. "Show me how you swim. After a lap, tread water in the middle of the pool."

Anger started to flare. How could he expect me to accomplish that task seconds after a mental attack which ripped my shield down?

He saw the emotion in my eyes. "That is an order." His voice was cold, his eyes piercing.

"Yes, Sir." I emphasized the last word and did not try to hide the anger in it. The pounding in my head was barely subsiding and the trials of the day were taking their toll, but I did what was ordered. Swallowing embarrassment, I swam a lap. To me it seemed a pathetic excuse – arm over arm, turning my head and trying to remember proper breathing. After the lap, I swam to the middle and started to tread water. My shield was still intact, and I took the moment to examine it for any damage.

James was still watching me with that frustratingly unreadable expression. I dared to meet his eyes, not holding back the anger, and for a moment we stared at each other. He blinked a moment later and launched into the pool. It took just over a second for him to reach me, and he grabbed my arm and hauled me to the side of the pool.

Enough. His mental voice was low and deadly. Before I could respond in any way he grabbed the other arm and pinned me to the side of the pool.

I froze, realizing a line either had been crossed or was dangerously close to it.

"Your behavior right now is completely unacceptable, Harlie. Despite whatever emotions are being triggered by these lessons, you must remember the two reasons why we are here. First, there is another empathic out there whom neither of us is prepared to deal with. Second, you are needed in Rio but must be left behind if you cannot get over your weaknesses in water." He watched my face, waiting for a response. I hid what I was thinking behind a blank face and mental shield that looked less opalescent and more like it was made of steel. The Commander tightened his grip. "I had planned for us to go back to the bunker once you had tread water for a minute. Instead, you are now going to swim and tread until I say you can stop."

He spun me back towards the water and pushed me away from him. I started to swim laps. Although I tried not to show it, his words had hit a nerve. I could have held my emotions in check and just followed along with everything instead of reacting. It would have prevented the mess I was in now. James was facing away from me, looking out one of the large windows.

When it was just the two of us, either on or off duty, the encounters seemed more intense. I did not understand why, but they were. There was something about James which brought out responses I could barely control. It seemed the same was happening with him. Perhaps it was because of our empathic abilities. We were constantly dealing not only with normal methods of verbal and body language expression, but our minds were also in-tune with each other. Could it really be just that?

"Tread." The Commander had not turned from the window. I stopped mid-stroke and started to tread water. From now until Rio I would just answer with an affirmative and do whatever was requested, at least for the lessons and most likely in the bunker as well. Our new-found friendship could

245

not be counted on in these moments and would have to be put on hold until after we returned from Brazil.

Several minutes later he spoke. "Stop and get out. You have four minutes to be at the bike." He still had not turned.

Getting out of the pool was difficult, my legs felt like jelly and hurt nearly as much as my head. My limbs were slow in obeying my brain's commands. At the four-minute mark, the motorcycle started, and I stumbled out about twenty seconds later.

The ride back was silent, his body tense underneath my arms. We were at the elevator entrance in the warehouse when he spoke. "Go straight to your quarters without talking to anyone. I'll explain how it was exhausting and that you have a headache. It won't be a lie."

Although it made me feel like a child being sent to her room, I followed the order. The others stared. I could sense their curiosity as I quickly shut the door behind me. Even though it made my vision swim, I focused my ability on Rick and felt satisfaction that he had not been fooled.

After taking my custom medication, which somehow had been placed on the counter, I showered then rinsed the suit and hung it up to dry. I was extremely tired but did not feel like sleep was possible. Instead, I sat up on the bed and reflected more on the situation between James, Rick, Jason and me. What a mess, and it looked to be getting messier.

The next day we were back into the same routines as before Panama. Jason's fever had broken, and he was expected to return to light duty the next day. Dara was under-the-weather though and was sent back to her room mid-day to rest. We worked until normal time and gave reports on our progress. The General was there and seemed genuinely pleased with how quick we were moving. After the evening meal, I went back to my quarters, put the suit and a towel in the backpack, and sat down in the lounge with yesterday's book. Forty minutes later, James walked past me with the pack.

Mitch called out, "Now don't you kids be out too late!" and we headed to the elevator with the sounds of laughter behind us.

James had not spoken to me all day, and there was no

way the team had not noticed. I sighed as we exited the elevator and tried to keep my frustrations under control. It almost felt as if he were punishing me, even after I served yesterday's consequences without complaint. At the pool, I went straight to the locker room and was at the waters edge within three minutes. James was in the pool already and starting a lap. Unsure of what to do, I stood and waited. After ten laps he stopped and climbed out.

"Your turn." He leaned his head toward the water.

I tried not to hesitate while getting in and starting my laps. While I wished he would comment or critique my swimming skills, he stayed silent. So, I thought about how athletes look when they are in a swimming competition and tried to mimic their movements. It surprised me when six laps did not feel as impossible as in the past.

"You are in better physical shape than you had been in the past."

I stopped mid-stroke and stared, curious. My shield had been up the whole time.

James was in the water, standing at the four-foot mark. "Lucky guess. You had to have been thinking along those lines soon."

Per my self-promise, I just nodded.

He swam up to where I was treading and did the same. "You have to be able to do more than just swimming laps though. The short-term above water goal is to swim a half-mile, tread for thirty minutes and learn how to rescue someone in the water. You also need to learn how to see and maneuver underwater."

"Yes, Sir." My reply was calm despite the sudden anxiety at the thought of being underwater.

James looked at me questioningly but continued. "Go to the edge of the pool and let's see how far you can swim under."

I came up farther than what was in my memories. He nodded, and we tread water a little longer.

"Take a deep breath and show me how long you can remain under the water."

Instantly, panic took over. No. There was no way I could keep myself still under the water and wait until my lungs started to burn. It took all I had just to keep calm enough to complete the previous task. Stupidly, I started toward the edge of the pool. A hand grasped my wrist and an arm went around my waist. I struggled to break free.

"Be still!" He hissed in Welsh.

The order to stop caused me to pause long enough for him to get both arms around me. I tried hard to pull away.

"Be still or I'll pull you down."

I froze. James did not let go though, instead, he dropped part of his mental shield and a sense of calm washed in around me. I stood in it, trying to breathe deeply, trying to stop the flight response. I could feel the warmth of his body and instantly became unnerved. My body tensed in preparation to struggle.

"I'm not letting go until you are calm." He whispered. Mentally he added; *Don't make me pull you underwater.*

Somehow, I was able to force my body to be still. My mind took a bit more time. Aided by the calming emotions coming from James, the flight response was tamed. When he felt me relax slightly, he let go but turned me to face him.

"That was interesting." He looked slightly amused.

I looked away, it was better than the instinct to look down.

"Harlie, you know I cannot let you out of the pool now, not until you complete that task."

I nodded, but still could not force myself to follow.

"So resilient, so brave, but then there are times like this and I remember how..." He trailed off, reaching out to place a hand behind my neck. "Look at me." His thumb directed my face back towards him. "Look me in the eyes, Harlie. I'll go under with you. Keep your eyes on mine."

I took a deep breath, looked him in the eyes and nodded. We were both under the water in an instant. I fought panic while keeping my gaze locked on his. Ten, twenty, thirty seconds went by before I shot back up and did not stop until I was out of the water. James followed me, and once we were both toweled off, he spoke again.

"We still have to practice with defenses."

Since screaming was not an option, I nodded.

"Let's build on that notion of fear. You said the

empathic sent an image of intense fire. I'll do the same, but with various negative images and you fight it off, push it back towards me." There was a hint of The Commander in his tone.

We worked on that for the next hour. It was awful and difficult to fight. Even though I was mostly successful, I was sure that nightmares would come later. James seemed pleased at how he could at times break through a portion of my shield, but even more so when I was able to throw the image back at him.

When we left to go back to the bunker, I noticed he was not as tense as before. It seemed the choice to be quiet had been a good one, and my panic attack had been forgiven.

At the warehouse entrance, he stopped me. "Getting over your fears will be hard but keep remembering that it was far in the past...another life. You are now Harlie Berryman, a woman who barely resembles the woman of before."

I thought about his words for a moment and decided to make an exception to my silence. "There is an error in your logic, Jamyson."

He looked curious, "And that would be?"

"While I might look slightly different physically and there have been enhancements to my brain, my heart and soul are still the same. Those," I trailed off at a sudden burst of emotion. "Those remember."

James frowned, "Yes. Yes, they do." He pressed the button for the elevator, and we were back in the lounge in time to watch Rick lose to Ryan in what seemed to have been a violent game of chess. We laughed with the rest of the team, and James updated them on what we had practiced before we both retired for the night.

The rest of the week went the same as the first two days. By Thursday I could complete the half mile swim and the treading water goal. Friday brought success in the water rescue, but I still could not force myself to get through the obstacle course underwater. As predicted, our practice sessions were leading to an increase in nightmares, but since I was taking the custom cocktail, I was not waking up screaming. However, I was tired and getting more so by the day.

On Saturday we were required to work until noon and

from there were free to go above ground. During the morning workout, plans were being made for dinner at the pub and a hiking trip after church on Sunday. While I said okay to the pub, hiking was out of the question. Sunday would be a true day of rest for me, even if I had to lock myself in my quarters.

Jason had been out of the medical bay since Thursday afternoon. At my declining of the hike, he turned a curious look in James direction. James had also declined the activity, saying the motorcycle needed work, and he had some other tasks to complete. When I went up to the research facility to grab a few printouts, Jason followed me.

"Harlie, wait up!"

I waited.

Jason came up beside me, and I started walking again. After looking out of my shield, I knew why he was following me. It was not fair to do so, but I wanted to know what I was up against. He was in full possessive mode.

"I know there was a lot missed while I was in the medical bay. It looks like you and James are practicing mental stuff at the pool. Is that right?"

"Yes. If he wins, I get wet." There was no reason for anyone to know the other details.

"Well, is it all defenses or are you practicing attacks as well."

Good question. I stopped and turned to look at him. His hands were in his pockets and he looked genuinely concerned. "Still getting the hang of defense and since neither of us is sure of exactly how to practice it at all, it's going as well as can be expected."

The concerned look deepened, "You need to know how to attack, Harlie."

"Yes, I know. We are working on it, Jason." I looked skyward. "I'll be fine. Quit worrying."

I picked up the needed printout and turned to go back down the hall to the elevator. Jason planted himself in the doorway. I looked around and, being Saturday, the room was deserted.

"Someone has to worry. I mean, look at you. The bags are back under your eyes, your stats are horrible on the circuit, and I bet you have lost some weight. I'm tempted to drag you down to the med-bay, hook you up to the machines and show The Commander what he is doing to you."

So that was what this conversation was about! Making James look like some evil dictator instead of a leader making sure all the members of his team were as prepared as possible.

"Jason, he is not doing anything wrong. Do you expect him to take me into Brazil without any preparation? Yes, all this mental training is tough work, but at least I'll be able to handle that empathic. And, I'm getting some great swim practice in while learning."

He wasn't listening, "You are not resting, not being given time to recover. He could pull you for practice during the day, not during our break. You need that time, Harlie. You are still getting used to this life." A desperate look came over his face. "Dangit! You should not even be here! You should be up there in the village, doing what you love, not down here preparing for war against a monster."

My heart caught in my throat. "Is that what I am too then? And Dara, Max, Rick, and Skull? All monsters?"

He stepped back, and I pushed past him. For a moment Jason stood immobile but then raced to catch up. He grabbed my arm and spun me around, pressing my back against the wall.

"Let go, Jason." I hissed.

"No. Not until you listen to me." He put his other arm against the wall to block me from darting.

"This is not the way to get me to listen. Perhaps you should be the one in the medical bay, seems like you're not over that fever."

He laughed harshly, "The only fever I have is the one raging to keep you safe. I insisted from day one that this world was not for you, tried to show you too. I thought you were listening, but then James got his talons into you." He was leaning closer.

I thought fast, "Jason, listen to me. You were so sweet when I first woke up, so helpful in my first weeks here. I took your warnings to heart. I know what is out there, what they did to me. No one is being fooled. While I appreciate you trying to look out for me, it is dangerous for both of us."

251

I stopped because, at that moment, James started tapping on my shield. He must have sensed Jason's emotions. I raised my hands and tried to push Jason away from me. "Let me get back to work. This is where I belong, at least for now. The Guardians needed another empathic, and I was put in their path." He did not budge, so I stated the obvious, "Your emotions are being monitored. We don't make it a habit to watch the team, but I've been gone awhile and..."

Jason pulled back, "He picked up on us, didn't he?"

I nodded, "Yes, one of us monsters picked up on it." With that, I practically ran down the hall, got into the elevator and let the door shut in his face.

The last hour was spent throwing myself into the research, not even looking up from the computer and reports I was printing and highlighting. When noon rolled around I sat as far from Jason as possible, wishing that he would quit sending apologetic looks and emotions in my direction. Most of the team went straight up and out of the bunker once the meal was over. I went to my quarters and lay on the bed.

Minutes later there was a gentle knock. I had expected the dark spot to be there, but it was Rick. So much for any attempt to be alone.

Rick, already dressed for off-duty leisure, stood for a moment and then sat on my bed. "James said you and Jason had it out in the upper level. I wanted to see if you were okay."

I sat up. "It was bound to happen sooner or later. He wants so bad to mean something to me, or at least enough to listen to and believe his rants about James."

Rick leaned against the wall and held out an arm. Surprisingly, I not only sat up, but went to the waiting one arm embrace. Rick had become a safe spot, someone who was there for me but made no demands of his own. I let him hold me, and something about that action soothed my ragged emotions. He did not say anything, just sat there quietly like a rock in a storm. My eyes closed, time passed, and when they opened again, Rick was gone. I could hear piano music coming from across the hall. He had propped both doors open. I smiled and promptly fell back asleep.

I was awakened again, this time by Dara who insisted

252

we needed a shopping trip before leaving for Brazil. When she gets into a mood like that there is no stopping her. She was like a woman crazed while making me pick out tank-tops, t-shirts, and shorts. She had more than enough outfits for the trip but commented constantly about how my own wardrobe was still lacking. Since the excursion took up the rest of the afternoon, we went right to the pub.

It was completely packed and noisy. A major sports game was on the oversized television screens and the voices rose and fell with each play. Our traditional seats were cleared, and we sat in the same order as usual. I smiled at Rick, who was taking careful note of my appearance. He was mentally happy with how I seemed well rested. James was trying hard not to glare at Jason and, while physically that was almost working, the dark spot was even darker. I nudged him.

Back off, Jamyson. No major harm was done.

He turned to glare at me, and I cringed. *It was totally out-of-line.*

I tried to make my mental voice sound light. *We all have those moments.*

Not like that, not what he called you.

Called us. I corrected. *And, it was a heat of the moment comment. I was more upset about him trapping me against the wall.*

James continued to glare. *You should have kicked him. If he does it again you can bet I will.*

If it happens again, I'll kick him. That is no way to treat a team member.

Thankfully, our food was ready. Afterward, Mitch and Ryan left for their wives. Max pulled Skull and Jason to the dart board and Dara went to show up the men at the billiards table.

Rick turned to me, "Where are you staying tonight, Harlie?"

"I'm picking up a frozen homemade meal from the cottage then staying at the bunker. Less to distract me there."

He nodded and excused himself for the night. James and I were alone at the table.

"Billiards or a walk outside?" He asked.

I looked at the rest of the team and felt a bit like an

outsider. The hum of all the minds inside the pub suddenly seemed like a roar.

"The walk outside."

We stood and made our exit together. I could not help but mentally glance back at Jason. He had noticed.

James and I walked to the cottage. There was a wicker couch in the backyard, and he walked out there while I was inside grabbing the meal and a few odds and ends. When I met him out back he sighed. It sounded like the weight of the world was on his shoulders. His green eyes stared out at the garden then shifted up to the stars.

"Never did get to show you the stars in Panama." He whispered.

I looked up too, "It's okay. There will be other times."

He nodded. I sat next to him and he dropped his shield. I did the same, basking in the relief that came with such a simple action. We were still close enough to the pub, and of course still in town, but the hum did not seem to bother me as much right now. We sat for the next hour, not talking, not reaching out to the others' mind, just sitting.

When I stood to wander the garden he asked, "Bored? Ready to go back underground?"

"No. Just looking at what grew this week."

He came over to me. "How can you tell what is what when it's dusk?"

Showing him took up the next hour, then we sat again in silence. Finally, he sighed again. This time it sounded more like a sigh of contentment and not the heavy one of before.

"You are amazing, do you know that?" He turned to look at me.

I glanced his way mentally, and his mind was calm. There were no emotions which, in my book, could be deemed dangerous. "You keep saying that, but I'm just me. Nothing amazing about that."

"There is plenty amazing about that." He laughed softly. "You just refuse to see it." James stood up and offered me his hand like a gentleman, "I walked here, so we better start back to the bunker."

I ignored the hand, rose and started out; James chuckling quietly beside me. We were past the main part of town when he spoke again. "So, I can't punch him because I'm his commanding officer, and you pushed him away before I could use the unwanted contact as an excuse. Am I supposed to let that kind of behavior slip? He is expecting retaliation."

"Let the encounter go, Jamyson. It's not worth the effort. You and Jason have been at each other's throats before, and it always passes. He does not understand our abilities and believes we should have never been enhanced. But, he is on the team and is really good at what he does. I'm not all that upset anymore, so you shouldn't be either."

I felt it more than I saw it, "That Look" had been gone for several days but was now back in my direction. When it faded, he spoke. "Okay. Just because you said so."

"Thank you." Now I was the one to sigh.

That night my dreams turned evil quickly: Pictures of mutants and monsters, images of people with radiation burns, fire and water. It all came together and was too much. I woke in a scream. Rick, James, and I had chosen to stay in the bunker. I glanced out. Rick had turned over in his sleep, but it appeared he had not heard me. I looked over for the dark spot and found it was not dark. On the contrary, James was awake and had lowered enough of his shield for me to sense his growing concern. I chose to ignore it, rolled over and tried to go back to sleep. An hour later I woke again, this time Rick had registered the scream and was awake too. James was no longer in his bed but was pacing his room. I started to do the same. Stubborn pride, the urge to be independent, those were what stood in the way of me asking him for help. I looked back out at Rick, he was sad over the nightmares and wishful, I guessed he wished that he could help. Turning my mind back towards James, I came across him staring back at me.

I sat down on the bed with a sigh. We were one week from Rio, and it looked like the team would be intact for most of the mission. There would be nights where I could not take the sleep aid, nights like tonight, where I did not want to. I hated relying on the stuff, but it could hurt our mission if I were to wake screaming.

James continued staring at me, watching the thoughts I was not bothering to guard.

I give up. My mind whispered to him.

James stayed still. The words were not acceptable, not what he had told me. I took a deep breath and let it out very slowly. *Jamyson, please show me how to control these nightmares.*

In the silence, I sensed a nod. He left his room, came into mine, and stood in front of me in the dark. Hands reached out and rested on my shoulders. I looked up at his face. His expression was determined, but his eyes were gentle. I stopped breathing, waiting.

"You need to go back to sleep. When the dreams come, look for me. I'll guide you through how to stop them from turning bad. If you are already in a nightmare, I will show you how to change it, how to divert the worst. Either way, look for me."

"How will you be there?" The thought of him interacting with my dreams was upsetting.

"Harlie, I won't really be there. It's a trick of the mind. I'll be here but putting just the slightest pressure on your shield. When you fall asleep, your mind should accept me as part of it, and then I'll be able to help you. I will only see what you are focused on; just sense what your subconscious is feeling. Your mind will fill in the blanks, so to speak, and put me inside the dreams. I really will be talking to you, just as when you are awake, but your subconscious will think it is all part of the dream. When you wake up, you will remember my presence, because those upper levels know I'm there at your shield. I know it sounds confusing but try to trust me." He reached up a hand and gently brushed the back of his fingers down my cheek. His touch felt like fire.

"How do you know these things? Did you come up with the theory and try it on someone or was there another empathic who taught you?" My voice was barely a whisper.

His eyes narrowed for a moment, then turned gentle again. "I knew you would be curious..." He hesitated, "But that is another story for another time. Right now, you need a peaceful sleep more than those answers."

James walked to the other side of the room, sat in my desk chair and waited. I thought there would be no way I could sleep with him in the room, but then his mind reached out and gently ran a mental finger down my shields. It almost

256

felt like a caress. I rolled over and looked up at him. He smiled and whispered both mentally and out loud.

"Sleep, Harlie."

It took just a few minutes to fall asleep, and the dreams started shortly after that. I was at the ocean, staring at the waves. It was something I enjoyed doing, watching the power, thinking about all the things in the universe which had to come together perfectly to make those waves as well as the rising and falling tide. I looked for James and found him nearby, throwing shells and stones back into the water.

"Hello there!" He smiled and held out his hand, "Let's go for a walk."

I took his hand and we walked along the beach. "This is a pleasant dream to start at. Do you come here often?"

I shook my head. It was actually quite rare for me to have this particular dream.

"Too bad. I like it."

We walked along for what seemed like several minutes, and then the scene changed. I was in a crowd on a boardwalk, looking for someone. I scanned the faces, not sure who I was looking for. All the faces were familiar but not who I needed to find. Suddenly, I saw James standing near a bench and remembered I was looking for him.

"Good!" He reached for my hand again. "Try to go back to the beach scene. Tell your mind that is where you want to go."

I did, and it worked. We were back in the sand and looking over the waves. I relaxed as we walked along a little more.

The scene changed again, and I knew this time there would be trouble. I was in the refugee camp, moments before my first assault. The rundown buildings, stench, and sudden fear was overwhelming. The dream started forward and I forgot about looking for James. My focus was getting away before the sneering guard grabbed me. I started to run and heard him chasing me. The dream changed again, and I was running from the nuclear blast, trying to get home as fast as I could, hoping the expanding cloud would not reach my village. It changed a third time and I was underwater, lungs burning. I opened my eyes and floundered about, trying to see

257

which way was up. A hand rested behind my neck and his face appeared in front of me. James looked up, and I moved in that direction. We came up sputtering.

"Focus, Harlie! You forgot to focus, forgot to look for me. I was there the whole time." He shook me slightly. "You can make this stop. You can tell them to stop, force the good memories forward. Go back to the beach, away from here."

I tried to make the beach scene come forward, but it was too similar to what I was trying to escape. Panic rose, and fire started coming around us.

"Look into my eyes, Harlie." He was so calm, even with the fire and panic. "If you cannot appear at the beach, go someplace else you feel is safe, someplace you enjoy."

I fought the urge to close my eyes and forced myself to look into his. Various scenes rushed past us as my mind searched for one deemed safe enough. It stopped on the front porch of my old house. I was there with Gareth, and we were looking out over our garden. Our dogs were there too, so both my hands were busy petting them. James stood at the tree line, an outsider. He nodded solemnly as I smiled at him.

"Don't let it move forward. Keep yourself here. It can be done." He stepped back into the trees. "I'll be close if you need me."

The scene lasted until my alarm clock made it end. When my eyes opened, James was not in the room. I mentally glanced into his quarters and found him sleeping on the couch. I thought back to what had transpired. It was bizarre and confusing, but it worked. The nightmare had been halted in its tracks. A small sense of relief washed over me; perhaps I could learn enough of James' method to keep the horror away.

After a shower and trip to the cafeteria for breakfast, Rick and I went to church. James had still not awakened, so we decided to let him rest. We sat with Jackson and his father, with Jackson and me passing notes like a couple of children would. After the service, Rick went back to the bunker, and I took Jackson and his father out to lunch.

Afterward. I rested and read a book, enjoying the quiet moments. The afternoon passed into evening and the team returned with a stack of pizzas. Rick pulled out the digital piano and a guitar. While the team knew from my file that I had been involved in music, it was not something I was quite ready to share. Rick insisted though and soon all of us were singing and laughing. Rick then started a favorite song, a duet, and motioned for me to sing it with him. After the last note there was silence until Dara said, "We had been told you had musical talent, but...wow." The others made me promise not to hold back again. I agreed, then excused myself to bed. My dreams were calm that night, and come daylight, I was refreshed and ready for the last-minute rush to Rio.

DANGER IS EVERYWHERE

Monday was spent with Max, Skull, and Ryan in the second bunker. We pulled all the needed supplies and carted them over to the training facility, which had been turned into a staging area. Everyone brought out their bags and backpacks, and we started the process of deciding who carried what, trying to maximize the amount of equipment we could sneak into Brazil. The U.N had provided us with documents which would exempt us from the security screenings and hopefully allow everything to be left unscathed during transport.

At the pool, James had me start to practice mental attacks. The idea repulsed me, but I knew it was something that had to be learned. Perhaps it would have been fairer if I could have practiced against someone who was a new empathic like myself, instead of against someone who had been born that way and had proper training. James never said who trained him, but his skills were obviously too advanced for someone to have learned it all alone. Going up against his mental shield was like attacking a titanium wall with an ice cube, all my attempts to get through just shattered and fell away.

Tuesday, we had a meeting with the General which lasted almost our entire shift. He was leaving again to meet up with the North American team and we finalized plans between the two groups. They would oversee the outskirts of Rio De Janiero, and we would be responsible for the area immediately surrounding the international conference.

We were all worn out from the long session with the General, but James still insisted that we practice. This time, I was not allowed out of the pool until I could pass the underwater obstacle course. The test took quite a few attempts, and James looked to be nearly out of patience when I finally made it through. I had been silent the entire time, just grimacing, nodding and trying again. Neither of us cheered when I came out the other side victorious. We climbed out of the pool, dried off and stared out into nothing.

I was still staring when James came up behind me and

stopped very close. He sighed, and I turned slightly to look up at the haunted green eyes.

"What's wrong, Jamyson?" I whispered.

"There is a struggle with helping you learn how to attack and defend effectively. I cannot figure out a way to teach you without causing pain." He looked down at me and I could see sadness.

Choosing my words carefully, I replied. "At this late in the game do we really even have another choice? I have to learn attacks and quickly."

He reached out and turned my head so that it was facing away from him again. "I don't want to keep causing you pain." Before I could reply, he continued. "Remember when I showed you those harsh scenes in order to get you to raise your shields and later when projecting death of an enemy?"

I nodded.

"As an empath, you should not be able to see those things. With the exception of empathic to empathic communication, your skills should only be sensing emotions. I've said before how your abilities seemed to run deeper, more like my own skill level." He reached out to put his hands on my shoulders. "I pray that they are."

His hands pressed down on my shoulders and a shock wave hit my shield. "Fight it off, Harlie. Throw it back at me!"

My shield shuddered under the pressure but did not fall. I gathered my thoughts and attempted to force the wave back to him but was unable.

"Picture something evil, something or someone that hurt you badly. Picture that and push the wave back."

Instantly, the sneering guard came into my mind, and I pushed the wave out towards him. James let go and fell to his knees.

Realization hit me. By picturing the evil and sending the wave in that direction, I sent it to the attacker, sent images and emotions to...I stepped back with a gasp. James sensed the change, stood up and shook his head.

"Don't do it, Harlie. Do not finish that thought." He stood up. "The only way to learn these skills is to practice and you must practice against me. You know that... you have known that. Yes, it might hurt me but..." He placed his hands back on my shoulders, "It is nothing near the pain I would be in if something happened to you out in the field."

I froze.

"You are going to have to fight dirty, Harlie. Attack with images of what horrors you have experienced. Once the person is startled, you can try to pull at the shield."

My head shook quickly. I had spent the last few months burying those horrors; to bring them back up and use them to attack anyone would be nearly impossible.

James stepped back. "You have no choice. If you will not learn on your own, it will be forced." The Commanders' tone left me back in a frozen state. His voice changed again and became almost tender. "Please, Harlie. I hate when I have to force something on you."

What else could I do? There really was no choice. I nodded, gathered images of the nuclear bomb and devastation and hurled it at him. He stepped back slightly, but his shield did not waver. I flashed images of the children I had seen with radiation burns, and his shield jumped. With all my mental strength I hurled out the final assault at the refugee camp, and James fell to his knees. His mental shield flickered, and in that instant, I reached out mentally and grabbed hold of it. When James looked up, I stopped and let go.

"You." He panted, "You should have kept going." His eyes shut. "That would have been the first time in decades that anyone forced me to lower my shield."

There was silence.

"Try it again." He ordered.

"No, Sir." I refused and started towards the door. He reached one hand out to grab my ankle, and I fell to the ground, instantly in battle to keep my own shield up.

"Try it again!" It was practically a scream.

So, I did, and this time his shield did fall.

We were both in an intense amount of pain upon reaching the bunker. This session had taken much longer than anticipated and the others had already retired for the night. As we exited the elevator, The General was waiting, his luggage against the wall.

"You both look horrible." He commented.

"We were successful though, Sir." James replied.

He gave us both a knowing look. "Get some rest. There will be more excitement tomorrow."

James looked angry for a moment, then nodded at The General, took my arm, and walked me to the common room.

"Get ready for bed, I'll be in shortly." At my expression, he added, "You know as well as I do that there will be nightmares, and it is too late to take anything other than something for the pain."

"Yes, but you need sleep too."

"Don't worry about me. I'll get enough rest."

The moment I sat on the bed, James came into the room and stood in front of me like before.

"I want to make sure no damage has been done. Any weak spot will take time to heal." Ever so gently, he reached out his abilities and inspected my shield. The touch felt almost real, almost as if his own fingers were brushing gently over my face. My heart started beating out a strange rhythm.

He finished and stepped back, "Nothing. Brilliant!"

"What about you James? Were you injured at all?" Concern laced through my voice.

He shook his head, "Always worried about the other person. Enough of that for one night, time for bed."

"Jamyson, why don't you go get some sleep first. If I awake with a nightmare, then you can come back over."

He chuckled quietly, "Okay."

He returned three hours later, but tonight the lesson in controlling my dreams went much smoother. He showed me how to change the image of himself to an animal or person of my choice. In very little time, I was hiking a trail at Yellowstone and James slipped back to his own quarters.

Wednesday morning, I awoke feeling uneasy. Glancing at the rest of the team I realized that several of them felt the same way. Something was different today, something was off. At breakfast, James announced what it was.

"Doctor L. is in the bunker today. It is time for Harlie's three-month scan, and he wants to examine the rest of us who have been enhanced. Dara, Max, Skull, and Rick are all to report to the medical bay immediately. Harlie, you and I need to meet privately before joining them."

We rose and started in our assigned directions. Jason leaned over and whispered, "Stay alert. I'm not allowed in there today."

James was right behind him and said, "Harlie will be in good hands. I'm not leaving her side."

The expression Jason gave James was enough for a standard military recruit to face court-martial, but I pleaded mentally for James to ignore it. We walked into the small office behind the training room. Once the door was closed, James sat on the desk, folded his arms and stared at me.

"Danger is everywhere, Harlie."

I thought he was referring to Jason's comment, but he wasn't.

"Doctor L. is very nervous today. I think it's because he suspects you are more powerful than anticipated. Whatever it is, he foolishly thinks I am going to allow detailed tests to be run on you. He's lucky I don't wring his neck or fire him for showing up unannounced. Yes, it has been three months since your procedure, but I sent him a notice last week stating you would be unavailable until our current mission is completed." He paused, looking thoughtful and I realized he was scanning the medical bay. "Jason is right, stay alert. Something is not quite right about him today. Give short answers, no details. He's looking for something, but I cannot decipher what it is." James then stood up and laughed, "I've always despised that man. He might be a genius, but he also leaves a bad taste in my mouth and mind." I nodded, and his eyes suddenly brightened. "Brilliant!"

At my startled expression, he laughed, "You really are not one for unnecessary conversation anyways, so you can get away with hardly speaking to him at all! I can state you have been that way since the procedure. Of course, you and I will keep up a mental conversation, but he will only hear one or two-word answers from you."

Before I could respond, he opened the door and we walked down to the medical bay. Flashbacks of my first days in the bunker came to the front of my mind and I hesitated. Doctor L. had come across as creepy to me in those few lucid moments.

What's wrong?

I showed him.

Oh. Yes, I can see how this impromptu exam could affect you that manner. Be brave though, I'm right here, and he will not be doing anything adverse to you.

We arrived at the medical bay as Doctor L. was examining Dara in the glass-enclosed room. If looks could kill he would have, at the minimum, be incapacitated with the expression she had on her face. He was clucking over her like a hen with a chick, running a strange device over her head.

"Very good, my dear. Let's get a working image and you'll be done." His voice made me shudder.

James walked up to him. "Not to interrupt your important work and research, but we are on a very tight schedule. I'm afraid there is no time for detailed tests today." His voice sang of The Commander.

Doctor L. looked over at James, "I'll see if General Smiths can clear up a few minutes."

The Commander handed him something written on our organization's letterhead. "I am currently in full command and there will be no schedule changes. You should be grateful that I'm allowing you to complete any type of exam at all since you ignored the notice I sent you."

The doctors' eyes narrowed. "I did not receive any notices."

James looked back at me and I nodded once. Doctor L. was lying.

"Ah, my prize patient!" His voice was a little too enthusiastic. "How are you? You look quite well." He waltzed over to me. "It looks like you put on about twenty pounds and your hair and skin are positively glowing!"

Dara rolled her eyes, hopped off the exam table and left without another word. Rick, Max, and Skull choked on barely contained laughs. Doctor L. motioned me forward and James took my hand, leading me into the room.

"How are you my young one?"

I stared at him. In my mind, James laughed.

He parted my hair and looked closely at the surgical site, the entry point for the tools he used to stimulate the overdeveloped, but inactive, part of my brain. While examining the plastic surgery spots, his mind swelled with self-pride. He then squeezed up and down my arms, poked at my shoulders and examined my legs and feet.

"You are in wonderful shape. Tell me, what has your adjustment been like?"

I just shrugged.

"Now, don't be shy. You do know who I am, don't you?"

I nodded.

The Commander spoke up, "Ms. Berryman has been very quiet since her release from the medical bay. Her ability to adjust has been extraordinary, and she has even been in the field with the rest of the team several times. She does not speak aloud often though."

Doctor L. gave a harsh laugh. "So much for your diplomat then."

James smiled at him and mentally winked at me. "She communicates with us all well enough."

Now I was the one who almost laughed. The doctors' eyes grew wide as he put the pieces of The Commanders last two sentences together.

"Just a moment ago she told me you were lying about the notice I sent." His eyes narrowed.

Doctor L. turned to me with a look of astonishment, and I gave him a small smile. He turned to the others. "Is this true? She does not speak aloud much but you still know what she is communicating?"

They played along and nodded. Max enhanced the scene with, "Rick and James hear her the clearest."

"Are you sure we don't have a few minutes for a quick scan?" There was a hint of pleading in the doctors' voice.

James turned to me. *If I stay with you and only gave him a few minutes to look at the results before kicking him out?*

I was hesitant but nodded.

Thank you. I've been wondering myself about what an action shot would reveal.

The large machine was turned on. The others were given their basic exams and allowed to leave while it warmed up. I sat silent, watching, waiting, and trying not to panic. True to his word, James did not leave my side. He was also watching the doctor and mentally observing every moment.

When it came time for the scan, James asked me to complete several mental tasks – but he did not let Doctor L. know which ones.

Tell me your name, birthday and position.

Harlie Anwyn Berryman, February 20th, team diplomat and spy.

James looked up at the surgeon. "Did you catch any activity?"

Doctor L. nodded.

Lower your shield and look around the bunker.

I heard a breath being quickly sucked in over at the station and grinned.

He is going to freak out with the next one.

I had the sense to not look panicked, but my heart raced.

Fight off my attack.

This time I was the one who sucked in a breath. James grabbed my hand and held it tight as the shock wave hit. At first, it was too much, and I thought my shields would fall, or I'd scream from the pain. But, I gathered my wits and memories from the first days in the bunker and sent the worst moments in a rush to the wave. It faltered. Then, as the emotions broke through, the wave just stopped. His shield lowered on its own, almost like surrender. I looked away to avoid any loose emotion.

Doctor L. did look like he was having physical issues. James stood up, still holding onto my hand. "I think that should be enough data."

The surgeon just nodded, eyes wide, and started going back over the images. I sat up, slightly dizzy, but not in too much pain.

Wait for me in the gym.

I walked out quickly, but the second the training facility door closed, I slid to the floor. Jason and Max reached me first. Jason started to check my vitals, but I pushed him away.

"Harlie, don't be like that."

I glared at him. "The monster just overextended her abilities while in a test because she was being closely watched by her creator. All I need is a dose of your cocktail."

"Dude, that was harsh." Max was giving me a disapproving look.

I ignored the comment, "Root, set up the guns, I haven't practiced all week."

They both got up, and Jason left for the medical bay. I continued to sit and gather my wits.

Jason came back a moment later with a syringe. "The Commander is escorting the surgeon off the premises. Doctor L. is ranting about something he saw on your scan, but James won't let him look at it again."

My only response was to hold out my arm. As soon as the medication took effect, I stood up and met with Max in the shooting range. He stared at me, disbelieving, until I picked up a 9mm semi-automatic handgun, knelt on the ground and took out the target. We spent the next 2 hours destroying more.

"Dang, Bear, you are a spitfire today!"

I turned to him, "Don't mess with it."

After we had eaten lunch, James had us wrap up packing and start on our circuits. Dara and I were working side by side when James joined us. Something was obviously on his mind, but I was uncertain about discovering what it was. When we made it to the mats, James took up a defensive position and Dara moved in to attack. When he shook his head and pointed at me, I became apprehensive. There was only a moment to think, though, because if I did not immediately make a move, he would. We circled around, and my first attack was a kick. It connected, and he responded with a punch aimed at my chest. I was able to block it, and we separated again, circling around. James then moved to tackle me, but I was able to avoid falling and my knee connected with his chest. We were always careful not to injure our opponents, but he was being rough. He stepped back, and I saw the warning in his eyes a split second before it happened. At the same instant he moved forward, he let loose a mental attack. It was not a shock wave but images. They were hard to ignore, some were very potent, but I focused on his incoming fist and swept his legs out from under him. As he went down, he grabbed my leg and the shock wave hit. I gave a short scream from the pain of the double attack, then turned and stared hard at him.

here, go someplace where you can properly process what we found."

We rushed out of the medical bay, up the elevator, and out of the warehouse. His motorcycle was outside, so we hopped on, and he took off at top speed. My heart was racing, and a scream was building in my throat. He drove to the end of the village and pulled off at a road which paralleled the river. We drove until the water was deeper and the hills gave more protection. At a dirt road, he pulled off and stopped the bike at the bottom of a hill.

I climbed off and sank to the ground. James leaned the bike against a small tree and came to my side. A hundred thoughts were going through my brain. I wanted to be angry, wanted to scream and lash out. Another part of my mind tried to accept the situation as something that was meant to be, and I might be able to help others with what I had become. But what had I become? Was I really a monster, something which should never have been created? I wanted someone to blame, someone to hate, but knew hate would get me nowhere. I had just become someone again, become part of an organization who could do so much good in the world.

My thoughts were interrupted when I realized that, at some point, those thoughts had become open to the person sitting next to me. James turned at my unspoken question.

"When you started to panic inside the med-bay, the shield did not drop but became more transparent from the intensity of your emotions." His voice was a whisper.

A new train of thought came forward, a part which wanted to blame him, blame the person who took me from the camp and allowed the changes to happen to me. My jaw clenched as I remembered the early days in the bunker.

James flinched, then dropped his shield completely. His thoughts were in as much turmoil as mine. "I would not blame you for despising me, especially since you showed me exactly how your first days were perceived."

I stood up. "I need time. Alone."

He stood up and started walking away. I walked in the other direction until I was sure we were out of range of each other. I curled up into a ball on the cool grass and started to scream and cry. Sobs racked my body and my thoughts

271

refused to settle down. It was at least an hour, possibly more, before the slightest bit of relief came and my eyes shut. When they opened again, the sun was starting to set. A sense of determination had come over me. I would make the best out of this revelation and train hard to make sure my abilities were strong but under control. Through my work with the Guardians, I would help as many people as possible.

James was another situation, one that was not easily resolved. He had rescued me from the refugee camp because of the potential for those abilities. While our relationship had been rough at first, he had taken responsibility for his early actions and we had been getting along better. He was kind and seemed to know exactly what I needed and when I needed it. James did not mean for this situation to happen. He had only meant for me to be a regular empathic in order to help the Guardians out in ways he could not. With all that he had been doing to teach me, to help me, I could not be angry at him. He really was a friend, and I could not see my current life without him. That made me wonder, with some of the events which had been happening and the intensity of our relationship, if something else might be developing as well. I shook the thought out of my mind; it was way too soon and there was too much emotion in recent months. I hoped that friendship was all he was looking for. Danger really was everywhere.

Minutes later I heard him at the edge of my mind.
Harlie?
I'm settled down, James.

We met halfway, but he stopped twenty feet out and waited. It was up to me to close the gap. I dropped part of my shield, and my emotions let him know how I had resolved myself to the situation. He nodded but stood still. Taking a deep breath, I closed the gap. Hesitantly, James opened his arms. I went to him and he held me gently.

"I'm so very sorry, Harlie." He whispered.

"It's resolved, and I don't hate you,"

"With all I've done, you should. I am determined to make it up to you as much as possible."

I just nodded, being unsure of what he meant.

He dropped his arms and looked me over, "You're a mess."

I grinned slightly, "Can't take me anywhere."

James smiled warmly. "Dinner out is not an option and you need to eat. Let's get back to my formal office in the bunker. I'll bring up a meal for us then find a way to get you past the others."

"Sounds like a plan." I was not in a state to deal with the questioning glances and emotions from the rest of the team.

It was the first time I had really been in James' office. It was professionally decorated with a traditional hardwood desk, leather chair, a book shelf, and against one wall was a couch. We ate dinner there in a comfortable silence. Afterward, I sat and waited while he checked in on the others. Most were in the common room playing on the video game systems. He returned with Rick in tow.

I explained some of the situation to him. I know the two of you are good friends and figured you need him here about now.

I need you here too, Jamyson.

You'll need me more tonight. I'm going to get some rest now, so I can be there for you then.

He was right of course.

Rick sat down next to me, "James left the images up when the two of you ran out of here."

"So, you saw I'm more of a monster than expected."

"Harlie, none of us are monsters, especially not you. Forget about what Jason said, he is paying dearly for it."

While we waited, he updated me on the rest of the teams' activities and how everyone was eager for the Rio mission. When the conversation faltered, he turned to face me. "You know that I'm here for you, whenever you need me."

"Yes."

"Life has not been easy on you. Not your past one and definitely not this one. I cannot protect you, but I can help you stand whenever life knocks you down."

I scooted over to him in response, and he opened his arms to hold me. No words were necessary because we both knew what was needed. The rest of the world faded into the background. Rick kept me safe, and he was not even trying to protect me.

When James returned I was half asleep, leaning against Rick's strong frame. He still had an arm around me.

"Thank you, my brother, for watching over her. The others have turned in for the night, but all are uneasy about my return without her." He looked as if he had just woken up, his hair tousled, and clothes wrinkled.

"Anytime. You and I both know how special she is."

I sensed James' nod, "Even more so now."

Rick moved his arm, and James came to stand in front of me, "Alright, Harlie, the coast is clear."

After stretching, I stood and followed him down to my room. He stayed in the hallway, speaking quietly to Rick, while I got ready for bed. The moment I sat down, he came in and sat next to me.

"A long, painful day," He sighed.

"One I would rather have skipped." I tried to make light of the situation.

"Me too. Next time we should do just that." He joked.

I laughed quietly. "It's a shame these abilities don't allow us to see into the future. We could have hung out at the beach instead of dealing with Doctor L."

It was his turn to laugh. "Ah, Harlie, your resilience makes this massive mess seem so small." When I just shrugged he sighed again, "Time to sleep, Bear."

Obediently, I climbed under the covers. Instead of sitting on the chair by the desk, James stayed where he was. He was perfectly still as the day's trials quickly brought me to the edge of sleep. I felt the gentle pressure of his mind and then the dreams took me. James did not allow the nightmares to even start, instead guiding my thoughts from one pleasant event to another. Sometimes it was something I had experienced, sometimes it was one from his own mind. I was aware of him backing away in the early hours of the morning, but the nightmares were far off, and I continued to sleep peacefully.

The next two days passed at a furious pace. The team was curious about what had transpired, but because either Rick or James was constantly at my side, no one had the nerve to ask. Saturday morning, we left the bunker before dawn. The battle for Rio had finally arrived.

RIO

Early winter in Rio De Janeiro is so much more pleasant than late spring in Panama. The first week of July brought warm, but not too hot or too humid weather, and we could feel the difference the moment we landed. The team had come in on two separate flights that were only a couple of hours apart. The cabin was full of a combination of tourists, protesters, and diplomatic support staff – all arriving for an early start to the International Summit. I was sitting next to Max, and we were looking out the window at the cityscape below us. There had been a recent revitalization due to several large sporting events, and he pointed out the newer buildings and parks.

Dara and Ryan were four rows back. They were also watching our approach. Like with Panama, we were portraying visitors to the area. Max and I were protesters, and the others were tourists, there to see the area during this international event. On the second plane, the rest of the team were doing the same.

We landed without issue and our quick exit through customs was all that set us apart from the others getting off the plane. Security was understandably tight, but we had not received information about the U.N. increasing security even more due to any particular threat. Skull had arranged for us to stay at a proper campground at the southern side of the city, right along the water's edge. We gathered our bags and traveled there via two separate routes. By the time the others arrived, we had checked in and set up the tent from Dara's bag. We had reserved four primitive sites, which were side by side, but only planned to utilize two of them. The others were to be left empty. With as late a date as they had been reserved, the team had paid a steep price for the spots.

It was late evening when the others arrived and set up their two tents. We ate dinner and discussed our next moves. The International Summit was in three days.

Our job would be to spend them split up into sectors, watching for suspicious activity. Rick would stay in the camp and monitor all transmissions. If the police, U.N. or other force noticed something, he would tell us, so we could investigate. We would be working eleven-hour shifts with two-hour breaks in between. Those breaks would be used to debrief and have a group meal. It would be exhausting but, with so few people and so big an area to cover, it was the best we could do. The North American team would be doing the same but on the outskirts of the city. Skull, Max, Ryan, and I would be working the day shift. Mitch, Jason, James, and Dara would have the nights. Max and I immediately started taking bets on who would antagonize who first, James or Jason.

Because of the mission and our shifts, we had brought two smaller four-person backpacking tents and one standard four-person tent for Rick and the equipment. This allowed us to pack more supplies. As soon as the meal was finished: equipment was handed out, final directions were given, and we split into our groups. Max and I were in one tent, Skull and Ryan were in the second, and Rick camped out in the equipment tent. As we did in Panama, someone would remain awake throughout the night. Skull started, and Rick would finish the shift.

In the minutes before they left, James pulled me aside.

"How are you feeling? Are you ready for this?" His expression was somber.

"Since we are already here, I have no choice but to be ready for it." I laughed quietly, "I'm feeling well enough, just a little jet lagged."

He reached up a hand and gently ran his fingers down my cheek. "You are going to do a something brilliant here, I can feel it." He laid his hands on my shoulders and gave them a gentle squeeze, "Get some rest."

I smiled up at him then reached up a hand to grasp one of his, "I will. Try not to get into too much trouble on the first night okay?"

He laughed then mock saluted me, "Yes, Ma'am."

The night team left for the city, and the rest of us quickly prepared for bed. Inside the tent, Max took one side and I took the other. It was nice not to be crammed like sardines, although that time was sure to come. As per habit, I put my handgun by the pillow and my knife under it. Max noticed.

"Nice."

My nod was the only answer needed.

He turned to me, "Bear?"

There was a mental cringe when I looked out to see what he was after. "Yes, Root?"

Max rolled his eyes at my expression, "Don't play stupid. You're empathic and know full well what I'm curious about."

"Yes, we found out something really disturbing about my abilities. No, I'm not going to elaborate. Yes, The Commander and I are friends and no, it is not something more." I laid down on top of the sleeping bag and tugged the mosquito net into place, "Close enough?"

"Scary."

"G'night Root."

His response was muffled by the sound of him getting inside his own bag.

Due to our long day of traveling, we were barely awake when the others arrived back at the campground. They had picked up some pastries and fresh coffee on the way and, with some quickly reconstituted eggs, the breakfast was more like a small feast. The other group looked exhausted, especially James, but they remained awake and told us what little had transpired. They had split up into two smaller groups to cover more ground but all that had been witnessed were a couple of scuffles between police and what seemed to be gang members. They had also contacted five of our undercover agents.

The moment the meal was finished, we grabbed our day-packs and left. Ryan and Skull took the northern region with the airport, Maracanã stadium, and the famous samba schools. Max and I stayed in the south, where the Summit would be held. The North American team called in and said they would be covering the western, more crime-prone, region. The General had been going over our plans and decided to move them closer to the city. Past evidence had proven that whoever was planning the attack would have to stay closer to the site as the moment approached. We would all meet towards the end of the shift in a set location downtown.

With so much area to cover, time flew by. Max and I rented scooters and rode along the beachfront. We also took them in and out of the Barra section. It was here where the Summit was being held. Many of the buildings were new or recently remodeled. Several sports complexes had been built in recent years, and the streets had been repaved. We walked along looking at the new apartments, parks, and storefronts. At one point I thought I sensed something amiss, but it was fleeting and could not be traced. As the day passed, we hardly remembered to eat, never-the-less get to downtown in time.

Meeting part of the North American team was uncomfortable. They had an empathic on their team as well, a man named Zane. He was short with shoulder length blond hair and many piercings. After a few moments of staring at each other mentally, the others started to laugh. We kept it up though, poking at the others shield and introducing ourselves mentally. His mind's voice sounded strained though, perhaps because he did not use it enough. One thing that came out of our silent conversation was the impression that Zane was "not quite right." I remembered how James had described other empathics as people who had to shut the world out to stay sane or had lost their sanity due to the strain. Zane's eyes constantly darted about and his responses were clipped. When I reminded him, the other empath might be watching for us, he shuddered.

The other members were much like the rest of our team. Their main sniper was a redhead powerhouse named Lucia. She was from Belize, and it quickly became apparent that she and Max were fierce competitors. Another female was their diplomat and was called Sarina. One of the men was of Asian descent and was a bomb tech. I missed his name due to a comment from Zane. The final member present was their leader, Rockwell. He was of average height with eyes as dark as his skin. His head was completely shaved, and he analyzed my every move. I observed that he had mental shielding but did not seem to be looking out as another empathic would.

We went over schedules and plans with them, and they handed us the latest information gathered from their own agents. One was a promising lead, and we agreed to look

279

closer into it. They were still in the middle of their shifts and ours was ending, so I promised Rockwell that James would contact him about what actions to take. Just as quickly as we met, we parted ways. It was not good practice to be in one location for long, especially with a larger group. Skull and Ryan split from us and took a more direct route back to the campground. Max and I returned the rented scooters and rode a shuttle bus.

Since there was so much to cover, we debriefed during the evening meal. James was quite interested in the lead and would investigate it as soon as he made contact with Rockwell. Dara and Mitch were going to meet up with the rest of our agents while the others worked their assigned part of the city. Rick took first shift tonight while Max was taking second. The rest of us were asleep within minutes of the night group's departure.

Come morning we knew things were heating up fast. The lead James followed was indeed a branch of the mastermind group. As far as he could tell, they were moving parts of equipment into Barra. He did not sense the empathic but warned us to be careful. James showed me mentally all he had seen, heard, and felt. He then showed Skull where the information had been gathered, and the decision was made to have Skull come with me while Max went with Ryan. Rick relayed the information to the North American team using a fresh code, and our second full day in Rio began.

It was not very long before Skull and I picked up the trail again. The great thing about having a walking talking atlas alongside was that we never needed to stop. He knew exactly where we were and how to remain hidden. Around noon we had to do just that. I sensed a vaguely familiar mind in the crowded streets, and Skull led me to an alley nearby so could I try to spot the person. Sure enough, it was the man from the office in Poland. Once I saw his face, I knew. He had the same nervous look as he did the afternoon when I mentally witnessed the meeting he was in and when he sat on the bench afterward. This time he was dressed in blue jeans and carried a reusable shopping bag. We could see a box inside of it. Even without words, Skull knew, and we started following him. The man took a twisted path through the center of the Barra, never pausing. Skull kept us on more of a direct route and our paths crossed the man's several times. When he paused ever so slightly and handed off the bag, I knew the place had been marked into my partner's brain. We started following the new lead, a dark-skinned girl in a mini-skirt, but she soon climbed into a white car and was gone.

Skull found us a quiet location nearby and I opened my day pack.

"You think it was live?" He whispered.

"Even if I had not sensed him, the clicking from the Geiger would have tipped us off. It started when we first got close to him. Whatever was in that box was live." I lifted the pocket-sized digital detector from the pack. "It jammed up my earpiece so badly when we were within fifteen feet that I couldn't hear anything else."

It was disconcerting to see a person that built and fierce looking shudder, but it was the truth. The man I had seen in Poland had been carrying something radioactive in his shopping bag, and it was poorly shielded. From what I had sensed, he did not know it was leaking radiation so didn't know he had a short time to live.

"They won't travel far. This is their target area." Skull looked around.

"I hope we can pick up the trail again. Perhaps there was some increased chatter Rick can translate." A passerby looked in our direction, and we quickly took out water bottles and drank to make it seem as if thirst had been our reason for stopping.

We wandered the streets until our shift ended but the Geiger did not click or chirp again. Once again, I sensed nothing. Frustration was mounting because all afternoon I had been fighting the urge to stretch my abilities and sense as many people as possible. It might have led us to a bomb site, but it also might have attracted the other empathic.

When the others heard of our encounter, Rick confirmed there had been an uptick on a particular frequency and he quickly went to analyze it. James and I repeated the mental sharing of information while Rick worked. We could feel the others trying not to stare and failing.

He smiled mentally. *They can't help it.* Then added.

281

We'll find them. This is a solid lead, and you're right. It won't be far off from the exchange point. Great work today. Pride flowed through him and out towards me. I sent caution back in his direction. *Always, Bear, always.*

Just as the night team was walking out of our camp, one of our undercover agents called. Since they were under the strictest of orders about when it was permissible to contact us, we all listened to what was said. The agent had just witnessed an exchange not even six blocks from where Skull and I had been. The piece was much larger and was moved from a pick-up truck to an unmarked white van. The agent was able to get a picture of the van, two of the handlers and the plate numbers. I fed the information to the North American team – who forwarded it to the Canadian bunker. Within minutes, their results were printed for us. James looked over it and frowned.

"They must be really confident that we will not find out for them to be this careless." He handed the picture and printout to Mitch and then Ryan. "This is part of the trunk bomb isn't it?"

Mitch nodded, and Ryan swore. "They must be assembling it there in the city! That way, if they make a mistake and it goes off, it still does significant damage."

James looked around at all of us. "This makes it look like the enemy is almost ready to attack. They must be planning to detonate early in the Summit. We must find the targets as well as the locations of the bombs. That has to be done without tipping off the empathic. At least it looks as if the truck mounted airborne nuke isn't here. That means we had some success in Panama. Day team, get a few hours of sleep while we set up. Be prepared to head out before dawn. We are going to need as many people on the ground as possible." At our nods, he added, "Time is running out."

I started to follow Max to the sleeping tent when James called me back. "Bear, I need you to contact the U.N. force here while Jaws works on translating. Give them an update on our situation but keep it brief. Tell them to keep a group of at least twenty on standby. We could need them to step in at a moment's notice. This is the latest contact code." He sent it to me mentally, and I quickly repeated back to him. Without another word he left.

It took only minutes to reach the U.N and a minute more to be patched into the proper channels. They were eager to hear from us. Two bodies had been found in an abandoned building just under an hour ago. It was a male and female and the bodies showed signs of radiation poisoning. They had been shot before it could kill them. I described the witnessed exchange and they verified the physical descriptions. I asked that they keep an open channel with local hospitals because innocents had been exposed as well. I quickly relayed the update, including the recently witnessed exchanges and the order to have them be prepared for our call. One of the officers wondered if they shouldn't be stepping in now. I reminded them that there was more to the situation than they had been briefed on and how it could sabotage our mission if the U.N. appeared with us. We did agree they could increase security around the buildings involved in the Summit, but not by so many that the enemy would be tipped off to our knowledge. Our plans would only work if we were to remain hidden until the last possible moment – hopefully, the moment of arrest. No one seemed appeased by that, but they had been told by the highest-ranking officials to obey us.

After the call ended, I turned to see how much progress Rick had made. He had stopped translating and was staring at me.

"What?" His expression was confusing me.

He smiled, came over and placed his hands on my shoulders, massaging them gently. "You just handled that call like someone who has been a diplomat for years. I wish you could have heard your tone, as it was perfect."

"I don't know about that." I started to squirm out of the contact, and he reluctantly let go, stepped back a pace and stared at me again. This time I was tempted to look through his light mental shielding and see what emotions were trickling through, but he did not give me time.

"Stay here tonight, Bear. You only have a few more hours, curl up here instead."

I thought about it for a moment then chanced a glance mentally. It seemed Rick was feeling alone here in the equipment tent. His schedule was more grueling than ours, catching naps instead of proper sleep. I wasn't sure how my staying would help him but nodded and left to grab my pack from the entryway of the other tent. Rick pushed his own sleeping bag over so mine would fit better.

I peeked out again and Rick's mood had improved. He must have sensed my intrusion, because he turned to me and smiled gently.

"Thank you." He whispered and reached out to tousle my hair before going back to his work. I climbed into my bag and watched him until my eyes shut in sleep. Sometime later, Rick stopped his work and prepped for bed. I woke up at the sound and scooted closer to the equipment to give him more room. It was a tight fit, but I was comfortable near him.

At four in the morning, I was awakened by Rick whispering into one of the headsets. At my stirring, he said, "She's waking up now. I'll make sure she is ready. What about the others?" After the response there was a brief "okay" and the conversation ended.

He stepped over me and knelt down on his bag. "Bruce needs you to suit up and meet her at the water's edge. You'll be going with her, via boat, to a dock near some warehouses. Boss Guard picked up on a dark spot heading out of there and wants you and her to investigate."

Rick left the tent, so I could have some privacy while undressing and pulling on the skin-tight swimsuit which had been tucked into the bottom of my bag. A pair of thin black pants, my gun belt and a black t-shirt went on top of that. Next was the earpiece, a black baseball style cap and last, I pulled my hair up into a hasty ponytail through the back. When I left the tent, the others were awake and in various stages of getting dressed. There would not be time for a proper meal, so we rushed through energy bars and water. We had to be really quiet since this was a public campground and we were breaking the curfew rules set in place by its owners. The others were given their directions, then Skull led me out of the camp and over to the water's edge. Thankfully, the beach was deserted, and Ryan was back in the equipment tent, hacking into any security camera that might pick up on our movement. After we walked a mile, we heard the short static burst, which was our cue to stop. Skull handed me a waterproof bag with a shoulder strap and I quickly stuffed my pants, belt, and shirt into it. Looking out mentally, I could sense the location of the stealth boat and knew it was not far to wade and swim. Swallowing the panic which threatened to make itself known, I mock punched Skull's shoulder and started my silent walk into the waves.

Getting beyond the waves was more difficult than anticipated, and my progress was slower than it should be. However, Dara did not seem impatient when I swam up to the side of the boat. She hauled me into it, we both crouched below the frame, and the boat started moving. I looked over to see who was manning the vessel and recognized one of our agents. The boat was nearly soundless as it cut through the water. I was once again grateful for the advanced technology we seemed to have unlimited access to. Dara showed me a map of the warehouse, as well as the path the dark spot took out of the area. For part of the time, James would be within the range of my abilities in case the spot returned. He had been at his own limit when the anomaly was noticed and could not be sure if it really was the empathic from my Panama encounter.

The agent slowed the stealth boat, and we coasted into the warehouse area. The massive buildings were the only real eyesore in this renovated section of Rio. They were old, with broken windows, torn up lots and holes in some of the roofs. Graffiti was sprayed on many of the exteriors, but it was too dark to see the details. Dara and I put our clothes on over the suits, along with a bulletproof vest, and prepared to disembark as the driver edged closer to the dock. The agent would be staying with the boat and acting as a lookout from the water side. It was up to James, and whoever was with him, to watch our land side.

"Be on the lookout for surveillance cameras or motion detectors. We cannot be too sure Ryan or Mitch has disabled it." Dara whispered as we prepared to leave the boat.

On the agent's signal, we climbed the old ladder he had brushed the boat up against then laid flat on the broken boards until it was determined that no one had heard us. Even though I had no real experience in this type of situation, I was the first to spot a camera and the path to take around it. Dara nodded, and we found our way to the first building. Our target was one building over and further inland by three. It was a long way to go without being detected.

There were two chirps in my earpiece, and Dara turned to nod that she received it too. It was the sign from Ryan and Mitch that the security system had been scrambled. She peered quickly around the corner, unholstered her gun and nodded again. We ran across the alley between the first and second row. The water was still on the one side and our agent clicked an all clear. Once we made the run down the row, there would be little he could do to protect us.

Dara motioned for us to move forward and hide behind some palettes. I stretched out my abilities about a hundred feet around and there was no one but us. At my nod, we made the dash and sank behind them.

"I need a moment to stretch out farther. We are guessing the empathic is not within range, but there might be other enemies." I whispered.

"Don't be careless. I'll cover while you do," Was her hushed reply.

I stretched out again, a few feet at a time, until I was at the target warehouse. There were a few scattered sleeping people in the building next to us. They seemed to be transients. The target warehouse was alive with activity though.

"Only a few sleeping homeless between here and there but quite a few minds at the target. I'll home in on specifics once we get closer."

"Let's hurry, I don't know how long we have with the scramble."

We dashed to a large garbage bin, then to the edge of the first building. No one was in the alley, so we crossed and continued up the side of the second building. It didn't take long, as there were plenty of debris to hide us. We were two-thirds of the way up when I pulled Dara to the ground. There was a mind about fifty feet in front of us.

"Guard." I mouthed.

She nodded and leaned out for a quick look. "Easy." She mouthed back. The moment the man had his back turned, Dara dashed behind him and knocked him out with one blow. I never heard her steps, and he never saw her coming. In a moment she had him tied, gagged, and hidden.

I met up with her, and we continued to the edge of the building. There was a door at the back of the target warehouse along with another two guards. This was the way we had planned to get into the building. Dara looked at me, held up two fingers, waved them back and forth, and then signed the letter L. I was to take the guard on the left. I gave a quick nod and she started forward. The guards spotted us only a second before we reached them. Dara knocked hers out with one punch. I kicked the gun from the others hand then put him on the ground. Dara finished the job, and we tied them up as well. There was an external stairwell to a second level, which we climbed up as quietly as possible. The door was unlocked, and we were inside within seconds.

We were on a small overlook and boxes hid us from those below, so long as we remained at a crouch. From what I could sense there were about ten men at the lower level. I homed in on each one to find out what they were doing. After the third person, I hit the button on the back of my earpiece three times. We had found something very important.

"Can I look?" Dara mouthed.

"Wait."

The empathic was not there, but he had been. Three people below were thinking about him. I lingered on their minds and was able to get a partial mental image of what the empathic looked like. The rest were focused on their tasks. They were assembling several items I could only assume were the bombs. I turned to Dara and mouthed, "Get pictures." She pulled out a thin camera the size of a flash drive, reached around the debris we were hiding behind and snapped a couple dozen shots without looking. She then reached into her pocket and pulled out an inch-wide monitor. She installed it into the corner, where it would stay hidden by the boxes. It would pick up conversation and transmissions from anyone who came up to this level.

Two chirps came out of our earpieces. The scramble had to be stopped, so it was time to make our escape. The guards were out cold and had not been discovered yet. We raced past them to the middle building and sprinted down the length. We had just ducked around the end when James made

287

contact.

Dyfodiad.

"Empath incoming." I whispered to Dara.

"Shielded." Was her reply.

We had to get one building down and one across to reach the boat. My heart raced as what we had just accomplished caught up with me. I quickly scanned for minds between us and the agent, but only found the same sleeping forms. I mouthed, "Run for it."

We did, stopping only at the alley for a split second. The moment we landed in the boat, the agent took off for safer waters. Not once did I sense the other empathic and hoped that meant our minds had not been noticed either. The only evidence of our presence would be three unconscious guards. However, I knew that would be enough and started to think about what had to happen next. It was disconcerting to say the least.

It was a fifteen-minute ride to the prearranged drop off location, time enough to get my emotions under control. The small pier was under U.N. watch and we safely disembarked. We did not want to take public transportation, and it took many minutes to hail a taxi, but eventually, we made it back to the camp.

James and Mitch were already there and recording the incident. Max, Skull, and Ryan were out in the field, while Jason was cleaning up. Dara handed the tiny camera to Rick, who quickly pulled up the images.

"Boss." He called to James. "You're going to want to see this."

James started towards him but then paused and came over to me. "I want your input on this."

We crammed into the tent and looked at the first picture. Since Dara had only reached her hand out to take the images, instead of possibly blowing cover by standing and properly setting it up, the angle was off a bit. However, it was obvious that we had indeed found an assembly point. The trunk bomb was there, and two men were leaning over it, presumably installing a detonator or other important equipment. We could see the warhead. The van our agent had taken images of was parked nearby, as was an SUV.

James swore then added, "That will wipe out a million people."

"Are there still no leads as to potential targets?" Mitch wondered, leaning his head through the door flap.

"They have to be planning for more than just the Summit because look at the next image." Rick clicked over.

The second picture showed a table with three open suitcases. Rick zoomed in and enhanced the image. There were definitely bombs inside. Some of the electronics sat nearby and another person could be seen working on it.

"They are almost ready." I whispered.

"I hope there are not more than these four." Rick looked up at the sky. "The trunk bomb will flatten four miles. Each of the suitcases will destroy a mile, so that's at least eight miles of the city gone. When you calculate damage zones and what the wind can spread it means almost all of the city will be affected in some way."

James sighed before responding. "The good news is we are still not seeing evidence of the flatbed nuke. They must not have been able to recover from the damage we did in Panama...although what is in these images is indeed enough to destroy Rio."

"The trunk bomb must be for Barra, and we have to assume one suitcase will be for the airport. They will want to cripple potential assistance." Rick looked over at James, who nodded in agreement.

"Barra is a large area. They will not be able to get close to the conference center, and the towers the representatives are staying at are heavily guarded. But, with a bomb that size, they do not need to get very close to either. Let's pull up the map and see if there is a likely spot between the two locations." We looked closely at the map and found several points where a van might be parked and left without suspicion and too many locations where the SUV could sit at.

"What are the chances that they can still remote detonate, even though we took out the transport with the major components of their device?" I pondered.

"They might risk using the same device they used in the U.S. attacks, even though they must realize we have the ability to disengage it." Mitch answered.

James spoke up again, "This group has been known for suicide bombs as well. It is more likely that this is their plan, at least for the suitcase nukes. I don't see the right equipment in these pictures for that type of attack with the larger warhead."

Rick enhanced the suitcase picture even more. "These need to be sent to the U.N. immediately. Everyone needs to be on the lookout for those cases."

"I agree. Bruce, assist Jaws with making contact and then get cleaned up and eat." James left the tent and went over to where Jason was heating up a pot of water over the fire. "You need to be ready for duty in four hours."

Mitch popped his head out of the tent, "Boss, I'm going to analyze the images to figure out exactly what they are using. I'll rest after that."

James nodded then motioned for me to follow him. He went into one of the sleeping tents and sat wearily on the ground. I sat facing him and waited. James stared into nothingness for at least a minute before shaking his head and making eye contact with me.

"Good job out there this morning, Bear."

"Thank you." I wanted to add how he had done well too, but that probably wasn't appropriate for one's commanding officer.

"What did you sense at the warehouse? Did they seem excited as if the event were about to happen? Or were they still focused on the work?"

"Most were focused on their work, three were thinking about the empathic." I showed him the partial image I had been able to pull from their minds. "It seems he is perceived as a boss of some type. We were not there long enough for me to gather more details, but we did leave a receptor behind."

James closed his eyes, "I hope they start talking about targets. This is coming down to the wire." His eyes opened, and I could see the worry pouring through the emeralds. "Unus Universium is being extremely careful with transmissions, and the bunker is not getting anything worthwhile from the cities cameras – even with the instant recognition software for the faces we know are involved."

Despite part of my mind telling me no, I reached out

and touched one of his hands. "We are going to have to take the warehouse."

He nodded, then grabbed my hand. "But how can we bring a team in when an empathic is keeping watch? He was not away very long, and we cannot sniper him because he is probably looking for an attack of that type."

"Bait," Was my instant response. I had been thinking about it for a couple of days and this seemed the best time to bring the idea up. "He is familiar with my mind already and I with his, so I bait him the next time he leaves the warehouse and try to keep him distracted. The downside is that he already suspects I'm an enemy, but there are questions I want to ask. If we time it well enough, the others can get into the warehouse and disable the nukes."

James closed his eyes again and shook his head from side to side. I began to think up ways to reason with him if he were to verbalize the movement.

"You cannot go alone. Skull will come with you and Root will station on that side just in case there is a chance." The eyes opened to stare at me.

I quickly realized the effort the decision had to have cost him, agreeing to let me become the bait without arguing about my protection. However, a smaller point needed to be addressed. "No, you are going to need Root for the firepower. Skull and I can handle it."

He let go of my hand and shook his head again. "I'll decide where he will go once we see how the situation is playing out." James then leaned forward, reached up and brushed the back of his fingers down the side of my face. I could feel him reach out mentally at the same time and hoped all he picked up on was my determination. There was no way I would allow anyone else to experience what had happened to my native country. The fact that an attack was so imminent and was planned to take out the heads of so many nations just made me even more determined to succeed.

James dropped his hand and smiled, "Don't let go of that feeling, no matter what."

BAIT

Once the rest of the team was informed of our plans, those who were in the camp prepared for the mission ahead. Instead of wasting time waiting for the others to arrive, we set up three meeting points along the way. I would split off and join up with Skull at one area. The rest would gather at the other two locations to wait for my signal. The North American team would also split up. Half would be dispatched to cover the airport in case the masterminds had a backup plan of body strapped explosives. The other half would station at the conference center for the same reasons. James ordered the U.N. standby group to make sure several snipers were in place around the center and for the rest to stay outside of range.

While this was happening, I added two extra clips to my belt, holstered a smaller gun at my ankle and changed into a proper outfit for my mission. My goal was to come face to face with the empathic, so street clothes were best, but I also needed to be prepared for a fight. The jeans and sneakers I put on worked fine for the bottom half, but I had to put on a tank top under the bulletproof vest and a dark button-up shirt to hide it. Once the earpiece was in, I left the tent and waited for the others. James looked me over and dropped part of his shield. He radiated confidence in our ability to be successful, followed by reminders of how to attack and defend, then ended with concern for the safety of Rio. At my silent nod, he walked over to me, looking like he wanted to say something. Instead, he stood silent then turned and walked away. I smiled to myself, no words needed to be said aloud or mentally. I already knew it in my heart.

Before noon we started to leave for our positions. In less than two hours, I was at the location James had been yesterday when he had sensed the dark spot. Skull arrived minutes later. I filled him in on my plan while taking his vest out of my bag along with another weapon. We were in a supply yard. Pallets, crates, and shipping containers were stacked in seemingly random piles. Some areas were fenced in while others were not. Security cameras were scattered about,

293

but there were many areas outside of their sight. We sat in one of those spots, next to a couple of crates along the southern edge. It was going to be a waiting game, but I was to determine how long of a wait. We knew that as soon as I stretched my abilities out far enough to reach the warehouse if he were there, the empathic would know. We were counting on his curiosity and hoped he would not bring more than a few people with him.

"Skull, are you ready?" I turned to him.

"Bring it on." He smirked.

"I'll need to focus, especially if he starts to prod. Cover for me."

"Not a problem." He pulled out his gun.

My earpiece chirped once, the others were in place. After several deep breaths, I started to look out. I made sure that all of the minds in the yard were registered. There were not many because the number of boats being allowed in and out were tightly restricted due to the Summit.

"Only a handful of workers here today."

Skull grunted in reply.

I reached farther out, closer to the warehouses. There was more activity in several buildings now that it was mid-day, and I sent out a silent prayer for them. At that instant I felt, more than saw, the dark spot. It seemed to be staring at me, and I guessed he had sensed me before I had registered him. Just as with Panama, I sent out a tendril of curiosity. However, instead of waiting for a response, this time I pulled my abilities back a couple of hundred feet. After counting to thirty, I moved forward again until I could see the spot. He had not moved. This time I mixed a little worry in with the curiosity. The spot wavered then moved closer several feet.

I pulled back totally and turned to Skull, "I'm moving in and out of his range, hoping to either make him curious enough or annoyed enough to come looking for me."

"Good plan." Skull was a man of few words.

I focused my abilities again, but this time the spot was prepared. He sent curiosity back in my direction. I ignored it and started to focus on the minds around him. Those were starting to become edgy. The spot paced back and forth a few times then stopped. I stared at it, hard, and I know he had to

294

have felt it. I backed off again.

"I have his attention now. He was waiting for me."

Another grunted response.

When I looked out this time, the dark spot was slightly closer and was not alone. Two other minds were next to him. Focusing on them I could tell they had been told to follow and be ready to shoot. The dark spot noticed my probe and sent out a wave of annoyance. I sent back a wordless question, just like he had on our first meeting, but did not wait around for a response.

"He is bringing two guards, be ready."

Before I could look out again, the other empathic made contact.

I know you. You are the stupid child from the jungle.

You must be mistaken. I am not a child and do not know you.

What do you want? The voice sounded annoyed.

I was curious. It's not often I sense another mind like myself.

The three minds were walking towards us quickly. I pondered briefly over how the dark spot was speaking mentally with much less effort this time. The thought was interrupted.

Who is with you?

My guide.

You lie.

Search for yourself, he is a guide.

I spoke aloud. "You are my guide. He's going to probe for that."

Skull looked very focused.

He likes maps! the mind laughed. *Another stupid child.*

"He just called you a stupid child." Now Skull was the one to look annoyed.

You are lucky that I am curious about you too. If not, you would be dead by now. The empath's mind reeked of overconfidence. It took extra control to keep my thoughts simple. I decided to start my distractions with a question.

Are you like me and born this way? It was a half-truth, and I hoped to keep the lie hidden.

No, stupid child, I was made. He laughed harshly.

Does that scare you?

"They are halfway here. Tell the others." I whispered aloud before answering mentally. *How?*

The other mind sighed and paused in his step. *It was the most amazing accident! I was scarred in a fire. My brothers heard of a special doctor and took me to see him. He said he would do the surgery to fix the scars for free. During a test before the surgery, he found something wrong in my brain and offered to fix that too. When I woke up, I could hear others' minds.*

Something about his story scared me to the core. This sounded all too familiar. Part of my mind reasoned that what he was saying could not be possible. The Guardians kept careful control over anyone they worked with. But still...

Ha! he laughed. *You are scared, I can feel it.* He started to press in on my shield.

I struggled to hide the reason behind my fear.

The surgeon knew what he had done and showed me how to use my new power. He also told me to look out for an old mind. That mind would try to kill me and anyone like me.

What is an old mind? I fought to sound dumb.

Stupid child! One who has had too much time alive. I was warned that he looks young but really is much older and very powerful. He laughed again. *I bet he is not as powerful as the surgeon thinks.*

The trio could be seen in the distance. I sat still, hopefully looking calm but curious. Skull had moved to sit about twenty feet away, mostly hidden by a crate.

Have you met other minds? He pressed harder on my shield in an attempt to probe my mind for the answer.

Yes. Honesty seemed like a right approach. *But it was not an old mind. It was someone else born this way. He taught me how to shield and talk like this.*

They were close enough now for me to see details. The middle person was young, perhaps in his early twenties. He appeared to be of South American decent with straight black hair pulled tight into a ponytail. He was dressed in black, as were the two taller men on either side of him.

He was looking me over as well. *Are you still in contact with that mind?* There was an edge to his voice.

Again, honesty seemed good, *Yes.* I withheld the details, though.

Interesting. His eyes took on a hard glint and the guards reached for their guns. *The day we last met, and I know you remember, there was an attack on some friends of mine. They were bringing supplies to my village.*

Is that why you were in the jungle with those other people? It took everything I had to keep the innocence in my voice, as I knew he wasn't telling the truth. *I wanted to ask, but you left so quickly.*

I left because you were lying like you are lying now! Mental fire rippled in my direction. I cringed but blocked it.

He laughed out loud this time but quickly stopped when one of his guards fell down, shot. The fact that he had been distracted enough to not sense Skull draw and fire registered in my brain.

"You were with them!" He screamed aloud. "More lies."

At the same time, the other guard opened fire on Skulls position. I tried to remain focused on the empathic while touching the button on the exposed part of my earpiece to signal it was time for the attack.

"Why are you trying to destroy Rio?" I asked over the gunfire. No more lies here, I was getting right to the heart of the matter.

"Why should you care? With our powers, we can rule over those around us."

"It was not an empath who led the attack on America so don't use that line on me. Are you part of the Universum?" I had to raise my voice to be heard.

"Oh, so you know about them? Too bad they are far too powerful to be threatened by your pathetic special forces." He was gloating now, his eyes wild.

"Don't be so sure about that. We seem to have had recent success in Panama. Tell me, how are you planning on detonating those nukes?" I hit where it hurt. His expression changed from one of gloating to one of grief, then to anger.

"Your people killed one of my brothers." He sent out another wave of fire. This time I not only blocked it but threw the wave back at him. He stumbled backward and sweat

297

started to bead on his forehead.

A pained yell distracted us momentarily. The other guard laid on the ground dying, and Skull had been shot in the leg. The empath scowled, then turned to me with an evil grin.

"Just you and me now," He laughed, then his expression became blank.

I waited, torn about being unable to see if Skull was in need of help.

Fierce anger lit the enemy's face. "How...dare...you!" He screamed at me. I assumed he had seen some of the truth in Skulls mind. This time the mental attack was much worse. It was flames from the sun itself, and I gasped at the pain. My eyes closed for an instant in the battle for my shield and, when they opened, his expression had changed again.

"There is always a backup plan. You have just proven your stupidity." He was holding a detonator remote in his hand. I recognized the design.

"We have codes for that." I challenged.

"But who's going to be around to put them in when there is only a twenty second timer on it? This will blow the warhead and your friends with it."

Before anything else could be said or done, I mentally sent out a single word in Welsh to James, knowing the empath would not understand what I said or who it was meant for. He looked confused for an instant but raised the detonator higher.

"It will blow us up too you know." I countered.

"I am not afraid to die for Unity. If you are afraid to die for your pathetic cause, then tell your friends to surrender."

Time was running out. He was insane enough to press that button and I knew it. Shielded or not, that much was leaking out of his mind. He was not stable. We stared at each other for a long second.

He had to be distracted from the detonator and quickly. His thumb kept inching towards it. I knew what had to be done and braced myself. Gathering all the horrible images from the nuclear attack on America, I threw them in his direction. I then pushed out the scene from the destroyed transport in Panama, followed quickly by the determination I felt. Behind that, I hurled images of Dr. L. The last part felt like the shock waves

298

James had used during my training.

It worked. First, the enemy's eyes grew wide in shock, then a wave of horror washed over him. The moment my images of Dr. L reached him, his shield flickered, and I grabbed hold of it and yanked. Somehow, while focusing on this, my hands found my gun, and I aimed for his hand. The instant his shield fell, I shot the detonator out of his hand and put a second bullet into his chest.

His reaction was to throw all of his emotion, a twisted souls worth, at me with the force of a bomb blast. It was his last action. My finger pulled the trigger again and he fell. However, before I could see if he were dead, he exploded in a gruesome display. Pain raced through my mind and body. I saw stars but managed to stay conscious.

Stumbling over to where Skull sat propped against a crate, I was vaguely aware of movement off to my right. I numbly tore open the bag we had brought with us and grabbed the med-kit. The gunshot wound in his leg was bleeding but not bad enough to make me worry about a damaged artery. There was a slight shuffle and a pinging sound, then nothing. I started wrapping his wound with gauze, ignoring the pain wracking my own body. Suddenly, I heard Max scream in the distance, "Bear, duck!"

There was just enough time to pull Skull down with me when a bright flash enveloped us. Smoke filled the area and shrapnel flew in every direction. I could hear it slamming into nearby objects, then silence. We laid perfectly still as I tried to process what had just happened. The silence was soon broken by the sound of Max's footsteps. He faltered several times before making it to us.

"One guard wasn't dead yet. When you turned your back to help Skull, he pulled the pin on a grenade." Max panted. "I watched the empath go down from my sniper scope and was on the way to you when he moved."

I looked up at him while Skull repositioned himself against the crate and saw that Max was holding his shoulder. The movement made me dizzy, but I reached back into the bag and grabbed a gauze pad. The dizziness became worse when I handed it to him.

"Thanks, Bear, took some metal there." It looked like

he had taken a few smaller pieces as well.

I tried to speak, but the words would not come out. The effort caused my vision to go white.

"Bear? Bear! Hey, what's wrong?" Max sounded far away. I heard him swear and felt him grab my leg. "Looks like you took a big piece, but it's not too bad." The shrapnel was sticking out of my lower leg, so he bandaged around it.

I nodded numbly. Whatever was wrong was not coming from my leg wound. We sat and waited for the rest of the battle to be over, Skull muttering about hoping we did not have to defend ourselves from this position.

"Bear, can you look out to see how they are doing?" Max's voice still sounded far off, and I could barely understand him. I made several attempts at taking deep breaths before trying to focus my ability. The pain it caused made me break out into a sweat and start shaking. The mental image was distorted, but I could sense Ryan and Mitch working on the bombs. James noticed and turned his thoughts towards me. I heard myself scream in agony but could do nothing to stop it. Skull leaned forward and slapped his hand over my mouth. I shoved him away, leaned the other direction and became sick.

"What happened?" Max pulled me away from where I had become ill and leaned me against a different side of the crate.

"Root..." My voice sounded choked. He handed me the canteen from the bag, and I took a sip of water. It was a full minute before I could try again; "Root...my h-h-head." was all that came out.

Sudden understanding came into his eyes. He plopped down next to me, gun in hand, and we waited silently until Ryan and Mitch finished their task. We heard the U.N. forces as they drove into the area and knew the mission was successful. A helicopter flew in overhead, the sound deafening. We continued to wait.

Jason, Dara, and two U.N. force members reached us nearly an hour later. Jason went over to Skull first, then started towards me. I pointed to Max and he obeyed. One of the other members gave me more water and asked where else I was hurt. I couldn't respond though, just stared at him and choked on the water. That got Jason's attention and he came back over

300

to me.

"That shrapnel needs to be pulled, but I want to wait until it can be properly sewn up." He took my vitals, paused and took them again. "What's happening, Bear? It's more than just the leg doing that." I shook my head and tried to shrug but it ended up as a cringe from a burning sensation that raced through my body.

He turned to one of the U.N. soldiers, "All three need pain medication, but go light on it because they'll need to answer when Colonel Davies arrives." It was the first time I had heard James' proper title in context. He frowned at me then went back over to Max.

An ambulance and van arrived shortly thereafter, and we were loaded into them. The drive seemed to take forever, with every jolt and bump causing me to almost black out. We stopped inside the U.N. post at the edge of the city. The group whisked Max, Skull, and I into one of the buildings. It was the medical facility and within seconds a U.N. nurse had me on a cot, barely dressed and with an IV line started.

A doctor came over to start examining me, but Jason hollered out, "Wait! Take the other two. She has a tricky underlying condition." Jason came over and started working on my leg. "We need to get the three of you stable. I have no idea how fast we are going to move out." At my questioning expression he added, "If we find information leading to others, we'll have to chase that lead before the enemy realizes we are coming."

I tried to nod but saw stars again.

"The Commander better get here soon. I have no idea what is going on with you, but right now your vitals are more critical than the others." He whispered. Loudly, he called to the nurse, "Prep her leg for me to remove that shrapnel."

Jason walked briskly over to the others, talked to them briefly, then hurried out of the room with his hand on his earpiece. Fog rolled over my mind again, and I barely registered the nurse commenting to me as he strapped my legs down, injected a local anesthetic, covered, and then swabbed the area. Jason came back into the room, and I forced myself to focus as he went to a glass-enclosed corner, scrubbed his hands and arms, then came over to me. After the nurse gloved and masked him he poked at my leg.

"Can you feel this?"

Again, my voice was paralyzed. I could not speak. He turned to me, eyes pleading. "Bear, please try to respond." Although I could not seem to focus on his mind, I knew my condition was just verifying his delusions about my presence on the team.

"Can't...feel...that." I choked before the same burning pain raced through my body again, and I flinched.

He hovered over me and the nurse looked concerned. I could hear beeps from the monitor showing my heart beating too fast and the chime warning that my blood pressure was too high. Jason sighed.

"Your meds are at the camp, aren't they?" He grumbled then turned back to the nurse and ordered several medications. The nurse nodded and rushed off. "Can't get this piece out with you reacting so badly, but I know better than to sedate you with The Commander on the way – even if it is the safest thing for you."

Three injections into my IV later and I was staring off into oblivion while Jason tugged the five-inch shard of metal out of my leg and started sewing up all the bleeders. Somewhere on the other side of the small building Skull screamed out as the bullet was removed from his thigh. Max was silent, watching both of us, as his wounds were sewn and bandaged. My eyes closed as another wave of fire washed over me and the alarms went off again. Far away, I heard Jason mumble, "Let her pass out, just monitor her vitals so she doesn't go too deep."

Fire, fire, and more fire. The more I looked around, the more fire I saw. Empty black holes were surrounded by flames. Doctor L was on fire, the empathic blew up, my leg was on fire. Oranges, reds, and yellows swirled around and around. I screamed, but it seemed that no one heard me. I tried to run, but my legs were immobilized. Panic and pain circled as the flames burned brighter and stronger...

A cool breeze whisked by me as I burned. It came again, and this time cold water poured around me. My screaming stopped with the relief of the water. A voice was

302

calling quietly.

"Bear, come back to me. Come back, Bear." I knew that voice. It registered in my mind as well as my ears. More cold water poured around me. I gasped at the sensation and opened my eyes.

The fire was not real. I was on a bed with a monitor beeping quietly beside me, not the alarms of before. James' fingers were on my temples, his green eyes blazing with concern. I gasped again and tried to sit up. The fingers moved to my shoulders, gently pushing me back down.

I looked around. It was night and the room was dim. Skull was snoring off his pain medication in the corner and Max was still watching me. James lifted a cup of water to my lips, and I drank like a person who had been in the sun all day.

"Easy, Bear." He gave me a small smile then sat back to look me over. "Now, before your body decides to rebel again, can you tell me what happened?" He clicked on a portable voice recorder and placed it next to my head.

I looked at him questioningly, then turned to Jason who was hovering at the foot of my bed. "You had a seizure, a bad one at that. You're pumped full of anti-spasm drugs right now."

I mouthed an O.

"Bear, try to talk to us." James met my eyes, "Your unique physiology seems to be the root of the seizure." He added in a whisper.

I swallowed hard, and James leaned back over me, resting his fingers back on my temples. A cool wave of relief washed over me again. I knew it was temporary, so I forced the most important fact out first.

"The enemy empathic was made by Doctor L."

James sucked in a breath while Jason spat out an "Impossible."

I started to shake my head, but James held it in place.

"He said he was made by a man who fixed his burn scars." I braced myself as a new wave of burning pain started to come and was stopped by the cold water, "In the fight, he went into shock when I showed him L's face." Thankfully, my voice was a whisper. No one outside of the Guardians would understand any of what had been said. "It's what distracted

303

him enough so that I could..." The world started to spin, and James' fingers pressed harder. "Could shoot the detonator from his hand."

"What happened from there?" James probed.

"He attacked back with everything he had." I gasped at the memory. "Then...then I shot him again. He was dead before he blew up." That part I was sure of. His mind had been silent.

James nodded. "We searched through what was left. He was implanted with a device set to go off at brain death. Makes sense, if he was enhanced, to destroy the evidence. Root told us what happened from that point on." He smiled softly at me, "I told you that you were going to be brilliant. When you've been healed you'll have to tell me the whole thing." He stood up. "Rest now while I work on getting us home."

Jason took James' spot by my side and grabbed my hand. My world was still fuzzy and there was no strength to pull it away. "How's my leg, Stitch?" I forced out.

"It looks like a smaller piece was imbedded deep in your leg. I couldn't get that out without doing more damage than necessary, but you'll heal around it." His eyes looked at my body, lingering on seemingly random spots. "There are numerous scrapes and smaller wounds. You are on heavy antibiotics because," He hesitated, "Some of the punctures were caused by bone fragments." I cringed, and he added, "We are running tests on the remains to make sure no anti-retroviral drugs are needed."

I sighed, and he squeezed my hand. "You saved the day, Bear. Those nukes were on a hair of a trigger. The plans were to set them off within twenty-four hours, so we got there just in time. Some story is being leaked to the media right now about a special U.N. team discovering and neutralizing the threat, and the Summit is still happening."

The wave of dizziness was returning. I knew there was not much time before I went under again. My other hand started to twitch, "What's wrong with me?" I forced out.

Jason looked at the monitors then at me, "You shouldn't go into a full seizure this time." My vision shook, and I flinched from the waves of pain, but stayed conscious.

When it passed Jason explained, "James thinks that the empathic attacked you literally with his dying breath. Everything he had was used to hurl his hate towards you. It ripped apart your mental shielding or something like that."

"What do you think?"

He sighed. "I don't know. Something happened to you that cannot be explained by the medical equipment here. If it is what he says it is, then I can only try to keep you stable." Jason squeezed my hand again, "I don't know how to fix it."

Just like that, whether it was how the words registered, the effects of the day, the power of the medication keeping me stable, or a combination of the three, I stopped being able to talk again. Worse than that, I could barely focus on anything around me: not words that were directed towards me or conversations hushed away, not the food placed in front of me, nothing. I laid on the cot and stared into nothing with no coherent thoughts going through my brain. James came to check on me around midnight and asked several questions, but I could not respond verbally or mentally. He looked as if my silence hurt him but only responded with a comment about getting us all out of Rio.

Although I did not sleep that night, at first light Skull woke everyone up with his demands to be discharged. Max threw a pillow at him and Jason humored the U.N. doctor with stories of past experiences involving Skull and injuries. James came in shortly after with the rest of the team behind him. I could see The Commander was here for business. Jason handed Skull some crutches and they all gathered by my bed.

"We are leaving in two hours. A straight through commercial flight has been arranged. Since we are technically part of the United Nations Forces, they will be providing us with uniforms as our cover. The story is that we were involved with the takedown of the nuclear threat and are traveling with our wounded back to our home base." He smiled grimly, "For once we get to tell the truth. We still need to hide our identities though, so it will be fake our ID's, hats, sunglasses, and no names will be on the uniforms."

The others nodded, but I was battling to process the words.

"Let's get properly packed up. I want all evidence

secured for carry-on. Stitch, you will obviously oversee the wounded and will have an aisle seat in order to roam between them. Ka, you will sit with Root. Bruce, you'll be with Skull and have permission to knock him out if he gets too loud." The others smiled. "Jaws, you'll be with Bear. Boom and I will manage any questions and run interference. Understood?" They all nodded.

I stared, barely understanding. James frowned and dismissed the others. They quickly left to prepare for our departure. He sat down on the bed and stared out, "That Look" coming into focus long enough for me to grasp it. I started to shake, and the expression disappeared, replaced by one of concern. James placed his fingers on my temples again and I felt the cooling relief.

"Do you understand what is happening around you?" He asked aloud and mentally.

It took me several long moments to put his words together. I slowly shook my head.

"We have to get you home. I think I can help you but not in this place."

More long moments passed while the words processed.

He pressed his fingers harder, and I could feel his presence at the edge of my mind. It was painful though, and I tried to curl up into a ball. He let me but kept one hand lingering. I shuddered as a wave of pain took me and felt him tense up. James waited until it passed before speaking again.

"Hang on, Bear. Keep hold of that determined feeling from yesterday. Don't let that go, don't let the pain take over."

I understood his words this time, and my eyes let him know.

"Good. Keep holding on." He moved away from me, going back to preparing for our departure. I wanted to scream for him, but words still would not come.

Jason came up minutes later and started to disconnect me from the monitor and IV bag. Next, he went and did the same with Skull. An officer came in with three U.N. uniforms, and I numbly started to put on the one she handed to me. It was difficult to sit totally up. My leg throbbed as I started to swing it over the side of the bed.

"Wait." Jason called out. I did not understand the word

but comprehended his tone enough to be still. He rushed over to support me as I tried to move again.

"You should be sedated and put on a medical flight up north." He growled when I cringed. Once the words registered, I shook my head no and reached for the uniform pants. Jason gently helped me into the uniform, as I had to pause often due to the waves of pain. He had just finished when an official came in stating it was time to leave. Jason reached into his pocket and slammed a syringe of something into my IV, tugged the jacket over my arm, then stood back a moment.

"Sorry Bear, I hate the stuff, but it will hold you over until we are off the plane." He grabbed my arms and held them to my side as my body started to twitch. "Don't seize," He begged. "Please don't seize." The twitching became worse and his grip tightened. "They won't let you out of here unless you can fake being stable. You have to be coherent. That stimulant I gave you has to work."

It did. I was able to understand him and forced my body to be still. Jason dropped his grip, checked my vitals, then looked me in the eyes. "Can you talk?"

"Yes." I croaked. My heart felt like it was racing out of my chest, but I knew whatever act I had to put on would be possible.

He handed me crutches, and I was up in moments, fighting through the dizziness to hobble outside of the building. Rick was waiting and helped me into the transport for the ride to the airport. The others loaded in, Skull swearing the entire time, and we were off.

Rick took my hand in his larger one, rubbing circles on it with his thumb as we drove. I looked out the window, trying to keep myself coherent by focusing on finding major landmarks. When the vehicle turned so that I could see the Corcovado mountains, I found where the Christ the Redeemer statue stood and stared at it for as long as possible.

We were driven to the airports' main building via a back gate and dropped off at the end of a long terminal. A jumbo jet was parked there, and people could be seen boarding it. Our larger bags were quickly secured in the cargo hold, right next to its door. Rick helped me out of the transport and swung my carry-on bag over his shoulder. Using the crutches, I climbed up a flight of metal steps and was escorted into the back door of the terminal. People turned to stare at us, many were smiling.

Rick leaned over to whisper, "The passengers have been told of our accomplishment and how the three wounded in the take down would be traveling with them." He grimaced, "The airline demanded the right to tell. Anything for positive publicity, you know. However, the demand was made for no pictures being taken, as it could compromise everyone's safety."

Many eyes were indeed on me and the now silent Skull. Max, arm in a sling, came to stand next to me. "Wish it were not such a serious situation," He grinned. "I'd give them something to publicize."

The crowd parted for us to move into the passageway leading to the airplane. Security was making them lower their phones and cameras. Rick kept a protective hand on my back, and Mitch nodded thanks to those who spoke out. Although the tickets we had been given said our seats were at the back of the plane, enough people had volunteered to give up their business class seats so that all nine of us were able to sit there. I sighed with relief. It would have been near impossible to hobble all the way to the back. Rick took a middle seat and helped me settle into the aisle one. We greeted the middle-aged gentleman sitting by the window, then waited. Many of those who boarded after us paused to say thank you. We smiled back, and I even shook a few hands. I was aware enough to recognize changes in the expressions of those who paused long enough to really look at me.

"Jaws?" I finally whispered.

"Yes?" He leaned closer.

"Do I really look that bad?" I turned to face him.

His slow nod left me frowning. "Keep your chin up. You'll be able to relax a bit once everyone is on board."

I turned back towards the incoming passengers, choking back tears. The sound of the sealing hatch was the cue I was waiting for. The moment I heard it, I melted against Rick – who quickly wrapped an arm around me.

The pressure changes as we lifted off caused so much

pain that I wanted to scream and ended up holding my fist to my mouth to stifle one. Tears were streaming down my face from the agony. The man in the window seat tried hard not to notice but ended up leaning over and offering words of encouragement in Portuguese.

James and Jason were by my side the moment we leveled off, a stewardess right behind them asking if we needed anything. James pulled my fist down, and I noticed the blood. Apparently, I had bitten harder than I thought. He pulled my fingers apart and wiped them up with water someone had provided.

"Oops." I mumbled.

He swore several times in Welsh and hovered over Jason as my hand was wrapped. When Jason moved to check on Max, who was shifting uncomfortably two rows down, I chanced a look into James' eyes. I was aware enough to see he was exhausted and also seemed to be in pain. Unthinking, I reached up and touched around his eyes. He looked deep into mine.

"I'm causing that." I whispered in his native tongue.

James nodded once, moved away from my touch, and brushed his fingers across my temples again. He answered in the same language to keep our conversation secret. "Your injury is. I'm going to try to rest. Be strong, Bear." He looked tortured.

I spent the rest of the flight leaning into Rick's embrace. Sometimes he would doze off, other times he would gently run his hand up and down my arm to help me relax. Sleep did not come for me though, and I still could not eat. Jason forced me to sip juice but even that was hard. It was difficult to be stuck in my own mind, not able to see out. I could not even use the talent I was born with, and it was unbearable. The fact that the stimulant made me aware enough to comprehend just frustrated me even more.

When it came time for the airplane to start descending, I knew there would be trouble. Whatever Jason had injected me with back in Rio was wearing out. James, who had been asleep for the past six hours, came over and looked deep into my eyes again.

He turned to Rick, "Switch seats with me."

309

Rick gently moved past me, "Be careful with her, Boss."

James and he communicated something silently before James came to sit next to me. "Just a little longer, Bear, I'll help you get through the landing." He paused and looked into my eyes again, "I'm not going to leave your side until you are healed."

Words were failing me again, so I just nodded.

The pain during landing was nearly as rough as what happened during takeoff. James wrapped one arm around me, pulling me as close as the seat would allow. The cooling relief from his mind was not enough though. When my bandaged hand started twitching and the other started to raise up in a fist, he reached over, lifted my left hand up so it was held by the hand around my shoulder. He then took my clenched right hand and held it down.

"Shh. Don't struggle. Focus on my words, focus on my touch." He spoke softly to me as the plane slowly made its way to the ground.

SANITY

We landed in London and the passengers applauded us as we stood to disembark first. The stimulant had completely worn off, so I could no longer speak and could barely nod as we were rushed through customs and into the waiting van.

Jason hovered over me as we rushed back to the bunker. Once inside though, everything changed. James' phone rang, he spoke harshly into it, slammed it shut, and ordered us all into the conference room. Jason started to protest but the look on The Commanders face stopped him in his tracks.

"The General wants a short debrief. I had been unable to contact him leading up to our departure. It is vital that he hears what we discovered, beyond vital that he hears what Harlie has to say."

Max spoke up, "She can't talk, James! She is barely conscious! Can't you relay what she was able to communicate with you?"

James response was to stand in front of me, staring at the crutches I was heavily leaning on. "I'm sorry this is happening, Harlie, being rewarded for your brave actions with torture."

From somewhere deep inside, I found the strength to fight the numbness in my brain and pain in my body.

"I...can...tell him."

Rick sat me next to the giant view screen in the conference room and The General's face soon appeared. James quickly ran through the events leading up to the warehouse discovery and my offer to be the bait that pulled the enemy empathic away. He continued through what little he knew of my side of the battle, but the General stopped him.

"That is for Agent Berryman to tell." He reprimanded.

James jaw clenched, and he turned to me.

"Sir, Ms. Berryman was severely injured in the ensuing battle. She is barely able to stay conscious, but she is here."

The General looked in my direction. "I am sorry for

your suffering, but have been told you learned vital information, and I must hear it straight from you."

I took a deep breath, "Sir. The empathic...was man-made. He told me the surgeon was fixing burn scars... and found something in his brain. The surgeon offered to fix that and it... changed the enemy to empathic." I paused, dropping my head and reaching deep into what little reserves I had left. "During our mental battle, I attacked with images of Doctor L. and his reactions..." My eyes shut in my effort to focus. "His reactions verified that he knew L. It was his shock which gave me the chance to disarm him."

The General looked furious for a moment then cleared his throat. "This is a very serious accusation you are leading us to Agent."

"I know, Sir."

Ryan stood up at that point, "If I may, Sir, there is additional evidence being processed right now, biological evidence which may verify Harlie's experience."

General Smiths looked from me, to Ryan, to me and then to James. "I will be leaving Canada within the day. If this is true, I want concrete evidence on my table upon arrival. Dismissed."

Jason jumped up, raced into the medical bay and returned a moment later with a wheelchair.

James met him in the doorway. "No."

"Get out of my way, Commander." Jason hissed.

"Jason, listen carefully. She is not safe here. If these accusations are true, and I believe they are, there are too many connections to L right now. If Doc sees her like this he might call over to the surgeon, not knowing what we are investigating. We cannot go after him until the evidence is processed." He turned to look at me. "Besides, I cannot do what needs to be done here. Get a bag together for me with her custom medication, morphine, something to keep her hydrated, and anything I might need if she goes critical. Do not leave your phone for an instant."

Jason looked skeptical, "What are you going to do? You are putting my patient in more risk than necessary by taking her out of here."

Considering the situation, James looked remarkably

calm. "I know how to help her. I might not be able to fix the damage to her mind, but I can get her stabilized enough for her to heal herself. And, you know I am well versed in the items you will be sending for her." Something about the way he said it, made me think he was holding back on the truth. Even though everything around me was numb, I still was able to wonder how he seemed to know more than what he was letting on.

"What if Doctor L. comes here looking for her?" Jason asked.

A deadly chill swept through the room, "You'll tell him she was stable enough to go home to recover and that I am with her."

Jason nodded and left to pack the requested bag. James helped me into the wheelchair and pushed it over to the elevator. I was having trouble staying awake as Jason handed him the bag and we rushed up to the warehouse exit. James' bike was waiting, and he helped me onto it before grabbing my arms and holding them around him with one hand.

"Stay with me, Harlie, just a few more minutes." He begged as he started the bike.

The ride out was a blur, as was the trip through town. I barely registered that we had passed the village when he pulled the bike up to the entrance of his apartment building. Leaning against him, I stumbled through the entryway, pain searing my leg, and made it into the elevator before passing out. He must have carried me to his top floor residence because, when my eyes opened again, I was on a couch. He had hooked the saline bag to a nearby standing lamp and it was hooked into my IV. James was kneeling next to the couch.

"Hey there, feeling any better?" he took my hand.

"Not really, can't...can't keep my eyes open." It felt like my eyes had lead weights on them.

"Don't try to, just rest." He squeezed my hand, "You know the injury happened to your mental shield, right?"

I nodded.

"I think I can make it better, can help you heal the injury."

"How?" My voice was a whisper.

James looked off into the distance. "It's complicated,

but you need to trust me." He looked back at me, and I could see the seriousness of my situation in his eyes. I could also hear what sounded like pleading in his tone.

"Promise that you'll tell me the details one day soon?" I asked.

"I promise." With those words, he released my hand and reached for the IV.

"Harlie, what I have to do is going to hurt. You are already in so much pain..." He looked away again, tortured.

"Jamyson," I struggled to reassure him, "It's more than I can handle right now."

He nodded and took out a pre-filled syringe. "Please forgive me if you still feel pain through this. You know I hate it."

Seconds later, my body and mind felt like they were floating. A pleasant dream started, and I smiled to myself. All around me soothing colors were swirling. I watched them until I saw a hole in the colors. I was curious and floated over to it. When I looked into the hole, there was a hideous image. I screamed and everything around me went black. I blinked, and the pale swirling colors were back. It reminded me of mother-of-pearl and something rang of familiarity. I noticed another hole but, before I could move away from it, I was dragged into a nightmare from the refugee camp. I tried to run, but a hand grabbed me, and I screamed again. The image broke up and returned to the swirling colors.

The cycle continued for what seemed like many hours. As the time passed the nightmares became less and less and the holes they were inside became fewer and fewer. Pleasant dreams started to take their place. The last dream was of the countryside, and someone was gently holding my hand. It was James, and he smiled while raising the hand to his lips and kissing it. When the dream ended, I drifted into true unconsciousness.

I awoke some time later. Rays from the morning sun were pouring through two windows in an unfamiliar room. I looked around and started to remember that I was in James' apartment, and he had brought me here to hopefully heal me. My eyes came across a figure staring back at me from his position on a recliner.

"Good morning." He smiled at me. "How's your head?"

I did a quick self-check and realized that much of the pain was gone and there was some clarity around the mental numbness.

"It's improving." I tried to smile.

James rose up out of the chair, came over, and brushed his fingers across my forehead. "It will take some time to heal completely but quite a bit was repaired. Don't look out and keep your shield down for now."

I nodded then focused my eyes on his face "Jamyson, you look exhausted. Haven't you slept at all?"

He gave me a small smile, "Always worrying about others and never about you." He looked up at the ceiling then back down to me. "Ah, Harlie! Do you have any idea how incredible you are?" His expression turned stern. "Or how close you were to quite literally losing your mind?"

I shook my head no to both, even though it made my head spin.

"Think you could eat a little, perhaps a piece of toast and some tea?" He asked.

"Yes, I am starting to feel hungry."

He stood up and walked over to the open plan kitchen. I watched and waited, still not aware enough to attempt conversation or focus on the details of what had happened to me. James prepared breakfast, looking in my direction every few moments. Once it was ready, he brought over a stack of toast and two cups of tea, placing them on the end table.

"Let's get you to sit up a bit more." He muttered. James gently wrapped his arm around me and helped me up. When I went to try to move my legs over the side of the couch, he stopped me.

"Not yet. Eat first." He handed me a cup of tea, put the plate of toast on my lap and sat at the edge of the couch. We ate in silence, sharing the stack. Once finished, he put the empty plate and cups into the sink and came to kneel at my side again.

"The General is in the air right now. I'll be meeting him at the airport and bringing him straight to the bunker." He paused, waiting for me to process his words. I nodded, and he

315

continued. "Rick and Jason will meet us at the cottage. Rick will be there the whole time; Jason until I return with The General." He waited for my response.

"What else is happening?" I knew there had to be more.

James grimaced, "Dara, Ryan, and Mitch are setting out in an hour to track down leads on this side of the ocean. Hopefully, Max will join them in a couple of days. They are taking several of our higher-level agents with them for assistance. I also have a team of agents tracking down Doctor L's location. We don't know if he has been informed of the enemy empaths death. If he has, then he will most likely be waiting for us to make the discovery of the creation and will be removing any evidence of his involvement." He shook his head a couple of times, as if to clear it, then turned to me. "Try to sit up properly. I'm going to change clothes and find my old crutches, so we can get you to the bike."

The world spun for several seconds when I moved my legs over the side of the couch and totally sat up. My wounded leg protested the movements, but it was tolerable. James was only gone a few minutes. Soon, I was standing with the crutches and slowly moving towards the elevator.

At the cottage, James handed me over to Rick with instructions to make sure I ate in a couple of hours, that I was to get cleaned up and to not let me sleep for more than an hour at a time. He then turned to me. "I'll be back soon, Harlie. While most of the damage is healing, what's left might cause problems. Rest, please."

I assured him that resting would not be a problem. James looked as if he wanted to say or do something more but just nodded before going over to a dark green car he had parked the bike next to. The keys were in the ignition and he nodded to Rick before climbing inside and driving away.

Inside the house, I was carefully sat down on the couch. Jason was waiting, and I was given a thorough but gentle exam. Once finished he sat down and sighed.

"Your vitals are much better than before...still off...but much better."

I turned to face him, "Whatever James did, it's working. It's easier to talk and I am able to focus more on

316

conversations and surroundings." I did not add how the pain was getting fierce but guessed my vitals already showed it.

"Have you eaten?"

"Two pieces of toast and a cup of tea."

He nodded. "Think I'm going to let whatever is in your system wear out more before medicating you again. It'll give me a more accurate reading on your recovery."

"Jason?" I waited until he was looking at me, "I have a feeling that my abilities will take awhile to heal. Those vitals are not going to have a dramatic change."

"Probably is the case, but I want to be sure. In the meantime, let's get that leg bandage changed into something waterproof so you can bathe. The same with your bite."

Jason had already brought over a shower chair from the med bay as well as a set of crutches. It felt wonderful to wash off the remnants of Rio and change into my own, clean, summer dress. The process exhausted me though and both my hand and leg were screaming. Jason took more readings, then said that, when he returned from checking on Skull and Max, enough should have burned out of my system. I wanted to ask for pain medication now but stayed quiet.

Once Jason was gone, Rick stood up from the seat he had taken at the kitchen table and sat down on the far side of the couch. He had been so quiet I nearly forgot he was in the cottage.

"What's wrong, Rick?"

He peered at me for several long minutes. "I was worried about you. Still am." he admitted.

"I'm recovering." I gave him a small smile.

"At what cost?" Rick wondered.

I had no knowledge for answering that, so chose to shrug instead. The movement set a small flame of pain through my body.

He tried to change the subject. "Rest for a little while, then I'll get you something to eat."

"I'll try, but now you have me confused." I settled back into the cushions, trying to look like I was relaxing instead of fighting off the pain. "Did you see a better option for taking out the empathic?"

Rick shook his head, "No. But it has been harder than I

317

thought it would be, seeing you injured and in so much pain." He held out an arm, and I gingerly worked my way across the couch and into his gentle embrace. Although I was still mentally blind, his touch felt more brotherly and less of anything more dangerous. I shifted so my legs were up and sighed. He started to hum quietly, and my eyes were shut in moments.

The rest of the afternoon was dull. We reheated and ate some of the frozen chicken and dumplings I had made before the mission in Rio. After the meal, we sat back on the couch and watched a kid's movie until Jason returned. Skull's leg was infected, so he was going have to split his time carefully. Doc was still being kept out of the picture. My vitals were slightly better in some ways and worse in others.

"How bad is your pain?" Jason was concerned.

"I almost didn't let you leave this morning." By now my head and leg were throbbing and the sudden bursts of fiery pain were coming closer together.

He looked apologetic, "Wouldn't have done any good. I would still have insisted on you waiting it out." Jason then set up an IV bag with the antibiotic in it and sent a dose of pain relief through my IV – making sure it was working before going back to the bunker.

It was at that point when something unexpected happened, but I was too far into the medication to respond the way my mind normally would. Rick held out his arm again. This time when he held me, the embrace did not feel as brotherly as before. I thought it was the morphine blurring my senses until he turned his head and placed a gentle kiss on the top of my head. Rick then mumbled, "I'm relieved that you are healing and not in as much pain."

Sleep took me again, and it was a struggle for Rick and later Jason to keep me awake until James returned with The General. I could tell from the moment he walked in that there had been new developments. Jason helped me sit up from where I had been laying on the couch, and the General sat in the chair next to me. James stood by the door, his face tight with the effort to control his emotions.

"Ms. Berryman, it is good to see you with a bit more color on your face." The General started.

"Thank you, Sir." My voice was still barely above a whisper and still required effort to use.

"Colonel Davies has informed me in greater detail about what occurred during our mission in Rio. The witnessed events were verified by the other Guardian present at the time of the encounter. Combined with the initial evidence, it is enough to make me concerned about the loyalty of our surgeon. Be that as it may, as we were pulling into the village, we received word from the bunker that the remnants of the device inside the empath's brain were indeed very close to the device we use on members of our team."

James looked as if he were losing the battle to control his expression. Jason's hands were both fists. The General continued, "Agents have worked through the night and have found a lead to when and where the betrayal took place. Mitch will be joining the agents on that trail. Because of his recent interest in you, and the timing of your enhancement versus the other empathic, you will not be alone until the situation is resolved." He glanced over at James. "Colonel, you have that covered, correct?"

"Yes, Sir." His voice was as tight as his expression.

"Then we will return to the bunker and leave Ms. Berryman to rest."

They left moments later, but James returned at nightfall. I was feeling quite lousy by that time. My head was pounding, and it was becoming harder to focus. I had been rotating between laying down with my leg propped up or leaning against Rick while sitting on the couch. Several times he threatened to call Jason if I showed any more signs of deteriorating.

I was standing up on the crutches, getting ready to hobble to the bedroom, when James opened the door. He looked haggard.

"Good to see that you are ready. Let's go." James turned and started to walk back out.

"Huh?" Someone must have forgotten to fill me in on some details.

Rick stepped in, "Sorry, my brother, she has been going downhill for the last couple of hours. I hadn't told her yet because just staying conscious seems to be difficult."

James turned around and came over to me. "You're coming back to the apartment tonight. As predicted, you are still unstable and might need support. Honestly, I'm surprised you are awake and standing."

Although speech was a struggle, I managed to respond. "It's not without immense effort and only because I'm going to bed." I did not want to leave the cottage. Whatever was going to happen with me, I wanted it to happen here.

He stepped closer, reading the emotions I was trying to hide, "You are too stubborn for your own good sometimes. Stop that attitude and humor me." He leaned over to whisper, "I am too tired to fight with you and will not hesitate to pick you up and carry you out." James then headed for the door again.

Rick came to my side. "Harlie, I'll see you tomorrow." He gave me a gentle hug and left.

I hesitated for a moment, but then followed James out. He had the green car again and helped me inside, throwing the crutches into the back seat. Once inside he turned to me, "Sorry for sounding harsh in there, it has been a long day."

If I had been in any shape to put up any kind of fight, the look on his face and tone of his voice would have taken the attitude right out of me. As it stood, just being able to get to the apartment was going to take any reserves left. "You need to sleep, Jamyson."

Since it was only three blocks away, we were parked at the large building when he responded. "Only after you are stable and resting."

Step by painful step we made our way to the elevator and up to his residence. He helped me onto the couch and propped up my throbbing leg. James knelt next to me and placed his fingers on my temples. I could feel his mental fingers tracing where my shield should be, looking for deeper wounds. I cringed as it set off another burning wave of pain. He noticed, but said nothing, instead leaning over to the medical bag from last night, filling a syringe with my custom medication and reaching for the IV in my arm.

"Sleep now, Harlie."

The next morning was cold and rainy. Despite being early July, the apartment was chilly. That was just registering

320

in my foggy mind when James came out of the bedroom. He looked as if he had just awakened.

"Good morning." The sleepy smile he gave me did something strange to my heart. I smiled back at him.

James went right to the kitchen and made breakfast, this time adding some bacon to the stack of toast. I slid up to a better position, and we copied the meal from yesterday. As he washed the dishes, I sat with my legs over the side of the couch. He stopped, came over and sat next to me.

"How is it?"

"Disorienting and still a bit painful." I was honest. He would have seen any lies.

James looked at me, then out the window at the pouring rain. He seemed to be mentally scanning the area.

"Can't do this in town." He added an expletive. "Let me check in with the bunker and get Jason to come here."

Instead of picking up on what he was planning, my injured mind could not seem to figure out what he was trying to say. So, I sat still and waited until he finished the call.

"The agents have not found L, but they seem to be close. Max is being discharged from the medical bay, but Skull is still feverish." He grinned, "Last night he broke one of the beds and threw a tray at poor Kayla."

I had to smile at that.

Jason arrived twenty minutes later and ran his tests. He looked at James, "Slightly better than yesterday."

James nodded then asked, "Yesterday, did you witness her flinching or cringing with pain not related to her leg or hand?"

Jason turned back to me, "Once. But I thought it had to do with her injured ability."

"I hope that's all it is." James mumbled. "I need to take her out of the town for a couple of hours. She should have it quiet when looking out for the first time and maybe getting her shield back up."

Jason nodded, "Whatever needs to be done. Just go prepared."

It surprised me how Jason was going along with anything James said but guessed that, since my injury was beyond his expertise, there really was not much of a choice.

They helped me to my feet, and James packed a small bag before we all headed out. He drove the car to the same spot along the river as our last time away from town, the day I found out that my abilities were much stronger. The memory sent another wave of fire through me. James shut the car off and turned to face me, his expression showing concern.

"When you are flinching, what is happening?"

I thought about it, trying to come up with something I could actually put into words. "It's like a wave of fire. It starts either in my head or at my heart and spreads everywhere. It's quick, but it's very painful."

James nodded but said nothing. He looked out at the rain falling around the car. I did the same and we sat for over fifteen minutes before he spoke again. "That is really bothersome. I have no idea what could be causing it. Everything about treating your injury is a theory, so I'm worried about making it worse." He turned back to me. "Try to look out."

It took another minute before I could gather enough strength to focus on the task. Everything that had been so easy was now very difficult. I turned my eyes to the hills and started to look out in that direction mentally. So far, so good. Slowly I turned my eyes and mind towards James. I registered the dark spot that was his protected mind and nodded to let him know.

"Good." James gave me an encouraging smile. "I'm going to drop it a little."

I felt the small shaft of light and emotion and started to focus on it. Of course, what was first and foremost was his concern, followed by some relief at my recovery. He opened up a little more, and I wavered. When I started to look away he spoke again.

"Try to focus on it, Harlie, you used to be able to do that."

My mind turned back to his and my breath caught in my throat. Was he projecting that as a test or was it really what he was feeling? His eyes registered my reaction.

"No, I'm not projecting anything false. That is really what I am feeling. I don't want to hide it from you."

While there were emotions towards the rest of the team

322

and towards the world situation, what was in front of his mind was still emotion about me. Worry, but also deep caring and behind it, desire.

I stopped looking out. "I'm not sensing things accurately."

James took one of my hands and slowly moved it to his lips. "There was no mistake." He whispered. He kissed it lightly then placed it back on my lap and looked out the windshield

"This is not the best time for my revelation, I know, but you would have found out soon enough. It was becoming difficult to hide it from you." He turned back towards me. "Don't panic or get defensive, Harlie. For now, its staying in my mind and away from my actions."

Mixed emotions ran through my own mind. I tried to focus on them but only succeeded in confusing myself.

James started the car. "Let's move slowly towards the village. Look out towards it but do not focus on any one person."

That was easy as I did not want to focus on anyone else. What I had seen in his mind was enough. We crept closer and closer to town. With each mile, I was able to perceive more and more minds. The hum from them seemed louder than they had been in the past though. As we reached the street the cottage and apartment were on, I put my hands over my ears. The normal hum was a raging scream, and I could not get the level to lower. James turned the car around to head back out of town.

"Guess I'm a bit oversensitive right now." I panted. My vision was hazy from the sudden noise and pain.

"Let's give it another day or two then. Try to look out if you want to but do not force it. I wish we could get your shield up though. I would feel better if you were at least protected that way."

The pain was still too intense to respond the way I wanted to, referencing all the protective males around here. Instead, I looked over at him. "We can try to get it up."

He noticed the plural and smiled slightly. "Are you sure? You seemed to hate the one time I tried it."

I nodded. "This seems like a situation where it would

323

be acceptable. There is too much going on out there for me to not be shielded." I cringed through a wave of pain. "What if L does come here? Or someone else we don't know about?"

James pulled the car over, placed his fingers gently on my temples and waited. I focused on my shield and tried to raise it. Mentally and physically, I was still weak and injured. The pain from looking out was still too fresh. I felt him reach out, and ever so carefully, he helped me raise the shield all the way up. Physically, I was shaking from the effort, tears streaming down my face from the pain. However, I forced myself to recall the worst moments of the battle and, true to form, the shield sealed shut in defense.

"Wow." James breathed, pulling away from me.

"Don't test it yet, it's likely to fall." I warned him.

"Not going near it, am getting you home and resting. We are out of time and Jason is going to have a fit at your vitals." He smiled grimly.

Sure enough, Jason was indeed upset at my condition when we arrived at the cottage. I quickly settled him down by asking for something to sedate me as soon as I forced down some lunch. James agreed, and it was late evening when I woke up again. Rick was watching me from where he was working on his laptop in the kitchen. Silently he came over and smiled. "The others are in the bunker and I'm remoted in. We are closing in on L and the rest of the tests came back proving he is the one behind the empath."

I sat up totally and reached for the crutches. My leg did not hurt near as bad as before, so it was easier to come stand by him. I looked into the webcam. Text came across the bottom of the screen. It was James commenting on how it was good to see me up and to go eat the pizza on the counter. I followed orders then plopped down onto the chair closest to Rick and watched the events as they unfolded. He took off his headset and turned up the volume.

The agents were at Doctor L's last known location. They had just broken down the door and were searching through the suite. All of L's movements had supposedly been under constant surveillance, but now it had been discovered that the agent watching him had been double-crossing us. He had been arrested that morning and was on the way to the

324

bunker to be interrogated. The Guardians knew of this residence in particular, but L was not there when they arrived, and reports from the arrested agent had said he would be. I followed along as they went room by room looking for evidence of his deception or information that would lead to his whereabouts. Mitch was hacking into one of the two computers there. It only took a few minutes before he called for someone with a camera to come over.

We sat in stunned silence as the images flashed across the screen. It was the schematic for the device we found in the empath's brain. Documentation showed that he hired someone to make ten of them, complete with the dead man explosive. Immediately, the research team inside the bunker was put to work tracking down the manufacturer. Mitch continued to search the computer at top speed. Another agent was tracking phone records from the line in the house and found recent ones to and from Bangladesh. Hours passed, and by the end, we knew that Doctor L. was there and had been for a week. The research team had found the manufacturer of the pirated device, and a separate team had used the phone records to discover what region L was in. There had been a monitoring device placed inside the residence when L. had moved in. It had been active in the past, but no evidence of it could be found and the last records of it being checked were over two months ago. James was pacing, and we could tell he was impatient for the arrival of the deceitful agent. I cringed at the thought of what the interrogation would be like.

Rick noticed my cringe and turned the laptop away from me. "You have enough to worry about right now. Go lay back down. Let us take care of it."

I sat stubbornly. He sighed. "You know I would normally let you get away with that, but not tonight. You are off duty due to severe injury." He waved his hands in a shooing motion. "I let you watch for several hours, now get back to the couch."

I did not want to stop monitoring the situation. However, it was difficult to stay awake. The burning flashes were coming again. I stood up on the crutches and replied, "I'd rather not."

He turned to look at me incredulously.

A smile lit my face at his expression. "I would rather just go to bed." With that I hobbled to my bedroom and over to my dresser to pull out one of the sweatpants and t-shirt uniforms.

I heard the chair scrape against the floor as Rick stood up to follow me. He was smiling. "Now I can see what you must have put Jason through when you first arrived." He leaned against the doorway to the bedroom. "You are going to be stubborn enough to put that on without help, I bet."

I hobbled to the door and shut it in reply. It took a long painful time to get the pants over my bandaged leg, but once it was on, the rest was easy. I opened the door and Rick was back in the kitchen. Someone had brought fresh milk over to the house earlier and a glass was poured and waiting on the counter. Rick half watched me, and half watched the computer as I drank it then turned to go bed. I was almost there when he stood again and came over to me.

"Harlie." His voice was low and laced with emotion. I waited but did not turn around. Hands reached out and rested on my shoulders. I felt him standing very close to me. Just when I was gearing up to look out, he backed away. "I'll see you in the morning."

After I was in bed, one thought kept going through my brain, making sleep difficult. If I had indeed avoided losing my mind, why did the world around me suddenly seem to have gone insane?

LIFE'S VOW

The morning brought Jason to my bedside, trying to get me to cooperate while he changed the leg bandage and removed the hand one. Once that was completed he did a thorough exam, taking notes the entire time. He said very little and that made my frustration rise.

"Are you going to say anything worthwhile, or am I going to have to get angry at you again?" I finally blurted out.

He jumped as if I had startled him then grinned at me. "I have to fill out a detailed report on your treatment and recovery. With Skull still having that fever, I have not had time to work on it."

"And you are going to be cold and calculating while doing it?" My mood was very poor this morning, due to a restless night thinking about the two people I was the closest to.

Jason frowned, "No, but you and I have not exactly been getting along lately either." I waited, knowing he was not finished. Sure enough, Jason put the notes down and sat on the bed. "I'm sorry, Harlie. Sorry for what I said upstairs and sorry for all the negative things I have been saying about The Commander."

"Who reprimanded you?"

He looked surprised. "No one. Watching you in action during this last mission, seeing how you work with the rest of the team, witnessing the effect you have on James – it all proves that I'm the one in error." He lowered his head and seemed embarrassed. "I had been hoping that we would become close, so when it looked like James and you were instead..." He broke off.

I took a deep breath before responding. "Stitch, it would not have happened anyway. I have been through too much right now to even think about something like that." I paused, trying to be gentle, "I just lost my husband and am starting a new life with a new persona and these abilities..."

Jason frowned. "I have to disagree. You have become close to Rick and James."

327

"Rick is more of a big brother and James..."
Flashbacks of yesterday made me stop and think. "James and I
are friends."

He looked doubtful, "If you say so, but I've never seen
him so obsessed before, and you two are spending a great deal
of time together."

"Jason! Most of that has been for training. It is much
easier to learn how to handle these abilities when there's not a
crowd screaming in your mind."

He still looked doubtful but gave me a small smile.
"Most of that?"

It was time to lead him back to the purpose of this
conversation, "I accept your apology, Jason. Now, can I get up
and have some breakfast?"

He stood up from the bed, picked up his notes and left
for the kitchen. I grabbed my crutches and made my way there
as well. As with the pizza last night, someone had dropped off
donuts this morning. We both ate and had just finished up
when James arrived.

My first hint that something was about to change was
due to him not being in uniform. James was constantly in
uniform or clothing which closely resembled it. The second
hint was that he was not alone. Jack and Mr. Phillips were
behind him and both looked serious. Of course, Jack's
expression instantly changed as he came over and picked me
up in an exuberant hug. As soon as he put me down though, I
chanced a glance out of my shielded mind. It caused a wave of
pain, but I hid it from Jack and his father. There was no hiding
from James though, and his head whipped around to face me.
We stood, staring at each other in silence until Mr. Phillips
cleared his throat.

"You look as if there has been some improvement."
James started.

I nodded, "Didn't sleep well though."

"With all the rest we have been making you get, that
does not surprise me." His words might be saying one thing,
but his eyes were saying something different. He motioned to
the couch, "And with that said, sit down." He smiled just a
little.

Once we were all seated, he quickly got to the heart of

his visit. "I'll be leaving shortly to go after our current target. Last night we found information which indicates a device to deactivate the implant chips was in the process of being developed. Since we do not know how developed it is, Dara has been totally pulled from that part of our mission. I'll be going into Bangladesh with Mitch and Max. Ryan and Dara will be working on supporting the agents who went after the Rio leads. Rick will be assisting both groups from the bunker." I understood completely what he said as well as what was left unsaid. Skull and I would be sitting this one out, along with Jason who was still monitoring our recoveries.

James continued. "Mr. Phillips and Jack have been temporarily reassigned to stay with you. While there is still no evidence that he has been informed of his project's death at your hands, L. has always been more interested in you than the others." His eyes added emphasis on the last phrase, due to our recent discovery about how powerful I had become.

I nodded again then turned to smile at Jack, "Just like old times."

Jack smiled back, "Except this time you came with a guide." He held up a stapled packet.

"Harlie, I do need to speak to you privately for a moment." James was looking at the back of Jason's head.

I stood up and followed him out the back door and into my garden. The moment we sat down on the wicker couch, he turned to me.

"This was not what I was expecting for the mission. However, I am going to take Doctor L. down. The information we got out of the ex-agent last night proves that L is deranged and completely out of control. He has tried to perform this procedure in three countries in the last five months. There is even some evidence of success. He must be stopped."

"You might have to kill him." I stated surely, and he nodded.

"I told you when you were injured that I would not leave your side until you were healed..." He started.

"Jamyson, even then I knew that would be impossible, especially with our line of work." I would not allow him to be put on a guilt trip.

James took my hand, gripping it when I tried to pull

away. "There is a lot to explain, and you are still trying to recover your abilities. It is almost reckless for me to leave."

"It has to be done, Jamyson, and you are the best person to take L out." I stopped pulling, drawn by what I saw in his eyes.

"When I get back..."

"You'll explain." I finished for him.

He reached up his other hand and brushed some stray hairs behind my ear then streaked his fingers down my face. Once again, his touch felt like fire and my heart started beating faster again. James smiled before looking towards the door.

"Jason." He sighed.

I nodded. "At least he apologized."

We stood up and went back into the house. Both he and Jason left shortly after, and I was once again under the protection of Mr. Phillips and Jackson.

Jason had hooked me up to the antibiotic drip before leaving, so I was stuck on the couch until he returned. We spent the time catching up. Jack had just finished a summer class through Swansea and had a two-week break until two more classes started. Due to his experience in the refugee camp and working for the Guardians, he had changed his mind about what to major in. criminal justice would be his major and he was going to minor in world history. After I rested, and Jason unhooked me, we spent some time in the garden before I wore out again.

Days passed by with very little information coming out of the bunker. Jack and his father stayed with me morning, noon and night. They left only when Jason would come to sit with me for a few hours while I practiced with my recovering abilities. James had left orders for me to keep trying to look out, but only with the medic present. While it became a little easier and less painful every day, I still ended up needing the custom cocktail before the session was over. Rick, who was supposed to be on high alert and therefore confined to the bunker, still managed to come by every evening to "check in on me." All he could tell me though was that James was in Bangladesh and closing in on Doctor L.

A week into the mission, Rick came to the cottage

330

earlier than usual.

"Been given the night off. They know where L. is and are running recon. As soon as James gives the word I will be on duty until they return." He explained. "Besides," He added with a smile, "You must be restless by now and need a change."

He was right. My leg was healing nicely, and I no longer needed crutches. My strength had also returned, and I had to have been starting to get on Jack and Mr. Phillips' nerves with my pacing about from garden to kitchen to couch and back again. We had spent the day before cooking and freezing various dishes to share between the two households, but I needed to get out.

I smiled back at him, "So is this a jailbreak?"

He roared with laughter, picked me up in a bear hug and swung me around. "Yes, dinner out then back to my place for music or a movie or whatever."

I felt my muscles tense up and quickly forced them to relax. Rick needed this night as much as I needed to get out of the cottage. There was no reason to panic, yet. Since I was already dressed in a t-shirt and jeans, I grabbed my purse and was ready. Jack and his father smiled as they left. It would be their first night back at their apartment all week.

Rick drove a small convertible, and we went straight to the restaurant in the village. Dinner was good, as usual, and we kept up a steady stream of conversation on various topics. When the check came, he grabbed it quickly.

"My treat," He smiled at the pouting expression on my face. "None of that."

I had been to Rick's residence several times before so there was no real reason for me to be nervous as we drove up to it. Or was there? Our conversation from last week crept into my mind, along with his actions. Again, I forced my muscles to relax and wished my mind would be convinced that it was nothing.

Once inside, Rick picked up a remote by the door and, a few buttons later, the lights were on and music was playing. I looked around the main room and noticed that Rick had disappeared. Shrugging off the beginnings of uneasiness, I sat down on the large sectional couch in the main living area and waited. He popped back into the room a moment later.

"Why don't you see if I have a movie you might want to watch?" He suggested, then left the room again. I stood back up and went over to the shelves that held his vast movie and music collections. I skimmed over the titles, pretending to really think about what was in front of me. In reality, I had decided to carefully look out of my mind to see what he was feeling. Inch by inch I stretched out. The instant my mind reached his I sensed that he had a surprise for me, but something serious was also on his mind, and it was not the current mission. I pulled back and wondered what it was.

Hands rested on my waist, breaking off my concentration and causing me to startle. Rick laughed quietly. "That wasn't fair, Harlie." He gently reprimanded me. Of course, he would have sensed the intrusion with his strong sense of intuition.

"Neither was scaring me just now." I muttered to hide the flustered feelings.

Rick sighed before dropping his hands. "Forget the movie. Go sit down. I'm going to tell you a story instead."

I did so, and he sat at the corner of the couch. I could see him gathering his thoughts and waited patiently – unsure of why he was doing this.

"Many years ago," He started. "There was a small town on the north-west coast of an island. Inside this town lived some of the wealthiest people on the island. The town also held many secrets. Secrets that its residents swore to keep, no matter what." He turned to see if I was following along, and I nodded. "A handful of children lived in the town, and on most days, they could be found playing at the water's edge. While they all got along well, two boys were close friends. One was older than the other by a couple years, but it did not matter. These boys both had something different about them, something they could do that made them stand out from the other children. It made the bond between them very strong. Nearly every day they could be found fishing, climbing rocks, chasing animals or playing army games. They ate meals at each other's houses and helped each other with school work.

These two boys knew there were more secrets in the town, and that their parents were very involved with it. Like most children, they wanted to know what it was and couldn't wait until they were old enough to find out. It seemed to them that other children found out when they were around fifteen. That was when playing stopped totally and they became serious like the adults. But these two boys were different from the others, and the town adults knew that. They looked at the boys differently, spent extra time telling them stories, and spoke to them in hushed tones instead of the voice normally used for addressing children."

Rick looked up, lost in thought for a moment. "When the oldest boy turned fourteen he was taken out of the town in the middle of the night and sent away. The younger was furious and the things that made him different became more pronounced. He was defiant and refused to do anything anyone told him, demanding to know where his friend was. Then the younger boy experienced the loss of a parent, and the sorrow of both losses broke him completely. The boy was quickly sent to a school far away. To his surprise, his best friend was there too. At the school, the boys learned there were others like them, and they took classes together to learn how to use what the teachers called "their gift." It was also there that they learned the secrets of the town. They were the youngest to ever be told. The knowledge was a large burden to carry, but the boys adjusted to it and put all their effort into using their gifts and learning how to help the adults in the town.

Over a few short years, the boys were transformed into responsible young men with an intimate knowledge of what was known as their "Life's Vow." It was a promise to keep the secrets, to work to make sure that the rest of the world stayed safe from the evil at the heart of those secrets. The boys went into the military for the vital training it would provide. Once again, they were forced to be apart – but this time they understood why. When their service was over, they stood in front of the elders of the coastal town and officially stated their part of The Vow. The boys had chosen to make the greatest sacrifices possible. Together they left the town, never to return, and the rest of their lives were devoted to the work involved with keeping those secrets."

Rick stood up, stretched, and turned to me. "You are

wise enough to fill in some of what was not said in the story. The rest must remain as vague as I made it, and for that I am sorry. It is a fine line to walk, and this is the first time I have ever voiced our past."

I stared at him, trying to process all he had said, filling it in with what James had told me about him and Rick. Some of it clicked together like a high-quality puzzle, other parts left me with more questions. Rick watched the process, observant as always. He sat down again, this time closer, and turned his body to face me.

"You know my gift is more linguistic, but I also have the same latent ability as you once had. You understand that you and James share a very strong mental talent. Since joining The Guardians, you have discovered there is more going on in this world than you could have ever imagined." His eyes flashed. "Harlie, it is only the tip of the iceberg!"

I found my voice, "Rick, why me?" He knew right away what was not said. Why was it me hearing this story, hearing what no one else knew?

"Because after seeing your scans and witnessing your sacrifice in Rio, The General demanded permission from those few above him to start filling you in on our reality, the side of the story that the rest of the team will never know."

I heard the omission. "You don't have an answer yet?"

He shook his head, "No. But we decided it would not stop us from letting you know that there is more, especially..." He broke off, and I saw his body tense for a moment, "Especially with more recent emotional developments."

And there it was. Instantly, my heart snapped its own wall up, and my mind started to come up with excuses to not feel what I knew would come.

"Stop it, Harlie. Hear me out before you get worked up." There was an edge to Rick's voice, and I had no choice but to listen. "James and I both want you to know our individual parts of the Life's Vow. While I cannot tell you some of the specifics, there are personal aspects of it which you can be told. Due to my upbringing in a single parent home and seeing what James went through with his own losses, with watching innocents die and children suffer, part of our personal promise was that we would not father any child, nor

334

would we adopt. I took it one step farther and vowed celibacy. I have never allowed myself to be in a relationship." His looked up at the ceiling then met my eyes. "You have always been and will always be safe with me. Right now, I wish it were different, but I will keep to that standard."

There wasn't anything for me to say. All defenses dropped as I looked out and felt the pain he was in. It caused a burning wave of fire to lash through my body. I forced myself not to flinch and to accept that pain. Rick looked away, and I could see him thinking hard. Just as the pain faded, he leaned forward and reached out to place his hand on the back of my neck.

"With all of that in mind, please forgive me for this." He whispered then closed the gap and very gently kissed me. It only lasted a few seconds but seemed much longer. When Rick pulled back, he dropped his hand and sighed heavily.

I waited, thinking about the weight of his personal disclosure, the taste of his kiss, the fact that I was now feeling sorrow. I watched the emotional struggle on his face but refrained from looking out again. Minutes later he looked at me and a small smile lit his face.

"You were okay with that, weren't you?" He asked quietly.

"It surprised me a little… but, yes." I smiled back at him. "My heart knew the truth, so I'm okay." It was confusing, but that part of me wanted him to kiss me again.

Rick took my small hands into his large ones. "Tell me, Harlie, what else is your heart saying? What has it been saying since we went to Rio?"

There was something in his tone that let me know what he really was asking had to do with how I handled James' revelation. I tried to pull my hands away, but he gripped them firmly.

"Did James put you up to this?" Now I was second-guessing the entire night.

"No." He looked pained at my question. "He didn't have to. I know how it is between the two of you. I'm happy you allowed his friendship, as it has been good for both of you." He took a deep breath, "His emotions towards you turning into something more intimate does not surprise me."

I cringed slightly, "It shocked me."

Ricks expression became reproving, "It shouldn't have. Think about it, Bear, from the moment you were rescued it has been you and him. He has never spent this much time with any team member. When the two of you are in conflict the whole team can sense it. When the two of you are working happily, so is the team. I've never seen two people with such an intense relationship before."

I dropped my eyes and head. "I know, it keeps getting me into trouble."

The grip on my hands became painful, almost crushing, and I looked back up at him. Conflict was in his eyes, and I realized my mistake. I had unconsciously assumed it was okay to lower my eyes around him – it was not.

"Don't ever...do that...again." He choked out.

I nodded quickly. He was still gripping my hands painfully tight, and I sat frozen until the storm passed.

"No, Harlie, it does not get you into trouble." Rick finally whispered. "Not at least what I would define as trouble." He let go of my hands. "This is going to sound a bit harsh and there is no way to lessen it."

I waited, wondering what he was going to say.

"You are not in what the mainstream knows as the 'real world' anymore. In that version of reality, it might be normal for someone who has gone through the grief you experienced to force herself to remain alone and emotionally isolated. In your past life, doing what you could to lessen a person's pain was something you practiced daily. But this life, this world where the blinders are removed, is different. You are not alone and will never be alone. Someone else here might have gotten away with being emotionally isolated, but not you, not with your talents. When you try to relieve another's pain, you are literally taking it onto yourself. I see you struggle day in and day out to make sure others are happy, all while isolating your own emotions. And James and I both grind our teeth and wonder when..." He stopped and looked into my eyes.

"When?" I whispered.

"When you will allow yourself to be happy. When you will allow yourself to be cared for, even briefly, by someone – anyone. When that wall around your heart will drop long

336

enough to see that there are people around you who love you...and I mean love in many forms."

"It's too soon." I fought to keep my eyes from dropping.

His eyes flashed again, and in an instant, he had my head in his hands, his face inches from mine. "Is it?" His breath whispered around me.

"Rick." I tensed up, preparing to pull free. "Don't do this to yourself, please."

"I'll do whatever I want, Harlie. The question is, what will it do to you if I kiss you again? Or how about when James comes home? You know in your heart that it is only a matter of time before your head agrees about him being something you need, something you want."

I wasn't giving in. "What will that do to you?"

He pulled back a few inches. "I'll be happy when you finally allow him to be what you need. I'll also be happy because he is more than willing to let me be here for you when you need me."

If there had been a response in my mind it fled the next instant, as he was kissing me once more. This time there was more emotion with it, a finality which said he would never allow himself to perform this action again. My heart reacted, and I had no choice but to respond. This kiss lasted longer, and the ending was so tender I wanted to cry.

He pulled back and moved to the corner of the couch. We both were breathing hard and were struggling to regain control. When he let out a sigh, I counted to fifty before scooting over to him and resting my head against his strong chest. He wrapped his arms around me and propped his legs up on one side of the sectional. I curled my legs up on the other side, and we stayed there until dawn.

I awoke first, slipping out from under Rick's arm and carefully sitting up. Looking over at him, last nights conversations ran through my mind. In the morning light, after a night for my subconscious to work it out, more things were making sense. While part of me still reasoned that the way James and Rick were feeling towards me should not be happening, another part accepted it. A small smile appeared as I thought about how comfortable I was around Rick, no matter what. If our situation had been just slightly different, I could see that kiss becoming so much more. The smile faded as I thought about the other half of my problematic equation, Jamyson Davies. As much as I tried to deny it, I had been reacting to him in ways which proved there was some type of attraction between us. The flip side was I still believed it was too soon, even with Rick proving that I was capable of deeper emotions. The walls around my heart were starting to crumble, though, and with everything that had already happened, I was not sure I was ready for it.

Ricks' eyes opened, and he stretched. "Hey there, beautiful, how did you sleep?"

I stood up, "Quite well, how about you?"

He smiled, "Wonderfully." He stood up as well and came over to me. "Thank you for last night. It is something I will treasure forever."

Stepping closer, I leaned my head against his chest, "Me too."

He held me gently before stepping back. "Breakfast here, then I'll drop you off at the cottage."

I nodded and followed him into the kitchen. We had a simple breakfast, and he went to prepare for the day. When he came out of the bedroom there was a cube-shaped package in his hand and a silly grin on his face.

"I forgot about this last night. Here." He held it out.

Inside was a stack of CD's which must have taken him months to find. It was the complete collection of my favorite inspirational trio. My jaw dropped, and he laughed.

"The last one came in yesterday morning. It should keep you occupied for awhile."

I ran up to him and kissed him on the cheek. He smiled down at me, "That reaction alone is all the thanks I need. Let's get you home."

Jack and his father were waiting for me at the front door. Rick gave me a long hug before driving off. I showered, changed, and was just getting the first CD unwrapped when Jason arrived.

"Hey, Bear, ready to get those stitches out?" He grinned. Minutes later they were gone, and I looked down at the fresh scar. It wasn't as bad as some others I had. Jason had

338

a glint in his eye and I could tell he was curious about last night, even though it wasn't any of his business.

"We had dinner, then he told me a story, and we talked until we fell asleep." That was all he needed to know.

Jason grinned. "Rick said the same thing, except he is smiling a lot today."

I grinned back, "Nothing happened, Jason, and you know it."

He nodded but did not look convinced.

The rest of the day was spent listening to the CD's and telling Jack the stories that went with the songs. We stayed busy and night came quickly. The following day brought changes, as the General came to the door first thing in the morning.

"Hello, Agent Berryman, might I come in?" Once the shock wore off I opened the door the rest of the way and motioned him inside. He nodded to Mr. Phillips and Jack, whom immediately went outside.

"I understand you have yet to be returned to any type of duty." It was not a question. "Our medic's report indicates that a full physical recovery is nearing completion. He is unsure about your abilities though. You still seem to be in pain while looking out."

"Only when I look far, Sir," I clarified.

"Agent Berryman...Harlie, I am here to clear you for light duty beginning immediately. You are needed with your research team to support information coming in from the recon teams in Bangladesh." He paused. "I also need your abilities to make sure that those in the bunker are staying true to us. The agent we arrested has me understandably uneasy. The surgeon might have had a contact here that allowed him to gain the information needed to make his own enhancement chip."

The same thought had crossed my mind several times as well in the last week, but I had not voiced it to anyone. With The General standing here with that same concern, what could I do but stand at attention and respond with a firm "Yes, Sir."

He looked me over from head to foot, "Something tells me you have thought along those same lines."

My shoulders slumped just a hair, "Yes, Sir. I have but did not bring it up to anyone."

He nodded, "In the future, please do not hesitate to speak what is in your mind. The Commander could have been on the lookout."

"Sir?" I waited for him to nod again. "He would have been too distracted by the other events happening around him. Chances are that between the continuing investigation from Rio, my experience with the empathic, and ensuing injury, and the search for Doctor L, any hint would have been missed."

The General placed his hands behind his back. "You are very wise for someone so new to this world." He took a breath and held it for a moment. "Our Linguist came to see me yesterday morning. I am pleased he was able to give you some insight so quickly. He had only been given permission after your arrival at his residence."

So that was where Rick had gone when we first walked in that night! The General saw the understanding in my eyes. "Yes, Ms. Berryman, I believe he still had something special planned for the evening, but judging by his mood, the change did not modify that plan much."

"Sir?" This might get me into hot water, but I wanted to know.

"Yes, Harlie?" He looked amused, perhaps my expression had changed.

"I am under the impression that you have also been informed as to the relationship status between Rick, James and me."

He gave me just the smallest of smiles, enough for me to understand that he did indeed know. I sighed loudly, grabbed my ID's and walked out the door to his waiting car. Mr. Phillips and Jack were already in the back seat, so I sat up front with General Smiths. We drove into the base and directly to the warehouse entrance. At my questioning glance, he explained.

"Mr. Phillips has been given temporary clearance to remain as your guard. Young Jack has his normal duties to perform but will be given the freedom to come and go from the tactical facility as you require him."

"Thank you, Sir."

We were in the elevator and everyone was taking out their cards to scan. The General turned towards me once more. "Our medic will also be standing by in case your primary assignment becomes too strenuous." There was much unsaid in that sentence, but all was completely understood.

Something was bothering me though. "General?" I started. "Wouldn't it be more effective if I stayed out of sight? If there is a chance of a mole, we would not want them to know someone was watching. That person might feel safe right now with James gone and me injured."

The General thought about it for a minute. "You are absolutely correct. I'll have you set up in James' formal office instead. It should not take too long to network into the research room and tactical facility. We will make it look as if you are working from the cottage." He clasped his hand on my shoulder, "Right there is more proof that I made the correct choice with you." He whispered.

We stopped the elevator at the upper level and quickly made our way to the offices. Thankfully, no one was in the hall. General Smiths made a few brief calls, and in minutes, Rick arrived with my laptop. As promised, it did not take long to network me in. The webcam was turned off on my end, so no one could see that I was not at home. Within a half-hour of arriving, I was being debriefed by the research team, and Jack was on his way to pick up print-outs. Mr. Phillips sat on the couch and quietly observed.

Once updated on the situation in Bangladesh, I made some quick decisions. I had Rick send out a code to James to delay Doctor L.'s capture until we had visual evidence. I also warned him about the possible mole. He agreed, adding that if they could catch him in the process of trying to perform the surgery it would be even better. He told me his team had acquired a local agent to make an appointment with the doctor to see about plastic surgery to fix up two facial scars and remove a supposedly unwanted tattoo. While in there, he would tag a piece of furniture with one of our small monitors. Mitch was working on hacking into the computer system without being detected.

With the debrief finished, I handed out orders on my end and faked needing a short break. In truth, I was going to

341

start stretching my abilities to see if I could detect anything amiss. Jason had arrived minutes before and had checked my vitals. Mr. Phillips sat silently, observing as my eyes glazed over and I peered out of the opalescent shield. A meter at a time I spread out until the entire bunker was covered. It took more focus than before Rio, and I could hear Jason grumble in the background. Floor by floor, hallway by hallway, room by room, I scanned. Briefly touching each mind and quickly moving onto the next, I choked back the fire as it raced through my body.

Thinking about the details of our situation, I decided the medical bay would be my place of focus. If the surgeon had been able to not only rebuild the chip, but modify it to have a dead-man switch in it, he was either getting help from there or from someone of higher clearance in Research and Development who had access to that technology. I let my abilities linger in that area while opening my eyes. Jason came over to me, but I raised a hand to halt him.

"Still working, seeing if I am still able to multitask."

Out of the corner of my eyes, I saw him shake his head. "Don't push it."

I ignored him, moved the laptop closer, and sent a message to my team. They had been backtracking our records of Doctor L.'s activities and matching them with information found on the computer. Apparently, he had deviated from approved plans and, with the assistance of the rogue agent, was able to make it look to us like he had followed along. While on the way to a guest house in Spain that he vacationed at every summer, he made a short trip to Portugal and performed a surgery while there. The same thing happened when he was supposedly at his residence. We found a forged passport which showed he had been in central America twice in the last year. It had all been very well hidden. I was becoming frustrated at how he played the system and, for a while, had gotten away with it.

Focusing back on my primary task, I noticed Mr. Phillips looking uncomfortable. "I'm not looking at you." I tried to reassure him. "But I am empathic and am looking out at the others."

Mr. Phillips looked away for a moment, "I don't

342

understand it at all."

Smiling at him, I replied, "I'll have to walk you through it when the crisis is over."

Two hours later, the pain was too much to take, and I had to stop looking out. Jason handed me something to take, and I didn't even look to see what it was. Jack came in minutes later with meals and we all took a break to eat. During the afternoon I had to stop looking several times and just put my head down. It was at four-thirty that something started to change in the medical bay. I could tell someone was uncomfortable, but it was fleeting, and I was too worn out to focus on the person. Nothing else happened, even though I continued looking out until most of the bunker was empty and all of the day shift went home.

Rick came into the room with a late meal and dismissed Mr. Phillips and Jack for the night. I was still at the desk, going over some files, and he sat on the couch and watched silently for several minutes.

"Harlie?" He finally spoke.

"Hm?" I was still absorbed in my work.

"Give it up for the night. You'll be useless tomorrow if you don't get some rest."

I looked up. "So, you will be sneaking me out of here and back to the cottage in case anyone is looking to see if I really still am there, then back again before the start of the workday?"

The look on Ricks' face was priceless, and I started to laugh. At my response, he started laughing as well. Back at the cottage he walked me inside and held me in a tight hug for a full minute before leaving. Exhausted and hurting from the day I took another custom dose and went straight to bed.

BETRAYAL

Before daylight, we were back in the bunker. I was sifting through files when something caught my attention.

"Rick, come look at this." I pointed to the screen. On there was an image taken from the computer in L's residence. It sent chills down my spine. "How could he have gotten these? James pulled him away and escorted him out when this was minutes old."

Ricks' hands were clenched, and he was holding his breath. I turned to look at him. This narrowed our suspicions down to only a handful of people in a bunker of over a hundred. Although the Research and Technology department was not totally out of the picture, it now looked like we really had a mole and that person was working in the medical department.

"Could it be a computer program pulling the information and passing it to a different department and then to him?" It was a long shot, but I had to ask before starting an intense hunt for the person.

Rick looked down at me and shook his head. "Mitch, Ryan or one of our upper-level techs would have caught it."

"Thought I would try," I shrugged.

He smiled and rested his hands on my shoulders. "Looks like a big day for us today, Bear. I'll see if the cafeteria is open yet and get us a supply of food."

I stopped him at the door. "Bring me a stun weapon too, all I have is my handgun."

Twenty minutes later Rick returned with food and the stun gun. Another twenty minutes later, the bunker started to buzz with activity. Mr. Phillips arrived, and Rick went back to his position translating for the Bangladesh team. I was trying to find a viable trail that would lead to whoever sent L my recent scan. It meant doing the same as yesterday, working on the computer and interacting with the research team while scanning mentally. I was completely focused on members of the medical department now.

It was early afternoon when James contacted us saying that, not only did his contact get inside and set up the monitor, but he was also set up for surgery. The procedure would be

344

tomorrow afternoon, their time. He was not the first patient of the day either. It looked like a neurological patient would be first. It was the moment we were waiting for. In Welsh, I updated him on our situation and could hear the anger in his voice at the thought of such a betrayal. As we were signing off he reminded me to be careful and, for some odd reason, it made me smile.

Two hours later I was munching on dark chocolate and focusing on the med bay when it happened. I sensed that same uncomfortable feeling, followed by a nervous sensation, and then determination. The person moved over to where I remembered was one of the computers and pressed a few buttons. Seconds later, the person felt pleased. I focused in more and was shocked at whose mind it seemed to be. I could sense the person become surer after talking to someone and then was on the move.

I contacted Rick before calling the head of our security team, a Nordic man named Henrik. I continued to follow the person mentally while informing Henrik of our situation. Having been warned by The General yesterday, he was prepared to follow my orders. Only a select few people would be involved. If there were more than one mole, we needed a better chance of that person staying in the dark. I had his people start running through surveillance video of the last days before we left for Rio and then the most recent week, looking for activity from that person. Henrik himself used the cameras to follow the supposed mole's current movement. Rick accessed the audio pick-ups in the medical bay to discover what had been said. The entire process took moments and I was back to focusing on my target.

The person had left the medical bay and was on the way up the elevator. Non-Guardians stopped at the cafeteria level and took a separate hall and elevator up to the surface. It opened up in the above ground cafeteria. The instant our suspect left the first one and walked to the second, I stood up. Mr. Phillips followed. I waited until the person was inside before leaving James' office and rushing into the main elevator. I kept my mind focused but stayed aware enough of those around me, just in case. Once at the surface, I paused and waited to see where the mind would go. The suspect walked briskly across the base and over to the above ground clinic the other members and employees used. I contacted Henrik, and he sent Mr. Phillips to the side of that building. Rick called at that point saying the suspect had claimed to have been called to the clinic to deliver a few supplies. The cameras showed something had been placed in that person's pocket, but the shoulder bag, which was being carried, was probably empty.

Keeping as hidden as possible, I made my way across the base to the clinic. Henrik accessed the security cameras there, and we waited. Sure enough, the suspect went in the back door and the cameras showed the unlocking of a supply closet door. Inside, several small boxes were being pulled from a shelf, behind them was a small computer pad. Henrik had seen enough and was going to signal an arrest, but I made him stop. I wanted to know exactly what the person was doing and how the information was getting out. I tightened my focus and, for the first time, was able to sense more than just emotions. I was able to see thoughts as the suspect entered in a series of codes, took a tiny flash drive from the pocket and started uploading its contents. I could see some of it in my mind as the mole's mind registered it. Rick quickly shut down most of the network, using emergency protocol, to make it easier to track the transmission. The person started to feel nervous again when the system hiccupped during the shut down.

The medical team member waited until there was confirmation of reception, placed the pad back on the shelf, and covered it with boxes. I sensed the person looking for something to take back to the bunker and listened as the heart and mind started to slow down. This person was very confident of success, and I could sense emotions about believing those actions were the right thing.

It was time. I contacted Henrik and told him to have Mr. Phillips cover me. I was going to handle this myself. I backed away two buildings and waited until the mole was in the open.

"Kayla." I called out to her.

She froze before turning to me. "Ms. Berryman! What are you doing all the way out here? You should be at home resting."

That set me off. In the nearly six months I knew her, Kayla rarely spoke a sentence, never-the-less two with expression. "Kayla, put your hands on your head and kneel on the ground. Now."

Her entire demeanor changed. "I can't do that." She whispered. She started to reach into her pocket, and I sensed there was a weapon there.

Although I had been hoping to get close enough to stun her, my hand quickly grabbed my gun. I aimed low, shooting her in the lower leg before she could grasp what was in her pocket. Mr. Phillips tackled her an instant later, cuffing her a second after that.

"Wait for the head of security to arrive, then take her to the holding cells. Have Jason check her wound." The cells were in the second bunker, as was the interrogation room. Once Henrik arrived, I quietly walked back to the warehouse and went back to James' office. If she had connections, there might be some communication once news of her arrest spread.

The General was waiting for me in the doorway. He shook his head sadly, "Kayla..." He did not finish.

I nodded. "She must have had inside help." My head felt as if it were in a vise, my vision swimming from all the effort, but I sat at the desk and looked out at the rest of the bunker. A flash of pain spread through my body, and I cringed slightly. General Smiths came into the office and sat on the couch.

His expression turned soft. "You must be in agony from all of this effort."

I met his eyes, "It is manageable, and the effort must be given."

"All the same, I am calling Jason up to make sure you stay stable." He took out his phone.

"Jason is making sure I did not wound Kayla too badly." I reminded him. "Sir, when I was out there something unusual happened. I was concentrating very hard on her mind and, during that time, I was seeing through her eyes. I saw the code she entered into the computer and heard her thoughts as the information uploaded." I shuddered through another painful wave. "It was frightening, but we might be able to use what was gathered." I took out a pad and pen and wrote it all down. General Smiths took the page and turned back to his office. "Sir?" I whispered. He stopped. "We should go on lock-down until this is resolved. The reactions of others might help with any secondary targets."

He smiled grimly, "Consider it done."

Seconds later a klaxon sounded, and I heard metal doors crashing down. I took several deep breaths and started looking out again. I still felt that, if there was a second mole, he would have to be in the technology department. As word started to spread and the lock-down sank in, my suspicions were starting to become solid leads. Since I did not know all of the employees, I sent locations to Henrik, and his team narrowed down visuals and sent them to me for confirmation. Jason arrived less than thirty minutes later and promptly started swearing. Of course, my vitals were way off from the effort and he took out the syringe.

"Easy, Stitch, I need to stay alert."

"You need to stay alive too. Right now, you are in danger of another seizure."

The General had returned ten minutes before and had been sitting quietly, watching me. At Jason's words, he spoke, "Is she really that critical?"

Jason turned to him, "It is hard to say, Sir. On any other person, I would say yes, but she seems to have a higher tolerance. However, that is just as dangerous because it might be her body overcompensating and she could crash."

"I'll be fine. Now both of you please be quiet so I can work." My voice was more confident than I was. Under the table, one foot was stepping on the other to stop it from shaking. I had to move. "Whose coming with me?" I stood.

"Jason should attend in case the strain becomes too much. I will come as well. We hired Kayla when she was barely more than a child. She was rescued from a horrible situation similar to your refugee camp. I want to know why she felt it necessary to betray us."

Rick met us in the hallway. "Some warning would have been nice. I was in the middle of a transmission to Dara."

I stopped and faced him, "Does James know about Kayla?"

His eyes roamed over my face, then turned to the General. "Could I have a moment with Ms. Berryman please?"

The General nodded, Jason looking confused next to him, and Rick pulled me back into James' office – shutting the door behind him.

"He knows that you were close to uncovering the mole but has been out of reach since then. But that is not why I pulled you aside." He took both of my hands into his. "You look like you are going to collapse any second."

I tried to back away, now was not the time. He pulled me to him, one hand at my waist and the other reaching for my face. "Stop looking out everywhere. Focus on me, right now." He took my chin in his large hand, raising my face so that my eyes met his. I reigned in my ability and looked only at him. Strength poured from his mind, a calmness that I had not felt in days. Minutes passed, and I could feel my body and mind respond, my heart slowing, my blood pressure falling. "Good girl." He whispered and kissed the top of my head before dropping his hands and stepping back.

Rick went back to his station to set up our emergency channel, and I joined the others at the entrance to the tunnel. With the bunker on lockdown we had to manually open what looked like a giant fireproof door. It was very heavy and awkward. We crammed into a battery-powered golf cart, because the high-speed trolley was now offline, and began a slow journey under the river. Since it would take at least five minutes, I shut my eyes and tried to rest my mind.

Kayla was sitting on the bed in one of the holding cells, her leg propped up and bandaged. Henrik and Mr. Phillips were nearby. They opened the cell door and went to stand on either side of her. I followed and stood against the far wall. The General stayed outside the cell.

Between the physical pain and the pain of the betrayal, I had little tolerance for the interview. I got right to the point, "Who were you sending that data to?"

She sat silent and calm.

"Who are you working for, Kayla, and who is helping you?"

She remained silent, but I could see her tense slightly.

"The bunkers are on lockdown. No one is leaving or

349

entering until we find out. We are still communicating with the away teams. You might as well tell us."

Kayla looked angry for a moment. "Why? You'll just pull it from my brain anyways."

Her words caught me off guard for a split second, "No, Kayla, I cannot just pull it from your brain. I can sense emotions and that is about it."

"That's not what your scans showed." She spat out.

I changed my tone to one I would use with a young student. "That scan showed communication and action between two empathics. It is not an accurate account of my abilities with the rest of society. It is only what happens between Colonel Davies and me."

Kayla's anger faltered for a moment but then returned. She pursed her lips and sat silent.

Turning to Henrik, I asked him to print out pictures of my suspects. Without a word, he left the room and The General took his place. Kayla's eyes grew wide at the expression on his face. I focused in on her mind, and she was feeling just a little guilty but resolve soon took its place.

"I did what had to be done. You were keeping the advancement of the human race confined to a handful of people under your command. The rest of the world needs leaders with enhanced skills like those here. You alone cannot decide who gets the procedure or keep those people under your control."

I sensed she was repeating the basics of a conversation she had been part of many times. "Kayla, what you are doing is just as bad. You are allowing a madman to go and enhance whomever he finds and then leave them with little to no guidance. It took me months to fully control this ability. He has also handed us the ultimate betrayal by enhancing someone for the enemy."

She looked angry again. "They are only an enemy to you. They are trying to unite the world, to bring everyone together."

"By murdering millions? Kayla, there are better ways to unify people."

Henrik came back in at that moment, but she ignored him, "No, there isn't. The only time your country ever came

350

together was during disasters. The same goes for most of the world. Those who survive are stronger and ready to live in a unified world."

Jason's hand on my shoulder was the only thing that stopped me from backhanding her. Sighing, I turned away, "You have become as twisted as he is." I waved a hand at Henrik, "She's all yours, I'm done," Then added in a whisper, "Show her the pictures, slowly." I gave her one last scathing look before leaving the cell and sinking against the outer wall.

He stood in front of her and started his part of the interrogation, repeating questions, probing for answers, threatening. She was fairly worked up by the time he showed her the pictures from earlier today.

"Are you working with this person?" He would ask each time. Each time she would shake her head no, but her mind said something else. He had succeeded in distracting her from my presence. After going through them three times, Henrik left and came over to me.

I could barely look up. "The one called Yoseph in Technology. It was the only person she responded to at all."

Jackson came running up moments later, a printout in his hands. He must have run the entire length of the tunnel. The papers showed that in the last six months Kayla had made five other trips to the clinic where there had been a surge in internet feed there. Henrik went over to the tiny office next to the jail and quickly typed up a warrant to arrest Yoseph and to take possession of his workstation. With a worried look in my direction, Jackson was in the cart and racing back through the tunnel.

The General came out of the cell and nodded to me. It was my turn again. Jason helped me to my feet and steadied me when I wobbled slightly.

Kayla was still looking determined but tired. She eyed me cautiously when I leaned against the wall again.

"Yoseph is being arrested as we speak." My voice was low and cold.

Her eyes widened for an instant then narrowed.

"You were so distracted by Henrik's interrogation that you forgot I was on the other side of the wall." I took a step towards her. "Oh, and since we now have him, I need to be honest. In a moment that surprised even me, while waiting outside of the clinic, I was able to pick out the codes you use out of your head."

She took a sharp breath and looked ready to leap from the bed.

"It's over Kayla. L will be taken into custody any minute now. We have your internal contact and there you sit. This twisted scheme is finished." Without waiting for her response, I turned to walk out of the room. However, on the way out, I sensed something. I stopped and turned back, "You did what to Skull?"

Her eyes grew wide again, and she answered aloud, "I switched his antibiotic for saline." Jason heard, and his anger ripped through my mind. I nearly collapsed while turning to leave.

Making sure she could hear, I added. "The moment lockdown is lifted, call the U.N. to come get her."

Just to make sure there were no more secrets, we stayed on full lockdown until both her and Yoseph's residences were searched, and we had processed most of the initial evidence. It was close to midnight when the doors were unlocked, and non-essential personnel were allowed to leave. Those with higher levels of clearance stayed and took turns sleeping in the bunkhouse.

Before going to my room for a few hours of sleep, I checked in on Rick. He had just brought the communication network back online and was reviewing what had been missed. Thankfully, the system was built with a program that recorded everything incoming, even when our side was shut down. James had sent two messages. One stated that they were in position and waiting for the first surgery to start. The other one simply said they were going in. I went to where Rick was sitting, forced the pain back, and rested my hands on his shoulders. He leaned back in his chair and looked up at me.

"No. You are not staying up. I am going to walk you to your room right now and make sure you are securely in bed."

"Securely in bed?" I had to smile and laugh a little.

"Sedated and locked in if necessary. There is no way you are getting out of there without at least 10 hours of sleep."

"That's absurd. There is so much more work to do,

and..." I looked at his computer and equipment willing it to squawk an update.

Rick stood, faced me, then wrapped me in his arms. "I will let you know when I hear from him."

"Not if I'm sedated." I pouted.

"Harlie, Bear, don't do this. You have strained your wounded abilities beyond their limits today. If you don't rest, you could do permanent damage. Please cooperate."

At my sigh, he let go and tugged my arm towards the door. He marched straight to my room and waited at the door while I got ready for bed. I shrugged out of my uniform and into the standard sweats and t-shirt from my early days on the team, just in case. Jason had dropped off a sedative and stronger dose of my custom medication, and I took them, hoping it would at least take the edge off. It felt like I could go crazy from the pain, but the situation had kept me from doing so. Now that it was ending, would the fires stop? What if it didn't?

Rick came into the room, pulled down my covers, swooped me up into his strong arms and plopped me onto the bed before I could take a breath. He leaned over and brushed a gentle kiss on the top of my head then walked out without a word. In the hall though I heard him mutter, "If she so much as sits up, call me."

Waiting for what I hoped would be relief was torture. Every part of my head hurt, my leg throbbed, and my stomach growled from barely eating. With nothing to distract me from it, I curled up into a ball and tried to breathe evenly but even that caused pain. It felt like hours until my body started to relax. When it did, tears of release trickled down my face and sleep came.

Without an alarm to wake me, I did sleep nearly ten hours. As I yawned and stretched, my hand brushed against something on the pillow. It was a note:

Good Morning Bear,
At 2:12 AM the call came in stating that Doctor L. was in custody and that James' team is bringing him directly to the bunker for interrogation. The U.N. will be making a direct flight and landing here via helicopter late

this afternoon. Be prepared for visitors. He asked about you and told me to make sure you were in better shape before he arrives.

Jaws.

After showering, I put on the least worn out polo and pants outfit then hung my dress uniform on the outer side of the door. The little effort it took to do those actions caused my body to rebel. It had been too long since I had eaten, and it was too late for a proper breakfast. I looked over to the empty refrigerator and microwave. All that was in my food basket was a pack of cookies and a granola bar. With a sigh, I left my room and hoped the cereal hadn't yet been put away upstairs. It had been, but a few donuts were in the baked goods section and fresh fruit was always available. In between waves of fire, I choked down one of each and a glass of milk. Moving slowly, I went back downstairs and peeked in at the workrooms. Every inch was being examined for devices and evidence of tampering. I knew they wouldn't find anything. This was purely between the three currently under arrest. What I wanted to know was who they were feeding the information to. The Guardians had been so careful! What knowledge had been obtained by this evil?

My next stop was the research room. Most of my assigned team was present, and my computer had been put back into its proper place.

"Good morning." I said in response to their salute. "Sorry for the deception these past few days. What have I missed in the last twelve hours?" There was not much to report, half of the team was waiting for the reception location of Kayla's contacts. The others were still reviewing files from the confiscated computers. I was just sitting down to log in when Jason came to get me. It looked as if he had not slept at all so protesting was out of the question.

"She could have killed Skull!" He hissed. "He was only getting sporadic antibiotics and could have easily bred an immune variety. As it is, Doc and I have switched to a more powerful one just in case. He has had that fever off and on for so long now that I am concerned about long-term effects on his health."

We were at the med bay at this point, and I walked into

354

the room where Skull was resting. One glace at his mind and I knew that part would be fine. With the crisis over, Doc had been allowed to return to the bunker from where he was normally stationed up in the clinic. He gave me a head to toe exam, told me to eat more, and recommended that I be given more time to recover. To the last part, I shook my head, there was no way I was going off duty until the entire team got to as well.

The activity picked up quickly after that. Everyone who stayed was given a chance to clean up, handed a fresh change of clothes, and were briefed on the incoming visitors. Shortly after four in the afternoon Rick, Jason, The General and I made our way to the landing pad on the edge of the base. As if on cue, three large helicopters landed within minutes. Inside the first one was three of the handful of U.N. officials who knew of our existence and one of the Founders of The Guardians. The middle helicopter held James, Mitch, Max, one soldier and the cuffed Doctor L. The third carried our agents and two more soldiers.

They came up to where we stood and saluted. The General shook hands with the Founder, a short-haired woman in her sixties who had a stern expression on her face. We saluted back and loaded up into two transport trucks. Even though we were seated apart, I could feel James' eyes and mind on me the entire way to the bunker. It was uncomfortable because there was still a great deal of pain, and I needed to focus away from it – away from him.

L. was taken straight to the second bunker and placed in the cell next to Kayla. The rest of us, minus the soldiers who were, of course, denied underground access, went right into debriefing. Because there were still suspects to question, everyone tried to be quick. James group had caught L. in the act of trying to enhance someone. They did not allow him to get far before breaking in. In those seconds of chaos, L. had gone to a computer in the operating theater and typed in a code. The system started to dump every file, but Mitch was able to quickly stop it. From that point on, L. had been cooperative.

The top officials wanted to know how something like this could have happened. We explained what we could, but all nerves were on edge and scathing comments were being slipped into conversation. When it finally ended, a meal was brought to us in the conference room. The entire team was silent as we ate, looking at each other and trying to communicate what could not be said aloud. How dare these people come in here in the middle of an investigation and start questioning us!

The moment the meal was cleared, The General called James and me over to where he was standing with the officials. "Take them to L. They will witness the interrogation."

James went in first and drilled him with questions. L. tried to be charming but soon became more and more curt. When he started to ask for a lawyer and refused to answer anything further, James had me come into the cell.

"My prize patient! I am so sorry you have to see me like this. Oh, child, I was so very proud of you. You must do something to clear this misunderstanding." He cooed.

I nearly vomited, "Proud that I was able to take down one of your creations? Proud that I caught Kayla in her act of betrayal? Proud that I used her mind to find the other mole here?"

He smiled, and I could see in his eyes that he was on the edge of insanity. "Imagine what you could do away from here!"

"No. I would not dream of being away from here. It must be horrible for those you have changed, to be out there alone with no one to teach them, to help them through their new reality." I walked out and did not stop until I was at the golf cart.

James came up to me minutes later. "The officials are going to stay here and continue to question him. Henrik will stay as well." He started to climb into the cart, "Our duty is done for now."

But it wasn't. We no sooner made it back to the conference room that an alarm started to sound. We rushed back to the holding area, but it was too late. While the officials were discussing what interrogation methods to use, L. had walked to the cell bars around the door and reached out enough to touch Kayla's outstretched hand. He had grasped

356

something, laughed hysterically, put the item in his mouth and bit down. He died within minutes, taking unspoken evidence with him. Kayla, it seemed, had a tiny pocket sewn into her cloth hair band. Even though she had been made to put on standard prison garb, no one had thought about her hair band. The pocket held a single cyanide pill.

We stood there in shock that whoever was behind this deception had planned so carefully. What if the trail of evidence did not stop at Doctor L. but continued onward and led us to the mastermind group? I sent my fear out towards James.

He glanced briefly towards me. "I don't think it will go that far. This was well planned, but there is little depth to it." He whispered.

It was nearly midnight before we left the conference room again. I had kept up a near constant observance of those inside the bunker, even the officials, and the Founder. There had been no deception sensed, just frustration at the situation. When we finally made it into the common room, we were too tired to do much other than sit and stare at each other.

Mitch was the first to speak. "Who would have thought that their twisted ways would have made it all the way out here?"

Rick responded quickly, "It was only a matter of time."

Max added, "New security clearances, everyone reevaluated, code changes, this is going to be a long week."

James nodded, "It's happened before. We will get through it." He then stood. "At least General Smiths has been able to keep the vastness of Harlie's ability out of the reports. Not even the Founder knows right now. Be grateful for that, we all remember what it was like when the others were leaked. Let's get some rest." On that cue, we went to our rooms and attempted to sleep.

Exhausted and in pain, it was a repeat of the prior night. The only difference was that this time I was being watched from the other side of the wall. As I tossed and turned, I wondered what had happened in the past to make James say that. Morning came too quickly, and we were all on-duty at the normal time. Paperwork, meetings, research, and tracking leads were the new routine. Dara and Ryan were pulled from the Rio work and joined up with Max to follow up anything we found. Mitch worked on the new security. Days passed and each night we were up until midnight. The U.N. officials and Founder watched from the upper-level offices.

We rarely had time to relax and barely had time to interact. It was hard on all of us. There were times I would be deep into my work and the flashes of pain would come so fast that I could not hide it. But it was in those moments that I sensed the calming, cooling presence at the fringe of my mind. James. It was not until we had been apart for those days that I realized how much of my life was connected to him.

Six days later the bunker was reopened. Kayla and Yoseph were transferred to a secure U.N. prison to await trial. Much to our chagrin, only two more arrests had been made, the manufacturers of the chip, and then the trail scattered. All of Kayla's uploads were only to the surgeon. It seemed that Doctor L. was a follower of Unus Universum's belief in one-world government and thought that enhanced people could be the leaders. He was quietly making himself part of their plan with his unlawful surgeries and hoped that they would discover his self-imposed importance. We were unable to discover if the Universum had been helping cover his tracks or if the empath was nothing more than an accidental discovery by them. As far as we knew, the knowledge of who had enhanced him had been left behind in the excitement of having the empathic man join their ranks. I was certain that he never knew L's real identity and that was some comfort. One of our top team of agents would continue to work on following the scattered trails.

The information gathered from the computer in the surgical center showed that there were three other enhancements which were titled "Successful." and four that were labeled as "Partial Failure." Dara, Max, and Ryan were called back to the bunker, and we sent out two more agents to track down the victims. I wondered what skills had been enhanced and if those four had gone insane. Would they be brought back to the base here? Would the Canadian bunker take them? What was the policy for when someone with immense skills was found in a situation where they couldn't be easily extracted? I wanted to ask Rick or James but never had the chance.

During those days, we took our meals together but were either too tired or too involved for small talk. At every meal, James sat on one side of me and Rick on the other, but we barely interacted beyond a professional level. In the few moments I caught him unaware, I was able to tell that James was a bit nervous about how I was handling my new knowledge. Rick was worried that James would be upset at him for kissing me. I was wondering how James was going to handle his feelings for me. If we were not being kept so very busy, it would have made me crazy.

On the day after the transfer happened, we had a formal dinner for the officials and Founder. It was the first time I wore the dress uniform, and my nerves were fried. I could barely get my hair into a professional looking bun. There had been too many late nights, too many days of stretching my abilities, of having to be careful to not let the others know what I was doing. It had taken its toll. But, all of us were together again, and the moment we gathered in the common room the laughter started. We just could not help it, looking at each other, all of us with bags under our eyes and battered from the tough days. It was a ridiculous sight, seeing us in our formal uniforms laughing so hard that tears streamed down our faces. When we were finally composed, which only happened when The General called inquiring what was taking so long, we marched into the transformed cafeteria for the event. Proper introductions were finally made, and we were presented an award for the success in Rio.

Max had told me that had this been a formal military operation there would have been individual medals and commendations, but from the start, the Founders had decided that if recognition were to be given, it would be to the team. He then added how I would have received at least two medals if it had been the other way around.

"Admit it, Bear, you saved the day both in Rio and here."

My response was to blush, "I could not have done any of it without the enhancement and hard training. It is only right to acknowledge as a team."

At the end of the presentation for the award, The

General stood up.

"Although I shouldn't have to say this, I want to reiterate how incredibly proud I am of you. Time and time again, in these last years, you have proven to be a solid force, a danger to anyone who threatens the destruction of humanity. Individual recommendations will be placed in your files." He looked at each of us in turn. "Take the next few days above ground. I think we can hold the fort while you rest and recover."

At those words, we stood and cheered. Skull and Max pounded the table and hollered until James silenced them with a look. We then calmly marched out and went back to the common room. On the way out, I heard the Founder mutter, "Smiths, they are completely awe-inspiring."

WALLS

There was a lot of celebrating once we were back in our corner of the bunker. All the doors were opened, and we chatted back and forth while packing and prepping. First thing in the morning our mini-vacation would start. Plans were made for the pub, and Dara warned me that she was taking me to Cardiff for a "real" shopping trip. Exhaustion soon caught up with us, though, and we settled down into our rooms. I had just curled up in bed when a thin shaft of emotion slid through the wall and into my mind. Pride. I looked at the wall and sent a reply. Relief.

Yes, a few days of relief. His mind smiled. *Harlie?*

Yes, Jamyson?

I missed you. His mental voice rang with the worry he had felt about leaving me injured.

I missed you too, but you should not have worried. I had excellent care and look what we discovered whist you were gone!

His voice filled with emotion, *Yes, once again proving that you are amazing.*

I smiled back at him. *You are over-tired. Get some sleep.*

You first. With that I sensed him sit on his couch, cross his arms and wait. I was asleep within minutes.

The next morning, we had breakfast as a team before going our separate ways. Although offers were made, I wanted to take my electric-assist bike back to the cottage. It had been inside the warehouse since before Rio. Throwing my near empty backpack onto my shoulders, I made the slow trek through town. It was a warm day but not as hot as it could be for the end of August. I slowed down several times to look closer at the village that was now my home. My only stop was at the grocery store, where a small purchase of perishables made the backpack bulge.

I did not look out mentally until the cottage was in sight and only then for security purposes. Just outside the back door, a dark spot lingered. Pretending not to recognize the way

361

my heart reacted, I parked the bike at the front door and went inside to put the items away. Mentally, he was watching every move – even though his shield was up. With a sigh that sounded more nervous than anything else, I went out the back door.

James was sitting on the wicker couch, looking out at the garden. At my approach, he turned and gave me a small smile before patting the spot next to him. I smiled back and sat. He turned away again, and I could see traces of that unknown expression in his emerald eyes. Unsure of what he was thinking or feeling, I waited, focusing on keeping my breathing steady. After a short time, seconds really, he shook his head ever so slightly and reached for my hand. I let him hold it and he gave my fingers a gentle squeeze before leaning against the back of the couch and sighing. We continued to sit, lost in our own thoughts. Unlike in the past, this time I was uncomfortable with the silence. So much had to be said on so many topics, but the ball was in his court.

At last James shifted his position, moving my hand to his lips and softly kissing it. "I am relieved about Rick being able to tell you about us." He began. "He did a much better job than I ever could, but then again, that is his talent."

I turned towards him a little. "I am relieved too...but."

He interlocked his fingers with mine, and I glanced down at them.

"But?" His voice was nearly a whisper.

"I don't know what is real and what is a global conspiracy anymore. It's hard to comprehend."

James was watching me closely now. "Some of what you learned did not surprise you at all, did it?"

Observant as always. Between him and Rick, my life might as well be an open book. "No. I've suspected some of it for nearly a decade now. It's those cover-ups and what is not reported that Gareth used to research." It had been so long since I had said his name. My heart skipped a beat and memories flashed through my mind.

I saw James' head shake and came back to the present. "I know. It would have been his position here."

My body tensed slightly, "If he had not died, what would my position have been?"

He looked heavenward and was still for a moment. "What you would have started as does not matter. The end result would still have been your enhancement and placement on the team."

I thought about the last six months and the transformation from Nicole Jones to Harlie Berryman. My mind then wandered to the six months before that. Tears began to fill my eyes and one started its trek down my face. James lifted his free hand and gently brushed it away.

I know. His mind whispered.

"Jamyson, I don't know what to think about anything anymore." Even with his shield still up I could sense the change. He knew I was referring just as much to the situation between him and me as to my changing worldview. His fingers brushed down my cheek, leaving fiery streaks in its wake.

Don't think. Let your heart guide you.

I turned away from him, *I can't.*

"Yes, you can." He whispered aloud. Mental fingers tracked in a feathery touch across my shield. Giving my hand one more squeeze he stood. "Get some rest. I'll see you tomorrow." He dropped my hand and left via the back gate. I went inside, curled up on the couch and let the memories come along with the tears. Eventually, my eyes closed in rest.

The following morning brought a normal waking time and I was ready to celebrate a day of freedom. Of course, that was the moment Dara knocked on the door. With an exasperated sigh, I invited her inside.

"Good to see you are up and kind-of dressed." She rolled her eyes at my t-shirt and jeans.

"At least it's easy to take off and on if you are really going to drag me to Cardiff." I pointed out. "Besides, what if I had other plans for today?"

She crossed her arms for a moment before marching into my bedroom and going through my sparse wardrobe. "Seniority. I've been here longer, and your wardrobe is a crime committed against all spies and diplomats. If you are going to hang around and talk the talk, girl, you better start walking the walk."

There really was no point in arguing with Dara when

she gets that way. I stood silently and watched as she took out a notepad and wrote out all I was supposedly lacking. She then grabbed my purse and pointed to the door. It was at that point I remembered about someone else wanting to spend time with me today, and he was coming up the road. He projected the question I knew would come, and I begged him to make Dara stop. When she saw James' arrival she looked from me to him then back to me.

"No way, Harlie, calling in The Commander to rescue you is not going to work." Her look dared him to contradict her.

"Actually, Dara, I was already on my way here. I had told Harlie yesterday to be expecting me."

"Tough luck, James, I got here first."

He looked at me for a moment, "She better be home by dusk."

Dara looked incredulous. "And what if we are not back by dusk? What are you going to do about it? This is free time."

His voice changed in an instant, "Do you really need to ask that question, Dara?" At that, he turned and walked back to his apartment. She glared at the back of his head until he was out of sight, then motioned me into the car.

Our first stop was the town bank where she supervised me taking out an absurd amount of cash. She followed with her own account, and we were headed to Cardiff. The moment we were out of town she asked the question I had been anticipating.

"Did you call him over?"

"No. What he said was true." I refrained from looking out at her.

"Why does he still think he can waltz in whenever he wants and control your life? You are not that passive of a person."

"Dara," Considering the frustration I was suddenly feeling, my voice was awfully calm. "He does not control my life. We are friends, just like you and I or Rick and I are friends."

"Jason seems to think it's something else." She hinted.

"Jason is full of himself. We are friends. Rick is great

364

for talking to and being comforted by. James is..." Now how could I describe the complexity? "James' mind is like mine. That gives us a connection and has helped build our friendship."

She did not push the issue and we made random small talk the rest of the way into the city. Once we arrived, Dara was like a woman possessed. Her plan was to make it so that I could blend into every major society. Ethnic clothing drew her like a magnet. I could only sigh and be subjected to what loosely translated into torture. She did let me pick out a couple casual dresses and some sweaters for the autumn, along with some jeans. The rest I did not even have veto power over. Once again, I found myself pondering how one person could go from shopping maniac to a deadly force in an instant.

We pulled back into the village just as the middle of the sun was reaching the horizon. The back seat was near full of clothes and accessories. She was going to drop all of the outfits off at the cleaners and bring them over later, so she could organize my closet. Whatever made her happy. At least our conversations were always good. It's what kept me sane for most of the day.

Dara helped bring the accessories into the cottage. She had no sooner left when James pulled up on his motorcycle. One look at my face and he was frowning. "She wore you out didn't she?"

"I'll be fine, but she just left, and I have not had a chance to unwind."

He appeared to be deep in thought for a moment. "How about watching the stars come out while resting at the river?"

I gave him a weary nod.

It was a clear night and while, at first, we were sitting on the blanket he brought, we ended up laying next to each other to watch the sky. We were far enough from the village that it was comfortable to lower our mental shielding. However, we both seemed to be more careful about what we were thinking. At one point he took my hand again, and I found it was easier to accept the contact. Once it was dark, he brought me back to the cottage, kissing my hand and smiling before leaving. I wondered if it was really so wrong to acknowledge that I was enjoying these moments with him?

The thought kept me up for a good part of the night. This past week, I had come to realize how connected our lives had become. I did enjoy being around him when we were off duty. He had apologized for our difficult start and seemed to be doing everything in his power to keep his word. The intensity of our relationship frightened me some. If we were so intense now, what would it be like if I did open up to his growing feelings? How would our abilities affect it? We constantly had access to the other's emotions. Would a relationship change how we acted around the team? My thoughts went back to Mumbles, our time at the river, the hike and those days at the hotel. Come dawn the conclusion was: I did not want it to stop and would wait and see what Jamyson had planned. If it still seemed too dangerous or too soon, I felt sure that I could back away.

The sleepless night led to waking quite late. I was wondering why no one had bothered to wake me when I felt the light tap on my mental shield. We did live within range of our abilities, so he must have been watching me some.

Can I come over? He sounded like a child asking to come and play at a friend's house.

I was planning on staying here and resting today, but if you want to...

Do you want me to? It was a weighted question. He was leaving it up to me. Perhaps some of my turmoil had slipped out during the long night.

I counted to twenty before replying, *Yes.*

I sensed his smile and hurried to make myself presentable before he arrived. The knock at the door came at the same time as the tap on my shield. He let himself in and came over to give me a hug, lingering there for several long moments.

"You look very tired." He commented, letting me go and placing his backpack on the table. "I brought over a few movies you might like, some popcorn, and a book you showed interest in back at the bunker."

I smiled at his thoughtfulness, and his eyes lit up in return. It looked like we might get the rest we both needed while still spending time together. We settled in to watch one of the movies, sitting on separate sides of the couch. It was

366

time for lunch afterward, and he followed me into the kitchen. I was nervous with him watching my every move, and he could tell. I saw him laugh quietly and threw a warning glance in his direction.

I was cleaning up from the meal when he came up behind me and rested his hands on my waist. I froze and felt him laugh again. "Settle down, Bear." James did not move. "I'm not going to do anything to press my luck. I'm enjoying this too much."

As with my evening with Rick, I forced my muscles to relax and struggled to get my mind to do the same. I relaxed my posture just enough so that my back touched his chest. It felt like electricity was flowing between us. His fingers gripped my waist for an instant, then relaxed. He must have felt it too. We stood there, frozen in time for over a minute. James moved first, dropping his hands and reaching for the rest of the dishes.

During the second movie, he sat next to me and held my hand. He seemed relaxed, and I could not help but be the same way. Once it ended he stood up and stretched, then reached for my hand and pulled me up into an embrace.

"I'm going to head out and let you nap. Don't forget we need to be at the pub tonight."

I grimaced and started to pull away, he hesitated before letting me go. "Do I look like I need a nap?" I asked.

His response was to trace the bags under my eyes with his fingers. "We both do." James looked like he was going to say more, but instead took my hands and kissed both of them before smiling at me.

I smiled back. "This was really nice, Jamyson."

"It was. We need to do this more often." I heard in my heart what his words were really saying. We need to spend more time together.

I nodded, and he gave me another hug before leaving.

The nap was indeed needed, and I was refreshed and ready for the pub. Skull and I were the first to arrive, and we made small talk with a few locals as the others arrived. After we ate, Max, Ryan, and I had a game of billiards that nearly turned volatile when they started to lose. The others laughed at the expression on Max's face when I won.

"Aw, poor Root lost to another girl!" Dara crowed. She was soon ducking under his half-hearted punch.

I sat back down at the booth with James, who had just finished a game of darts with Rick, and we watched the others. Even though we were the only two there, we sat close enough that our shoulders brushed. I felt him smile mentally and responded with the same.

It was not too long before I noticed something different in the team's behavior. While Jason had a habit of shadowing Dara, tonight he seemed to be nearly hanging onto her. She was allowing him to do it too, something I had not seen before.

"Am I missing something?" I asked when James eyes and mind turned to them as well.

He frowned. "No. It comes and goes with those two. There are no deep feelings, they just use each other for..." He paused, and I filled in the blanks. James watched my reaction to that knowledge. "Yeah, I wish they wouldn't, but within the hour she will start hanging onto him, and then they'll go back to one of their places. It's not right in any sense."

The concept bothered me. Of course, I had seen that kind of behavior before but never with anyone I was close to. The idea of them using each other for sexual release with nothing deeper rubbed me the wrong way on all levels.

"Want to get out of here?" He whispered.

At my nod, he stood and went to tell Rick, who made a gagging motion before turning and giving me a sympathetic smile. James and I walked to his apartment, hopped on his bike and went back to the river. High wispy clouds impaired the view of the stars, so we watched reflections on the water. James sat so our shoulders were still touching.

He broke the silence first, "I'm glad you feel the same way about that situation."

"I can see why you tried to keep Jason and me apart." A small shudder came forward along with that train of thought.

He nodded and put his arm around my shoulder. It was a battle not to freeze up, but my heart won. "Rick relayed a lot of what the two of you discussed in my absence." He was looking out at the water. Did Rick tell him that we had kissed?

368

As if he heard the question, James turned to me, "I know you think it is too soon, but Rick did a good job of talking you through our point of view." He added under his breath, "Wish it had been me."

"Jamyson, that conversation would not have gone as well if it were you and I having it."

I felt him smile, "No. It probably would not have." He leaned over and kissed the top of my head, then dropped part of his shield. I felt again what had been in his mind when I was recovering. This time it was less concern and more of his other emotions towards me. My mind started racing through the thoughts of the night before, and I barely hid the burning flash of pain that followed it. "Can I hear you?" He whispered.

I shrugged out of his one-armed embrace, my shield acting like the strongest of walls that even I could not break. His head shook slowly at my reaction.

"Time to take you home then."

The struggle continued, part of me wanted to tell him no and that I wanted to stay. Another part of me wanted to run away. I followed him back to the bike, torn. When we arrived at the cottage, he walked me to the doorway then turned me towards him.

"Harlie, it's okay. I understand what you have to work through. In a way, I am experiencing those same emotions. Remember what we have told you though." He pulled me into an embrace. "Sleep well. I'll see you at church tomorrow." With that, he was gone. I fought tears while getting ready for bed. The walls were crumbling, but it was a very painful process. I slept that night with a photo of Gareth and me in my hands.

The next morning, while I wanted to be at church, I did not want to be near James. Thankfully, the pastor's wife saw me arrive and waved me to her side before the others arrived. James, Rick, Ryan, and Max all sat towards the back. I could feel James and Rick's questioning stares but ignored them and focused on the service.

The afternoon was spent cooking and freezing a few meals and working in the garden. While it felt good to have true alone time, it was oddly unsettling as well. Without someone to interact with, my thoughts turned to the past. I tried to force myself to think of happier times, but the last three years constantly intruded. The back to back plagues, the bombs, the collapse: Running, hiding, saving, surviving, it was so hard to push those aside and think of the years before it. I was back inside, staring at nothing when there was a knock at the door. Per habit, I looked out and frowned. Not now, I thought to myself, please just leave me alone. I sat on the couch and pretended not to hear. The tapping at my shield came next, harder to ignore but possible. And then he spoke.

I wasn't going to come by today, especially after seeing how you were at church.

Silence was my answer.

You need time away, time to process, and I want to give you that. But, Harlie, an answer just came from the higher-ups. Still silent, I turned my mind towards his, knowing he would sense it through the shield. *Rick and I have permission to let you know more and want to do that before things get crazy again.*

I nodded. He sensed it.

Come with me to his place for dinner. We'll tell you what we are able.

This time I opened the door. His beautiful green eyes were tortured. Even though he wanted me to feel for him what he felt for me, James understood. My defenses crumbled a little more. The emotion from it caused me to turn away, feeling as if I were choking for a moment. He saw and quickly stepped inside, shutting the door behind him.

Regaining some composure, I started towards the table to pick up my bag. A hand gently wrapped around my wrist and another touched my waist, turning me to face him. I stared at his chest, willing myself to avoid the tortured eyes.

"Your pain right now," His voice matched my choked feeling. "It's on your face and in your movements. Even your shield is rippling from it."

"Took a walk down memory lane," I whispered. "But I could not get beyond the last three years."

He nodded, and I could see his mind working on a response. "It is a lot to overcome, your past life, and should not be downplayed." I looked up at him, confused at his words. "However, it should not be allowed to stop you from

370

building your future." The hands drew me closer, despite my tensed posture. Calming thoughts washed over me, positive memories from the last six months. "Focus on what is in front of you." He smiled, "And I don't mean just me, although I would not mind in the least."

I relaxed just a bit, and he pulled me the rest of the way to him. My head rested against his chest as the memories continued, some which I had not realized were so positive for him. One hand held me to him, the other traced up and down my back. The moment my mind caught up with what my heart had allowed, I flinched. He quickly let me go and nodded at the door.

Dinner with Rick and James was a fascinating event. Away from the others, I could see glimpses of the childhood friendship: playful jibes and comments, smiles, and laughter. The meal was excellent, and afterward, we retired to the living room. I was almost to the corner of the sectional when James raced past and plopped down with an exaggerated sigh. I turned towards one end and Rick was placing a box there. My eyes met his and he started to laugh before pushing me out of the way and claiming the other side.

"Not fair!" I pouted.

Rick laughed harder, "Get used to it, Bear. There are very few rules here."

James nodded, "You might as well give in now and come sit by me. It's not worth fighting over."

They underestimated my stubbornness. I took two steps back and sat on the floor instead. That stopped the laughter, and they quickly turned serious. I felt bad about the action but did not let on to that emotion.

Rick spoke, "What do you know and understand about the science of time?"

What an odd question to ask. I thought about it for a moment. "It is the forward movement of all things and has a predictable pattern."

"How about lesser followed theories?"

"You mean things like bending space so that time travel is possible, that certain galactic events can stall time and anything moving faster than the speed of light goes back in

371

time?" James nodded, and I continued. "I know nothing of the potential science behind it. It seems too fictional." I saw both their expressions change at the same time. "But then again, nothing seems impossible these days."

Rick nodded this time. "About thirty years ago there was a well-hidden event that happened not too far from here. It was quickly covered up with some random believable explanation, but that event has had far-reaching consequences. You see, a man showed up at a casual luncheon between two high ranking United Nations employees. He was very calm and pretended not to know whom he was speaking to, but he dropped hints as to knowledge of classified situations. When they grew suspicious, he somehow prevented them from calling the authorities. The man told them that he was from their future, and he provided enough evidence that they believed him. In his time, a group of radicals had taken over most of the world through violence and threats. While they had recently been overthrown, it was almost too late to save mankind. The radicals had been so set on their domination that they had poisoned most of Earth with the results of their attacks and attempts to keep power.

The visitor was a scientist, living with others like him in an isolated community. Even though the rest of Earth was practically in the Dark Ages again, they developed technology to fold space and time enough so that he could go back 100 years and warn us. The process, while it worked, caused a fatal breakdown of human tissue. The members brought him to the base in this village. In the days before his death, he taught the people here some the advances he knew, told them about who to look for to help change the outcome, showed them how to use a device he had somehow brought along, and wrote out a basic timeline. He was careful not to give too much detail but enough for them to see the signs." Rick paused and sighed. "He sacrificed his life to warn us what to look for and when we would be out of time."

James took over, "It took years to convince a select group of what would come. This was something that had to be hidden from the world. Using the visitor's advances, this bunker and the one in the Canada were built. Money was quietly filtered out of various budgets and became our funding. Using his guidelines, those with special abilities were chosen to lead it. Your enhancement was possible using his device. This is the Guardians' history."

I was stunned. Was nothing sacred anymore? Had the world been turned inside out while we slept? Was this insanity going to stop? I sat and thought it over. There was an omission in their story, a hint that it did not quite go that way, but it quickly became a moot point. The more I thought, the more it made sense with my experiences these last few years. So many were still so blind, so many had to stay that way, even those I worked with every day. Responsibility weighed heavy on my shoulders. Whatever reason those in power had for making me privy to this information, I had to make sure I lived up to it.

I looked up at James, "How much time do we have to prevent it?"

"We have been doing much to prevent the most catastrophic event. The first major attack never happened. The second was made lesser by our efforts." I saw the pain and knew it was what happened to the United States. "The worst of the attacks, fifteen large nuclear blasts on the same day...it's less than two years off."

"That's not a lot of time."

Rick shook his head, "No it's not, but every success we have, in places like Rio, puts them farther and farther behind on their goal. As of right now, we don't see any way for them to acquire all fifteen, and we keep destroying their technology. We have some evidence that they are in possession of what is needed to make around nine bombs. But there is not enough information for us to be able to decipher the locations and go after them...yet."

"Fifteen blasts, if they were placed properly could, in fact, contaminate a large portion of the planet." I whispered, thinking it over.

James nodded, "Even if they were placed outside of a country's capital, less than fifteen could bring the human race to its knees."

"And you have known this since you were teenagers? One of the first enhanced to follow the visitor's instructions on how to save us?"

Rick looked at James and James stared at him, silent

communication flowing between them. "James was not enhanced. He is one of only a handful born with that kind of talent. As far as we know, he's the only one who is not insane. The visitor said that in the future more and more children are being born with empathic and other special abilities, as an adaptation to the chaotic world perhaps."

I sat in silence, thinking over their words. In some strange way, it all made perfect sense. There were still questions about why and how I played into all of it, but those would wait for now. Even with my shield up, James was somehow able to follow my train of thoughts.

"Harlie, did you ever think that perhaps everything you have been through, all of your trials, all of your experiences both good and bad, were somehow guiding you or molding you into what we see in front of us today? As heart-wrenching as all of it was, your past appears to have happened for this future." He waved around him, "And this is where you belong."

There had been times when those same thoughts had occurred to me, times when I was almost convinced that my life had been designed for my time with The Guardians. Hearing it from James and Rick started to solidify the concept. Others had mentioned how easily I adjusted to this new life, perhaps it was because my entire past was in preparation for this future. Thinking again of my faith, I realized how my life had been allowed to play out that way in order for me to be ready for this part of my life. James saw the conclusion in my eyes and smiled warmly. He held out a hand to me and I willingly went to sit next to him, needing security as yet another wave of reality washed over me.

James wrapped an arm around my shoulders and pulled me closer to him. His shield lowered, and I was surrounded by projections of what he saw as evidence. From there, soothing images and comfort wrapped around me. I sat absorbed in the projections, my facial expressions changing with each received thought or picture. When James finished, I was much more at ease with the concept and let out a small sigh.

Rick had been watching the interaction, and out of the corner of my eye, I saw him smile. It bothered me that he had such strong feelings for me and how he kept them hidden behind his "Life's Vow." On the other hand, he seemed to be telling the truth about not only accepting James' feelings for me but wanting me to be with James as well. I turned to give him a small smile, and he nodded.

James and I left shortly afterward. We were both lost in thought during the short ride back to the cottage. At the front door, I turned towards him, knowing he had more on his mind. It was moments like these where the holes in the wall around my heart glowed like a beacon, nearly begging for someone to release more of the light. It was also those same moments that set every part of my mind on edge. The opposing sides stared each other down, waiting to see who would make the first move.

He looked at me quietly for several seconds, then reached out a hand to touch my face. I smiled at his touch and he smiled back. Stepping closer, he rested both hands on my waist.

"Back to our old routine tomorrow," His voice sounded a little strained.

"I hope we have enough of a break in the action to make it seem like routine." My voice was hoarse.

"It has been awhile since we've really just worked out of the bunker." He was standing so close I could feel the heat coming off his body.

"Not since my training." Now my voice was a whisper.

"Should be interesting, hope I don't mess up."

I knew what he was referring to, keeping our feelings hidden. "Just don't be too hard on me."

He looked up to the sky, "They expect it though."

"Then mentally let me know it's a show or take me away from them so they only think the worst."

James' eyes met mine and he smiled, "Brilliant."

My brain attacked at that moment, sending a fiery flash through my body so fast that I tensed up and a small gasp of pain escaped. I saw several expressions cross his face, disappointment, confusion and then concern.

He did not move, instead asking, "Is that the same thing as what was happening right after your fight?"

Just as fast as it started, the pain stopped. I nodded, then added, "I think it is. The pain seemed random before but

375

now seems to have triggers."

A frown appeared on James' face, "Too much stimulation, too much emotion, your mind is still trying to protect itself." He touched my face again, his fingers lingering around my lips, "Protecting itself from me it seems." He looked bothered, "I'll let you get some rest."

Unable to stop my mind from stepping on my heart, my mouth refusing to tell him of the times it acted up while he was away, I stood and watched him leave. Arguing with myself, I prepared for bed. Sleep came but so did nightmares. What would it be like once we were back at the bunker?

As if we were all empathic, the entire team arrived at the bunker within minutes of each other. Somehow, we had all decided that breakfast in the cafeteria was better then what was at our residences. We had also all been on the same wavelength when it came to clothing, and everyone was dressed in the green polo shirts and black pants. Doubled over with laughter, we caused quite a scene as we entered the large room.

"Honey, we're home!" Max called out to the agents gaping at us from a far table. There were many sets of eyes rolling and muttered comments about why we insisted on being so dramatic, but we didn't care.

After the meal, we stood in unison, sighed in unison, dropped off our trays in unison and crammed into the elevator without a word. Playtime was over, when those doors opened, again it was back to business.

The General was waiting for us in the hallway. At his nod we filed into the conference room and sat. "Welcome back. I trust you are all well rested and recovered from our latest adventures?" He looked at each of us and waited until we responded with a "Yes, Sir." or nod. Only then did he continue. "Just as quickly as the latest threat sprung up, it has disappeared. I wish I had conclusive results for you, but our field teams are still struggling to find out how, or if, our surgeon was involved with the masterminds. Of course, we still have Unus Universum to follow and are still working with leads from Rio. They have more resources than previously thought, enough to plan a larger scale attack like the one in the

376

U.S." He paused to let the words sink in, "We need to find and remove those supplies, make it so they cannot build their weapons.

Because there is no current mission to prepare for and we are back to a research and recon stage, there is no reason to keep you underground full-time. You will be allowed to leave at the end of your normal shift."

We reserved the cheering for after he left and just thanked The General instead. There was gravity to our situation, but we were happy to be allowed our version of a normal life at the end of the day. He dismissed us, and we went right to work in the training facility. It had been so long since we had followed a schedule that the rest of the day was spent figuring who was working out where and when each person would be at the tactical facility.

I was happy to have a routine to follow and made sure Max and I were in the gun range at the same time. Just as with my old schedule, Rick, Mitch, and I were working on our research at the same time as well. The only difference was that I was permanently working with the group of research agents assigned to me since Panama. I would meet with them every day and go over what they had found, guiding them to the next steps, and following up on promising leads.

By Wednesday, we were completely back to our version of normal during the workday and were looking more and more like the team we had been before Rio. James and I had been paired up on the mats for martial arts practice and true-to-form he held nothing back. I ended up on the ground several times before finally getting him down. The others were trying not to watch and failing at the attempts. We figured they were waiting for us to take it to a mental battle like before, but my mind was still not ready for it. After our end-of-shift debrief, Rick came up to me like he was going to ask something but just gave me a quick hug and walked away. Seconds later, James inquired mentally if I wanted a ride home. Even though part of me wanted to stay away, my heart won, and I answered with an affirmative.

At the cottage, I walked around and started checking all the raised beds and landscaping. It had become a routine when I was actually home and was something that helped me relax after a long day. Even though I had not asked him to stay, James followed closely behind. Sometimes he asked questions about particular plants, the rest of the time he just watched. When I reached the back of the house and started harvesting tomatoes, he placed his hands on my waist. I froze.

"Keep working, I'm enjoying watching." He grinned.

"If you want to eat dinner anytime soon, I suggest you not distract me." I looked over my shoulder at him.

He turned me to face him, "I don't recall any conversations about dinner."

"You've followed me long enough that I figured you were planning on staying."

James turned serious, "Only if you want me to stay. It was rude of me to invite myself to tag along." His hands squeezed my waist gently, "You did not seem to mind though."

Before my head could try anything, I nodded at him, "I want you to stay." Turning back to the plants I added, "Looks like pasta with homemade tomato and vegetable sauce."

He let go of me but did not stray far as I finished harvesting, prepped the vegetables and made the sauce. He offered assistance, but I only allowed him to help wash the dishes. We both enjoyed the meal and sighed in satisfaction when our plates had been emptied.

When I sat down on the couch, he came to sit beside me. I had been planning on reading, but he took one hand, then the other, and tugged them towards him. I turned to face him.

"You are so beautiful." He muttered, "I know you don't believe it, but you are beautiful both inside and out."

I shrugged.

"These last three days have been interesting for me. A large part of me knows my responsibility and wants to fulfill it. Another part is trying to watch your every move, while a third part is coming up with excuses to pull you away from the others."

The internal war was on but each side called a short truce for me to say, "I don't want this to be a struggle for you."

James' expression grew intense, "Harlie, we do need to decide sometime soon exactly what this is and how we are going to handle it."

My head held an invisible hand over my heart to prevent it from speaking. "Jamyson, right now this is you admitting your more intimate feelings for me and trying to get me to feel the same towards you."

"Do you feel the same?"

I could barely handle his burning eyes and fought not to look down, "I...I like us spending more time together, and I missed you while you were in Bangladesh." Try as I may, I could not say the rest, that I did have stronger emotions for him. He saw the conflict.

"I wish you would stop thinking it's too soon, stop making it so you cannot accept what others feel for you." His eyes turned sad. "You don't allow yourself to feel anything positive."

I tried to pull my hands away, but he tightened his grip. "Jamyson, I do let myself feel positive emotions." But, I could not deny the rest. It was easier to keep my strange new world at arm's length.

As if he read my shielded thoughts, James pulled me closer, "You can't deny it, can you? You know you are keeping us all away from you." He then dropped his shield and there was no escaping the cascade of emotions. Even if I tried to look away some would still wisp about. I cringed at the onslaught, and his thoughts were protected again. "You can't stay that way. At some point, you are going to have to say yes or no. One will be the truth, the other a lie, and I will know the difference."

I jerked away from him and he let go, leaning back against the couch. Anger flashed briefly across his features. It was a long minute before he spoke. "I wanted tonight to be positive and now I've gone and ruined it."

My head shook back and forth, "No, you did not. My head and heart are in conflict, and that is what messed it up."

The fierce expression was back, "You are not going to take responsibility for tonight. I came here knowing that conflict, hoping to guide you towards your heart. Instead, I was too firm, and the other side won."

The tug-of-war was growing painful. Something had to be done, "James, if you want my heart to win, stop grumbling

379

and hold me."

His eyes widened, "Show me you meant that."

I pushed the conflict back and let that part of my emotions come forward before dropping part of my shield. I really did want to know what it would feel like in his arms. James shifted to the corner of the couch, and I scooted over to rest against him. We stayed there for an hour, lost in our own troubling thoughts. When I stifled a yawn, he kissed the top of my head.

"I should be heading out." His voice was muted. His lips found my forehead and placed another kiss there.

My heart started racing and my brain turned to mush – I could only nod in reply. He ran his fingers up and down my arm several times before moving to sit totally up. A hand reached up and rested on the side of my face.

"Good night, Harlie. Sleep well." With those words, he stood and left.

The rest of the week picked up the pace as increased research led to us planning a few quick out-of-country trips to check some leads out. Friday evening, I was exhausted. James had planned to come over, and I hoped he would understand that I was just too tired. He did. We went hiking Saturday and rested with a movie and a book on Sunday.

The following week was the same. We spent several evenings together, and I was becoming more and more comfortable with having him around. He had pulled me from the group twice to see if I could still defend mentally, following it up with a visit to the house afterward to try to soothe the pain it caused. The week after that we spent two evenings out at the river. He would sit against a tree and I would sit between his legs, resting my back against his chest. We talked for hours, shields down and relaxed. However, the moment his mind turned to the idea of holding me closer or kissing me, my body would be enveloped in a blinding flash of pain. I could sense his frustration. I was feeling the same. Some of the excuses my mind was using were just not working anymore. I was beginning to feel for him the same way he felt for me.

BY FIRE

As August ended, I was called up to General Smiths' office. He had a sealed envelope for me. It appeared to have been something which had been mailed, and it had my old name on it. Since I did not really exist to the outside world, I panicked as The General told me what it was. A subpoena. Those who had hurt me were going on trial, and both sides had been told I was alive and under witness protection. I had to appear and testify against the man who had raped me. At the same time, a military tribunal on the condition of the camps and treatment of its residents would be happening. My presence had been requested there as well.

"Much has happened since your attack. Even though it is policy to avoid our past, much good can be accomplished by those men being convicted. I had to allow you to testify."

"How can that happen?" I was confused.

"You will be led, in disguise, to a separate part of the building where a closed-circuit camera will show your masked face to the courtroom. They want DNA to prove you are you and insist on a psychological evaluation beforehand. You'll arrive before the trial to provide those things and at least one of us will be with you at all times."

"When will this occur?" My attempt to be professional sounded pathetic.

He smiled sadly, "To be honest, I have held onto this letter for several weeks now. It arrived right after you returned from Rio. The trial starts in eight days, you will be leaving here in three."

I stood silent, angered at having information withheld from me, desperately fighting flashbacks which threatened to overtake me. The General walked around his desk and came to stand in front of me.

"The decision to hold the letter was solely mine. James knew I was keeping something from him but did not know what it was. I told Rick earlier this morning because he will be the one coming with you. Is there another member you would have attend for support?"

I knew that since Rick was coming with me it meant James was unavailable. I thought it over briefly. "Dara, Sir. It would be good to have female support."

He clapped a hand on my shoulder, "Consider it done. Doc is going to walk you through what types of tests they could perform and how you need to react. Dara will be handy in helping with your disguises as well as the support she can provide. You may be relieved from whatever duty necessary in order to prepare."

Stepping back, I snapped, "There is too little time, Sir."

He frowned. "With all that has been going on, I believed it was best to give you less time to ponder over that part of your past. As of late, you have seemed more relaxed here, and I did not want to jeopardize it."

There was no denying the truth of what he said. If I had known about it for longer, I would indeed be thinking about that time and worrying about the trial. There was also no denying how I had indeed been more relaxed in the past month than before. This bunker was feeling more like home and The Guardians were my family. Of course, the time spent with James played a part as well. I gave The General a curt nod, "Will that be all, Sir?" So much to do, so very much to prepare for.

"Best of luck to you, Agent Berryman. You are dismissed."

The elevator seemed to be a mile away, the trip to the lower level like a trip down a skyscraper. Dara was waiting at the bottom, a questioning expression on her face.

"You'll know soon enough." I told her as we traded places in the elevator.

Even though I should have gone straight to my quarters to start preparing, I walked into the training facility and picked up where I had left off in the circuit. James was out of town, meeting with one of our contacts, and would not be back until later today. That meant I could get more of my work done before dealing with what I was expecting to be an explosion of emotion when he found out. After running, I marched straight to the firing line and took my frustrations out on numerous targets. Apparently, it was a dramatic scene because, when I paused to reload the empty line of handguns, several pairs of

383

eyes were watching from the other side of the glass. Max came into the room, removed the gun from my hand and stared at the carnage.

"I think it's time for a break, Bear. Whatever is going on, it's not worth damaging my range over." Wood, paper, and ballistics gel-stuffed targets were in various phases of destruction. I had gone through in minutes what the I would normally destroy in a week.

Looking just slightly embarrassed, I walked out of the line and towards the mats. Rick met me there, and I knew it was time to face the situation. Here was the person who knew more about me than anyone else in the room – someone who knew exactly what was upsetting me. Although I could have effectively defended myself against someone of his stature and power, I was too distracted. In just three moves I was on the ground, my shoulder taking the brunt of the fall because I could not get my body to respond fast enough to roll. I laid there for several seconds, fighting back pain-filled tears.

Rick knelt next to me and, despite the stares of the others, brushed the hair away from my face. "Get up and we'll take a break." He whispered.

I sat and pulled my knees to my chest. "I want to finish the day."

In front of everyone, he rested a hand on the side of my face and lifted my head to better meet his eyes. "And you will after you have a break." He dropped his hand to take one of mine then stood and pulled me up. "Dara, we are all involved in this unusual circumstance. Please debrief the others."

She nodded, and the rest of the team followed her to the conference room. Rick did not even wait until they were out of sight before wrapping me in his arms.

"General Smiths' judgment was way off in this situation. He should have given you more time so that, by the trial, your mind could have been desensitized to the concept. Now, you'll still be in the middle of raw emotion."

"When is James due back?" I wanted to see him but, at the same time, I was afraid of his reaction.

"This evening and you'll be back at the cottage by then."

I looked up at him, "Shouldn't I stay here? It is a

mission of sorts."

He let me go, taking my arm to lead me to our living quarters. "We'll stay here the night before departure. Besides, most of what you need is at the cottage." At my questioning expression, he added, "The ethnic clothing Dara and you purchased will make great disguises. Even though she did not know about the trial, she was right to have you add those items to your wardrobe. You are a spy after all." He smiled.

Rick stayed with me as I packed what few items I needed from the room. It was our normal lunch break, so we went to the cafeteria. We sat apart from the rest of the team, who now looked at their food instead of at me. I tried to see the situation from their perspective. We had all given up our past lives, our history, and all that we had been. We had sworn to never again go back to those we knew, those we had loved, from that time in our lives. Now, one of their own was being forced to relive that past, forced to resurrect a ghost.

Doc came to get me as the meal was finished. We talked about what the evaluation would be like and started practicing responses to make my answers seem more natural. It would be difficult because for many things I would have to simply respond with "I cannot say at this time." or "I cannot say due to regulations surrounding my protection." The same responses would be used during my time on the witness stand. Our session lasted the rest of the workday.

Emotionally exhausted, I wordlessly let Dara take over with whatever she had planned. She stopped first at her apartment and grabbed two proper suitcases.

"Our normal bags will not work in this situation." She commented while placing the large sturdy items in the back seat. Her next stop was the pub where she forced me to eat and sat stubbornly until I had a drink as well. At the cottage, she went right into my bedroom and opened the closet.

"I knew these would come in handy!" She exclaimed a moment later, pulling out two saris and matching headscarves. "No one will recognize you under these." She also put together two jean and sweater outfits as well as a pants-and-blouse combo which matched the headscarves. "Your face will still be hidden."

Looking at the outfits, I was fairly sure that no one

would recognize me. I was starting to think about who might be present when my mental shield felt like it was on the edge of a blast zone. I flinched at the sudden shock and shut my eyes.

"Harlie, what's wrong?" Dara's voice was alarmed, "Your face just turned white!"

Forcing my lids open and my eyes to turn in her direction, I whispered, "The Commander is home." A fiery flash ripped through my body, and I cringed against it.

She stared at me, questions on her face. I had to protect all of us by answering her. "When either of us is overly emotional, like when something dramatically shocks us, our mental shield is not enough to keep the powerful responses hidden. He was just told by The General, and..." My eyes darted around like the danger was here. "and... he is very angry." Focusing on her I added, "He'll probably come here next. You might want to leave."

Dara stood ramrod straight, and her eyes held a determined expression. "I'll leave when we are finished packing and not a moment sooner. If he is angry, well that makes nine of us." Her expression softened, "You are in deep with those two, aren't you? I saw how Rick handled you earlier today, just the right amount of compassion and discipline. He obviously cares about you and knows you better than the rest of us."

I looked out to make sure James was still out-of-range. It was scary how far outside that range his anger traveled. "Rick and I are good friends. He is there for me when I need him and seems to know exactly what that need is. He is very caring and gentle."

"But nothing else?"

"No, nothing else. Nothing more than close friends."

She went back to searching through my belongings for items I might need while we were away. "Rick and James are on the team with us but, at times, have seemed to be separate from us as well. It's almost as if their mission is different from ours. You are starting to seem the same way too."

Dara's accurate observation put me on edge. "It's just because they knew each other in their past life. They have been like brothers most of their lives."

She nodded, throwing a pair of shoes into one of the bags. "Harlie, the way you reacted to James' anger right now, it makes me even more concerned about the two of you."

At that moment, James came into range. Keeping my shield tight, I chose honesty again. "Dara, sometimes I'm concerned about me and James too. The intensity of our early days and now our friendship..." I looked towards the door. "He's left the bunker."

True to her word, Dara did not leave until she was sure everything I could possibly need was packed. James had arrived fifteen minutes before and was sitting on the wicker couch behind the cottage. Anger was no longer leaking from his shield, but I was still hesitant about going to him. I paced the kitchen, thinking it over. James had done nothing wrong. If he had come home to the normal day-to-day, he would have been here anyways. Taking a deep breath and slowly letting it out, I opened the back door.

He was hunched over, head in his hands. The image reached straight into my heart and nothing else mattered at that moment but him. I went to stand by the couch and, when he did not look up, I placed a hand on his shoulder. One of his hands left his head, reached over to that spot, took my hand, and moved it to his lips. James then looked up, and I nearly choked at the pain in his eyes. Slowly, he stood up and I put my arms around him. He held me dangerously close, his face buried in my hair. We stood there, letting the shock of the day catch up with us, and soon both of us had tear-stained faces. I had not seen him that emotional before, and it frightened me. At long last he pulled away and sat back down again, pulling me next to him.

"I'm guessing my tantrum leaked and is what caused your hesitation?" The eyes turned tortured.

I nodded but added, "That and Dara refusing to leave until she had me packed."

A grim smile crossed his face, "Yes, her mind was basically yelling at me to wait my turn." The smile turned to a frown, "I can honestly say it has been many many years since I have been that angry and never towards a superior officer."

Although I knew it would not be, I rested my head on his shoulder and replied, "It's going to be okay. I'll make it through the trial and be back here in no time."

His mental shield rippled, and I quickly sat up and scooted away. "It is not okay, Harlie. What the General has decided is wrong at the most basic level. His claim of the good it will do for those left at the camps and not thinking of the consequences to you is asinine. The fact that he has scheduled me to be far from here while it happens is the worst." His fists clenched. "No one should have to relive their past the way you are going to have to. You'll be drilled over and over on some of the worst memories of your life."

I held up a hand to stop him. "James, anyone who has to testify in any trial has gone through the same thing."

He reached out and took my raised hand, lacing his fingers through mine. "But they are not you." His voice had gone soft. "They are not a strong empathic who will realize that the best way to get through the trial is going to be by listening in to the minds around her. To use her ability for gaining the exact results needed to not only achieve the maximum amount of good for those left behind but to make sure there is no doubt in anyone's minds that those charged are guilty."

The day had been so busy, the efforts to keep me distracted had worked so well, that I had not thought at all about how my ability could be used in the trial. The idea of seeing into the mind of the sneering guard, of listening to what lies his lawyers would be weaving, sickened me. I tried to pull my hand free, but James' fingers tightened. I stood, needing to hide before the waves of panic hit me full force. James stood too, reaching out his other hand to take my arm.

"Now you see why I am so angry. The others are upset over you having to become Nicole again, over you having to resurrect that ghost. I'm angry because you have too little time to prepare for the burden, the horrible test of looking into their minds while acting as if you are not." He pulled me closer to him. "I don't even have time to start preparing you for it. The General is leaving you nearly helpless, and I can't make it right." His eyes flashed, and his body tensed up.

The situation was becoming too intense for both of us and something had to be done to stop it. My free hand reached up to touch his cheek, and I slowly lowered part of my shield so he could see for himself exactly what was going on in my mind. I heard him gasp then hold his breath.

"Yes, I am afraid. Yes, I am close to panic. Yes, there are more questions than answers, but do you see what else is there? What else I felt today?" My mind focused in on the emotions concerning him.

The held breath was slowly released. Eyes turned to meet mine, and his arms encircled me again.

"James, we both need time to process this day. Go get some sleep and I'll do the same. Tomorrow will give us a better perspective." My voice was a whisper.

The emerald eyes looked tortured for a moment, but then his entire expression turned soft. Before my brain had a chance to set up its barrier, James tenderly kissed my cheek. I did not want to leave the security and comfort of his arms but knew our emotions ran too high right now.

"I'll see you in the morning, Jamyson."

Reluctantly, his hands dropped, and he stepped back. "Call out for me if it gets too bad tonight. I can be here in moments." He was referring to the nightmares we both knew would come. I nodded before backing up towards the door.

Three hours later James was back at the cottage. I had not called out to him, at least not consciously, but had been awake when he started his silent trek. The nightmares had been bad, to the point where the methods he had shown me were not working. I could not find him or the image I frequently used in his place, an eagle.

I met him at the front door and walked with him to the living area. Although slightly nervous at his presence, I also wanted the comfort I knew he could provide. James looked as if he had barely slept at all. One glance at his barely shielded mind, and it was obvious nightmares had come to him as well. I started to reach up to touch around his tired eyes when he took my hand and led me to the couch. Sitting at an angle, he pulled me next to him, my back to his chest, and wrapped his arms around me. I pulled a blanket off the back of the couch and tossed it haphazardly over us. No words were exchanged, none were needed. We were asleep in minutes, and this time the nightmares stayed away.

At the first rays of light, we awoke. His arms tightened

around me for an instant when I moved to stand up. Again, words were not exchanged. He needed to return to his apartment, unnoticed. We both needed space to breathe and think after the last few hours. The moment I had awakened a fiery flash had threatened to make me cringe. A battle was brewing, and I did not want James to witness it. As if reading my thoughts, he gave me a brief hug, then left.

The moment he was gone, I ran into the bedroom and nearly doubled over at the new wave. Something had to give. What had started as a reaction to the shield injury at Rio was becoming my mind's favorite way to punish me. It felt almost as if I had a split personality, and it was frustrating. Forcing the pain back, I staggered to the shower then finished preparing for the day.

Doc and I started the shift by going over my response training from yesterday. From there, I went to the training facility and started the circuit. James was watching my every move, and it was obvious to everyone. Of course, they were glancing in my direction every few minutes as well. Throwing myself into the workout, I tried to tune them all out. However, being alone with my thoughts meant thinking about what was coming. In just a week, I would be facing my attackers, the people who expedited my conversion to an empathic and made it necessary to become Harlie Anwyn Berryman. Even though I would testify from another part of the building, would there be moments where I ended up seeing them? Would I be given a chance to address the sneering guard? Was I strong enough to endure the emotional and physical strain?

James was now working alongside of me, almost hovering. Rick was not far off either. My frustration level was rapidly increasing as we stopped for lunch. Although I wanted to escape, I sat with the others. Some attempts at small talk were made and failed. I looked out and could sense their turmoil at the situation. It made me wish there were something I could say to relieve their stress, but nothing came to mind, and anger joined the frustration.

Back at the training room I was finishing up a five-kilometer run when The General and a stranger walked in. Simultaneously, nine pairs of eyes turned to the door and nine bodies stopped moving. He motioned to me and I started in that direction.

"Agent Berryman, this is Gerald Trone. He is part of The Guardian's legal team and will be working with you during the trial."

I nodded in his direction.

"Mr. Trone would like to meet with you to start going over potential questions, the answers to those questions, and your legal rights during the trial."

Without taking my eyes off the lawyer I asked, "Will he be available during the days between the psychological exam and the start of the trial?"

General Smiths looked from me, to the lawyer who nodded, then back to me. "It seems so."

"Then we can discuss those details in length at that time, Sir." I turned towards the tactical facility. "There are other things which need to be completed before departure."

Max was already in the hall and held up his hand for a high-five as I walked by. "Brilliant revenge, Bear! Keep it coming."

James walked in behind me, "Not sure it was a good idea to show such a level of disrespect in front of a visitor."

Max rolled his eyes and laughed, "He's not a visitor. We've all seen him before."

I stopped to face James, "And don't tell me you were not a tad disrespectful last night."

His green eyes turned to ice and we glared at each other. "Uh huh." I nodded. "That's what I thought. The General deserved it."

As the shift ended, Dara decided our pent-up emotions could use some release via hand-to-hand combat. The others agreed, and we set up four pairs and a spotter with a rotation system so everyone had a turn against everyone else. It was nearly impossible to keep my emotions under check and focus enough to stay on my feet. I was mostly successful though. Jason, Rick, Mitch, Max, and Ryan all ended up on the ground. I have never won against Dara and Skull came at me like a charging bull. Somehow, I ended up against James last.

His eyes lit up. *If I win, we go where I want tonight. If you win, it's up to you how tonight will be.*

I nodded once and started to circle. He wasn't finished.

391

Under the circumstances last night went quite well didn't it? A feign to the right was the only response he received. *Did your mind cause havoc once I left?*

He jumped forward and tried to connect a punch. I blocked it then nodded.

We are going to have to do something about that, you know.

James' mental chatter was grating on my nerves. I spun about, trying to land a kick to his side, but he jumped back. *Missed me, missed me...* His mind laughed as it started the famous rhyme.

Despite the audience I knew we would have, I stomped my foot and glared at him. He laughed out loud and attacked with a series of quick moves, which I blocked. We started to circle around again. *What will it be? Dinner? River? Garden? Or will...*

"Jamyson!" My voice was loud and harsh. "Unless you want me to repeat out loud everything you just mentally said, kindly be quiet and fight."

Within ten seconds I was on the ground, emerald eyes laughing above me. I shoved him away and stood up, "Who's cheating now?" I spat.

He looked apologetic only for an instant, "It could happen. Practicing a fight with mental distractions is a good thing."

You sure seem bothered by some of the things I said. He added where no one could hear.

I glared at him until Dara stepped in, "It's past debriefing. Let's just call it a night."

The others agreed, cleaned up, and headed towards the surface. I stayed in the gym and started running again. It was not long before I sensed two minds there with me, one calm but concerned, the other a dark spot. I started running faster, willing my frustration to run itself out, hoping my head would clear of its' turmoil. Footsteps thumped behind me, but I ignored them. Tapping was felt on my shield, but I ignored that too. Only when the tap became a tug at the same time a hand reached out to grab my arm did I slow, but not stop. When James pulled mentally and physically, I was forced to halt. He spun me around, and I froze at his expression. It was

The Commander.

"Enough, Harlie, running laps will get you nowhere. Go clean up." He dropped my arm, and I walked out, turning towards the living quarters. James stopped where Rick stood in the entryway. I paused at the door to my room, listening in to what was being said.

"Are you sure now is the best time?" Rick was asking. "She is really on edge."

James sighed before responding. "No, I'm not sure, but it's tearing her apart. Neither of us can keep denying..." He realized I had stopped to eavesdrop and glanced over at me. I stared at him, mentally daring him to finish the thought. Instead, he dropped part of his shield, flashing the tender moments from last evening and his happiness at how the night turned out. He was such a cheater. Despite the turmoil, I gave him a small smile before going into my room to clean up.

When I stepped out of the warehouse it took a few seconds to process what was in front of me. James was there, but the standard motorcycle which was his near-constant companion was not. In its place was a sleek, fresh-from-the-factory, electric motorcycle. It was black, red, and silver and practically glowed in the early evening light. James started to laugh again.

"I would have been back three hours earlier yesterday if I hadn't stopped to pick this up. After waiting three months for it to arrive, and not knowing what had transpired here, I was eager to drive it back." At my questioning expression, he added. "I still have the other one, but it's loud and getting worn out. This one is great for local driving and is so quiet." He handed me a new helmet, "Let's go get some dinner."

We drove to another town, to a restaurant I had never been to. The bike was almost silent and rode like we were on a cloud. For the first time ever, I enjoyed being on the back of a motorcycle. James gave me his most brilliant smile when we parked, and he saw my expression.

Dinner was excellent, and James seemed to enjoy educating me in the world of motorcycles. It was a regular conversation like regular people would have – so very different from the world we had been living in. Despite myself, I started to relax and was not as worried about what was happening in just a day.

We went to the river from there and walked hand in hand at the water's edge. We kept talking about automobiles, discussing past cars and trucks we had owned as well as sharing stories of events that happened with those vehicles. The night air was cool, with just a hint of autumn on the breeze. At some point, both our shields dropped. I could sense his contentment more than the other more potent emotions that had been present. I was feeling the same thing; the edginess and frustration had been pushed aside. As we were turning to go back to the bike, James stopped. His thoughts became more guarded as he turned to me.

"Harlie." His voice was gentle and calm. "Once again, this has been a wonderful night." He smiled, and I returned it. He took my other hand and raised it to his lips. "Our friendship, the ability to just spend time like this," He looked around at the river and hills. "It has come to mean so much to me." His gaze then turned back to where we stood.

"I enjoy these times too, James, and have even been looking forward to them." While my heart sang at the admittance, my mind sent out warning signals.

His expression became one of mixed emotions, "How come sometimes it seems like that, and other times you act as if you want me as far from you as possible?"

The stirrings of defensiveness came forward and my posture stiffened. His hands tightened around mine, eyes pleading for an answer.

"James," I started but could not seem to find words. There really were no terms to express what was happening internally. "You know I am starting to feel for you the way you feel for me." What I was trying to say caught in my throat, my mind sending painful fire to every part of my body. "But there is so much going on...it..." I could not handle his penetrating gaze and ripped my hands from his. I quickly turned away, as the emotions were too strong.

He sensed it, saw it all flash through my mind. The moment my back was turned, he stepped forward and wrapped his arms around me. I had to put distance between us before a full-blown war started inside me. I tried to pull away but, unlike in the past, this time he would not let go. Instantly, panic took over and I started to struggle. However, the more I struggled the tighter he held me. Waves of fire came, and I flinched and cringed, unable to fight it off.

"I'm not hurting you, Harlie. Stop struggling. You are only hurting yourself." His voice was calm, as though he had expected this to happen. I thought back to what had been overheard earlier between him and Rick and struggled harder. I had to break free, had to get away. It was too soon, too soon. What I wanted, what he wanted, was too dangerous. I had to stop it!

Suddenly, I realized my shield was still down and he was able to witness all of what was happening inside my mind. Horror and embarrassment filled me, and I started to raise my mental shield. Just as quickly he reached out and pulled it back down, holding it there. I briefly contemplated stepping on his foot in an attempt to get away, but he saw the thought and showed me the position I would end up in if that action had occurred.

Instead, my mind and my heart kept battling it out inside my body: wanting James to be close, wanting to keep him away, wanting to be cared for, wanting to be independent. The war raged for several more minutes, but he never loosed his grip, never backed down. Exhausted, I faltered. When that happened, he let my shield go. It did not matter much though; my heart was winning. The pain was diminishing as my mind could no longer deny what my heart had been saying. The struggling slowed down, then my heart claimed victory and it stopped altogether. There really was no valid reason to fight him.

"Thank you." He whispered as I half collapsed against him. His lips brushed the top of my head. I looked out and discovered he had been feeling as if he were being stabbed, watching my struggle. "Harlie, what you are feeling all makes sense...except for one thing."

Somehow, I still had a voice, "What?"

He was holding me gently now, "You have every right to be happy with someone again, even if that person ends up not being me."

"It's too soon." My voice sounded like a whimper.

"No, it was another life in another time. We want...I

want you to be happy in this life." My body tensed, readying for another battle. "Bear, shh, listen." He held me a little tighter. "You seem to be happy when we are spending time together. It seems to have made you happier on the team too. You have deeper feelings for me and me for you."

"That's the problem." *Why should I be happy when so much sadness is happening?*

Slowly, James turned me to face him, keeping his hands locked behind my back to hold me there. His mind reached out and mental fingers ran gently over my shield until I let it drop just a little. He was not looking out at my mind, and I wasn't looking at his.

"It should not be a problem. Just try, Harlie, try to let go. Don't over-think when I reach out to you. I am well aware of the dangers this can hold, but I still want it. Right now, it is the only thing outside of my Life Vow that I want. I know in your heart that you feel the same."

Realization hit me then. I understood fully what he was saying. It was a much smaller part that wished it did not, but my feelings for him squelched it.

"Harlie Anywn Berryman, look at me not through me." He waited until my eyes fully met his. "We will be careful; we will go as slow as you need. But please, say yes to taking **us** beyond friendship and into a relationship."

Heart welling over, I nodded and leaned against his chest.

"Let me hear you." He whispered.

I let my shield totally drop and projected my emotions towards him. James' hands moved from my lower back to hold me in a proper embrace. We both sighed. The battle was over, my mind stopped its painful self-defense. Cooling relief flowed from his mind, followed by the gentle warmth of his desire. There were so many levels to it: caring, protecting, attraction, cherishing, compassion, the stirrings of love. I focused my mind on several and felt him smile.

We stood there, holding each other, lost in the others' emotions for what seemed like hours but really could only have been minutes. One hand held me close; the other ran through my tangled hair. When our shields rose again, he looked into my eyes and smiled his brilliant smile.

"Let's see how fast the bike can go before heading back to the village."

I smiled back at him and hopped on. We raced through villages, over hills, and across bridges, laughing like children until the bike was low on power. Coasting into the village at midnight, he stopped the bike at his apartment, then walked me to the cottage. At the doorway, he pulled me close again. I saw his eyes change a moment before he leaned forward to place a feather light kiss on my cheek. I smiled up at him, and he pulled me into a tight embrace before kissing both my hands and turning to leave.

Beautiful dreams filled my mind that night. The concerns and frustrations about the upcoming trial had been scattered. I slept deeper and calmer than I had in years.

Dara came to the door of the cottage just as I was waking up. Still tired mentally and physically from yesterday, it took me several moments to answer her insistent pounding.

"Rise and shine, Bear!" She grinned at my grumpy expression.

"How about I rise and, once some caffeine has been ingested, we can talk about shining?"

"Deal." She chuckled. "I brought the car over to get your bags, didn't think you could balance them on the bike or on James' motorcycle."

At the mention of his name, my mind replayed last night in fast forward. Surprisingly, no pain was involved, and I smile slightly before turning away from Dara.

"I saw that." She snapped. "What happened?"

Grinning, I turned back to her, "Nothing."

"I sure hope it was revenge for whatever he said to you yesterday."

Perfect! "Yes, and I'm quite proud of myself for it too." It had to be a lie. There was no way a member of the team was finding out any details.

After breakfast in the cafeteria, we tried to start the daily routine as if nothing were happening tomorrow. However, Doc and the lawyer were constantly in sight, probably discussing the way I was avoiding them. The team had given up trying to ignore the situation and joined me in glaring at the perceived intruders. We worked closely, and I was never alone. James was preparing for his, Mitch's, and Max's departure to the Middle East. In some ways, his absence made the morning a little easier.

After lunch, we were all called to the conference room where a very stern looking General stood waiting for us. "Although this should only be a meeting for those preparing to leave for London, the entire team's behavior these last few days needs to be addressed. While I am pleased to see you rallying around our newest member, the open dislike and defiance I have witnessed cannot go unmentioned."

If he had more to say, it never stood a chance. In an instant, Rick stood up. "You should have thought about the consequences beforehand, Sir. When you go back and think over what founded The Guardians, the code we follow, the life we have been living, did it even come to your mind that what you chose to do would have a negative effect here? Our performance these last days could not have been worse if we were freshly into boot camp. Our morale is down. We are all wondering, Sir, why in this twisted world did you hold back on telling her?"

General Smiths stood rigid. "The reasons are between Agent Berryman and myself."

Max stood up, "No, Sir, it is not. If it affects one of us it affects all of us. We are a team. Would you have waited until the last possible moment if it were me? Or Dara? Or Jason?"

Dara joined them, "Sir, what is happening here is exactly what you should have expected."

I sat perfectly still, watching to see how far it would go. Although it shouldn't have, the level of support I felt coming from all of them surprised me some. They really were my family… my brothers and sister, and in this moment, we were all bonded against a wrongdoing.

James, who had been silent, stood up with The Commander's air around him. "Team, cease and desist." The three sat and the others leaned back in their seats. He turned to The General. "I assure you, this response was of their own device. However, it is also my own belief. You and I have exchanged words already. We do not expect an apology for

398

what you have done to one of our own but reprimanding us for our understandable actions will not be tolerated." He turned to us. "Those not traveling to London are dismissed."

The others stood, saluted and left. The General remained standing until the last member was out then turned to James.

"Colonel?"

"Sir."

"Your point has been made."

"I would hope so." With that, he also saluted and left.

Rick, Dara, and I stayed to go over hotel arrangements, security detail, the tentative trial and tribunal schedule and other things that might come up. It was at that time I found out Jack had been subpoenaed for both as well and would be joining us next week, along with his father. It made me wonder if others I knew from the camp would be involved and if I would be able to see them.

As if knowing, The General added, "Remember you are Harlie Berryman, Guardian. You will be answering as Nicole Jones, using her memories, but at no time will you be her. You may not acknowledge those from your past life if there is accidental exposure. It is a very serious and very dangerous situation. Do you understand?"

"Yes, Sir." But deep inside, I doubted. I looked over at Rick. He seemed angered by something.

Come the end of shift everyone decided to stay underground for dinner. We tried to enjoy the time but knew that, come tomorrow, we would be separated again. Jason, who had been near silent for days, pulled me aside after the meal.

"Doc's been too busy prepping you to remember anything. Here, you'll need this." It had been weeks since I had needed the custom cocktail. He handed me a small canvas bag containing both liquid form as well as pre-filled injections. Next to those was a small electronic blood pressure cuff and other equipment to check my vitals. Jason pulled me in for a one arm hug. "Take care of yourself, this is going to be one of the hardest things you'll ever face, and I'm worried." He looked around, "All of us are."

After more well wishes, the others went top-side,

leaving only Rick, Dara and myself. James had disappeared after the meeting and had not returned. I was becoming worried about not seeing him before we left. Back at the common room, Dara decided to retire early. Rick stayed, watching me as I flipped through channels.

"You both are being very vague today." I turned to see his questioning eyes.

"By both, I believe you are referencing Jamyson and me?" I questioned back.

He nodded.

"It's been an interesting few days." How was I going to tell him? Why couldn't James be the one? I thought back to the night Rick and I spent together, to him kissing me. I knew immediately when James had mentioned me being happy with someone other than him that he meant Rick.

"He is going to be here soon. You know he won't let you leave without seeing you again, even if last night went poorly." Rick's eyebrows came together as he frowned slightly.

Why was he being so determined? Sighing loudly, I turned to him. "How do you think it went?" He stood up, glaring as he towered over me. Obviously, being vague was not going to work. "It was very emotional, and the internal battle was brutal, but Jamyson and I have decided to take us past friendship."

Rick sat back down and faced me. "Good. It's about time." Then, reaching out to brush a stray strand of hair out of my face he added. "I am here for you, whenever and however you need me. Remember that."

I leaned forward to hug him, "That's why I'm happy it's you coming with me."

We parted and went to our rooms. James arrived shortly after. We wandered to the cafeteria for a snack then into the darkened training room. Sitting as we normally would at the river, we relaxed. He held me close, placing occasional kisses on my head and running his fingers up and down my arms. It seemed odd to me that the place of my first lessons as a Guardian, the silent massive gym, was now a place where James and I were sharing more intimate moments. I shared the thought with him mentally and felt him shift.

"It seems so long ago, doesn't it?" He finally responded.

"Yes, but at the same time it feels like yesterday."

"If we had only known then, what today would be."

He shifted again and this time I had to move with him. A lantern was flicked on, and I smiled. "Planned that didn't you?"

James moved to his knees, motioning for me to do the same before facing me. "Look and listen to what is around you." He started, just like in our first lessons. I did, waiting for the rays of light from his mind. It did not take long, and the levels of desire were all I sensed. My eyes shut for a moment, knowing I could block the emotion but choosing not to. They opened briefly when a hand was gently laid against my neck, and he leaned in to kiss me. The kiss was gentle and sweet. He held back mentally, although I could sense it was a struggle. With just the slightest of hesitation, I responded to him.

Afterward, he stood and pulled me to him. "You are so beautiful." James murmured into my hair. "Being apart is going to be painful, but you will do well. I know Rick will take good care of you." He leaned in to kiss me again. When we parted he smiled, "Better get you to bed."

He walked me to my quarters and smiled. "I'll be watching over you tonight and will be in before dawn."

True to his word, at five in the morning my door near silently opened and shut. I opened my eyes to him kneeling at my side, running his fingers through my hair. We stayed like that, staring at each other until my eyes closed again. Before the others awoke, I felt him kiss my head before tip-toeing back to his room, and I smiled.

THE TRIAL

We left for London shortly after breakfast, taking two vehicles. One held Rick, Dara, me, and a driver. The other carried three security detail agents. It felt as if we were driving in slow motion, and I soon felt restless. Once inside London proper, we stopped for a late lunch before checking in at the hotel. Those in charge of planning the details of this trip must have had a better understanding of the team and situation than most. A two-bedroom, two-bathroom suite had been secured in one of the higher end hotels near the courthouse. One of the bedrooms had separate beds, so Dara and I took that room while Rick took the king-sized master bedroom. We joked about all the extravagant extras and how it would be impossible to stay in a tent after this mission.

The lawyer arrived shortly after we settled in and all three of us met with him. He had written down a list of potential questions the defense might ask and had me start recording my answers. Later that night, he would turn those into print and make any necessary edits. We would then drill those in hopes that something close would be asked. Evening came quickly, and we stopped for a meal. From there, I was reminded of what would happen during the psychological evaluation tomorrow. Tired and overwhelmed, I grumpily kicked him out of the room at that point.

Once the door shut, the room's environment became a little uncomfortable. Dara had turned on the television, expecting that I would go right to bed. Perceptive Rick knew sleep would not be possible in my current state of mind. While I was escorting Mr. Trone out, he had gone into the shared bedroom, went through my luggage, and found the medical bag. He came out of the room the same time I started to go into it.

"Not yet, Bear." He muttered, holding up the bag. "Need to get a reading after that exercise."

My answer was to growl at him, which caused Dara to turn and stare. Plopping into a chair in the suite's kitchenette, I held out my arm for the blood pressure cuff. Grumbling the whole time, I used my other hand to dig through the bag until the bottle of sleeping pills was in my hand. Rick grasped my wrist when I started to open the bottle.

"A bit early for poor behavior isn't it?" He looked serious.

"In this situation? No." I jerked my arm away, stood and went to the water cooler, poured a small cup full and swallowed the pill. Rick came to stand very close. My hand stopped halfway into crushing the paper cup.

"Look out and listen." His voice was nearly a whisper. There was something in his tone that prevented me from disobeying.

I looked out over the inches between us, focusing on the calming pattern of emotions he pushed forward. When a small smile came to his lips, I looked away again.

"Now, to bed with you," He shooed me away. I turned towards the bedroom and saw that Dara had been watching. The look on her face betrayed her emotions. It was a cross between confusion and reproach. Deciding that now was not the time or place for long explanations; I nodded to her and went to bed.

Early the next morning, Mr. Trone arrived with our driver and another agent to escort me to the courthouse. When Rick asked why it wasn't he or Dara providing the security, the lawyer replied that it was not their legal assignment in this mission. They were assigned to provide emotional support. I sent Rick a look of apology before being led out. Inside the courthouse, we were sent to a room which looked like a doctor's office. Two doors on the far wall led to other, smaller rooms. I quickly figured out that one was where the psychological evaluation would be taking place and the other was a viewing room.

The evaluation staff arrived several minutes later. Immediately, I felt like a bug under a microscope and fought back the urge to be ill. A man in his sixties and a woman in her forties would be proctoring while two professionals and the lawyers would be watching. A speaker hooked up between the rooms allowed for instant communication should the need arrive. It all felt very cold and sterile. I pulled the headscarf closer around my face and waited.

Formal introductions were made before the day was

explained. I would be given a series of verbal and written tests to evaluate my psychological well-being. The hope was to verify stability and adjustment to my new life as well as prove that I could indeed answer questions as Nicole Jones. The DNA test would be taken whenever the assigned nurse arrived.

Some papers needed to be signed and witnessed before the tests began. I read through each one carefully, asking Mr. Trone to clarify anything confusing. Taking a deep breath, I picked up the pen and slowly signed Nicole Maria Jones. The papers were copied and placed in various binders brought by the lawyers and evaluation staff.

For the next seven hours, I was drilled on everything from basic information, to what I saw in pictures, to events in my life that they had been previously informed about. It was difficult to not look to their emotions for perceived answers, remembering that what they want might be the wrong thing. Quite a few times I had to reply with "I cannot answer at this time." The most memorable moment was when the woman asked me to describe my current life. They seemed surprised at my peaceful answer describing the village, my cottage, new friends, and the activities we enjoyed.

When the testing was over, and the lawyers had conversed with the psychologists, we began the drive back to the hotel. I was exhausted mentally, and my head was throbbing. Not wanting to show weakness in front of the lawyer or agent, I stayed straight and silent until we arrived.

As we waited for the elevator, Mr. Trone stated. "You did really good today. I'll be by in the morning to continue working on our tactics for the trial. Once we are set on the answers, you should be able to rest and perhaps see some of the sights before it starts for real." I just nodded in return.

Rick and Dara were watching a movie and, although they paused it and stood to greet me, I waved them off and went right to the bedroom. Rick followed a moment later.

"No greeting, no waiting for us to ask how it went?" He looked put off.

"Hi. It was long, grueling, and painful." I flopped down on the bed, not even bothering to turn down the covers.

Dara came in behind Rick and stared at both of us.

404

"It was bad, and I really need to lay down. Give me an hour and I should be able to act human again."

"I sure hope you are not planning on acting this way the whole time." Dara snapped, "If so, I'm calling it quits and returning to the bunker."

I sat up and glared at her. "Huh?"

She looked up and sighed loudly, "This gruff, rude, shut-out-those-who-want-to-help-you attitude. Your insistence on being too independent, pretending to be so strong, which we know is a total lie." Dara came over to the bed and very roughly pulled me off of it. I barely was able to get my feet under me. "No, none of us have had to go through this kind of situation before. However, we have had years of experience with burying the other side and the pain it causes when certain days or nights makes our past life wake up. We have also had to do things during missions which would make the average person go insane." She went to the bedroom door and pointed out of it. "So, out you go. We are going to the fitness center here and not coming back until I'm satisfied."

I looked from her to Rick and back to her. Rick shrugged and left the room when Dara threw sports shorts and a shirt at me. "Keep your headscarf on." She grumbled and walked out.

We worked out for nearly two hours with Dara barking at me to run faster on the treadmill or get my heart rate higher on the elliptical machine. The only time she left drill-sergeant mode was when she noticed the faint bruises on my arms. I sensed her pause and ponder over how or where I could have been injured, but she didn't ask.   When my empty stomach growled so loud that anyone within twenty feet could hear it, she let us stop. Strangely, my head no longer hurt, and my emotions had settled down some. Rick had called for pizza before we stopped and, thankfully, the delivery came only minutes after we returned to the suite. After the meal, they went to finish the movie while I unpacked my mp3 player and relaxed.

The next two days were spent mainly in the suite with Mr. Trone, going over the trial. I was becoming more and more confident with the planned answers as well as potential situations that might arise. He had secured permission for

405

either Rick or Dara to be within visual range of me when I had to be on the stand. The original plan for my testimony to take place in the separate location had been canceled due to the defense team's protesting. A mesh privacy screen would be used instead so everyone could see me walk up and take the stand. Dara showed me how to pin the headscarf so only my eyes would show, and Mr. Trone reminded me that I would have to speak louder due to it being in place. On days I would not be testifying, we would still be at the separate location.

Once the lawyer would leave for the day, we would head to the fitness center to work off pent-up energy and emotions. The evenings were spent either watching movies or playing card games.

For the last day before the start of the trial, we were given the freedom to tour around that side of London. Of course, freedom meant having not only our own agents but also local security assigned to "keep us safe" from possible retribution - since this was supposedly my first time away from government protection. Neither side was very aware of the other, and we joked about how we could easily take them all out and be free. We came up with all kinds of crazy plans to ditch them. It kept us laughing throughout a history museum and then through a market. We even purposely lost the local security detail. For nearly an hour we ended up behind them, following as they chased after fake trails. When Rick decided it was time to be serious again, we stepped out right in front of them as if we had been there all along.

Day one of the trial was just preliminaries. We were placed in a sparsely decorated room on the top floor. A door led to a smaller room where I would be spending the day. The charged were introduced, the charges read, both sides read opening arguments, and then the day was done. It was there I learned the name of the man who assaulted me, William Abramavich. From my seat in the secured room I stared at him, silently observing his emotions. He was being charged with not only my rape, beating, and attempted murder but as the leader of the group involved. I also found out that there had been a second victim, a teenager living in the single's bunker. My heart went out to her as she was still living in the camp.

After the adjournment, Jack and his father met up with us. They had been given a room at the same hotel. Yesterday, Dara had suggested that we all purchase the same book to read and discuss during the evenings. I had made sure to purchase a copy for both Jack and Mr. Phillips. Since it was better for us to lay low during this part of the trial, we all spread out in the suite and started on it. Room service took care of the meals, and the rest of the day was relaxing.

Because we had to arrive at the courthouse long before the others, I looked out from my secure position on the second day. I scanned each mind as they entered the courtroom. The exercise was going well until four people arrived at the same time. I sensed pain and confusion first, followed by anger and frustration. When I focused on one of them I sensed something familiar. Looking at the person next to her, I sensed it again and suddenly realized who it was. Suddenly, Nicole took over, and I lost control.

"Rick!" I screamed.

He rushed over and knelt next to where I sat, concern on his face.

"It's them! They just walked into the courtroom. They know, they know!"

Hands gripped my shoulders and shook me. At the screaming, Dara and the lawyer had entered the room.

"Who Harlie? Who is here?"

A sob started in my chest, and I fought for control. "Gareth's parents." It was a whisper.

All three started to swear, Rick in several languages. He then pulled me up into his arms and held me tight. Caught up in the desire to run to them and explain everything, unable to sense anything else, I started to struggle. His arms turned to steel, like chains and shackles, bruising as I tried to act on the overwhelming emotion. Dara stood at the door in case I somehow broke free. I was still looking out towards my family but forced my mind to turn to those in the room. All three were a mixture of grief, compassion, anger, and concern – and those emotions were all due to the discovery. I stopped struggling and took several ragged breaths.

"They are confused as to why the charge is attempted murder." I continued. "They had been told I was missing and

407

presumed dead." The arms around me tightened again.

Mr. Trone spoke, "A very unfortunate situation here. The organization tried to keep the trial a secret from them, but the media has recently taken an interest in the camps. Your family has every legal right to attend the trial, Ms. Berryman, but it does put more strain on you."

Dara looked as if she were going to commit a serious crime on the lawyer. "That is an understatement. She will have to be in the same room as them in a few days. No one should have to go through that!"

An idea was forming amidst the chaos of my mind. It was dangerous, but I allowed it to keep coming. It helped to calm me.

Rick must have sensed the change. "No, Bear. You cannot allow yourself to think like that." He whispered.

But I had. It was those thoughts that allowed me to make it through the day. I watched the accused as he was questioned, listened to the minds of those involved, and glanced at the four familiar minds during any break in the action. That evening, I read with the others but could not focus enough. I ended up breaking away early, choosing instead to sit on the bed and write. I wrote a letter to my in-laws, one I had every intention of sending to them. Even though it was against policy, I was not going to turn down a chance for closure – a chance to say goodbye. I told them about what happened after they left for Wales, what we experienced in the camp, how Gareth died, and about how they had been grandparents for three days. I let them know that I was being taken care of and had made friends under my new identity. Without giving away details, I told them my new job was very important and took a lot of training, but I was well suited for it. Through those words, they would learn I was not only adjusted to this new life but also happy. I ended the letter with how much I missed them and loved Gareth, adding that they could relax knowing I was in good hands and would be watching out for them.

Just as I signed the letter, Rick walked in and shut the door behind him. "You wrote them, didn't you?" It really was not a question.

Holding the pages tightly, I nodded.

"I'm guessing you are going to attempt to find someone to hand the letter to them. Someone who will not give away your location here or at the courthouse."

Another nod, this one much firmer.

He stared at me for a long time. "Mr. Phillips and Jack have left for the night and Dara will be heading in this direction soon. Take your mp3 player, the notepad and those pages out to the main room. Pretend to be writing out lyrics. We'll talk about this infraction once she has retired." His voice was stern enough that I wondered if there would be real trouble. However, I did what was ordered and waited.

Once Dara had shut the bedroom door, I waited anxiously to see what Rick would do. He had ignored my return to the living area and mindless following of his directions. Minutes passed before he stood up from the seat he had taken in the kitchen and came to sit next to me.

He held out a hand, "Let me see the letter." It sounded like an order, but I still hesitated before giving it to him. I watched him read it several times before he looked back at me. "It is very well written and does not give anything away."

Of course, it was! I wasn't going to let out the secrets of our existence. I just wanted to tell them goodbye in the best way possible. In response to his comment though, I just stared back at him.

Rick sighed loudly, "If you were looking out, you would see how tortured I am right now." His voice held an edge of accusation. "I should rip these pages up and reprimand you for attempting this. Instead, I find myself planning how to get the letter to your family. It's not just because I hate the situation The General has placed you in, or because I expected something like this to happen." He put the letter down and reached out to take my shoulders, turning me towards him. "It's because I cannot seem to tell you no." He whispered. "Who are you to have such an effect on me that I would consider bending our laws just to make you happy – to give you the closure you want?"

For a moment, I couldn't believe my ears. Was he saying he would be the one to deliver the letter? One look into his eyes, along with a glance into his mind, and it was verified. He had every intention to do just that. I smiled timidly at him, and he opened his arms. I hugged him as tight as I could, fighting back tears of relief. His response was more reserved.

"We could get into quite a large amount of trouble if this were to be discovered." He whispered.

"I know, that's why I was planning on trying it alone."

"Harlie, you are never alone. It would not have worked, and you know it. Even with me handing off the letter there is still a chance at being caught."

He stood and pulled me up with him. "Get some sleep. I'll make sure your family gets this." Rick patted the pages before picking them up and walking into his room.

I thought it would help, knowing that closure was coming. I thought it would bring relief to know that my family would soon have light shed on their son's last days, on my final days as Nicole. It had the opposite effect. Until I knew the letter was in their hands and sensed their response, I was anxious. So anxious that it was hard to hide it and I worried our plan would be discovered just by my behavior.

The next morning, the first witnesses were called. The girl who had also been attacked testified about her assault. The defense lawyers chewed her up and spit her out afterward, trying to prove she was meaningless and that it was a business deal. The truth was her silence had been paid for by being given extra supplies for the single women bunkhouse. Only two witnesses were called for her, women who had seen the bruises and seen him following her. I paced the small room the entire time, anger mixing with the anxiety.

As the judge was preparing to dismiss for the day, Rick slipped away from the secure room and made his way to the courthouse exit. I followed him in my mind, listening to each flicker of emotion. He waited until my family had exited the building and were heading towards their car. As they came within visual range, he stepped back against a building so that he was hidden in its' shadow. When they walked past him, he took a step out towards my father-in-law, pressed the letter into his hand, whispered something, then backed away into the shadows again.

Their car was parked near the outer edges of my range, but I was able to pick up their confusion at the letter,

410

questioning if it were safe to open. I had put, "To Mum and Padre" on it, just like I used to address them in person. That was the key to getting them to believe it was me, and it worked. Once everyone was in the car, he opened the letter and read it aloud to the others. Mum and her sister began crying before the first page was finished. By the second, it had been handed off to Gareth's uncle because Padre was tearing up as well. Although I somehow maintained a neutral expression externally, internally I was crying too. Rick arrived shortly after the letter was finished, and we were driven back to the hotel.

Looking out at Dara, I sensed that she thought I was too quiet but attributed it to anger at what the defense did. I tried to make myself echo her expectation. Once we were secure, I set about looking busy with catching up on what I had missed in the book. Rick surprised me by suggesting we all go to the hotel's fitness room since it had been a few days since our last visit. Jack and Mr. Phillips backed out, saying they were going to watch TV and to call them when it was time to read. Mindlessly, I undressed from the sari and put on the proper clothing, taking care to keep the headscarf in place.

As I came out of the room, I overheard Rick tell Dara to go on ahead of us and that we would be right there. He wanted to check my vitals first. After looking out, I quickly realized his words were a ploy. The instant the door shut, Rick turned to me.

"Was it worth the anxiety?"

"Yes." I nodded for emphasis. "They were heartbroken of course, but I sensed a little relief when they read about my life now. It was difficult to witness but there are no regrets." I turned away. "They miss us. Seeing their minds these last two days is making it very difficult. I miss them too." I was going to add how I missed Gareth, but my voice caught in my throat.

Rick sat down on the couch and pulled me to him. Although I wanted to be resilient and brave, tears started to fall. Embarrassingly, I started to sob. Rick held me closer, mumbling words of comfort. Images of my past life flashed in my mind, positive memories of a time I had to learn to forget. They were impossible to squelch, so I let them keep coming and the tears continued. Time passed, and I struggled for control, exhausting myself in the process. My swollen eyes shut and stayed that way as Rick carefully picked me up and placed me on the bed. I heard the door click shut and sleep took me. I awoke only for a late dinner then went right back to the room and the memories.

Come morning, I thought I was ready for what was ahead. Today was my turn on the witness stand. Dara pulled out the skirt, blouse, and headscarf combination she had designated for this day and pinned the scarf so that only my eyes showed. We arrived at the courthouse early, but there was media already out front. I had learned that, because of my experience, several scandals had been exposed not only at Camp Iachâd but at the other six camps in Great Britain. The British military had been forced to either turn over the camps to private organizations or face a major overhaul at those locations. Both groups of agents circled us, and we were hastily led into the courthouse.

I was halfway up the steps when I sensed Mum and Padre amidst the minds – my pace slowed. When Mum started to cry I stopped for an instant, wishing I could turn around and run to them. But then responsibility kicked in and I rushed the rest of way into the building. Mum noticed the hesitation and a flash of hope ghosted through her mind. Dara and I were kept in a room that led into the side of the courtroom. Rick sat in the front row of the courtroom as support for when I was called to the stand.

Mr. Trone started out with the questions I had been prepared for, and I made sure to look out at the defense team's mind while carefully answering. The events which led up to that last fateful night, the last night of Nicole's life, were told in careful detail. I tried to keep the two personalities separate, but whenever I looked past the team it became almost impossible. Mum and Padre were hanging onto every word. I also made sure to look at my attacker's mind too. His mind confirmed much of what I had said and reminded me of a few details I missed but quickly added. It took all morning to get through my testimony. After lunch, the defense team started their cross-examination. As anticipated, they tried to disprove the moment where I was tripped and threatened. They blamed the guard's superiors for not placing me with the rest of the

412

singles and leaving me open to attack. They made it sound like it was an open invitation – as if it were expected. They had a much harder time with the night of the assault. I was using every ounce of my ability to cross-examine their own words and what they anticipated. Rick prompted with his mind as well. There was no way the defense could prove the innocence of Mr. Abramavich. The DNA evidence proved I was who had been assaulted, even though they practically taunted me about the headscarf. Mr. Trone would have none of that and motioned several times. It was grueling and frustrating. I wanted to stand up and tell everyone in the room the real story of what happened in the camp but had to settle for just this one person and his actions. My only consolation was knowing the military tribunal was next, and I could tell all at that point.

When it was over, we waited until the others were gone before leaving the side room. I was once again focused on my in-laws. Mum was still crying, she wanted to see me, to hug me and say how proud she was of what I did today. It was more than I could bear, and I paced, tense and ready to fight anyone who got in my way. Rick watched me, silent and contemplative. As we walked out he grabbed my hand and held it tight until we were back in the hotel. Dara watched, wondering about us, and I had to smile a little. If only she knew! My thoughts turned to James and I wondered how his mission was going, if he had been in any fights, and if he were thinking about me. A flash of guilt at how little I had thought about him these last few days made the situation seem more out-of-control.

Somehow, despite the physical pain from stretching my abilities all day and emotional pain from seeing my family, I managed to stay with the others and read. The liquid form of the custom cocktail Jason packed helped immensely. Rick, never leaving my side, helped as well. When night fell, and it was time to retire, he pulled me aside again, making sure I was in as good of shape as possible before bedtime. This time, when I went into the bedroom, Dara was waiting.

"You're doing better than I would be at this point." She stated.

"It's only on the surface." Already in a sweat suit, I brushed my teeth and climbed into bed.

413

"If our timeline had been the same, and I was only six months into military life, they would have had to court-martial me. But by the time I made it to The Guardians, there really was nothing that needed closure."

I rolled over to face her, "But you still have family out there."

"Yes, but because of my positions before joining they had already emotionally detached themselves. I was not as close as you were to your family. That made my decision to be declared dead easier. They know I'm gone."

"I want to see them one last time, to have that final goodbye. I know I'm strong enough to go on without it, but..." I let my voice trail off.

She looked worried, "I don't know what it is between you and Rick, but he looks to be on the cusp of letting you do just that." She paused, "Despite the potential consequences."

Hope rose within me but was quickly crushed by the thoughts of those consequences. "He can't do that. It would be too much."

"When it comes to Rick and James, nothing seems to be too much when it comes to you."

I looked away, "I'm still not sure why it's like that." For the most part, it was the truth.

Dara shrugged, then scowled, "Harlie?"

I propped myself up a bit and turned to her in response.

"Where did those bruises on your arms come from? I know what they look like but want to hear it from you."

Thinking quickly, I came up with something that wasn't a lie but wasn't exactly what happened either. "My emotional outburst where Rick had to hold me back? That wasn't the only episode this week." I let out a long sigh, "As stated before, I'm doing well only on the surface."

I could see Dara thinking hard, going over the days in her mind to see if my story fit. After several minutes she near whispered, "It wouldn't be a bad thing to let the rest of us in on these moments. We are a team, a family really, and we are here for each other. Despite what you think, you aren't any weaker than the rest of us. In some ways, you are stronger." She looked around the room, as if it were an example.

Her words struck a cord. I had heard similar arguments

414

from James and Rick, but this was the first time one of the others had addressed it. "Thank you, Dara." She nodded before turning over and shutting the light off.

Although I tried to think of other things, thoughts and dreams of seeing my in-laws filled my mind all night long. What would I say? How would I act? What would they do?

We had a break for the weekend, and I was a restless mess. Security on both sides encouraged us to stay inside the hotel. The five of us rotated between movies, reading, working out, and playing card games. I tried not to let the long hours of no action get to me, but it did. By Sunday night I knew the others were also at their wit's end and ready for the trial to pick up again.

On Monday, Mr. Trone went to the courthouse with Jack and Mr. Phillips. I wanted to be there, to hear what would be said, but we had been called to the military tribunal. Protected by agents, as before, we arrived and were brought into a very large room with tables set up in a "U" shape. In the middle was a smaller table with two chairs. It made the person feel like they were under a microscope. Against one wall was a separate table with four chairs. Against the other, a woman with a sketch pad was set up. While no photographers or media were allowed inside, the hand-drawn pictures would be allowed so long as those under protection were blurred. One of Mr. Trone's associates met us at the door and would be sitting next to me, just in case something came up. These people knew that I was now employed with the United Nations but did not know the position. I had been warned that one member knew of The Guardian's existence in some form and had been told I was with them. A few others knew the rumors of an anti-nuclear task force with special ops agents, but it was just that, a rumor.

We were seated, and the officers were brought in and introduced. I was surprised when the camps' commanding officer, nurse, and two other former camp staff officers, as well as a lawyer, were brought in and were seated at that far table. Suddenly, I became quite nervous. It would be difficult to deal with the emotions coming off of them. They were radiating confidence, and I caught bits and pieces of the lies

415

they had twisted themselves around. Grimacing, I braced myself and waited to have the floor.

The process took all day, with constant interruptions on all sides for questions, comments, and clarifications. It felt more as if I were on trial then those in the corner. Some of the minds proved it to me as well. A third of the people there were intent on covering up the scandal and those were the ones who drilled me on every detail. However, I had been prepared for them and never changed my story, repeating the facts again and again: the conditions we lived in, the babies not being brought home from the hospital, what it took to start a school, and how we managed to get supplies. I told of the disappearing rations, the food we were served, and the pay of those allowed to work inside and outside of the camp. All of it was told, including Gareth being a citizen and being refused the medication he needed. I choked on the retelling of Sarah's birth and death. They wanted to know how I was rescued, how this secretive military group came to know of the details of the camp and why they chose to secure my release. I had to tread lightly. There was so much that needed to stay hidden but so much which had to be said.

I was exhausted and in agony by the time they dismissed. The lawyer warned I could be called back in a day or two and that he and Mr. Trone would have more information on what could happen next.

Back at the hotel, Dara was fuming. Jack had also been torn apart by the defense because he had not actually seen who hit him over the head. They tried to portray it as an accident, something falling from the warehouse roof – even though evidence showed his injury was blunt force trauma. Mr. Trone had done well with proving otherwise, showing how Jackson was a target for helping keep me secure after the second assault. Mr. Phillips was called up to testify about my injuries and how he scheduled the volunteers to guard over me at night. Kris, the wonderful nurse who helped me, had also been called in to verify my injuries from the second rape. Dara found out that Kris would also be called in at the military tribunal the next day. Hopefully, she would be able to validate not only what happened to me but to what happened to others in the camp. I suspected much more went on than the stolen

416

babies and wished I could be there to hear it.

We skipped reading in favor of a long workout. Even Jack and Mr. Phillips joined in with us. They were all watching me closely, and I kept faking calmness. It wasn't until Dara went to bed early, and Rick motioned me to the couch, that I let the real me show with silent tears and clenched fists. Even with Gareth's life and death so forward in my mind, I was missing James and the security of my new life.

We were in London for four more days. On the third day, the trial ended with a guilty verdict for Mr. Abramavich and his surviving cohorts. Several witnesses, the soldiers' family, my in-laws and the legal teams were present. Before he was led away, the other victim and I were given a chance to address him. She chose not to, but I stood up. After a deep breath, the words I had so carefully planned came out.

"Today I have learned that the British justice system can be fair, and that lies and cover-ups can only go so far. You, the person I only knew as the "sneering guard," will now experience what it is like to be locked away, to have only the most basic rights. However, while in prison you will not likely know the hunger we felt or know how cold it really can be at night. You will have a proper bed and toilet there in your room, a room which may be larger than the shack I lived in. You will be behind a locked door that only few can enter, and if someone wanted to hurt you, you will have the ability to fight back. But you will watch from a distance as the world collapses around you, watch from a place where very few can reach you.

You raped me, a widow who had also lost her newborn baby, someone who could be considered the weakest of the weak in the most desperate of situations. Someone who is as human as you, someone with the same basic rights as you, a person you were supposed to protect, as we have helped protect you in the past. Shame on you for what you did to me and that other young woman. Shame on you for believing you had that much power. But as to trying to kill me to cover up your shameful actions, I have only one thing to say..."

I paused, waiting several seconds for emphasis. "Thank

417

you." Those around me gasped and muttered, wondering why. "That night you made a critical error, but either way it would have been a positive outcome. Either I would have died physically and those coming to rescue me would have known something sinister happened, or I would have been rescued in time. You know that the latter happened, but no matter what the outcome was, the scandals in Camp Iachâd would have been exposed. Neither you or I had any idea of who was really out there, watching and waiting to turn those evil acts into something positive."

Then, I turned around to face those who came to support me, my gaze lingering on Gareth's family. Moving slowly, I turned again to face the judge. "Nicole Jones can now rest in peace. The person she became can live knowing justice is being served. We both thank you for that."

There was silence in the courtroom. The guilty were led out and, with a near silent gavel tap, the judge dismissed us. Solemnly, I walked to the side room and waited for everyone to depart. The desire to run after my family was dulled by the lingering emotional impact of my words. Dara stood, holding one hand and Rick held the other. No one spoke. I looked out at my family long enough to know they were trying to understand, and I gave a grim smile knowing that one day they would. When Mr. Phillips came into the room to let us know it was safe enough to leave, he gave Rick a peculiar look and nodded in his direction.

The following morning, we were called back to the military tribunal. It was my third time in the presence of the committee. Jack and his father had also been called in during past few days as witnesses to the conditions of the camp and to retell actions of the staff and guards. Until that point, I had suspected, but had not confirmed, that Jackson knew of the outside help before my arrival. He had actually been hired on in June to be the eyes and ears inside the camp. No one suspected the New England teenager had witnessed so much. The tribunal officers were flabbergasted when he produced video evidence from a camera which had been hidden on his hat. They took it, hoping to find it was staged, but those who analyzed it said the footage was the real thing.

On our final day at the tribunal, they gathered all those

who had testified against the camp. Kris was there and, after one long look and a nod from Rick, I went to stand next to her. She startled when I took her hand and squeezed it tight. I turned to look into her eyes. It took only moments before I felt her sharp intake of breath and sensed recognition.

"Shh." I quickly whispered, watching the tears fill her eyes. "I'm being well cared for and am learning to live again."

She faced forward again and barely nodded.

"Don't let the others know you have seen me."

She nodded again.

I squeezed her hand once more then faded back to stand with Jackson and Mr. Phillips.

Fifteen minutes later, we were called into the main room. Those who had spent days trying to disprove what had happened at the Camp Iachâd, who had turned our words around and questioned the validity of our claims, all stood at our entrance. They took turns making formal apologies to us for the treatment of those in all of the refugee camps. In the corner of the room, the artists' hands moved furiously fast.

After the formalities were over, the people we had accused were brought in, this time several of them were in prison garb. We were told then that the camp nurse had admitted to arranging for documents to be forged stating that the expectant mothers willingly gave up their parental rights. The babies had been located in their adoptive homes, but any attempt to return them to their birth family would likely end up in a horrible battle. She had also been charged with medical neglect in Gareth's case. Although her neglect affected more than just him, she was only charged because of his citizenship. I found that fact incredibly disturbing. What about the others in the camp? They were just as human as Gareth, so it should not matter what their citizenship status was. Our countries were allied, and Britain had offered to take in refugees.

The head officer was also charged with various crimes ranging from accepting bribes, to confiscating supplies meant for the residents, to negligence in the monitoring the behavior of and failure to discipline those under his command. Once the charges had been explained, they were led back out again.

At that point, one official stepped forward. "Those charged will pay for the crimes they committed, and we will pay restitution for damages done to all in the camp. The private organizations who have taken over management of the camps will have our support."

I grinned up at Jack, who grabbed me in an exuberant hug. Kris turned her head and caught me in the act. I winked at her and she started to smile as well. This was a clear victory.

As much as I wanted to talk to Kris, to see how she was doing and if she were still in the camp, I knew that would be impossible. Mr. Phillips however, was not tied by the same laws and promised to get an update from her. We left them and one of the agents behind.

When we returned to the hotel I started to take off the headscarf. Rick caught my hand and said, "Wait." At my puzzled expression, he added, "Look out."

Dara stared at us disapprovingly then shrugged and addressed Rick. "For the record, I am against this violation of our laws." She looked over at me. "But I also do not agree with what The General did. If I were in your position, I would want this as well."

My jaw dropped as I looked from Dara to Rick, back and forth. Were they saying what I think they were saying?

Rick explained, "Mr. Phillips and Jackson will keep an agent or two busy. Dara is going to go shopping and do the same. You and I are going to appear to go on a bit of a celebratory date, which should cause those following us to keep their distance. All but one of the local guards have been sent home already, so it's just our own. Gareth's family did go home yesterday, but they left there this morning to meet us at a set location at a set time. You won't have long, but it will give you time to have the closure we all know you need." Right in front of Dara he placed a hand to my blood-drained face, whispering. "Love in many forms. Remember?"

I could barely nod, staring into his eyes and looking out into their minds. They were both serious and the event was happening very soon.

"Do you have the jammer?" Dara interrupted the moment.

Rick pulled a device out of his jacket pocket. "It will scramble the cameras for a few seconds at a time, just enough for us to get in and out without being picked up."

"Then let's go."

At the hotel exit, Dara went to the left and hailed a cab. Rick and I walked down the road to a nearby strip mall before doing the same. We asked the driver about places to eat and told him to pick someplace fancy. He seemed to enjoy that and told us about a place his cousin worked at and drove us there. We had a fabulous meal and played the part of a couple quite well. It was never far from my mind that if it were not for his "Life's Vow" our relationship might be more romantic, more like this moment. Then again, it might not be, not with the chemistry between James and me. I tried to convince myself that Rick would have found someone before I came along. Thinking like that seemed to make our situation more bearable.

From there, we hailed another cab and had him drive us to random locations where we had him wait while we quickly popped in and out of shops then came back and had him drive us elsewhere. We convinced him it was a scavenger hunt game and he seemed happy enough to follow along once we showed him a large tip. Finally, it was time. Rick showed the driver a slip of paper with the address on it then took my hand.

"The Commander is going to have our heads for this." He muttered.

"I have a feeling it won't be as bad as it could be. He is angry at The General as well."

"Don't underestimate him, Bear. He is very good at keeping personal feelings away from professional responsibility."

I was suddenly very nervous. "How bad can it get?"

His hand tightened around mine, "Not so bad that it will not be worth this moment...look."

We were pulling up to a very old church. Rick instructed the cabbie to wait in the small village we just passed until a certain time, then placed his hand into his pocket. We quickly stepped into the church and the cab pulled away. Minutes later, a second vehicle pulled up and stopped. They were here!

Rick stood just below the pulpit and pulled me to stand in front of him. He kept his hands on my shoulders, and we waited. It seemed like hours until the footsteps came closer and four figures came through the darkened doorway. They stopped, and for a moment, all of us held our breaths.

"Mum?" Eyes met mine and I could see her working through what was in front of her. Here was a stranger. Hastily, I lowered the headscarf. "It's me. It's Nicole."

She nodded, and I could see tears welling in her eyes. We rushed towards each other and embraced. Padre and the others came forward and did the same. Rick silently moved towards the front door to stand guard.

Through the tears I was able to choke out, "I know the secrecy, plastic surgery, and all, must make it seem unreal. I'm so far into this new identity, trying so hard to forget, that it has been difficult."

Padre spoke, "Why were you not allowed to see us before? Why all the secrecy?"

"I wanted to contact you from the moment I awoke in the hospital, but it is too dangerous. Some people in power were angered by the discovery of what happened in the camp. They were making money off it and enjoying the control it gave them. There was fear of retribution. I had to keep you safe but hated that it stopped me from saying goodbye. Even now, I am still not supposed to see anyone from my past." I grabbed their hands, "So much was out of my control for so long."

"So, you were given a new identity and job and everything?"

"Yes. I'm adjusting really well. It's eerie too, almost like I was always supposed to be in this line of work."

Mum spoke again, "You look remarkable. Whoever you are with seems to be making sure you are being taken care of."

"I am, Mum. I have my own place to live in, with a small garden and nearby village. They are keeping careful watch over me."

"But you cannot say who it is?"

"No. It's like witness protection back in the States. I'm breaking a lot of rules by seeing you right now."

All four of them nodded and we hugged again. I looked over at Rick who pointed to his wrist, time was growing short.

I took a long look at all of them, taking in every detail, knowing I might never see them again. There was so much I still wanted to say but decided to state the most important. "I miss Gareth. Sarah looked so much like him."

This time we cried. They mourned for their lost son and granddaughter, and I cried for losing all of them. These were tears of closure; of the goodbye I had been previously denied.

Hands rested on my shoulders, gently pulling me back. "We cannot linger here much longer." Rick whispered.

As if awakened from some dream, my family looked startled and stared at the tall stranger. I leaned back against his chest for a moment, tilting my head up to look at him. "I know, Jaws. Thank you for arranging this final meeting for us."

The others nodded and muttered thanks. Tears flowed freely again. "While another face to face meeting is unlikely, I know where you live. Look for things that I leave for you, signs that I'm still okay. If it ever becomes safe for me to return, I hope you will take me back."

Padre replied, "You've never left us."

It was almost impossible to get the words out, "I love you. Please stay safe." We hugged once more, and Rick rushed me out.

My family stayed behind, pretending to be looking at the ancient architecture of the church. We walked quickly to the cab, preparing to continue the same pattern as before the meeting. As we were leaving the village, I saw a tiny tourist shop. I had the cab pull over and inside was a small painting of the church. Hastily pulling out the needed cash, I purchased it and hurried back to the vehicle.

It was late when we returned back to the hotel. There was no way to tell if we had avoided detection or not. While I had not sensed that the agent assigned to follow us had seen the encounter with Gareth's family, I was not sure if he would report how we had obviously been up to something.

Dara was already back in the room, as were Jack and his father. I sat and listened as they talked about the progress which had been made at the refugee camp. Kris had to leave almost immediately, but she had told them some of the changes. The organization who had taken over seemed to be doing great things.

"Wish I could go there without having an emotional breakdown. It would be great to see all of the progress." It sounded wistful but was the truth. The others gave me a knowing look.

We had finished reading the group novel the night before so split up early to focus on packing for the ride back to the bunker. The emotions of the day were starting to weigh heavy on my heart. It was difficult to concentrate, and I kept missing items. Several times I caught Dara looking my way and frowning. When I dropped a shampoo bottle for the third time she came over. Picking it up and handing it to me she said, "How long has it been since you took that stuff Jason sent?"

"A few days. It's not something I take unless I have to."

"You have to, right now." She pinned me with an expression that dared me to contradict her. In a low voice, she added, "Go to him. He's worried about you."

With all that had been going on today, I had not been very observant. Of course, Rick would be concerned! Thinking about the team I realized that, in some form or another, they would all be wondering how these last two weeks would affect me. I hesitated at the doorway, my thoughts lingering on James. Would he be back from the Middle East? How would he react to me since I had to resurrect Nicole? How would I react to him? What if he found out about this evening? My hand gripped the doorway, and it was several moments before I could propel myself forward to the other bedroom.

Rick was closing his suitcase when I stumbled in. Hastily placing it on the ground he came over and pulled me to him. "I was wondering when it would all hit. Honestly, I'm surprised you're here so fast."

"Dara said something that set it off." My thoughts and emotions were in such turmoil that the fiery waves were starting. I cringed through the pain then looked up at him. His eyes verified what Dara had said. "No regrets though. Actually, that part of me is at peace."

He smiled gently, "I'm happy for that." The smile faded as he added, "It's the team causing the issues right now, isn't it?"

Instinctively, I started to look down, but his fingers quickly reached under my chin and stopped the action. "Oh no, you don't." His tone was firm, "Not now, not ever." I raised my eyes back up to his. "Harlie, those feelings are completely understandable. We've all been through this painful step...we were just given better circumstances than you."

He stepped back and took a deep breath. I dared to glance at his mind, even though I knew he would sense the intrusion. His hands came up and rested on my shoulders, almost as if he were holding me away from him. "Yes, it's like that sometimes. I'm thrilled over you and James being together, but there are times I wish our situation was different." I saw in his mind what his words did not say.

I stepped back away from him physically and mentally, becoming wrapped in my own thoughts again. Another wave of fire came, and I braced myself, trying not to cringe. Rick saw it though and left the room, coming back moments later with the small bag. I sat on the bed and watched as he took my vitals. A few numbers were in the red zone on the chart he was given.

"Dangit, Bear, when will you learn to take this stuff preemptively?" He sounded angrier than he should have, emotions running high. I shrugged and watched as he reached first for the liquid form of the custom cocktail but soon moved his hand to pick up one of the syringes. The first was bad enough, but the injected form I hated. I scooted away a bit and tried to stand up. A hand grasped my arm tightly. "I don't think so."

"Let me go, Rick. It's not bad enough."

He didn't move, "Your vitals and the chart say something else. You might be covering it up with that calm exterior you're so good at, but internally..." He shook his head.

"Please?" My voice sounded pathetic.

"No, and that's final. I promised both The General and Jamyson that I would make sure you made it through this mission as unscathed as possible."

I twisted in his grasp, but he did not let go. The injection dose was too strong, and I didn't want to be knocked out. I needed to have time to sort all of these feelings, to make a plan for what to do when we returned. My head started to pound, and my vision swam for a moment. I wanted to struggle but couldn't find the strength. Shoulders slumping, I sighed in defeat.

Rick let go and went back to the medic bag. He pulled out the syringe and prepped my arm. "Shouldn't this happen in the other bedroom? Jason put a large dose in, and I won't last long once it's in me."

"I'd rather you stay here for a bit. Once we're all packed, I'll help you back to your bed."

I gave a harsh laugh, "You'll end up carrying me."

He smiled gently, "Exactly."

NO REGRETS

Our return to the bunker was met with cheers and celebration. Since the media had been present at the trial, everyone knew about the guilty verdict. It was the same for the tribunal. Jack basked in it while his father looked embarrassed. While I was happy that we had seen justice done, all I really wanted was to go back to something which resembled normalcy.

When we reached the training facility the rest of the team was waiting for us. James and Max had returned from the Middle East the day before, so all nine of us were together once more. Hugs and high fives were exchanged, with James lingering during our embrace.

I missed you. He whispered tenderly.

I missed you too.

After a few minutes of reunion, we quickly settled back to business. It was a break in protocol to have met with them anyway. We were always supposed to debrief first, no matter what the mission. Hurrying into the conference room, we took our places at the table and started filling in reports. The three of us had discussed how to handle the infraction and made sure we put the same story on the report. Although there would be some minor consequences, we chose to keep it somewhat honest and admitted to playing tricks on the agents. Because we had returned after lunch, it took until past the standard work day to complete the papers and discuss the mission with The General. I had expected James to be there, but he had been called upstairs to assess some incoming transmissions.

It was past eighteen hundred when we were finally dismissed. Dara went straight home but Rick and I chose to have dinner in the cafeteria first. James met us there. I kept my shield up tightly, knowing that emotions were still too raw, and I was too emotionally drained to maintain the level of caution needed. When the meal was over, we made our way up to the top level. In the elevator, James started tapping on my shield. I sent a question mark back to him.

May I drive you home?

427

Thinking about my options and what paths led where, I nodded slightly. He left to bring the bike around, and I stood at the entrance to the elevator with Rick.

"Thank you so much for everything these last two weeks." I looked up at his strong frame and gentle eyes.

"It was difficult at times, but I'm pleased to have been there for you." With a quick hug, he was gone.

A gentle hum was the only sign that the motorcycle and its owner were pulling up. Smiling tiredly, I left the warehouse, put on my helmet and hopped on the back. Wrapping my arms tight around him I sighed. What was another secret in this world I now resided in? It was just one more thing to keep from the everyone else. The only difference, and it was major, was that I had to keep my actions hidden from another empathic. That would be tricky, at least for the time being. As time went on and the raw emotions of the infraction faded, it would be easier. I would tell him the truth, one day, but not now. Our relationship was still so new and my hold on this world still tenuous.

He stopped the bike at the cottage and walked me through the front gate. The moment it shut, he pulled me towards the high wall and held me close. I felt the longing from our time apart. Even though Nicole had to be resurrected, even though I had recently thought of Gareth and the love we had shared, I still had missed James. The realization confused me. It should be much more difficult to return to this reality. I rested my head against his chest and focused on the one hand running up and down my back and the other at the back of my neck.

"Your muscles are really tight, Harlie." He muttered, chin on the top of my head.

"It's been more stressful than I thought it would be." That was the truth.

"I haven't seen the report yet but have no doubts." He leaned back to look at my face. "I can see it in your eyes."

Although part of me wanted to make this moment last, the other part knew I had to get inside and start working on my scattered thoughts and emotions. Being sedated last night put me at a disadvantage.

"I need sleep and time to think."

428

He nodded understandingly. "It will take time to bury the dead again."

Yes, it will, I thought, especially since I had just seen and spoke to those to whom I was supposed to be dead. Hastily, I stopped that train of thought before he perceived a problem.

"I'll say goodnight then. Have you been given time off to recover?" His eyes showed concern.

"Tomorrow obviously, then Wednesday and Thursday."

"The same as what we got." He smiled wickedly, "Wednesday is mine, don't you even think about filling it with something else."

Despite everything, I smiled back. "Wouldn't dream of it, but you might have to hold Dara off. Oh, and Max said something about going to a range, and Rick was talking about a concert in Llanrumney."

The smile faded slightly as he moved to press my back against the wall, "They can all shove off. Wednesday is you and me and no one else. That is an order from your commanding officer." With that, he kissed me.

I could feel a fiery flash starting and flinched mentally. Too much was happening, and I needed time to reflect and recover. The wave hit, and James pulled back, frowning.

"Hope sleep takes care of that." He seemed to be pouting.

I nodded, hoping it did as well.

The next day was Sunday, and I was grateful when no one came to call. On Monday we arrived at the bunker, eagerly anticipating our first day back together.

As we ran through our daily workouts, I could see Dara start to relax. Rick was still tense, though. James had gone upstairs to go over our paperwork, so I walked to where Rick was lifting weights.

"What's wrong?"

He raised the bar, held it up, then dropped it down before answering. "Concerned we are not in the clear."

I scanned around the bunker, focusing on the dark spot who looked back at me, lowered his shield, and smiled mentally. The day went by without a hitch. We finished the daily workout, worked on our individual projects and debriefed. Since it was a beautiful autumn day, I chose to walk home instead of riding with James. I stopped to get some fresh food from the grocery store and enjoyed the chance to be outdoors. At my doorstep, there was a single rose, and I sent a mental smile in James direction.

May I come over? Although his voice was gentle and inviting, I really wanted the night alone. My emotions, while settling down, were still shaky. Any mention of the trial had made my heart rate increase all day.

Not tonight, Jamyson, sorry. Still some bothersome leftovers from the trial.

Let me help you through it.

His help was the last thing we needed. The visit was too close to the front of my mind, and he would sense it.

I'd rather deal with it myself. I was betting on the fact that he knew how independent I could be, how I had been in the past.

If you change your mind... The words were laced with multiple meanings. I picked up the rose and went inside, sighing as the door shut behind me.

It was eight-thirty Tuesday morning when I noticed something was amiss. I had been looking out when a sense of strong uneasiness came over someone in the upper levels. It faded but was then picked up by another person. Nervous, I glanced up at the General's office, but he seemed calm.

I was running the track an hour later when the shock wave hit. The power of it caused me to stumble and fall forward. Rick looked up, alarmed. I stared at him wide-eyed and nodded. They knew. A second wave hit, this one more focused. James was not trying to hurt me, but the overflow of his emotions at the discovery of our law-breaking hit hard. His mind turned towards me and one question came in a tortured whisper, *Why?*

Closure.

All three of you to Smiths' office. Now.

Dara had joined Rick in staring at me. The others were sending curious glances in our direction. I was still on the ground. Standing up, I stumbled towards Dara.

"They know, not sure how, but they know, and we

430

have been called upstairs."

Choking down the urge to go in on the defensive, I led the way. The expression on The General's face was enough to know that we were not going to get off lightly. He had a computer pad in front of him and held it up for us to see.

"You almost got away with it." He started, "The agent was suspicious but thought you were just playing around. On a whim, I researched where you had gone and came across a one-paragraph report of some cameras acting up. A repair team had been called out to see what was scrambling the reception. I almost missed it too, it was so insignificant." He paused to show us the footage. Sure enough, it was from the camera in the village. "I saw your purchase of the painting and just as you left, look..." Driving past the small shop was the car Gareth's family drove. Dara moaned at the sight. What were the chances of that happening? Of course, we would have missed it!

He pinned me with a glare that made me lose my breath. "Would you mind telling me why that camera was acting up and how you and your family were in the same village at the same time? It could not have been a coincidence."

I stood straight, trying to appear braver than I felt. They could not take me from this life I had been living, I knew too much and had seen too much. That made the thought of any consequence more bearable.

"As my report stated, Sir, Nicole's in-laws were present in the courthouse. As also stated, it led to a struggle between me and Rick as her emotions took over. To be honest, I did not plan this second offense."

James' eyes widened then narrowed. "Second offense?"

I proceeded to tell about the letter and my plans to have it delivered.

"Who did you end up giving it to?"

Rick stepped forward, "I realized what she was attempting and took the letter. After weighing the pros and cons, the conclusion was made that it was her only chance at closure. Since the rest of the team had been allowed some form, it was only right to place it into the proper hands."

431

The General glared, "So when did the plan to meet them come about if the letter was supposed to be closure?"

I started to speak, but Rick interrupted me. "Harlie was in agony over their presence. With her abilities stretched out during the trial, she kept picking up on their confusion, questions, and their longing to see her. While she put on a calm facade, it was destroying her inside. I made the decision, planned the meeting, and put all of the pieces in place." He stood ramrod straight. "And I have no regrets, Sir. You know our pasts, know our files. We were all given a chance to reconcile our old lives before starting this new one. Harlie was not given that opportunity. You placed her in this situation unprepared, there were bound to be consequences."

James spoke, his voice flat and deadly, "She was dead."

Rick glared at him, "Not to them she wasn't, and you should have seen her in the trial. In those moments, Nicole was alive again."

The General turned towards Dara. "And your part in this?"

"I stated my opposition several times. However, if the roles were reversed, I would want the same thing. In the end, I helped distract one of the agents."

The General looked to us, to James, and back to us. "These reports are falsifications and you violated our laws on two counts. Until a proper punishment is arranged, you are all confined to quarters. Dismissed."

Without saluting, we left the office and went right to the common area. Dara chuckled as she reached the door to her room.

"What's it been Rick, three years since the last time we did this?"

He thought it over, "Three for you and Jason. Been a little over four since I was last confined." He turned to me, "You have every reason to be concerned. While The General's form of punishment is more militaristic, if he has James deal the consequences..." He broke off.

"James' idea of consequences can be much more personal. You don't have to be confined to quarters to know that." Dara finished for him. She walked into her room and quickly shut the door.

Rick stood by me. When I went to open the door, he reached out to touch the back of my hand. "The Commander and James, one and the same. This is going to be a hard test so early in your relationship. I hope you do not become angry with us for it."

I turned to face him, "I could never be angry at you for what you did. You made it so I could see my family one last time. Whatever the punishment, that moment will be worth it. Hopefully, it will not be so harsh as to destroy what James and I have. I understand he has to keep professional and personal more apart than the rest of us."

Rick smiled sadly and went to his room. I did the same, going straight to the bed and screaming into the pillow. Up in the office, I wanted to tell The General off for being the reason why this situation ever happened. Anger flared, and hot tears fell. Physically, I was in pain from the shock waves James had sent. Emotionally, the look in his eyes and expression on his face caused their own wounds.

To calm myself down, I thought about the short visit. My mind went through moment by moment, reflecting on their appearances, words, and actions. It would have been so easy to continue to think about other times with them, but that would just cause more pain. Seeing them in the church brought peace. That peace allowed me to close my eyes and truly rest for the first time in weeks.

Lunch was quietly brought to the door by a clearly upset Jackson. I looked out to the rest of the bunker and saw how rest of the team was confused about why we were being confined. No one could figure out what we could have done. When he came to pick the tray up, Jack had an envelope for me. Inside was a copy of my original report and a note:

This official report is a falsification of the events which unfolded. You are ordered to accurately complete a new report along with the additional pages.

General Smiths

The added pages were basically a series of essays where I would be attempting to justify not only my actions but those of Rick, Dara and the others involved. It seemed a combination of something a student would be assigned and a written version of a trial. I laughed at the irony of both, and then started on the task at hand. Two hours later I was finally finished the actual report and on the first of the justification essays. It was emotionally draining, and my hand was cramped from hand-writing the reports. Normally, all our paperwork was typed.

I put my head down on the desk and closed my eyes when I sensed James approach the common room. The dark spot stopped first at Dara's room and then at Rick's before coming into mine. Aggravated by the essays, I did not bother to look up. He stood silently for over a minute before stepping forward and placing his hands on my shoulders.

"Sit up." The voice was James, but the overtones were The Commander.

Slowly, I obeyed, and he reached over to take the completed report. I stared at the wall as he read, wondering which persona would be dominant. The hands rested on my shoulders again, and I had a split-second notice to brace myself before his shield dropped. I was exposed to the full onslaught of his own tortured emotions, and it was excruciating. While I knew he would be torn between being our commanding officer and the friend he was off-duty, the pain at the level of conflict from our relationship versus my disregard of Guardian law was much worse. I tried to cringe, to pull away, but the hands held me in place.

"Stop it, James! Don't you think I knew that ahead of time?"

The shield did not rise, "Then why, Harlie? Why force me to choose? Why do something you knew would lead to me having to hand out the consequence?"

Fiercely, I pulled his hands off, stood and turned to face him. "You read the report; you know what happened." I pulled up the sleeves of my shirt and pointed to the fading bruises from the struggle when I first sensed the presence of my family and the new one from resisting the injection four nights ago. "I did not plan the meeting."

"You agreed to it." He snapped, shield still down. I shuddered, but he did not relent.

"We both knew if my family showed up there would be no way to return here without some kind of rule breaking."

434

I moved to step around him, but he blocked the way. "Tell me, Jamyson, if it were you there instead of Rick...what would you have done? Or if it were you in my shoes how would you have responded?"

His shield snapped into place, but not before I saw the answer. He would have let me have the closure that was needed, in some form or another. I sat on the top of the desk, placed my feet on the chair and tried to hide the pain. James paced the room, running his hands through his hair. It was over five minutes before he stopped.

"You need more closure in order to effectively move on. How to give that to you without you hating me afterward will be difficult."

"I don't think it is possible for me to hate you. Fear you? That has happened before, but hate you?" I shook my head.

He pinned me with "That Look" then closed his eyes.

"I can think of one thing." James started to walk out, paused, then turned back to face me, "Have a small overnight bag packed and be ready before dawn. Dress business casual, but warmly, and wear the headscarf. No gun, just your knife. We'll take the bike." The look on his face froze me in my tracks.

I finished the essays in time for the evening meal to be delivered. After eating, I showered and packed for whatever was happening tomorrow. James had gone back into Ricks' room, and it seemed they went to the second bunker. I was concerned about what his punishment would be. With them being close friends, I knew that whatever it was, it would be very hard on both of them. While there were still no regrets at writing to and seeing my family, I was starting to feel guilt-ridden over what my friends would be experiencing.

James came into the room at five-thirty the next morning. I was already awake, anxious about what would happen today. He stood in the doorway as I hurriedly dressed and grabbed the bag. When I hit the elevator button for the cafeteria level, he took my hand and shook his head.

"We'll eat once we get to our destination." He paused, head tilted as if listening to something. "You are correct in being so anxious. Today is going to be painful...for both of

435

us...but it is necessary." Still holding onto my hand, he led us up and out of the bunker. It was warmer than normal for a September morning, but there was still a chill in the air – a sign that autumn was here. His old bike was standing ready a hint that, wherever we were going, it was going to be far. James put my bag into his and attached it to a backpacking frame. When he handed it to me I noticed that there was a small tent with two backwoods sleeping bags attached. I hoisted the frame on and climbed behind him on the bike.

It was an uncomfortable and long ride. James made a lot of strange turns and seemed to be back-tracking some. I kept a close watch on the signs, though, and noticed we were approaching Newtown. He turned off a few kilometers before it and headed towards the hills. We drove into a large village, and he parked the bike next to a bakery.

"Stay here. I'll be back in a few minutes with breakfast." Confused and anxious, I placed the frame on the ground, sat down next to it, and fidgeted with the scarf until he returned. We had pastry, fruit and coffee drinks. It was a silent meal, as he seemed to be watching me for some kind of reaction. I was unfocused on anything outside of trying to figure out what he was up to. As I stood to clean up the small meal, I started to look out mentally. A shadow came across my mental line of sight.

"No, not yet." It sounded like a command, so I backed away. "Put the frame back on, we are not far from our destination."

He was correct. We went less than two kilometers to the foot of a hill. It seemed a strange place to park, as it did not appear to be a recreational area. I placed the frame down and fixed the scarf so only my eyes showed. James put on a baseball cap and took my hands in his.

"Try not to hate me for this, you mean too much to me, and it would be devastating." One hand reached up and he brushed the back of his fingers down my cheek. "I'd like to think it would be the same for you as well." He looked deep into my eyes, his own emerald ones penetrating into my soul.

Letting go of my hands he pointed to the hill. "For the record, I was not going to take you here for a few more months, but your recent actions and words gave me no

436

choice."

Nervously, I started up the hill. He followed close behind. I heard sounds coming from the other side and something about the air around us seemed familiar. Just before I crested the top, it hit me. I spun around to race back down only to find that James had anticipated the move and caught me.

"Go the rest of the way, Harlie. Go and take a good long look from the outside. In less than an hour, we will be back on the inside."

I stumbled to the top and fell to my knees. In front of me was the refugee camp, and I was on the hill where James once stood and watched. Tears and panic blinded me from seeing any details. All my mind knew was that I was at the spot where my old life ended, and it wanted to be far away. Nicole was screaming in my head, and my hand covered my mouth to keep her inside.

James stood behind me and waited as I rocked and stared. "You are still Harlie Berryman and will not be staying there. Today you are a visitor, someone coming in to see the progress made and, hopefully, offer assistance. Only the woman in charge knows who you really are."

"I can't go in there, James." It was a hoarse whisper.

"You do not have a choice. It is an order." The Commanders tone left no room for argument. He sat down next to me, "Look at it, Harlie, really look at it."

I turned away from the camp, away from him. "Believe me, you do not want to behave like that." The Commander threatened, "Turn back around and look at the camp."

I partially complied by turning physically towards it and pretended to look in that direction.

"What do you see?"

"Barbed wire, tents, shacks, debris, some warehouses and people."

A string of profanity-laced phrases was spat out. He grasped the back of my neck and forced me to face the camp. "You are making it more difficult and more painful than it has to be."

I twisted out of the contact and turned towards him, eyes flashing. "You want to tell me how this can be any more painful?"

He dropped his shield before answering, "I could make you go in there alone, overnight, just you and the ghosts." I doubled over, and he raised it back up. "That's what General Smiths thought would be best." Then The Commander took over again, "You won't be alone, but your Jamyson will remain buried for the time being."

His eyes proved that it was the truth. While having him with me would help with feeling safer inside the camp, the coldness of The Commander would make it difficult on all other fronts.

James looked at his watch, "Time to go inside."

It was another short ride to the front gate. We left the bike behind the gatehouse and walked up towards the main building. A woman, who appeared to be in her late fifties, was waiting outside the door.

"Welcome back, Colonel Davies." She smiled at him.

James stood stiff and formal at my side. "Thank you, Margaret. I am very interested to see the positive changes which have occurred since my last visit."

"You will be impressed for sure...although we were not anticipating your visit for another month or so." She then turned to look at me. "Is this her, the key to our success?"

At his nod, she held out a hand, "Welcome back as well." We shook hands, and she added, "I hope today will help give you the closure you need. It is because of you that everything we have accomplished here has happened so fast."

Margaret looked back over to James, "Are we still keeping her real identity hidden? It would be wonderful if the residents could know that she is here and well."

He frowned, "No. Mrs. Jones needs to remain dead, especially now. They know she lived because of the recent trial. That will have to be enough. She is Harlie Berryman and will be addressed as such." He pointed at my headscarf, "Hopefully no one will recognize her."

"Well, even if they did, these are an amazing group of people, and I'm sure whoever it is will keep the secret."

Listening to her talk about the refugees as if they were real people made me start to relax a little. "Madam, I am very interested in hearing about your organization and the work being done here."

She smiled brightly at me, "I am eager to tell you. Although what happened to you is tragic in many ways, it was the opening we needed to take the camp from military control." Margaret started walking past the main building, "Shall we begin?"

I turned to look at James, who gave a curt nod. I frowned. This was going to be a very long day. The first thing I noticed was that the walkway leading from the main building to the rest of the camp had been fixed up. It was no longer a roughly cut path but had been lightly paved. I took a quick look around me. The soldiers' barracks had been painted and landscaped. I paused and stared.

Margaret stopped, "We still have a small military presence here for security purposes, but most of those barracks now hold volunteers as well as our paid staff."

"They all live here with the residents?"

She smiled again, "Yes, even I live here."

Wow! I was really alert now, looking out mentally for signs of deception. Next to me, I heard James give a harsh laugh. I turned and glared at him. Instead of responding, he faced forward and started walking again.

The warehouse where I was attacked was still standing, and I hesitated. Margaret noticed, "Let's tour the rest of the camp before we go inside there." Her voice was gentle. I agreed, and we started towards where the tents and shacks were. I noticed that there were very few people roaming around. Those who did seemed to be in much better shape than when I left. I recognized a few faces and pulled the scarf closer around me. They did not seem to be concerned about our presence.

The shacks and tents were still present but in much fewer quantity. I stopped, amazed at what was in their place. The organization had acquired dozens of the shipping containers used to transport items overseas. They had been placed in the most ingenuous method. Two were set parallel to each other a set distance apart. Two more were placed perpendicular on top of those, one at the front and one at the back. The open area in the middle was turned into a simple courtyard with a raised bed and bench. The bed looked to have had various food-bearing plants in it. The scene was repeated across the back wall of the camp and had started down the side with the shacks.

"All of the residents with children are now out of the tents and we are now working on married couples. Sixty-four are set up, with four more going in every two to three weeks." She walked up to the closest container-home. "Come take a closer look."

One of the large metal doors had been sealed and the other was made so it was easier to open and close. Two windows had been cut out on each of the long sides. The exposed roofs had water collectors installed. On the second level, stairs led to a small landing and that container houses' door.

"Come inside, this family has offered their home for our tour."

The inside had been SIP paneled and turned into two rooms. The back one was a bedroom with bunks for children, the trunk from the tent, dresser, and a full bed for the parents. The front room held a worn couch, bookshelf, rough-made table with chairs and a tiny kitchenette. There was a sink with a hand pump, a single burner stove and small electric convection oven. Each room had two little light fixtures. It was a drastic improvement over the tents and shacks of just six months before but still seemed like something out of a third-world country.

I turned to Margaret, "They must be so happy to have a proper place to live."

Her smile grew wider, "Long-term goals are to add a second container to each home, giving them four rooms each. Our goal is to make this a self-sufficient community. The water collected is used for the renovated community bathrooms, and plans are being made to install solar panels on the roof to power the homes. The families are enjoying the chance to cook for themselves again with food raised here or purchased."

"Purchased how?" Very few had been employed before.

"Come and see." We left the residential area and walked back towards the warehouses. Along the way, she explained how two meals a day were still provided, but for the third, the people were expected to make using rations, food donations and what was raised. Monetary donations that had been collected since the first camp was opened had been used to provide salaries for some residents. The cafeteria workers, cleaning staff, and land management employees were all residents. Even many of the construction workers were residents. All were being paid at least minimum wage. Many companies had been willing to provide items and services, but the military had been turning them away or stealing the resources, even the assistance coming from the government itself.

We arrived at the warehouse which had been the female singles bunkhouse. I looked back at James and frowned again. He still stood formal and quiet.

Inside the warehouse, I saw just how the refugees were earning money. It set me on edge at first, until I realized they looked quite content. Some women were on one side of the room with sewing machines, making various items, and next to them were others who were knitting. More were next to them at a rug loom and, farther down, some were making pottery on a proper wheel. Several more women were making beaded jewelry, and others were making paper out of recycled material. A few of them looked up and smiled or waved. I walked around and inspected each station. It appeared to be a safe area, with good lighting, and my mental scan showed that most were very content with the work.

"They were given micro-loans to start their own businesses." Margaret explained. "They barter in the camp for other products like furniture and we have contracts with stores all over the country who are selling these items. We are starting an internet store soon. Some local shops have decided to participate as well, and sales have been good. Ten percent of the profit goes back to paying the loan, ten percent goes into a community fund, and another ten percent goes into a savings account for the person. They keep the rest. It isn't much, but at least they are able to help their families more, and it's allowing them to be productive members of society."

The warehouse which held the single males now was filled with wood-crafting machines, welding materials for metal crafting, a center for sculpting and several painting easels. As with before, when I looked out mentally, I could sense that they were happy about being able to work. Some were staring at me and two were wondering if it were me under the headscarf. I smiled as I recognized them as two of my nighttime guardian angels.

"We have a lot of talent here, and it's nice to see it being put to good use. About two dozen residents have jobs outside of the camp as well. We would like to see more, but the area is just too rural."

That made me wonder, "All of these changes have been so amazing. How can you be sure it will last?"

She looked serious as she replied, "With making the camp a self-sufficient village it means less money will be needed for maintenance. These people will always need some kind of assistance until a way is found to integrate them into society without them being taken advantage of. We hope that, by making them desirable with skills and experience, it will happen. Next spring, enough of the camp will have been renovated that we can safely bring in some food animals to raise. The school is completed, so education is being provided all the way through secondary."

That caught my attention, "May I see the school?"

"Of course!" I hurried to follow her out when a hand grasped my arm and held me back.

"Use caution in this next situation." The Commander muttered in my ear.

We were not far from the location, and my jaw dropped when we rounded a corner. One of the older buildings had been razed, and in its place, were two brand new modular classrooms! I thought back to my early days at the bunker and mentally thanked Dara for her generous donation. Behind the school was a proper playground, complete with swings, slides, and bars to climb on. Tears came into my eyes as I saw the name in big block letters on the first building, "Nicole Jones Primary." The other was called "Jackson Phillips Secondary." I felt a hand brush against my own and looked back to see that, for an instant, The Commander had disappeared. James gave my hand a gentle squeeze before dropping it and turning away, presumably to gain control of his own emotions.

Margaret waited as I brushed the tears away. "Are you able to go inside? I think it would be good for you to see it."

I nodded eagerly and followed her up the ramp and inside. Proper desks in various sizes were placed in groups all over the large room. Dividers separated it into four sections and each section had a new chalkboard and cork board. Children, my students, looked up at the intrusion. Catherine was leaning over one child, helping her form cursive letters. Two of the mothers who had helped me were with other groups.

"They all have a salary now." Margaret whispered. "Four curriculum companies have donated their programs, complete with workbooks. We are in the process of getting a few computers for the primary. We already have five in the secondary but need more there as well."

"Consider it done." I whispered back, nearly choking at the scene. Catherine was looking annoyed at our presence. When I made eye contact with her she froze, a question in her eyes. At that moment a tiny girl, I remembered she was called Ginger, came up and hugged my leg. I wished she could have seen my smile through the scarf. I bent down and hugged her back.

"You smell like my old teacher." She said, "I miss her."

I stood up, and Catherine came over. At her expression, I nodded before placing a finger to my covered lips. The Commander inhaled sharply, but I ignored him. I took her hand and squeezed it tightly.

"Your class is amazing and so well behaved. It has been a treasure to see, and you should be very proud of them." I managed to say.

Catherine, tears in her eyes, whispered, "They came from the best teacher who gave them an amazing start in the worst of conditions."

"Your computers are on the way." I gave her hand another squeeze then dropped it and stepped back.

We went to the secondary school where a stranger was teaching. Margaret told me he was a retired teacher from Cardiff who wanted to make a difference. He was living in the camp and doing his best to instruct what was needed to get the

443

students at least through their basic diploma. Three students sat at the computers.

"They are completing online courses for their A levels. Won't it be wonderful to see them in University?"

"The school's namesake is taking classes at Swansea right now." I told her.

"Wonderful!" She exclaimed, and all heads turned.

We went back to the main office for lunch. After the simple meal of sandwiches and crisps, The Commander took Margaret aside and they spoke at length about something. I could tell he was starting to struggle again and hoped that James would return. I wasn't blind to what was happening during this tour. All the positive things had been shown to me first. That left one more positive stop and the two which could break me.

Sadly, it was The Commander who came over to me. "The clinic is next." His voice was cool, his eyes guarded.

This was going to be an interesting stop since I had recently revealed myself to Kris. Because I was already here as punishment and would most likely be called out for the scene in the school, I shrugged it off. What was one more offense?

The clinic had been renovated and added on to. A secretary was at the front desk, working on files. At the sound of the door, Kris peered from around the corner. In seconds, she was by my side and we hugged.

"Can I talk to you this time, or is it still silence?" She asked, looking from me to James.

I looked that way as well, "She recognized me at the trial and tribunal. On the final day, there wasn't a way to keep us separated."

To my surprise, James nodded in understanding. But then added, "She cannot speak as the person she once was."

Thinking quickly, I asked Kris if she would take me on a tour of the clinic. She was positively bouncing as she showed me the "new" equipment, older model donations that were still in good shape. There was another nurse on staff, and between the two of them, they were able to set broken bones, stitch up cuts, treat minor illnesses, do wound management, and they even delivered two healthy babies.

"The organization makes sure a doctor comes in to check on the very young and old and all have been updated on inoculations. We have only had one person who needed surgery, and he was back here in a few days."

"This is great, Kris." I complimented. "It must be nice to be back in the field."

"It is." I could see the questions before they came and shook my head. How was I? Who was I?

"It's all good, really, just as I said in the trial. It's an entirely new life, but I am enjoying living it."

We said our goodbyes, and I braced myself for what was next.

"Is there a place where Ms. Berryman and I can be alone for a moment?" The Commander asked Margaret. She pointed to an empty outbuilding, and he led me into it. I did not give him a moment to speak.

"I know my limits, Commander, and this next part of the tour is beyond it. Please, please, if you are going to make me go through this today, please either go as Jamyson or not at all. The pain is nearly unbearable right now, even with all the improvements here."

A hand reached out to touch my cheek where the scarf had slipped. Eyes turned from cold, to warm, to guarded and then shut. When they opened, I was instantly lost in them.

"I cannot let you go through this part without me. It nearly killed me to stay The Commander for as long as I did, but the point needed to be made. I'll be here with you for the next steps." Fingers touched around my eyes, "Harlie, darling, it's time for you to go say goodbye."

Step by painful step we walked towards the graveyard. When they died, Gareth and Sarah had been laid side by side in a simple grave with their names carved on a piece of wood. I should not have been surprised but, as we neared, I could see that proper gravestones had replaced the wood and grass had been planted over the sites. Margaret stepped away to give me privacy, but James stayed close. I knelt down and touched the words on the stone:

Gareth Jones
Beloved husband and friend
We are forever grateful

Sarah Jones
Precious Daughter
You came and left too early

Once again tears flowed. I kept running my fingers
over the words, knowing there were things I needed to say,
things I needed to ask. This could be my last time with them.
Taking a halted breath, I whispered. "I love you both so much
and miss you terribly. Gareth, my love, if only you knew what
was waiting for us. We would have been rescued, and you
would have enjoyed it so much. The organization is amazing,
and the people are so good to me. You might not like me
being enhanced, but I think you would have understood.
Sarah, my sweet little girl, you never had a chance to see this
world. I only wish I had seen you smile..." I could say no more
and sat, staring.

The touch on my shoulders was almost imperceptible,
but the figure kneeling next to me could not be ignored. Tears
were in his eyes as he too spoke. "Gareth, we never met
formally, but I was watching you, trying to get you and Nicole
out of the camp. I promise to take care of her, to continue to
watch over her. She is safe with us, with me. I have feelings
for her and hope that you are okay with me trying to make her
happy..." He looked over at me, "Perhaps to the point of
getting her to feel love again."

Even though I knew those feelings would take time, as
I looked at him, looked into the mind he was now leaving
unshielded, I knew that those feelings could be possible. I
leaned against him, and he wrapped an arm around me, lips at
my hair. He protected his mind again, "I'll be nearby, take all
the time you need."

I stayed for a while longer, allowing myself to think
back to the good times before the bombs. I closed my eyes and
pictured Sarah, so tiny in my arms. A cool breeze reminded
me that daylight was short, and we had one more stop to
make. Shivering more from that thought than the breeze, I
stood and went to where Margaret and James waited.

"It is slated to become a recreation center but not much
has been done yet. The project is all volunteer-oriented and

446

school is back in session." Margaret explained. I heard her hidden apology, that she was sad it was the same as the night Nicole died. My steps slowed then stopped.

"Commander, James, I can't do this." Panic started to fill my mind. Even knowing the sneering guard was in prison, knowing so much good had come from that night, I could not make myself move forward.

James turned to face me, "Although what you went through is much worse, you have also seen it from my perspective. This is going to be hard for me as well. We will go in together. You will not be alone."

He took my hand in his, interlocking our fingers and started walking towards the warehouse again. Margaret had paused and looked back at us, her gaze lingering on our hands. The front was boarded up so tight that I could not see the hole from the rescue. At the back entrance, she stopped and said she would be at the main office when we were finished. I stood and stared at the door, torn through in two places by bullets – more evidence of that night. Taking a deep breath, I let James pull me forward into the nightmare.

Very little had been done to the small room, the table and wooden crates were still there. Faded blood stains could be seen in a few spots. My eyes roamed to one particular location and a stain was there too, the spot where my own blood had spilled on the floor. The memory came, and I leaned against the wall, unable to breathe. My head felt like it was going to explode, and I turned towards the door, ready to bolt.

"No, Harlie. Let it come. Remember when your life finally came to the path it was designed to take. Remember not the pain of the attack, but the rescue, the changes that happened since then." His arms wrapped around me and turned me back towards the room.

"I can't James." I started to pull away, needing air and not finding any.

He turned me to face him, "Then remember it with me, you from your point of view and me from mine. Let them blend together. I'll guide us through that night." His shield dropped enough that I could sense the memory being pushed through. It was a struggle, but I did the same. Together we relived the night, seeing it from both sides. It was amazing and

447

horrifying all at the same time, but we made it past the part where I passed out, and he ended with a memory from the med bay of him watching me sleep.

My eyes opened, and I looked around the room before walking over to touch the spot where my blood had spilled. It was surreal – like someone else had been there and not me. Nicole really was dead in every sense, and there was no reason to fear this room or that night. James saw the realization in my mind, and I sensed him agreeing. We stayed, scaring off ghosts until the cold night caused me to give an involuntary shiver through my thin jacket.

"Time to go back to the hill," He whispered, rubbing his hands up and down my arms to help warm me. At my questioning expression, he added, "To set up the tent and get some sleep. We'll go back to the bunker tomorrow."

We met up with Margaret to thank her for the tour and opportunity for me to have closure. I promised to order the computers as soon as I got back home. It felt weird to catch myself calling the bunker that term, but it was the truth. This day made me realize that it was indeed home.

I helped James set up the tent on top of the hill, then sat outside and watched the refugee camp sleep. It was a cold night, but when James came out with our dinner, he brought his black leather jacket. It felt ironic as he slipped it around my shoulders, and I sat where he used to stand. I looked over the camp for nearly an hour before he reminded me that sleep was needed after such a long day.

The tent was small, but there was enough space for both sleeping bags and the frame backpack. I took my shoes off and climbed into my bag, turning over only when I felt his gaze on me. He smiled gently before taking the baseball cap off and turning it over.

"Did you wonder at all what Ricks' consequence was?" It was a strange question to ask at that moment. I had thought about it though and told him so. He handed me the cap and I stared at him in horror. Inside the embroidered design was a tiny camera. "Rick had to watch."

I turned away again, thinking over the day and what he would have seen. It must have been hard to witness. James reached over to brush a stray strand of hair out of my eyes.

448

"Do you hate me?" He asked. His expression showing that he was serious.

"No, Jamyson, I don't hate you. It was very difficult today, especially with The Commander present, but I knew you were fulfilling your responsibility."

"Please, don't ever break the rules like that again." He whispered.

"I won't." I promised and meant it. Closure had come, there was no reason to look back. There was only the future, and, despite the weight of our positions, it looked bright. I had lived through midnight and now knew what morning would bring.

AFTER THE FIRE, BEFORE THE STORM

Nightmares had come as soon as sleep did, but James was there. Like with the first time he had shown me how to divert the worst scenes, he guided until peace came to both of us. I did not want that peace to end, but the sounds of the waking refugee camp rose up to the crest of the hill and shattered it. I curled up into a ball and shuddered, waiting for the waves of memories to attack. It never came, though, at least not as an attack. Instead, I was able to think through the bitterly cold mornings of the past and reflect how, right now, those still in the tents had better resources to stop the harsh temperature.

On the other side of the small tent I heard James stretch, then sit up and move to my side. "Show me those mornings, I want to experience it from your point of view."

I complied, and he showed me the days and nights he spent in this very tent, on this very spot. After packing up the tent, we went into the village for food and facilities. I assumed that afterward, we would be returning to the bunker. It was confusing when James started to head towards it, but then turned and headed farther south.

"Close your eyes so I can take a more direct route to our destination." He ordered.

When I was allowed to open them again, I knew exactly where our location was and looked at him in shock. We were on the small dirt path which ran behind Gareth's uncle and aunt's house. He motioned for me to remain still as I heard them open the door and leave for some unknown destination. Once they were out of sight, James came around the side of the house and pointed up to the power lines. There, on the pole, I saw the reason why we came. A brand new, tiny, security camera had been installed.

"The cost came out of your account and the monthly maintenance fees will as well." There was a hint of The Commander in his voice, but his eyes were kind.

I looked over at the house and smiled, "It's worth every pound and pence."

450

We were back at the bunker before sundown. Rick and Dara were still confined to quarters, missing the days off because of the infractions. We picked up meals from the cafeteria, and James let them move into the common room. After pulling me aside for a long hug, he left.

Rick had told Dara what his punishment had been but had not told her any details. The moment James was out of earshot, she turned to me. The rest of the evening was spent going over the events of the day before. Rick seemed relieved that I appeared to handle the visit and retelling, but his mind was laced with anger. We talked late into the night, then turned in and waited for Friday to come.

Friday was a day of settling back into a routine. With the trial and its consequences out of the way, we were back to "business as usual." My research team presented a lengthy report on what they had uncovered during my time away. They had been scanning media throughout Europe, hoping that coverage about the trial would lead to an increase in internet chatter about the need for better government or more unification – anything that could hint at Unus Universum's current activity levels.

After the meeting, I wandered back into the training facility. Silently, with barely a hesitation, all eyes turned to my entrance. No one said a word. They just watched as I made my way to the first station and started the circuit. Without looking out, I knew they wanted to know more about the trial and more of why Rick, Dara, and I had been confined to quarters. As I picked up the first weight, I gazed over the massive room and made eye contact with each person there. Silent messages passed, no words were needed – one by one they looked away and went back to work. All but James that is, he continued to watch as he ran the track. I wished he wouldn't and told him so, but he was determined to keep an eye on my readjustment back to the world of Harlie Berryman.

It did not take long. On Monday, I realized an entire day had passed without me thinking about the resurrected ghost and her life. By Wednesday, she was no longer in my dreams. Nicole Jones had silently slipped away in the night. I knew I would miss her, would have moments when I longed for her life once again, but she was gone. I allowed a single tear to slip down my cheek on that final morning. Once in the training facility, I gave a knowing look to James and dropped my shield enough for him to see. He smiled grimly and stopped his near-constant watch. Back at the cottage that night, he stayed later than normal, holding me close.

The days passed with very little information from our field agents and even less coming in from our research teams. It seemed as if the masterminds had gone farther underground. The thought agitated all of us, because we knew it meant they were planning and preparing. We could do nothing more than secure our allies and prepare for an unspecified attack. When work ended each day, we left the bunker frustrated. It seemed as if none of us could relax, and in that frustration, we had turned to other activities. Dara was going to the base's fitness center and teaching a martial arts course. Jason had decided to take an extra university course. Max was teaching Jack all about firearms. Even off hours, they were still in some form of work.

If it hadn't been for Rick, I would have been in the same situation as they were. However, a few days after we returned he had mentioned how winter was fast approaching. That realization both shocked and saddened me. I was in the midst of grief as winter started last year and wondered if I were strong enough to get through the anniversary days. Seemingly knowing what was going on inside my head and heart, he came up with the perfect distraction. We both missed using our musical talents, so he asked if I would be willing to help arrange and sing a series of older songs and hymns. The idea even came up of going into a proper studio to record the results and give the finished product to the others as a gift. On the nights I was not with James, I was at Ricks' townhouse, working on song ideas and writing out the arrangements. The Commander was curious about what I was doing, especially since there had been tension between them since the trial. He accepted my half-truth explanation, though, and did not press for details.

It was mid-October when the masterminds made themselves known again. Our researchers had intercepted part of a disturbing radio commercial, and we wanted to check the source. It came from a rural station with only a fifty-mile range in the midst of Lebanon. While various propaganda commercials or radio shows were common, there was something about this one which set my nerves on edge. Rick also seemed bothered by the little bit of content he had caught and translated. He and I were sent to investigate. We set up in a small motel in an even smaller town and waited.

Rick had been sullen since the decision to send us to investigate had gone through. It was a far cry from the creative energy and spontaneous laughter of our after-work sessions. I planned on cornering him about it, but he spoke first.

"How are you and The Commander doing? I want an open honest answer." At my hesitation, he added, "Don't cheat."

I looked up at him, "Jaws, I was just about to ask something as well."

"You answer my question first."

In the month since James and I had been in a relationship, Rick had never asked how we were doing. I thought carefully before answering. "The Commander and I are doing well. On the days you and I are not hanging out, I'm usually with him. We've been having more random discussions, and that has been a pleasant change of pace."

"How about mentally and physically?" He pressed.

I wanted to cheat, to glance at his mind and see why he was acting this way. It really was not his business as to that part of the relationship, but this was Rick: Rick who had befriended me instantly, Rick who had been there for me in my hardest hours. "We are being very careful with our mental abilities. We don't really know how those might enhance or interfere with our relationship. We still drop shield now and again, but not when we are being close." He waited for me to elaborate on the word close. "The Commander and I set up boundaries for our physical contact right after we returned from the camp and are sticking to it. He isn't pressuring me on anything." I did not add that when we were together, we were almost constantly in some form of contact: holding hands, leaning against each other, hugging, or touching. I found it to be very comforting amidst the turmoil.

453

Rick nodded then spoke, "I have been upset with him for how he handled the trial and its consequences. He is very fortunate that you did not turn away after such a harsh punishment. It had to be agonizing."

"When I found out that he made you watch, I was horrified."

He turned away and started pressing buttons and turning dials on the equipment. "I was angry at how he was treating you, and it was horrible having to watch."

I placed my hand on his arm. "Is that why you are so somber right now? Is it because it's just you and me here, far from his range?"

Rick gave a pained sigh before turning to me. "I said I wanted you and him to be in a relationship and that I would be happy because he would still let me be there for you. Those things are true to this day, but..."

I spared him the agony of having to say it aloud. "You wish it were the other way around. That your "Life's Vow" didn't seem to prevent a serious relationship. I don't have to be empathic to see that." Rick nodded once then sat on the bed. I sat next to him and waited.

He placed an arm around my shoulders and pulled me closer to him, "I'm sorry for being so sullen. I kept thinking on how it could have been, just you and I here. Bear, I cannot see my life without you in it and will continue to be here for you, whenever and however you need me." I wrapped my arms around his strong frame and gave him a big hug. I could not see my life without him in it either.

All the next day we listened to the local stations. Rick taught me keywords to listen for, writing them down phonetically. We would record an hour, and if the commercial or other information was not there, it was deleted. Late the first night, we heard the keywords. I rewound to it, and Rick translated. I jumped up startled when he slammed his fist down so hard that the table nearly broke.

"It's them all right. The whole commercial is full the masterminds' propaganda. It seems that a local cell has gone public instead of hiding underground." His eyes were haunted, "Bear, this can be very bad for our remaining time."

"What does it say?"

454

He shut his eyes and recited the announcement, "Children of Lebanon, it is time to come together. It is time for all of us to be equals, no classes, no more poverty, no more corruption in the government. We can erase those lines, make it so everyone has everything they need to be happy. Imagine an entire world like that, imagine not having to be afraid of our neighbors, of everyone working together for a greater good. We have already started forward with success. Join us children. Join us in unity." Ricks' eyes opened, "It goes on with some details, and gives a contact number, followed by the word for unite, and ends."

My mouth opened, then closed in shock. It was a blatant message straight from the enemy itself. I could barely believe how open the message was, how easy it was for us to find. But maybe that was the point. Perhaps they were getting ready to make their message public, to gain more support before making their big push for power.

Rick was thinking the same thing, "We were warned about this potential. They would make it seem like they were attempting a peaceful take-over and then set off the bombs and blame it on others, so the world has no choice but to unite or face a nuclear war. If our contact was correct, then interviews and entire programs will be soon." He stood and started packing.

"Wait!" I called out. Rick turned, looking slightly annoyed. "Jaws, be ready to leave at a moment's notice, but I want to go out there and sense if there is any reaction. We need to know how the public is responding."

He thought about it then nodded. I grabbed my headscarf and earpiece, put on the darker contact lenses and headed outside to walk around. I walked for two hours, stopping to get coffee and browse a few stores that were still open. Looking out from my shield, I observed anything which seemed to be a reaction to the commercial. When Rick beeped that it came on a second time, I stood still and opened up to my full range. It was at that point when I sensed it, a penetrating darkness which pierced me to the core. Cautiously moving towards it, I narrowed my focus. It came from inside a house, and I crept close enough to see it. Leaning back into the shadows I waited, taking in all that I could. There were seven

455

men inside and all were answering phone calls. They were radiating pride, arrogance, and belief in what they were doing and saying. I focused on each mind, trying to read them like I did Kayla. Several were offering financial help to whoever was on the other side, showing me a way they gathered recruits. A couple more were convincing the listener that their way was best. Then my heart and mind froze. One person had hung up the phone and seemed to be looking around at the others. He walked to the window and peered out. In that moment, I heard his thoughts. He was remembering a warning – a warning about watching out for someone with an old mind. Reaching into my pocket, I took out the stick camera and snapped a handful of pictures before fading back and rushing to the motel.

Suddenly, getting back to the bunker became the most urgent thought in my mind. We needed to scan more of the world to see if it was just this isolated cell or if we had a much larger situation on our hands. Without speaking, we packed the equipment and headed towards the airport. I could see the stress on Rick's face, it reflected my own. It was a two-hour drive, and we were able to book seats on the only flight from there straight to London. I had called from the road to tell the bunker we were on the way back, so a car and driver were waiting.

Since the trip was short, the reports took only minutes to complete and we were debriefing within an hour. Both The General and James were visibly upset at the discovery of the cell group becoming more public.

"This calls for more effort on our part to discover if anyone else is being this brazen." The General said when we finished presenting. "Call the others in here."

Two minutes later, we were all gathered around the table. Two minutes after that, the Canadian team was gathered and linked to us. Each Guardian was assigned to a region of the world and reassignment of research and technical teams were made so that every member had at least three people under him or her. If the enemy was starting to broadcast publicly, instead of their underground methods, it meant they were nearly large enough to plan a global scale attempt to take over.

We were in the middle of the reassignments when the Canadian team was interrupted by a runner. Rockwell looked at a print-out then called for silence. "It is worse than we thought. We have been tracking the political situation in the United States very closely. As you know, there has been a major uproar due to the Chinese take-over of the west. The elections are in just a couple of weeks for those who are still free enough to vote."

The General's hands turned into fists in anticipation of the results we knew had to be bad. Rockwell continued, "Current projections put nearly two dozen one-world supporters winning at the state level and seven winning at the national. With as poorly as they did last cyle, we were not anticipating this."

It took quite a few minutes to settle all of us down. The levels of anger and frustration were almost painful to witness, and my shield shuddered under the onslaught. James silently came behind me and placed his hand on my shoulder, helping to protect me with the power of his own strong abilities. No one seemed to notice, and that was a good thing, as he gently brushed the back of my neck with his fingers before letting go.

The General dismissed the others but requested that Rockwell, James, Rick and I stay. "We know more than the others what this means. Older Guardians and our newest addition, time is running out. We have less than two years if our source is accurate. I only hope we can prevent the disaster this time."

He sounded like he meant more than just referencing the attack on the United States, but I shrugged it off, instead choosing to ask what was burning in my own mind. "Sir, while in Lebanon, I used my abilities the way I did against Kayla. In the mind of a man looking out the window, I heard him repeat a warning about someone with an old mind." I paused, looking at all three. "It is the third time now that I've witnessed that situation. Shouldn't we take it into account?"

The General looked at James, then turned to me. "Agent Berryman, I know you are concerned about this reference, and we are as well. However, I don't believe it is something to focus on at this time." His tone and expression said that the discussion was over, but once again I sensed

457

omission. However, we were dismissed and went to assemble our new work groups.

Because of the urgency of the situation, we all moved back into the bunker. From dawn until dark we worked, scanning radio and television stations, setting up software to record as many as possible and red-flagging anything with particular phrases or words. Rick and the rest of the linguistics team were constantly updating the program with dialects and less common languages. Saturday came, and we chose to work a full day, then went to the pub for dinner. Because the software had to be closely monitored, we all came back to the bunker in order to check on it throughout Sunday.

James and I had very little time together during the week. On the first night back, he had slipped into my room after everyone was asleep. He gently woke me, pulled me into his arms and held me close. It was only a few minutes before he left. The rest of the week we talked mentally when possible, but physical contact was nearly non-existent. It was becoming painful for both of us.

On Monday, General Smiths had us gather all the mastermind commercials we had recorded and translated. After each team presented their evidence, he stood and looked at each of us in turn.

"We are going to put a kink in their recruiting. I want each of you to plan out and implement sabotage missions from your assigned region. The goal will be to destroy radio towers – their tool to spread the propaganda. We will only have a few days at the most before our plan is discovered, so choose just three sites to attack. If we are successful, it will be twenty-four targets in key areas that will be taken down on our side. You will have three days to plan out all the details, two days total to travel, five days to take out your targets and two more days to return back here. Those whose regions are closer will understandably not need as much travel time and will be departing hours later."

He paused to let his words sink in before continuing. "You must move quickly once on the ground. I can almost guarantee that, after the first or second wave of attacks, they will realize it isn't random terrorism. We can only speculate on what their reaction will be, but they should have the capability and resources to defend our other targets.

I have notified The Founders, and they have put our people in the U.N. on standby to assist us. You shouldn't have the need for commercial transportation until you are in the country of your targets. This will allow us to fly the needed equipment along with your groups."

Without asking if we had questions or something to add, he dismissed the others – again asking Jamyson, Rick and me to stay. I sat, glancing around mentally, and waited to discover why we were being retained.

Once the others had left, The General sat down with a sigh and put his head in his hands. Several long moments passed before he raised it again and spoke.

"I don't know why it keeps surprising me when something happens from the traveler's list. I keep hoping we have damaged the masterminds enough, prevented them from completing enough of their agenda so that the outcome won't be as he said. Then, something like this happens, and I become both shocked and saddened. So many years, so many successes, and we are still staring down the barrel of a loaded gun."

James and Rick both turned to see my reaction to The General's words and actions. I just nodded solemnly, there were no words to express what was going on inside. He noticed and continued.

"Time is very short, young one, very short. We are going to need your skills more than ever to locate the evil and eliminate it. Never forget that they possess enough nuclear weapons to permanently damage the world. We have to destroy that potential as well. From what we have been told, once they go to broadcasting, we have under barely a year until the catastrophic event occurs. Time is moving faster here than anticipated." He looked at James and nodded at what seemed to be an unspoken question. Turning back to me he smiled slightly, "James and Rick will fill you in on more details as the situation requires. As Jamyson said from the first moment, please remain open-minded. You are very important to our organization and there are strong emotional attachments as well." With that he dismissed us.

James spoke mentally as we walked to our quarters, *Dress warmly, we are going to the river.* I did as he said, and we hopped onto the bike. He had packed two extra blankets. One we sat on and one we wrapped around us whilst leaning against a tree. Traditionally, his back was against it while I sat in front of him with my back pressed against his chest. We had not been to the river since the night he asked to take us into a relationship, choosing to have our few proper dates in various hiking locations or going out to dinner someplace away from town. I tried to relax, but the strain of The Guardians' situation was eating away at me. James dropped his shield and beckoned for me to do the same. Needing the time to rest it, I complied.

This is what I've needed for weeks. His mind whispered. The next hour was spent in his arms, see-sawing between discussing the situation and sitting quietly while enjoying the contact.

Towards the end of the hour, I felt a slight shift in James' mind. "Harlie?" He asked lips at my hair.

"Yes, Jamyson?" I turned my head to look up at him.

"Even before we were committed to this relationship, there has been something about the times we spend in close contact." A hint of the famous look was in his eyes.

"I noticed that too. I wonder if it has to do with how our mental abilities play into our friendship or how our pasts make the present more intense."

He kissed my forehead, "It might be a combination of both. For being formally together for less than two months, it is quite painful to be apart. Being around you is so easy, so natural."

"Somehow, it seems we have been together longer," I thought it over, "Perhaps because of that intensity and our friendship."

He shifted again and turned me to face him. "More proof that you were meant to be here." He kissed me tenderly then held me close. "Please be cautious out there. Rio was close, but you are yet to come face to face with the pure evil behind the endeavor."

"It is a bit frightening, the idea of leading my own team in the field and being away from the rest of the

Guardians."

His arms dropped from around me and he moved to kneel in front of me. "You should be frightened, for it is the worst type of evil out there. They will not hesitate to kill millions more just to see their agenda come to fruition." James took my hand in his, "But you are well prepared for the responsibility of leading a team. I believe in you." He raised the hand to his lips while adding mentally. *Remember that you are never alone.*

He went back to holding me, and we sat wrapped up in the blanket. It was late evening, and the colors of the setting sun were awe-inspiring.

"I know you hate to hear it, but you are so beautiful and so amazing." He spoke quietly, holding me close to him. "Think of all you accomplished in just over a year. Think of what you have become in just eight months. Think of what your future could be." His rested his cheek against my neck. "No wonder I have fallen so hard for you. No wonder I am starting to feel what I thought was impossible." I held back the fire which threatened to ruin the moment. He sensed it and leaned back again, "Yes, I know, darling, I know. What I just said was very dangerous – about as dangerous as this upcoming mission."

I turned to face him, gently placing my hand on the side of his face and kissing him. "Yes, Jamyson, it is. But I am looking back on this last year, and it is astonishing to me. I have seen darkness and evil, have witnessed the midnight of my life. Now..." I turned to look over at the river, "Even though we face such a work of evil and potential devastation, I cannot help but see the dawn – the light of a new day." I spread my hands to show what was around us. "This is where I belong, no matter what may come." Leaning back into the arms of the man who freed me from the camp, the man whose life was somehow tied with mine, I smiled.

SPECIAL REQUEST

Independently published authors rely on reviews and social media to help spread the word about their books. If you enjoyed reading "Midnight to Morning" please write a review for it. The novel, plus its sequel "Sunrise to Shadows" can be found on Amazon, Goodreads, Self-E Virginia and other e-text outlets. Thank you from the bottom of my heart for helping to shine a light on this work.

About the Author

Holly Glogau-Morgan is a part-time teacher in the Piedmont area of Virginia. She lives with her husband and their precious pets on a small homestead. Despite the physical limitations from having Ehlers-Danlos Syndrome, she enjoys being able to grow much of their food and loves the outdoors. In her free time, she enjoys mentoring area young adults and chatting with her friends and family while playing various online games. While she has written some minor works, this is her first novel. Her blog, Morgan's Musings, covers various topics and can be found at www.ddraigswife.blogspot.com

Acknowledgements

This book obviously did not write itself. Many people were involved in the process and I would love to thank them. Crystal, for all the editing work you did and for your patience in teaching me. To my mother who encouraged me from a young age to put my vivid imagination onto paper and made sure I kept all the binders of my "early works." My wonderful husband who sat night after night, listening to me read out loud and dealing with the pauses as I found mistakes. To my "online friends" who have been my lifeline through all of this and mean more to me than you will ever know.